She Who Remembers

She Who Remembers

LINDA LAY SHULER

ARBOR HOUSE | William Morrow   New York

Library of Congress Cataloging in Publication Data
Shuler, Linda Lay.
She who remembers.
1. Indians of North America—Fiction. I. Title.
PS3569.H768S53   1988   87-19570
ISBN: 0-87795-892-0

Manufactured in the United States of America

Published in Canada by Fitzhenry & Whiteside, Ltd.

10 9 8 7 6 5 4 3 2 1

For my daughters

*"Time is a great circle;
there is no beginning, no end.
All returns again and again,
forever."*

Acknowledgments

$\mathbf{M}$uch is known about the remarkable Anasazi of Mesa Verde; yet much is not known and experts disagree on many points. This is my version of what may have been, after extensive research and information generously given by knowledgeable people. However, this is a book of fiction and does not necessarily reflect ideas or opinions of anthropologists, archeologists, historians, and others who have advised me.

I am especially grateful to: Linda Martin, Mesa Verde National Park; Dr. J. Richard Ambler, Northern Arizona University; Dr. W. W. Newcomb, University of Texas at Austin; Dr. E. C. Krupp, Griffith Observatory, City of Los Angeles; and Douglas Elmy, The Society of Archer Antiquaries, Bridlington, Yorkshire, England.

My warm thanks to those special people who reviewed the manuscript: my daughter, Linda Shuler, whose contributions were invaluable; Linda Martin, Naomi M. Stokes, Joe Stokes, and Victor Harrap.

My thanks, also, to Jean M. Auel for her encouragement and research materials she sent me, and to Louise Miller for helping me with research at Santa Fe.

What would writers do without libraries and librarians? I am indebted without measure to Laura Holt of the wonderful library at the Laboratory of Anthropology at Santa Fe, and Pat Todd at the Brownwood Public Library, Brownwood, Texas.

I appreciate the gracious permission of Rose Allen to quote from *America's Ancient Civilizations,* by A. Hyatt Verrill and Ruth Verrill, Capricorn Books/Putnams-Coward McCann & Geoghegan, Inc., 1953.

My thanks also to my indefatigable agent, Jean V. Naggar, and editor par excellence, Liza Dawson.

Finally, I am indebted to those writers and scholars, past and present, upon whom I depended so much. Especially helpful were J. Richard Ambler, *The Anasazi*, Museum of Northern Arizona, 1977; Don Watson, *Indians of the Mesa Verde*, Mesa Verde Museum Association, Mesa Verde National Park, Colorado, 1961; Gilbert R. Wenger, *The Story of Mesa Verde*, Mesa Verde Museum Association, Mesa Verde National Park, Colorado, 1980; Michael Zelkik, *The Sunwatchers of Chaco Canyon*, and E. C. Krupp, *Light and Shadow*, both of Griffith Observer, June 1983, City of Los Angeles; Ruth Benedict, *Patterns of Culture*, Houghton-Mifflin Company, New York; Adolf F. Bandelier, *The Delight Makers*, first published in 1890, Harvest/HBJ, New York, 1971; and the extraordinary Swedish explorer, Gustaf Nordenskiöld, *The People of the Mesa Verde*, first published in 1893, translated by Lloyd Morgan, the Rio Grande Press, Inc., Glorieta, New Mexico, 1979. I learned about buffalo from Tom McHugh in his fascinating book, *The Time of the Buffalo*, University of Nebraska Press, 1972. The account of the Snake Dance is from Arthur C. Parker's *The Indian How Book*, Dover Publications, Inc., New York, 1927, and the incredible Tipi Shaking Ceremony is from *The Religions of the American Indians* by Åke Hultkrantz, translated by Monica Setterwall, University of California Press, 1979.

To you, Bob, my thanks for all the reasons you know best.

Anasazi is a Navaho word meaning "The Ancient Ones." Pueblo Indians of today prefer the name *Hi-sat-si-nom,* "The People of Long Ago." Because *Anasazi* is the name commonly used, it is used in this book. "Utes," "Apaches," and other tribes mentioned are ancestors of those who came later; names given are today's.

Who knows what they called themselves, those ancient ones, the people of long ago?

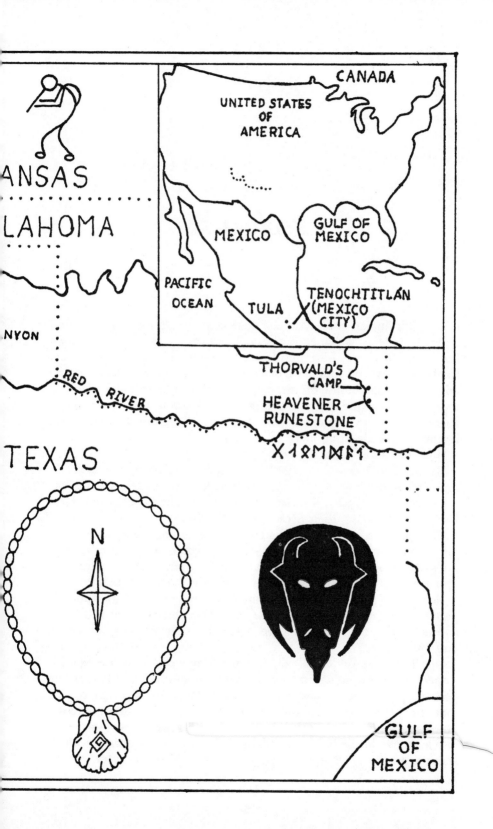

Prologue

The Indian crawled to the edge of the stony slope and peered down. In a deep, V-shaped ravine, tall trees showered red and golden leaves into a stream hurrying down the mountain. Eons ago, a great sandstone slab had toppled from the mountain and now stood on its edge, embedded beside the stream. The slab was huge: taller than two men, nearly as wide, thick as the length from elbow to fingertips, and speckled with the moss and lichens of centuries. The Indian knew it well; it stood in the dwelling place of spirits.

Now the place was occupied by gods!

He gazed in fear and wonder. There were three strange beings, tall, broad of shoulder, with pale skin that gleamed in the shadows, and hair the color of falling leaves. Masses of hair covered their cheeks and chins. Under bushy brows, their eyes shone blue. Blue!

The garments of the gods glistened in the autumn sunlight. Among his people it was said that magical garments could destroy arrows. The gods had arrows that flew straight and far from strange bows, and were tipped with a substance black as flint, hard as stone, but neither.

Now one of the gods used implements of the same hard substance to pound indentations into the stone slab. The others talked in an unknown tongue, polishing their spears and bows, or shooting at random targets.

One bow, the oddest of all, was small and set crosswise upon a wooden bar. The Indian watched in astonishment as a god looped the bowstring on a two-pronged hook suspended from the waist, placed his foot in a stirrup fastened to the bow, and pushed his foot down until the bowstring was caught by a notch on the crossbar. The arrow was fitted into a groove in the bar to be released by a trigger mechanism which sent the arrow speeding to its target with wonderful accuracy.

The Indian marveled. To have an arrow held in place by the bow, ready to fly at a touch!

The pounding continued. Seven strange marks had already been made; another was nearly finished. All were cut deeply into the stone in a straight row. It must be their sacred medicine, he thought.

They might see him! He pressed himself against the stone and inched into shadow. But at last the gods finished and slipped away, following the stream, disappearing among the trees. For a long time he remained still, listening, watching for a manifestation of displeasure at his intrusion into this holy place. But the spirits did not speak.

Cautiously, he clambered down and faced the stone from across the stream. The medicine of the gods was potent. Dare he touch it to absorb its magic properties? He fingered the talisman he carried in a small pouch dangling from a yucca twine cord around his neck.

"Give me a sign," he prayed.

For a time, there was no reply. Then a jay flew down and perched on the stone. It scrutinized him with its sharp, black eyes, but made no sound, no exclamation at his trespass. The spirits welcomed him here.

The Indian gestured in reverence. "I thank you, bird spirit," he said. The jay flew away.

The Indian waded the stream and faced the stone. Slowly, slowly, he raised both hands and pressed them against the medicine marks of the gods.

Centuries passed before the inscription was deciphered and the great slab with its carvings became famous as the Heavener Runestone. The inscription was a cryptopuzzle, deciphered as a date, November 11, 1012. The place was eastern Oklahoma in the Poteau Mountains above the town of Heavener.

Scholars theorized that the Vikings sailed up the Mississippi River, then up the Arkansas River, and, finally, up the Poteau River which leads to within a mile of the runestone.

What became of these Norsemen who ventured so far from the fields and fjords of home? Did they leave a legacy other than a date to mark their presence?

Kwani knew.

❖ PART ❖ I ❖

Kwani

*1270*A.D.

◆ 1 ◆

She crouched, waiting. Something, someone, was out there.

Through the cave opening she could see Sunfather's last light dissolving behind the mountain. The dank odor of the cave blended with mountain fragrances and the smell of nightfall—and of something else.

The nostrils in Kwani's round, red-brown face dilated with intense effort to scent a dangerous presence. She balanced the spear in her hand, ready to throw. She had never used a spear before, and it felt awkward and heavy; but it was all the protection she had now.

Her heart beat hard, and she tried to quiet her breathing. Something, someone, was out there.

Above the cave, a rocky ledge protruded. The cougar crouched there to ease her wound. In the cold sunset light, the open gash in her side oozed red. The wound was not healing; its constant throbbing gave her no rest. She had been unsuccessful in her hunting and she was ravenous; without food she would die soon.

The wind shifted and she lifted her nose to it. Instantly she became alert, the wound forgotten. There was a scent she recognized. She inched to the cliff's edge and leaned over, scanning the area below. Footprints led to the opening of a small cave. In the deepening shadow, the cougar could not see inside, but she knew what was there.

She crouched, waiting.

Inside the cave, Kwani listened. There was a rustle, a stirring, as night rolled from the horizon like a dark sea. The quavering call of a night bird echoed faintly and faded to silence. The bird's call said that all was well; but Kwani was uneasy. Nervously, she brushed the long, black hair away from her face. Usually she wore it in the conventional squash-blossom

3

style, a large roll high over each ear. But it had tumbled hours ago in her desperate run to escape Maluku, the Medicine Chief, and in her scramble up the mountain.

She strained to hear. Silence, deep and total. It was unnatural.

She retreated deeper into the cave. Her yucca fiber sandals whispered and scratched against the rocks as she clambered up a small rise at the back. Shivering, she wrapped her rabbit fur robe closely about her and pressed her small body against the cave wall.

I must leave room to throw the spear.

She raised her arm, thrusting the spear back. But it hit the wall. She climbed down a little and tried again. If only she had brought wood to make a fire, to keep animals away.

From a distance came the hoot of an owl, long and low.

Terror boiled in her stomach. The owl's cry was a harbinger of death. *What was out there?*

The cold night wind carried a taste of rain. The cougar trembled as the wind probed her bones without cooling the burning of her wound. She longed for the warm comfort of her den, but she was starving and food was tantalizingly close. All she had to do was wait.

There was distant thunder, growing closer. Raindrops fell, a few at first, then a downpour.

Kwani listened with relief. If an animal waited outside, rain would drive it away to its den. Her arm ached and she was weak from hunger now; she could no longer hold the spear. Cold seeped from the walls of the cave and her fingers were numb as she laid the spear beside her and lay down. Hunger ached clear to her backbone. But she had only a small corn cake left in her pack and she must save it for morning.

A terrible loneliness shook her. Never in her life had she been unprotected by a man. Always her father, or uncle, or brother, or Wopio had stood between her and danger. Protection of women and children by men of family and clan was a woman's right, necessary for the survival of the race. Always women had known the contentment that such protection brings. But now she had only her protecting spirits . . . and they could not warm or comfort her as had Wopio's strong body at her side.

Wopio . . .

The cougar lay on the ledge through the night, too weak to retreat. The searing fire in her side was unquenched.

Daybreak. The rain stopped. She tried to see inside the cave. The scent of prey grew stronger. There was a light scraping sound of footsteps. The sound stopped. A head appeared; was withdrawn. The cougar gathered her failing strength and crouched in readiness.

Kwani stepped outside. The cougar sprang; but the ledge was slippery, and in her weakness she landed several feet from her prey. As she turned to attack, a fierce pain stabbed her as a spear ripped into her wound. She screamed like a woman tortured, and clawed at the spear; it fell clattering to the ground. With all her remaining strength, the cougar retreated up the mountain.

A shout of triumph and fear followed her as she disappeared among the rocky crags. She climbed higher, and still higher, ignoring a rabbit bounding by. In her den, she lay in the comfort of its security and closed her eyes. The pain of the wound surged through her body. She tried to open her eyes, to raise her head, but she could not.

Slowly, a gentle darkness fell. The cougar could not open her eyes to see it, but she sensed its quiet approach; she could feel it enveloping her, taking away the pain bit by bit. She sighed, and rested her head on one giant paw.

Ravens were inching closer as she died.

Kwani shouted again in wild triumph, throwing back her head so that her dark hair fell nearly to her waist.

"Go! Run before my spear bites you again!" Her voice echoed eerily . . . "bites you again."

Suddenly, it seemed too quiet. The cougar's mate! Where was he? She darted to pick up the spear. Its point was stained dark red. There was a rustling sound on the overhanging ledge, and she whirled to look up. *Where was he?* She strained to hear, to discern a scent. But there was only the smell of earth after rain, only the sigh of wind and the bark of a distant coyote.

Quickly, she retreated inside the cave and climbed to the rise at the back. If he came, she must be ready. She grasped the spear again; its solid weight was comforting.

The spear had become hers when Maluku, the Medicine Chief, drove her from their pit home in the valley.

"This was your uncle's weapon, better than his bow and arrows," her mother had said. "It is heavy, but well balanced. Learn to use it, and you will survive to find the Blue-eyed One who will protect you."

Only then had her mother whispered the dangerous secret: Generations ago, blue-eyed gods with pale skin destroyed a village, raped the women, and disappeared into the forest. Their Chief had said that his men were colonizing the country with their seed; he promised that they and their descendants would offer protection to anyone who could prove this divine ancestry.

But the tribal Chiefs cursed them, swearing to destroy any child born of them, gods or no.

"It is your eyes!" Kwani's mother whispered. "Only you have the blue eyes. Kokopelli told me in secret—I paid him well—he told me a blue-eyed Chief lives far away, there." She pointed to the southeast. "Go! Find your protector!"

Kwani remembered how her mother's voice trembled, how tears ran down the deep creases of her cheeks.

"Witch!" Drumbeats outside had grown louder, the voices of Kwani's clan more insistent. The cry rose to a chant.

"Go!" her mother whispered. "Take the spear and go before the drumbeats stop. They will kill you!"

"But I am not a witch!"

"Aye-e-e!" her mother wailed. "I know. But Maluku believes you caused the sickness—the fever and deliriums—that kills our people. When you were born he said that eyes the color of blue sky were an evil omen—and now he says the killing sickness proves you are the witch responsible. Ai-i-i!" She rocked in terror. "Go!"

The drumbeats suddenly stopped.

"Now!" her mother whispered. "Go quickly, quickly!"

Kwani lifted the basket filled with her belongings and shifted it to her back. The carrying thong was across her forehead.

"Mother . . ."

"Run!" Her mother pushed her desperately. "Hurry!"

Kwani clutched the spear and stepped from the pit dwelling that had been her home all sixteen years of her life. She swallowed with fear and hope as Wopio, her mate, emerged from the kiva with Maluku, the Medicine Chief.

"Wopio, protect me!" She stretched out a hand to him. But he turned away, covering his face with his blanket to save himself from the death spirit—and to hide his smile.

For some time, Wopio had planned to leave her and take another mate, one who would give him sons. A bewitching twelve-year-old was already pregnant. Kwani was barren.

Maluku raised his bow; the medicine arrow would pierce her heart and destroy the evil spirit. With a cry, Kwani ran. She stumbled, and fell; the arrow missed its mark, embedding itself inside her basket.

A cry rose from the clan. "The spirits protect her!"

Maluku reached for another arrow, but the Clan Chief raised his arm. "Let her go! Her spirit is too strong. If you release it, it will remain here forever, calling our own spirits away. We shall die!"

For a moment, Maluku, the Medicine Chief, wavered. Kwani's spirit was strong—but not stronger than the power of his medicine arrow. Once the arrow pierced her, her soul would be destroyed and the evil would die with it.

Kwani was on her feet now, rounding a bend in the trail. A perfect target. Maluku knelt on one knee. The girl's figure ran awkwardly with its burden. Maluku's arrow leaped from the bow. Too late. Kwani's mother darted into the arrow's path, her arms outstretched, her mouth agape in a scream that never sounded as the arrow pierced her through.

A moaning rose like wind in the valley. The old woman was respected and loved. The medicine arrow had killed her soul. Never would she see her ancestors, never would her spirit greet those to come, never would her campfire burn in distant night skies. Never, never, would she return to counsel with them in dreams. She was killed unjustly; her spirit would prowl in the night, steal among them during the day, and haunt them forever.

Kwani had rounded the trail before her mother intercepted the arrow; she did not know her mother was forever gone. Now, as she huddled in the back of the cave, she was comforted by the memory of her mother's withered face, warm with love, and felt reassured that all would be well. The cougar's mate had not come.

She reached into her pack basket for the corn cake her mother had made, and for the little packet of ceremonial corn meal. She would honor the Six Sacred Directions and all the deities for saving her from the cougar.

She pulled her hand back as if it had been stung. Protruding from the back of her pack was the shaft of an arrow to kill witches. Maluku's medicine arrow! She opened the pack. The arrow was embedded against her scraping stone. Her heart beat wildly. The arrow's spirit had refused to find her!

Overwhelmed with gratitude, she removed it and laid it respectfully beside the spear, tipped red with the cougar's blood. She opened the small packet of ceremonial meal and tossed a pinch to each of the Six Sacred Directions: North, East, South, West, Above, and Below.

"I thank you, oh spirits, for your protection," she intoned in her talking-to-spirits voice. "I thank you, oh spear, for your strength and for saving me from the cougar. Most of all, I thank you, oh medicine arrow, for sparing me."

What else could she say? Girls did not have training in talking to spirits, as boys did. She would give the arrow a present, the best she had. It was a shell, an ancient marvel she had found at the foot of a rocky cliff. It was small and round, with a delicate spiral swirling from the center, a gift from Sipapu where ancestors dwelled.

She removed the shell from the small pouch that hung around her neck, and tied it to the shaft of the arrow. Now the arrow's medicine would be invincible.

Ceremonies completed, Kwani devoured the corn cake greedily. It was all there was. She must gather roots and seeds and berries for her journey. The journey would take many days. But surely she would find the one whose eyes were blue as her own, who would make her forever secure at last. Kokopelli, the traveler, the magician, he of the sacred seed, had told the secret to her mother. So it must be true.

She placed the arrow carefully in her pack, and swung the pack to her back. All would be well. No harm would come to her . . . no predator would find her . . .

But the spear stained with the cougar's blood seemed heavier as she lifted it. Her feet were reluctant to take her from the shelter of the cave.

All her life, Kwani had known that tears were unworthy of an Anasazi; she would not shed them now. But it was her own people who abandoned her, who had forced her into the wilderness, to die alone.

"I will not die!" she cried. "No, I will not!"

Who would know, who would care, if tears overflowed?

✦2✦

Following the faint trail that circled the mountain, Kwani headed south. Her mother had said the Blue-eyed One dwelled in the southeast. She might find a hunting trail. Meanwhile, she would look for food. At home, she knew where things grew, but in this unknown area it was hard to find edible plants and roots and berries, especially this early in the spring.

I must learn to hunt.

She assumed a throwing stance as she had seen the men do. Her spear had hit the cougar because the animal was so close. But could she hit a running rabbit?

On the bank of a cliff, a cluster of small flowers grew, the first of early spring. Instinctively, Kwani paused, captivated by the flowers' beauty. As she gazed, a field mouse scurried by. Dropping the spear, Kwani pounced on the small creature; it would be a tasty tidbit. But the mouse slipped from her grasp and disappeared into a crevice under a rock.

Frustrated, she continued down the path. The rabbit skin robe was wrapped snugly around her sturdy body and tied at the waist with an ornately braided belt from her own hair and the hair of her mother. She was a small woman, well built and firm, erect in carriage and graceful in movement.

She paused and gazed toward the southeast. Her journey would be difficult and dangerous, especially now when melting snow from icy peaks could flood the rivers. The Anasazi men who made long journeys to trade blankets, mugs, and other valuables with distant pueblos, and even in the great trading centers of the south and southeast, often told of the mountains, forests, canyons, and swift rivers that must be conquered.

I'll find other people, other clans to stay with on the way, she told

herself. But what if I encounter Apaches? Kwani glanced around nervously. The nomadic Apaches, ruthless and feared, could be anywhere,
hidden and silent, until they appeared suddenly like evil spirits.

She stopped abruptly. Directly in front of her, drying in the sun, were
cougar tracks no more than a few hours old. Her nostrils dilated, but
there was no scent. Still, she would find a cave till it was safe to go on.
Cautiously she crept forward, spear balanced. Ahead was a cave with a
small opening. As she stepped inside, she gave an involuntary cry.

A man crouched there, skinning a rabbit. He looked up, growling, and
rose, hands bloody, stone scraper still held in one fist.

They stood staring at one another. He was Ute, she was Anasazi—
ancestral enemies. He approached, snarling a threat. Matted black hair
hung over his forehead. Behind scraggly hanks of hair, black eyes
peered from ambush. His muscular, dark body was well formed except
for one leg which was shorter than the other, with the foot twisted
inward—a cripple, cursed with evil spirits.

An outcast, like herself.

Kwani stood uncertainly. She could outrun him if he attacked with the
stone scraper. She raised her spear, poised to throw. But he did not
retreat. His eyes glowed with the force of a blow, and he stepped closer.

Torn between fear of the animal outside and of the man in the cave,
Kwani stood hesitating. Food was here; the flesh of the rabbit lay pink
and gleaming just beyond her reach. If he could catch rabbits, he was
a hunter. Here she must stay. She lowered the spear and entered the
cave.

The Ute stepped in front of her, raising the bloody scraper.

"Go away!" The scraper whipped the air. He spoke Ute, but his
meaning was clear.

She backed away. Again she raised the spear. But he darted forward
with unexpected agility and wrested it from her hand.

"My spear! Give me my spear!" Kwani cried, reaching after it. But he
threw it behind him.

"Go away!" He slashed at her with the stone scraper.

She retreated in rage and frustration. Outside the cave she huddled
miserably against the cliff. She had no food, no spear; and the cougar,
the cougar, was near. Timidly she crawled to the cave's entrance. The
Ute was preparing a fire. A pile of twigs and leaves and several dead
branches lay near the entrance. From a pit in the cave's dark depths he
carried a live coal, holding it carefully between two small stones. She
ducked out of sight. Soon a delicate gray wisp floated out and up,
followed by the wrenching fragrance of roasting meat.

Kwani groaned and salivated, clutching her stomach with both hands.
Nearly fainting, she crept again to the cave; the spear lay beside him.

He gnawed a hunk of juicy meat and licked off juices that ran down his arms. As he tore the meat from the bones, he grunted contentedly.

She withdrew to the cliff and forced herself to wait. Perhaps he would permit her to have the bones and what bits of meat might be left.

Gradually the contented sounds ceased. Once more she crawled to the cave's entrance. He was licking the juices from his hands. He saw her and jumped up, but not without reaching for her spear. Faint with hunger, Kwani inched inside.

"Go away!" But it seemed to her that the angry glare was not as fierce as before.

Whimpering, she lowered her head so that her long, black hair brushed the ground. She reached one hand upon the rocky floor and crawled forward slowly, dragging her knees. There was no sound. Not daring to look up, she reached out her hand again and suddenly cried out. Her hand was pinned down by a twisted bare foot.

She looked up. He stood over her, spear raised, eyes mocking.

Terrified, she sprawled on the ground, face down. She heard his snarling growl. Would a spear thrust follow? She tried to pull her hand away, but the foot held it fast. She rolled to her back, an animal in a trap. Her hair covered her face; but she could see his glare, she could see the raised spear.

Their eyes met; hers through the long hair over her face, his through the matted cover of ambush. Abruptly, he leaned forward to brush her hair away. He stared into her blue eyes. He grunted.

Still whimpering, Kwani slowly parted her legs, and waited.

The spear fell to the ground, and the eyes in ambush came closer. She smelled the blood on his breath; she was engulfed by the odor of his body.

She knew he would take possession.

❖3❖

There was a sound. Instinctively, Kwani jumped up, reaching for her spear. Then she remembered. Crooked Foot was here. He still slept, his own spear close by. She was safe.

Five times the moon had been full since she came. She had planned to stay only long enough to stock her pack. But each had learned a little of the language of the other. With sign language to supplement, they discovered common ground. Each had been driven from their clans, deprived of family, home, friends, protection, and the pleasures and benefits of tribal life.

But Kwani's emotions of compassion and kinship were mingled with distaste because he was Ute.

"Why were you sent away?" she asked.

For a while, he did not reply. Kwani was afraid she had made him angry again. Fury seemed always to simmer under the surface in him. Finally, he said, "The shaman, my father, sent me away."

She was shocked. "Why?"

Black eyes smouldered. "I do not speak of it."

"The Medicine Chief tried to kill me so I ran away," she said. "He thought I was a witch."

Crooked Foot grunted and picked up a snare he was mending with twine made of yucca fibers, bending over it, weaving the twine expertly. As if to change the subject, he said, "Kokopelli will come this way soon."

Kwani had never seen Kokopelli; he visited their remote village seldom and left quickly. He was the one her mother had told of—magician, teacher, healer, a trader who traveled from far places bringing news and telling stories. Some considered him to be a god who assured fertility and good fortune for the tribe.

"When will he be here?"

12

"Soon. One cannot know until the flute is heard."

Kwani's round face glowed. She loved music. "He plays a flute?"

"Yes. He plays as he comes. We hear him before he is seen. His magic bird tells him when to play."

Kwani was astonished. "A bird flies with him?"

"Sometimes. But usually it rides on his shoulder and talks to him."

"My mother did not speak of a bird!"

"Only last time did he bring the bird. The bird and Kokopelli talk to one another."

Kwani was awed. "You heard them?"

"Yes. They speak a magic tongue."

Kwani pondered this. If Kokopelli knew such magic, surely he would know where the Blue-eyed One dwelled. "Does he travel to the southeast?"

"He travels far, far."

Kwani remembered this the next morning as she watched Crooked Foot sleeping. She visualized Kokopelli as a handsome young warrior who would whisk her away; their nights would be devoted to ardent and masterful lovemaking and their days to her amusement. She fantasized his sorrow when he turned her over to the Chief, the Blue-eyed One, an old but kindly elder of the tribe. She imagined, with pleasure, Kokopelli's last, lingering embrace as he said goodbye, and her brave acceptance of the inevitable.

Yes, that is how it will be, she thought as she gazed into the haze of dawn. A tawny animal trotted into view. It was Brother Coyote on his morning rounds. She wondered if he could be the same coyote who led the wounded hunter back to camp.

Her people often related this event at the campfire. It was a favorite story—how the coyote spent the night with the wounded hunter, licking his wounds, and how he led the hunter back to camp by a shortcut the next day. Some said it was the hunter's protecting spirit in coyote form.

She wanted to call, "Ho, Brother Coyote!" but she was afraid to waken Crooked Foot. The coyote darted into the brush and disappeared. She looked at Crooked Foot again; even in sleep his face was sullen. She would stay with him only until Kokopelli came.

It was late summer and Kokopelli had not come. Crooked Foot's moody furies grew more frequent, and Kwani became increasingly uneasy. She returned from root gathering one day to find him pulling at the sandal on his twisted foot. He jabbed his spear at it, tearing it off.

Kwani was appalled. "Why do you do that?"

"It is torn and useless." He flung it at her. "Make me another."

"But—"

"Now!" He fingered the spear.

Kwani examined the sandal. It was worn, but serviceable.

"I can repair—"

"No!" He spat out the words, raising the spear. "Make me a new one!"

She ran from the cave. He hates me, I must leave before he throws that spear one day. When will Kokopelli come? Soon it will be the time of falling leaves, then snows . . . I cannot go alone in the cold and snow, searching for a Blue-eyed One I have never seen, in an unknown place. . . . Mother, what shall I do?

An inner voice spoke. "Make the sandal, and wait. Kokopelli will come."

Not long after, Kwani was grinding corn on her metate when Crooked Foot burst into the cave.

"Come! Come!" he shouted.

She was alarmed. "What is it?"

"Hunters at the spring! With a magic bow! Bring something, something to trade!" He glanced about the cave and ran to the rabbit skin robe. He jerked it so that the basket on it tumbled over and corn spilled on the floor.

"Come!"

"No," she cried angrily. "No. Come back!"

But he was gone, running with his awkward gait down the path. She stood at the cave entrance, watching him disappear around the mountain. She was worried; he carried no weapon. She took her own spear, and followed.

At the bend of the path she paused, listening. Voices shouted. Cautiously, she peered around the mountain. Four hunters from an unknown tribe were shooting arrows in target practice at a distant tree. One bow was like none Kwani had seen before. It was small, set crosswise on a wooden bar into which the arrow was set and remained in place. When the hunter was ready to shoot, he raised the bow, sighted over the knuckle of his right thumb, moved a finger of the hand holding the bow, and the arrow sped like a flash of light to its mark.

Kwani watched in astonishment as the hunter replaced the arrow, tilted the bow downward, and looped the bowstring over a double hook hanging from his waist. He slipped his foot into a stirrup fastened to the bow, pushing his foot down until the bowstring was caught in place by a notch on the bar. She could see that the arrow was fitted into place in a groove on the bar, with its end resting against the bowstring. To release it, the hunter only squeezed a trigger that controlled the bowstring. Kwani saw that, though it took longer to fit an arrow into the bow, having it held in place ready for instant release was a big advantage in hunting.

No wonder Crooked Foot wanted to trade for it!

He waved the robe before their eyes. They ignored him.

"See this fine robe!" he cried, and repeated it in sign language.

The hunters snickered. They were four and he was but one, and crippled at that. They would have sport with him. They shot their arrows closer and closer to his head. Frightened, Kwani withdrew. He needed his spear. In close fighting, he was adept, she knew.

Quickly, she ran back to the cave and found the spear, longer and heavier than her own. At the hidden place above the spring, she stopped, listening again. Crooked Foot was shouting, "My robe! Give me the small bow for my robe!"

Kwani peered around the bend in the mountain path. A hunter yanked at the robe, trying to pull it from Crooked Foot's grasp. The others stood by, laughing.

They would tear her robe, her beautiful robe! In a furious surge of strength, she stepped clear of the mountain and flung the spear. It soared in an arc, fell, and pinned the robe to the ground. She ducked out of sight before the astounded hunters glimpsed her.

Instantly, Crooked Foot grabbed the spear and brandished it, shouting fiercely. He snatched the robe and flung it behind him.

The hunters regarded him with new respect. His tribe was watching! Finally, the leader approached and indicated he wanted to examine the robe.

After more loud talk and sign language, Crooked Foot agreed. He held the robe in one hand, spear in the other, as the leader examined the workmanship of the robe. There was more shouting as the hunters argued with one another and the leader tried to jerk the robe from Crooked Foot's grasp.

Instinctively, Kwani knew something must be done. Swiftly she ran back to the cave, and gathered up a week's supply of dried meat into a basket. She ran back down the path. At the bend, she paused and placed the basket on her head. Regally, seductively, she walked down to the spring.

Still they argued loudly, jerking the robe back and forth. When they saw her coming, they stopped, surprised. She approached, blue eyes glowing, and with a single, fluid movement, she lifted the basket from her head and offered it to the leader.

"Why do you give him my meat?" Crooked Foot cried angrily.

"We trade."

She smiled at the leader, who gaped at her as he clutched the robe in one hand and the small bow in the other. Kwani drew out a large, particularly tasty-looking piece of meat. She held it under the leader's nose while he sniffed hungrily. Gently, she pushed the meat into the hand that held the bow.

"I will hold the bow while you eat," she told him in graceful sign language.

He hesitated, trying to decide whether to relinquish the robe or the bow. He looked her over—only a woman, and small, at that. Quite delectable, besides. He grunted, released the bow to her hand, and took the meat. He could snatch back his bow whenever he chose.

He took a large bite, chewed. The others gathered around the basket, helping themselves. But though Kwani—with an inviting glance from under her lashes—offered him the basket as well as the robe, in exchange for the small bow, he continued to eat, shouting insults at Crooked Foot meanwhile.

Kwani was concerned. Already much of their meat was gone. She searched for a solution.

Babies of her clan nursed until they were over two years old. Sometimes, boys were unruly, even at the breast, and mothers quieted them. She would do the same. Crooning softly, she lifted the leader's loincloth and stroked him caressingly.

She was gratified to note he was not displeased.

Slowly, with mixed emotions, Kwani retraced her steps to the cave. The leader had not been brutal and he had refused to share her. The others were angry, but they obeyed.

Her feet dragged. She did not want to see Crooked Foot again, not yet. While the hunter was straddling her, Crooked Foot had snatched up the bow and run back to the cave. Her female nature, demanding protection, was outraged.

The bow means more to him than I do. And it was *I* who obtained the bow.

Her chin lifted. Confidence surged in her, intoxicating and new. She had succeeded where Crooked Foot had failed. He had run to his cave like a rabbit to its hole.

She would not be afraid of him again.

❖ 4 ❖

Crooked Foot sat at the door of the cave, making a new arrow for Strongbow, using the one obtained from the hunters as a guide. Admiringly he examined the hunter's arrow. It was short, and instead of feathers there were insets of hide. From what animal? Deer? Buffalo? He couldn't be certain; the tanning was different. The arrow's tip was strangest of all, made of a smooth, black substance, hard as stone but not stone, and when he touched the tip with his finger, he drew back in pain.

The bow was obviously very old, but it was so well made that it worked perfectly. He had carved a long, two-pronged hook from wood to resemble the one the hunter wore, fastened at the waist. It took some practicing with his twisted foot to push down on the stirrup until the bowstring was caught by the notch in the crossbar. But he was learning how. All he needed now was a supply of arrows tipped with flint.

He smoothed the arrow's shaft with his rubbing stone. From time to time he glanced at Kwani who avoided summer sun in the shade of a juniper tree. She was making a basket; her nimble fingers wove the pliant reeds swiftly, and she hummed as she worked.

Making noises like that, unprotected and out in the open! A Ute woman would know better. He fumed in festering irritation. Ever since the day of his brilliant trading with the hunters that gave him Strongbow, she had changed in her attitude toward him.

He watched her. That too-light skin of hers . . . he preferred women to be dark, like himself. She was a bore. She and her eternal baskets, her Anasazi ways! He spat.

Lately, she had been pestering him with questions about Kokopelli. He had told her that Kokopelli was a magician, a healer, a teacher, a sharp trader, but *he did not tell her the rest.* No, that he refused to discuss.

She seemed especially interested in Kokopelli's magic. Could it be that she wished to learn his magic so that she might use it? Was she, indeed, a witch? But if she were a witch, she would know magic already. No. She was nothing, only an Anasazi squaw.

Muttering, he polished the arrow. He, a Ute, whose tribe was master of vast distances, master hunters, master warriors—he, who should be roaming free, squatted in a cave like a sow boar. While a woman—an *Anasazi woman*—endangered their safety and sang as she did it!

He picked up Strongbow; the arrow was ready to fly at a nudge of the trigger. Raising it to his eye, he sighted over the knuckle of his right thumb. Only a touch and the arrow would slice her heart, silencing her forever.

She shifted position, raising her hand to brush a strand of hair from her forehead in a gesture of unconscious grace. She crossed her ankles and shadows played on her small feet in their yucca sandals. A bird flew from the tree; she turned her head to watch, sunlight dappling the shiny black coils of her hair rolled tightly above each ear.

She was beautiful.

He loved her. He hated her.

He laid Strongbow on the rabbit skin blankets Kwani had made for barter with Kokopelli. He should arrive in another moon; perhaps this time he would bring for trade objects of stone-that-was-not-stone, the substance that tipped Strongbow's arrow. Crooked Foot frowned impatiently. More blankets would be needed for objects of such value. He needed the help of the Anasazi woman still. He hated her.

He had not had a mate before. Because of his foot, women of the tribe ignored him. And he had been caught stealing a flint knife, which should have been his since he saw the flint first. But he was not as agile as the others . . . It was only because his father was the shaman that Crooked Foot's offending hand was not cut off. His father convinced the people that unupits, those mysterious beings who caused illness and had maimed his son's foot at birth, had influenced Crooked Foot to steal; he was not to blame.

Later, during the heavy snows, unupits attacked his father and took the life from both his legs. He was left crippled, helpless, old, a shaman no longer.

The Chief called a council of the clan. Crooked Foot sat in a corner, staring impassively, determined to show no feeling. The Chief faced the clan with dignity, and raised his hand in the gesture of silence-before-speaking.

"Unupits killed the foot of the son of our shaman."

There were murmurs of agreement.

"Unupits caused Crooked Foot to take that which was not his."

"It is so," the flint knife's owner cried.

Crooked Foot's impassive gaze did not waver.

The Chief continued. "Unupits possessed Crooked Foot. Now they have killed the legs of our shaman, they have killed his powers, they have made of him this." He gestured toward an old man huddled on a blanket. "Shall we permit unupits to linger here, killing the rest of us?"

"No! the clan cried.

"Kill Crooked Foot!" the flint knife's owner shouted. "Unupits reside in him!" There were murmurs among the clan. Crooked Foot gazed fiercely over their heads.

A young man spoke. "We must destroy the unupits."

The old shaman raised a feeble hand. "I shall speak." His voice was steady and strong.

"It is true. Unupits are among us." He raised his hand again, and waited for silence. "If my *son*"—he emphasized the relationship—"is killed, will unupits go away? No! No, they will rejoice and stay, to find more mischief to do here. Send them away, far away, with my son . . ." His voice trembled. "Send my son away. Forever." His old face crumpled. "I have spoken."

Crooked Foot rose, wrapping his blanket around him, and strode with his lurching gait into the night. Flint-knife owner's voice shouted after him. "If you return, you will lose more than your hand!"

Was there laughter?

When he was far enough away, Crooked Foot wrapped one arm around a tree, leaned down, and gagged and vomited until nothing was left.

But he could not empty his heart of tears.

Remembering, Crooked Foot grasped Strongbow. His foot might be weak, but now his hunting arm was strong—stronger than any of theirs!

Recalling how Strongbow was acquired, he experienced an odd emotion, one he had not known before. He remembered how tantalizing she was with the hunter, and how she curled her legs around him when he rode her. He felt his man part swelling.

Kwani's voice, humming, drifted by.

"Come here!" he shouted. He would show her! This was one time a crooked foot didn't matter.

The humming stopped, but she did not come.

He strode toward her. She continued her weaving, ignoring him. How dare she—an Anasazi squaw! Fury surged in him—and something more.

Kwani observed the bulge under his sage bark apron, and put the basket aside resentfully. She disliked being disturbed at her work. But he was on her before she could rise, throwing her down again, penetrating her savagely. She did not resist. But she did not respond; nor did she wrap her legs around him.

"You are *my* mate! I make you Ute!" he growled, and thrust harder. He visualized his organ as a knife, stabbing. Only when she cried out in pain was the man fluid released at last.

Kwani lay rigid in the darkness, pretending to sleep. Premonition lay on her, smothering like a blanket. Her heart beat irregularly and perspiration trickled from her body. Furtively, she glanced at Crooked Foot. Was he asleep? She couldn't be sure. He could crouch motionless for hours, like an animal, then spring to attack.

Her mind struggled like a rabbit in a snare. When will Kokopelli come to take me away? This man is my enemy. His spirit putrefies. He does not want to grind his own corn, make his sandals, cook his food. But he likes to hurt me; he will kill me one day. I still hurt, inside.

Pretending to sigh in her sleep, she turned on her side to look at him. His eyes were open. They stared at her like a wolf's eyes in the dark.

·5·

Clouds swept from the horizon at last, trailing mantles of rain over the mesas. Gods shouted, pounded thunder-drums, and threw fire spears to earth. Each day, Sunfather walked lower in his sky path; each day, heat and lassitude of summer faded in anticipation of a new season. The sky, a deep and dazzling blue, pushed mountains closer, outlining them sharply.

Crooked Foot stood at the door of the cave and gazed beyond and beyond, seeing in the eyes of his mind the place of his people, his homeland. Autumn was the good time of rabbit drives, of socializing, gambling, dancing, courting.

With a pang of longing, he turned back to the cave. Kwani was gone on some trivial female errand, but her handiwork was everywhere. Baskets lined the walls and skins lay in a neat pile awaiting Kokopelli. Other baskets held dried meat or herbs and roots, seeds, berries. Her implements were arranged neatly: flint knives—which *he* had made—awls and needles of bone, gourds dried, hollowed, and fitted with snug lids. Others held useless things she liked: bits of bright stone, sweet smelling leaves, and small objects carved from wood and wrapped in yucca twine dyed with the red of the cactus fruit. He suspected they had something to do with her wanting a child. She often hunted for the special herbs to make her pregnant.

Crooked Foot yearned for a son, who would be the swiftest runner, the strongest and best of all Utes, whose legs would be strong and straight. Then, he and his son would return to the tribe in triumph, assuming its leadership as son and grandson of the shaman.

If only he could return to his clan! If only he had a power to make them forget the past! His glance slid over the floor. Strongbow! With a surge of excitement he snatched up the bow and assumed a posture of dignity and importance, rehearsing his appearance.

Yes! He would return to his people, appearing with power and riches. Look at these fine rabbit skin robes, and baskets woven so tightly they would hold water! These awls and needles and all these other things! He was a rich man! He would select a woman of his choosing. He would become an important personage, respected, an influential tribe member. Never would he, a Ute, be burdened with an Anasazi squaw!

He would be gone before Kwani returned!

Kwani climbed the path to the cave, hurrying, weary with the weight of her pack. She could hardly wait to show Crooked Foot what she had found. She called as she approached, but there was no answer.

He must be hunting.

But when she entered, she saw immediately that something was wrong. Her belongings were in disarray; many were missing. Carefully she slipped off her pack, from which protruded her prize, a slab of wood pried from a fallen tree. The wood was just the right weight and size. Smoothed and polished and fitted with thongs, it would be a beautiful cradle board.

When her monthly flows had ceased, she was unbelieving, thinking a mischievous spirit was playing a trick on her. But when her abdomen began to swell she experienced the first wild hope. Then, later, she felt life move within her. She was pregnant—at last, at last.

To share her joy, she had planned the cradle board to be a surprise for Crooked Foot. His attitude toward her was sure to change now. He would be easier to live with until Kokopelli came.

But he was gone.

Where?

And it looked as if he planned to be gone for several days. Perhaps tired of waiting for Kokopelli to come and trade, he had taken things to barter at some distant village. My belongings! she thought in a flash of anger. He took them without even asking. An Anasazi would never do such a thing.

What if he never came back? A sliver of fear pierced her.

I am alone. Again.

She placed both hands over her abdomen. No, I am not alone. I have one I must care for . . .

As if responding, the baby moved within her.

Still holding her abdomen, she sank to the floor. "I will protect you," she whispered.

Resolutely, she told herself it would be a relief not to worry about Crooked Foot's rages. Not to gather food for him, or prepare his corn cake and corn gruel and meat stew. Not to have to tan skins for him, make his garments and belts and sandals. Or to comb the lice from his hair or make poultices for his wounds. Now she was free to prepare for the baby.

She began to unpack her basket. There were herbs for the birthing brews and poultice; cedar bark to be shredded finely to line the cradle board and to serve as diapering; and yucca roots for soapsuds. There were seeds, berries, and pinyon nuts. And a tiny prairie dog she had captured and killed, whose skin would make a fine pouch for salt. Kokopelli always brought salt when he came. *If* he came . . .

But now there would be no meat unless she became a hunter. When her belly grew big, how could she chase game? She would use snares. She glanced around; Crooked Foot had left a snare hung from a small outcrop on the cave's wall. Good! She could catch rabbits as well as Crooked Foot did, or almost . . .

She placed the birthing herbs in a little hollowed-out gourd with a lid, thinking of her mother preparing the poultice and brews. *I wish I could go home.*

She sat down to think about it. She missed her people, her home. Now that she was pregnant, the evil spirits must be gone. That would surely prove she was not a witch. Babies were an occasion for rejoicing—a sign that the gods were pleased and were increasing the tribe. How happy her mother would be!

Remembering her mother, Kwani was overwhelmed by loneliness. She thought of how her mother must stand looking down the trail where Kwani had gone, waiting for her to come home, and how it would be if she returned for the birthing, bringing another child to the clan. Wouldn't Wopio be surprised! And Maluku, the Medicine Chief . . .

Thinking of Maluku made her uneasy. But winter was coming, when she could not journey alone to the southeast with a baby inside her, searching for the Blue-eyed One. Even if Kokopelli did come—which she doubted by now—it would be difficult to travel the rugged terrain in winter storms, snows, and cold. Marauding animals . . . she remembered the cougar, and her palms grew sweaty.

Suppose Crooked Foot did come back? Would a baby really change him? Perhaps he would hate the child as he hated her.

No, I cannot remain here. Mother, I am coming home.

❖6❖

Just to be sure, she offered a pinch of corn meal to the Six Sacred Directions and murmured a prayer for a safe journey. Pausing at the spring to fill her deerskin water bag, she sent a final glance at the place she was leaving forever, and headed across the mesa.

Sunfather was higher now; although his breath was cool, she perspired under her heavy pack. Her sandals of yucca fiber protected her feet from sharp stones and gravel. But brush caught at her, scratched her arms and legs, and reached for the spear to seize it from her grasp.

There was no trail. To escape Maluku, she had run like a frightened rabbit all those months before, scrambling through the ravines. But her sure sense of direction told her she should be home the next day. But many rugged ravines dissected the mesas. Somewhere there should be a trail down; she would follow the ravine homeward.

Was that a sound behind her? She whirled. There was movement in a bush not far away. Her heart jerked. Apaches! She grasped her spear firmly. Maybe there was only one; if so, she had a chance.

"I see you!" she shouted. "Come out!"

She ran forward, spear ready. There was a rustle and the bush moved. Kwani drew back her arm for the spear thrust. A tawny brown figure darted out. A coyote!

She dropped the spear and sank to the ground in relief, laughing. Brother Coyote! Wiping the perspiration from her face left a muddy smear. What if I had hurt him? The thought was sobering. Coyotes had supernatural powers. Some were healers who licked the wounds of warriors and led them back to camp, but some were not coyotes at all, but evil ones who assumed coyote form. Was that not a coyote at all . . . but Maluku?

She trudged on, glancing nervously behind to see if the coyote followed. There was no sign of him.

At midday, she stopped to eat and rest on a rise, under a bushy juniper tree where she could see in all directions. It was cool in the shade, but when Sunfather disappeared into his mountain home, cold night winds of autumn would sweep the mesas, chilling to the bone. Soon she must find shelter for the night.

She munched a corn cake from her pack while she gazed over the countryside. In the distance, a flock of ravens flew upward, screeching. Something had disturbed them. She hunkered down and peered through the partially concealing branches.

A deer burst from the shadows and ran toward the rise where Kwani crouched. Three hunters followed. *Apaches!*

Frozen with terror, Kwani watched the deer approach, and the Apaches running after it. Her pack was only partially concealed under the tree, and her spear lay beside it. Surely the Apaches would see them! She tried to control her trembling so that no movement would betray her presence.

But the deer swerved and ran madly in another direction. The Apaches followed swiftly, silently, with indomitable ferocity. Eventually they would overtake the exhausted animal, she knew. For a long time, Kwani crouched motionless. The Apaches might return. Shadows grew long. At last she rose carefully and looked in all directions. They were gone.

Murmuring prayers of gratitude, Kwani made her way to the mesa's brim. The ravine was shallow here; she could find a way down if she were careful. Already, a cool wind rose.

The sandstone cliffs beneath the mesa had many small caves. She walked along the brim, anxiously searching for a place to climb down. She had to find shelter before it was too dark to see.

Her pack felt heavier. Her step slowed as she forced her way through the brush. There was a small cave near the bottom on the other side of the ravine, with brush nearly covering the entrance. It would provide protection from the cold and the eyes of hunters.

The slope was steep and rocky; she would have to use the utmost care and skill, so she paused to rest. There was a sound behind her. A footstep! Kwani whirled around to look. No one was there. But she *knew* she had heard a footstep. Apaches!

She stumbled down the slope, the rocky soil, crumbling under her feet. She slipped off her pack, but she was sliding. Helplessly, she dropped the spear and grabbed at brush. But loose gravel sent her hurtling downward. Over and over she turned, scratched and torn, thrown from rock to rock, each pounding a hammer blow on her body. She landed at last at the bottom of the ravine.

A fierce pain, different from any she had ever known before, knifed her back and abdomen.

She fell into unconsciousness.

It was dark and very cold when a terrible, writhing pain woke her. Her baby was coming! But it was too soon, too soon!

She tried to rise, but her leg hurt. She tried to stop the birthing contractions, but her body had a will of its own. Black dark pressed down; never had she felt so totally alone. She cried out in primal fear and agony as grinding spasms wrenched her again and again, leaving her panting and weak. There was a warm gush between her thighs, but she did not feel it. She was unconscious.

She woke again much later. The sharp pain had subsided somewhat, but her entire body felt like a throbbing wound. She was not as cold as before; something warm nestled beside her. She raised her head to see, and gasped. An animal like a dog lay with its back against her body. She moved, and the animal turned to look at her. A coyote! Brother Coyote!

Her baby. Where was her baby? She wanted to see it, to hold it. Brother Coyote was moving away. She felt with both hands, exploring the area between her thighs. There was no baby.

Then she knew. The spirit coyote had taken the child into himself so it would enter the spirit world with him.

She drifted into darkness again.

Dim light. Juniper smoke. Warmth. A sound, a strange sound like a bird squawking, close by. Again, pain shot up her leg. Her leg was moving, but not of its own accord.

She was in a cave. A person—a man?—wrapped a long strip of soft buckskin around her leg from knee to ankle, strapping it to a pine bough. She lay on a pad of grasses and cedar bark, and a fire burned nearby.

Again there was a squawking sound. A large, brilliant bird waddled forward. The feathers of its sleek head glowed red, its back and tail were vivid green, and the wing feathers were streaked with blue. Kwani had never seen such a creature and she was astounded as the bird walked up the person's arm to the shoulder and perched there.

A man's deep voice spoke impatiently in a foreign tongue. He reached up, removed the bird, and set it, not too gently, on the floor where it squawked in protest and waddled away.

Kwani gave a little cry of surprise and pain. The man laid her leg down and bent over her. Firelight illuminated him. He was like no one she had ever seen. His face was not round like an Anasazi, but long and narrow. A great beak of a hawklike nose protruded from between heavy eyebrows, swooping down to full lips that curved downward in the corners. Tawny, lion-colored eyes slanted above high cheekbones, seemed to throw off sparks. Heavy hoops of something bright and shiny hung from each ear. An ornate necklace of the same substance lay on a broad, bare chest.

Above a sharply sloping forehead his heavy black hair was coiled in a knot on top of his head and covered with a woven cap adorned with bright feathers and turquoise beads.

He had an odd smell, not unpleasant. He bent closer, and touched her face.

"Anasazi," he said in an unfamiliar accent. "You are Anasazi."

Strange though he was, something about him was reassuring. "Who are you?" she asked.

He did not reply, but turned to the fire, took a burning bough and held it over her face so that he might see her more clearly. He bent close, and Kwani saw that his cheeks and chin were ornamented with an elaborate pattern of black dots.

He lifted the lids of both her eyes, peering closely into each one. Then he pulled down her chin to examine her mouth. Grunting, he tossed the bough back into the fire and finished bandaging her leg.

"My baby!" Kwani moaned, suddenly flooded by overwhelming grief.

The man gave her not a glance, but finished bandaging her leg. Then, as the moaning continued, he vanished into the shadows and returned with a flute. Sitting down, he leaned against the wall and began to play. It was the sound of birds in springtime, of water in a stream, of wind in grasses, of the beating heart of a lover. A sweet, passionate song of life.

The music flowed over her like a magical balm, lessening her pain. She stared at him. Was it possible? But he was so strange.

"Are you Kokopelli?"

He inclined his head briefly.

"How did you find me?"

"Brother Coyote found you." His strange accent made him difficult to understand. "He led me to you."

The coyote was not really a coyote, Kwani thought. It was the spirit of an ancestor. I wonder which one? Aloud, she said, "You brought me here, to the cave I tried to reach." She smiled. "I am grateful to you."

He took a gourd dipper from beside the fire, raised her head, and held the dipper to her lips.

"Drink."

She sipped and turned her face away. It was a hot, bitter brew.

"Drink!" he commanded. "It will destroy the evil that makes you weak."

His voice, his presence, the look in his amber eyes, the way he held her head in one steady hand convinced her.

"Now, rest," he said.

The macaw squawked from the shadows. Kokopelli held out his hand. The bird waddled to it and climbed up on the outstretched finger. Kokopelli raised the bird so that they looked eye to eye. He spoke to it rapidly in his foreign tongue. The creature cocked its head, then replied in a wonderfully human voice.

Kwani was thunderstruck.

He lifted the bird to his shoulder where it settled itself and stared at Kwani with beady little black eyes.

"What does it say?" Kwani asked fearfully.

Tawny eyes under black brows regarded her silently for a moment. "He says you are beautiful."

He was making fun of her! A wave of nausea and pain surged over her, and she turned her face away.

Once more he lifted the flute to his lips. There was the melody of darkness falling softly, softly; of evening when day is done, stars appear, and families gather on rooftops to sing and tell stories and be happy.

Slowly her eyes closed and she fell into a deep sleep.

K okopelli sat looking at the sleeping girl, at the hair flowing like dark water around her face, and the lashes curving on her cheeks. Beneath those sleeping lids he knew the eyes were startlingly blue.

Blue. Like those of the Chief with whom he had traded in moons past. Who was she? From the contents of her pack he knew she was on a journey. Alone. Why?

Early that morning while he was bathing in a stream, a coyote had appeared. Kokopelli was accustomed to animals; he communicated with them in spirit and was never harmed. Courteously, he ignored the coyote until the animal saw fit to address him.

The coyote sat on its haunches and watched Kokopelli splash in the water. Finally, Kokopelli returned the animal's intent gaze. For some moments they stared at one another. Then the coyote rose, trotted a short distance, and sat again until Kokopelli dried himself with grasses. The sun had not yet risen, but the golden loops hanging from each ear, and the ornate necklace upon his bare chest reflected shimmering light. Kokopelli's bronzed body was hard and lean; legs displayed muscles developed in countless miles of walking through deserts, over mountains and vast plains during his wanderings from Cem-Anahuac, the One World, beyond the great river of the south.

As a Toltec nobleman, he was entitled to a life of luxury in Tula. But after the Chichimeca barbarians overran his homeland, he had had no desire to linger there. Even though his home and family—brothers, sisters, cousins—were safe, and his ancestral lands intact. Or had been the last time he returned for a visit. He preferred the life of a wanderer—a trader, healer, magician, a teacher of arts and sciences. When simple people revered him as a semi-supernatural being, it amused him. He used their adulation to his financial—and physical—advantage. He was, after all, a Toltec.

The coyote rose, trotted farther, and sat again.

"Very well," Kokopelli said.

He tied on his soft cotton loincloth and wrapped himself in his woolen mantle of bright colors. He had washed his hair in yucca suds; now he wound it into a tight knot and fastened it on top of his head with golden pins. His cap, placed on a rock while he bathed, was inspected carefully for the hated lice of the foreigners before he replaced it, smoothing the short, sleek feathers that gave it a luxurious, colorful sheen. The brim was edged with turquoise beads suspended to quiver impressively with each movement. He was proud of that cap; it was like no other. A Maya woman he had loved had made it for him.

He had loved many women and was ready to love another. That would be taken care of when he reached the Place of the Eagle Clan, as it was at every city and village he visited. A man's juices must be bestowed to be replenished. Otherwise, they dried up, and so did he.

The coyote waited, looking back as Kokopelli shouldered his pack and followed. At the mesa's brim, the coyote paused. When Kokopelli arrived, the coyote trotted away, smiling his coyote smile.

Kokopelli looked down in the ravine. A girl lay sprawled among the rocks, her clothes bloody and torn. Nearby, tiny bones lay about, and an infant's skull was being picked clean by ravens. They flapped away as he approached. Halfway down the bank a pack basket was alive with ants foraging for food. Nearby lay a spear. A spear of all things! No one used spears anymore; certainly not a girl.

He slipped and slid down the gravel bank. The girl's cheek was burning with fever.

I cannot leave her here.

A small cave was partially concealed by brush, and he carried her into it. The ceiling was low but the cave was deep enough. Beginning with the skull, he began a careful examination, inch by inch to the feet. She was cut and badly bruised, but the only break he found was between the knee and the ankle of her right leg. But she had given birth and was in a coma, with high fever.

He squatted on his haunches to think about it. As a member of the Toltec ruling caste, he had learned the sciences, including astronomy, mathematics, engineering, and medicine. He also had learned much from medicine men during his travels.

She has injured her head. Or else a sickness is in her blood, he decided. Again, his long, strong fingers examined her skull, pressing through the tangled mass of her hair. Her skull was flattened in back due to the Anasazi custom of placing infants on a cradle board. He knew that only a head suitably flat in back was considered to be beautiful. A barbaric custom, Kokopelli thought, as his fingers probed her skull. He found nothing to indicate serious injury, but of course one could not be certain about the skull. Surgery might be necessary. Trepanning instruments were in his medicine pouch.

However, treating the blood sickness might be sufficient. It took some time to find the berries, leaves, roots, and bark he needed, as well as a suitable bough for a splint. She was still unconscious when he returned. Hastily, he built a fire, mixed the medicinal substances in his pottery cooking bowl with water from his water bag. While the brew boiled, he would bandage her leg.

With his sharp flint knife he scraped the bark from the bough, smoothing the side which would rest against her leg. The pungent scent of the boiling brew filled the cave. From his medicine pouch he removed a long, white, very soft strip of buckskin, pressed the splint against her leg, and began to bandage carefully but not too tightly. One did not insult the circulation.

He was gratified when she woke, and congratulated himself when her spirit responded to his flute and she relaxed to natural sleep. The strength of her spirit would quicken her healing.

But the problem of time had to be confronted. It would be at least forty days before she could walk without a crutch. Meanwhile, she could not travel the rugged terrain. Winter approached, and it was time, past time, for him to return south.

Either he would have to leave her while he traveled to the cliff cities for someone to return and care for her, or he would have to remain here himself.

He stepped outside and sniffed the air. It was black dark; clouds concealed the constellations. A chill rode the breeze. Yes, winter was coming. He would head south to warm seas and sands and winter trading.

His gaze wandered to her pack basket. He had emptied it, inspected the contents, disposed of the ants. The basket was the finest he had ever seen, even of fine Anasazi baskets. For a long time now most Anasazi had preferred to make pottery containers. This basket was an outstanding exception.

He reviewed his travel route. He could barter many such baskets, many indeed. But he would need a woman to carry such loads, as well as to prepare his meals and attend to his clothes and other needs between villages. Kokopelli had long considered taking a mate. He was getting old; soon he would be forty-three, no longer able to challenge the horizons. But any animal, any bird, had a den or a nest, a place of refuge, a home. What woman would willingly wander homeless in heat and storms, living as he lived? Besides, he enjoyed choosing a different woman in every village and city he visited. When he bestowed his seed, he assured the fertility and well being of the tribe. He had taken great pains to convince them of this; he had no wish to sacrifice the fruits of his success. He had seen enough of marriage relationship to know that no woman of consequence, certainly not one worthy of his choosing, would be content with a nomad life like his. A discontented woman was a burr in the sandal.

He had thought of taking a boy as bearer. But sharing his trading secrets would result in competition. He had enough of that as it was, with all the trading going on, some over distances even greater than his. No. Only he was Kokopelli, teacher, magician, medicine man par excellence, bestower of sacred seed.

So it would remain.

But this girl. She traveled alone. Why? She had given forced birth. Did she have a mate? If so, where?

Her pack contained an excellent blanket woven of rabbit fur strips wrapped around fine yucca twine. Among the Anasazi, he knew men did the weaving usually. However, with baskets and blankets such as hers . . . His lips twitched and the nostrils of his beak nose flared as if to the scent of greater riches.

The girl stirred. Yes, she was beautiful. He laid aside her fine blanket and lifted her torn and bloody robe. Her small breasts had blossomed with pregnancy; they were round and full and tipped with the color of cactus fruit. He bent to taste them. Even after birth her waist was slim, her hips swelling in a lush curve to lovely thighs.

He felt a stirring in his loins. But it was only a few hours since she had given forced birth. He slipped the robe from under her and pulled it off. It was badly soiled; he would wash it in the stream. And her, too, in the morning.

Dawn. Kwani opened her eyes. She was weak, and she hurt all over, but the sickness in her stomach was gone. For a moment, she was bewildered by the ceiling hanging low over her. Then she remembered—the fall, the pain, Brother Coyote . . . Her baby.

"My baby!" she moaned.

There was an answering sound, like her voice but without the words. Startled, Kwani struggled to raise herself on her elbows.

It is the bird, she thought. Yes, there it was, perched on a ledge. Each beady little black eye was a malevolent spirit, watching her. Where was Kokopelli? Her frightened gaze probed the dimness, and she fell back, exhausted. He has left me, she thought. I am alone with this evil bird.

Or was it he, taken the bird's form?

Again, she saw his face bent over her—the glowing eyes under heavy, black brows, the eagle's beak of a nose curving down to sensual lips. She glanced nervously at the macaw. Was it he?

The beak was much the same. The eyes were of a different color but they had an equal intensity.

"Kokopelli?" she whispered nervously.

The macaw fluffed its feathers and ignored her. She closed her eyes so she could not see it. Her leg ached; she ached all over. She pulled the blanket aside to inspect her leg, and realized for the first time that she was naked.

My robe! He has taken my robe!

She pulled the blanket closer under her chin. Where was he? What was he planning to do to her?

In her weakness, fears became magnified. He knew she was Anasazi. Maybe he had gone to find her people . . . her robe would identify her . . . maybe Maluku would come. She was helpless, trapped, at the mercy of an evil bird spirit. Kokopelli was nothing like she had imagined him to be. He was so *strange.* She was afraid of him.

Then she remembered his music, magical and sweet; her heart slowed a fraction in its pounding. Perhaps he will return . . . perhaps he has gone for water. But why has he taken my robe?

Again her eyes searched the shadows. Her basket too was gone. But its contents were neatly arranged, and his own bulging pack was still there.

She relaxed. *He has not left me.*

It grew lighter. It seemed to Kwani that she lay swallowed up inside the cliff. She was hungry and terribly thirsty, and it hurt to move even a little. The low ceiling hung ominously above her.

I have angered the gods, she thought. *What have I done to offend them?*

My amulet! I have not fed it as it requires! Since giving it to the medicine arrow, she had ignored it. Now she was being punished. I will feed it when Kokopelli returns.

If he returns.

Time passed. Fear and loneliness pressed down like the cave ceiling. She thought of her mother, waiting for her to come home.

Mother, I cannot return; I have lost my baby, my proof that the evil spirits are gone. I cannot walk to find the Blue-eyed One, who will give me what I have never had. Never, since the day of her birth, had she known true security—her eyes, her hated blue eyes, made her always suspect. She was trapped.

But maybe if she had something to lean on she could walk. *My spear!*

That is what I need. Perhaps tomorrow, or soon, I can find my way back to the cave and to Crooked Foot. She thought how angry he must be to find her gone. But at least it was a home of sorts.

With effort, she raised herself on her elbow again. There it was, her spear, propped against the wall, next to—

She gasped. Strongbow was there! Her heart lurched. Crooked Foot and Kokopelli were together in this. A conspiracy! *What will they do to me?*

She fell back, her heart fluttering like a bird in a snare. It was Crooked Foot's footstep she had heard before she tumbled down the bank. He was tracking her.

Her mind raced. I need my spear. She tried to stand, but pain shot up her leg. She dragged herself over the rough cave floor, pulling the throbbing leg. The shadows grew dimmer. Weakness and darkness enveloped her. As if in a nightmare, she heard movement at the cave entrance.

"Crooked Foot!" she cried.

Helpless, she felt herself lifted in strong arms. Fearfully, she opened her eyes. "What were you trying to do, foolish one?" The voice was musical and deep. Kokopelli's. The foreign face, so close, with the pattern of black dots . . .

He laid her on the blanket and squatted beside her, his amber eyes intent. He inspected her nails; he leaned close to peer at her lips and to smell her breath.

Instinctively, Kwani grasped a portion of the blanket to cover herself. With a sharp word of annoyance, he jerked the blanket from her grasp and examined her leg inch by inch, probing the buckskin bandage with his fingers. He bent to inspect her groin.

"No!"

The parrot bleated after her, "No! No!" and squawked triumphantly.

A glint flickered in Kokopelli's eyes. He pressed his hand on her abdomen. "Is there pain here?"

"No."

He pressed harder. "Now?"

She tried not to wince. "Not much."

"Do not move."

She stiffened with fear as he gently separated the lips of her woman part and bent to examine the area.

"You will heal." He sat back on his haunches, appraising her with a gaze that was not altogether impersonal.

Nervously, she reached for her blanket. He did not object, but amusement tugged at his mouth.

"Where is Crooked Foot?"

"Who?"

"Crooked Foot. He who owns Strongbow."

His gaze was inscrutable. "You know him?"

"He is—was—my mate. We obtained Strongbow in trade with hunters. Where is he?"

"Only you and I are here. And, of course, my companion." At his nod the bird approached with his obscene gait; Kokopelli held out his hand, and the bird rode the hand to his shoulder.

"But Strongbow is here. I saw it, in the shadows." Her voice squeaked like a wounded mouse. "Where is Crooked Foot?"

For a long moment, Kokopelli was silent. Blue eyes probed his; he turned away. "He is in Sipapu."

She gasped. Sipapu was the sacred underworld from where all people came and to where they returned after death.

She stared at Kokopelli. "You killed him!"

Sparks flared in his eyes. "Kokopelli has no need to kill for what he wants!" He paused. "I traded for it with Apaches."

Kwani remembered the Apaches . . . how they pursued the deer . . .

"They said that the crippled one tried to steal from them. They took revenge. He was near the place of his people."

Kwani was shaken. Crooked Foot was returning to his people, leaving her alone once more.

"Kokopelli," she whispered.

He turned to look at her.

"I am grateful to you."

He smiled. It was the first time she had seen him smile, and she was surprised at his teeth. As far as she could tell, all his teeth were there, which was quite remarkable for one so old. Among the Anasazi, teeth sickened and crumbled, causing much pain, at an early age.

He rose and went to his pack. He brought his cooking pot filled with blue and red berries, and his water bag to her. She drank until the water ran down her chin. Her body felt as Earthmother feels when raindrops fall after drought.

"Eat." He set the bowl of berries beside her.

She stuffed a handful of berries into her mouth. The tart and juicy red ones, the sweet blue ones, were both her favorites. The bowl was nearly empty before she remembered her manners. She offered him the bowl.

He accepted it gravely, sharing a berry now and then with the bird, who gulped it down with a sharp little jerk of its head. As Kokopelli chewed, the black dots on his chin bobbed up and down, and his ears moved, the golden loops swinging gently.

She thought, how odd he is! But she felt more at ease in his presence.

Kokopelli put the bowl aside and he and the bird conversed as he glanced at her from time to time. Kwani yearned to know what they were saying, but refused to ask. Finally, Kokopelli spoke matter-of-factly.

"My companion suggests you would feel better if you bathed."

His companion, indeed! "He could probably use a bath himself," she said tartly. "Please, may I have my pouch of sacred meal and my medicine arrow?"

Kokopelli examined the arrow curiously when he found them. Its decorations were mystic symbols of white and black.

"Where did you get such a thing? It looks like an arrow to kill witches."

"It is." She sprinkled a bit of sacred meal on the amulet fastened to the arrow.

"Accept my gift, oh powerful spirit. Protect me from the spirits of evil." She tossed a few more grains to the Six Sacred Directions. She handed the arrow and meal back to Kokopelli who replaced them without comment, his face expressionless.

He set the bird down and they watched as it circled about them, turning its scarlet head from side to side. Light shimmered on the blue and green of its wings and the vibrant green of its long tail.

Finally, Kokopelli said, "So you are a witch? I am not surprised."

"I am not a witch!"

He saw the pulse jumping in her throat. "The arrow. How did you acquire such a thing?"

"It was my eyes, my ugly eyes. When the sickness came—"

"Ah. And the arrow?"

"Maluku . . ." Remembering, she began to shiver, making hiccupping sounds like a child.

"Tell me."

But she could not. Kokopelli pulled her to a sitting position and folded her in his arms.

"You will tell me."

She buried her face against his chest. The steady beating of his heart, the feeling of being held, embraced by a strong man with command in his voice filled her like water poured into a pot that had been too long empty. Her shivering ceased, and she spoke softly so that he had to bend his head closer to hear.

"They were going to kill me. My mother told me to run away to the southeast to find the Blue-eyed One who would protect me."

"The Blue-eyed One? She knows of him?"

Something in those amber eyes was disconcerting.

"Yes. Do you know him also?"

"Tell me of the arrow."

"Maluku, the Medicine Chief, shot it at me as I ran away. But the arrow refused to find me and hid inside my basket."

"Your mate did not protect you?"

"No. He, too, thought I was a witch. Wopio . . ." She realized with surprise that she had not thought of Wopio for some time.

"Are you?"

She sank back in anger and frustration. *He will never believe me.* She said, "I must find the Blue-eyed One. *He* will believe me!"

"Perhaps he, also, is a witch." The full lips twitched in a smile, and he laughed. It was a pleasant sound. He threw his head back and opened his mouth wide so that his teeth shone white in the large, red cavern of his mouth. Kwani could not help herself; she had to laugh, too.

"I will take you to the stream to bathe."

He reached down and pulled the blanket away. This time she did not tremble but lay, scratched and bruised and splinted, in beauty.

He lifted her easily and carried her outside into the cold sunshine. The odd smell of him, the hard, shiny necklace that creased her cheek, the fabric of his multicolored mantle, so different from anything she knew, the cold air swirling about her bare body, and the way he held her, effortlessly, stirred mixed emotions. She felt both secure and insecure, pleased, but fearful of the strangeness of him, fearful of his intentions.

He climbed down to the bottom of the ravine and followed it to a stream. He laid her on a smooth place by the water. The stream looked wonderfully inviting. But he thrust out an arm to stop her from going in. "The bandage must not be wet."

He pushed the bandaged leg to the side. Removing his sandals of strong hide, laced crisscross to mid-calf, he waded into the stream, his mantle draped over his shoulders. Using his hands as a scoop, he poured water over her face and down to her toes, scoop by scoop. The water was icy, but it felt wonderful, especially on her bruises.

The yucca root had been softened by pounding. He soaked it in the stream, rubbing and squeezing it to make suds. Then, beginning with her face, he rubbed in the cleansing froth. She felt his hands following the contours of her cheeks, her nose, her chin, around her lips.

She thought, I could do this myself. But she did not suggest it.

His hands were on her throat, her shoulders, on each breast in a lingering massage that was a caress. She felt her nipples hardening, responding, as he kissed them with his fingers. Down the slope of her waist to the swell of her hips and her abdomen, his hands massaged, possessing. As his fingers slid between her thighs in gentle motion, a sensation, almost a pain, stabbed her within.

If he noticed, he gave no sign. His hands continued down her legs, carefully avoiding the bandage, to both bare feet where arches and insteps and each small toe were given tender attention.

"Now for the stream. Keep the bandaged leg dry."

He stepped into the stream. Holding her in his arms, the bandaged leg raised out of the water, he lifted her up and down until the suds were rinsed away.

The shock of the icy water, his glowing amber eyes, the sensual mouth so near her own, the possessive strength of him . . . Never before had she felt this way.

He placed her again upon the bank, turned her upon her stomach, and washed her back and round little buttocks. Kwani lay with her head upon both arms, glad to hide her face. Almost, she wished she had not given birth so recently. Almost, she wished that Kokopelli would take her as his mate. But her body could not yet receive a man; she was still sore and weak. And he was so strange. She still feared him a little.

On the bank she shivered in the cold. He wrapped his mantle around her and carried her like a papoose back to the cave, stopping to retrieve his sandals and her clean robe spread out to dry on a bush. The macaw squawked as they entered, protesting at having been left alone, and Kokopelli spoke to it. The bird ruffled its feathers, watching sullenly as Kokopelli laid Kwani on the bed of grasses and helped her to put on her dry robe.

Her leg and her whole body hurt, but she knew she would get well. Magical hands would heal her. She was safe.

Kokopelli sat in the shadows, satisfied. She would be useful, very useful, to him. He smiled, remembering her beating pulse, her cactus-fruit nipples responding to his touch. He would plan the future carefully.

Taking his flute, he raised it to his lips and played a thoughtful melody.

❖8❖

What does he want of me?

Kwani stood at the doorway of the cave, leaning on the crutch Kokopelli had made from a forked tree branch. The arm rest, padded with grasses and bound by buckskin, was comfortable enough if she did not use it too long at a time.

How many days had she been confined to the cave with an enigmatic stranger? She could not remember. Earthmother had discarded her summer robe now for one of sunset colors. The sky throbbed with blueness, and the air carried the scents of seed pods, of dried leaves and grasses and crimson leaves fallen, of earth preparing for winter rest.

Always, the beauty of this season had made her sing with happiness. But now unease prowled inside her. Kokopelli . . .

She had suspicions about the foreign one. Instinct told her he was playing with her, as a dog plays with a sickly turkey hen. Her people raised turkeys for feathers and for food, but sometimes dogs stole the weaker ones and devoured them.

What does he want of me?

His eyes said she was desirable. But never again had he touched her as he had that day at the stream. Remembering, her body told her it was awake, declaring a need.

The times when she watched him as he slept, his lean body and straight legs in graceful respose, one arm flung out, inviting embrace, she wanted to lie beside him, to rest her head on the chest that rose and fell in serene rhythm, to caress him and waken his desire . . . But instinct jangled a warning bell.

What does he want of me?

Kokopelli had become increasingly restless. He often went over the contents of his pack, making adjustments, as though he were ready to

39

leave. He spent much time in silent concentration, fingering his long fringe of knotted cords of different lengths and many colors, with the knots at varying intervals.

"Why do you do that?" Kwani asked one time.

He shot her an annoyed glance. "Do not disturb me at my calculations."

It was all quite mysterious, Kwani thought. A part of his magic.

She was curious to know more of the contents of his pack that bulged so intriguingly. But except for the first time she awoke in the cave, he had taken the pack with him when he left; when he was there, it lay by his side.

A footstep and rustle of brush made Kwani retreat inside the cave. Shadows moved at the entrance; Kokopelli stepped inside, the bird on his shoulder. Kwani wondered why Kokopelli never acknowledged the spirits of a dwelling when he entered. Her people were meticulous about this. Perhaps his magic made it unnecessary.

"I welcome you," she said.

He nodded acknowledgment of her traditional greeting, and placed his pack on the floor. His gaze was a confrontation.

"You are stronger."

"Yes."

"Good. We are leaving here."

Her heart jumped. "When?"

"Before dawn."

"Where are we going?"

"To the cliff cities, to the Place of the Eagle Clan."

Kwani knew of the Anasazi cities high in cliffs under the mesas. Her people spoke of them often around evening fires. But only traders had seen these cities of wonder, and never tired of relating their marvels. Kwani yearned to see them also. But she could not, not now, when all would know she was cast out from her clan as a witch.

"I cannot go there, Kokopelli."

"Why not?"

"They will have heard—"

He dismissed her concern with an imperial gesture. "You will be safe because I will take you there." He tilted his head back so that he looked down at her over the beak of his nose. "I am Kokopelli!"

Her voice trembled. "The Blue-eyed One—could not we go there instead?"

He shook his head. "It is too far. Soon the snows—"

She hobbled to him on her crutch and stood close. "When you leave to go on your way I shall be there alone. In their hearts they will believe

I am a witch. Always they will watch, waiting . . . Please do not take me there." Tears threatened and she put one hand on his chest, touching the ornament warmed by his skin.

"There is no choice." His voice grated with irritation. "Because of you, I have lingered here too long. We cannot find the Blue-eyed One before high snows block the passes. Because of you, I must hasten home by a longer way, and even then—"

"Take me with you. You need not go to the cliff cities at all. Take me to your home!" She stepped close and flung both arms around his waist. The crutch fell to the floor. She buried her face against his chest. "Please!"

He disengaged her arms. "I cannot."

She sank to the floor, wrapped her arms around his knees, lying there, trembling, head bent, dark hair flowing.

He stooped and lifted her, holding her so that her feet dangled in the air as she faced him. She could not look into his eyes, those lion eyes so close. "Even with two strong legs you could not travel so far a distance as quickly as I must. I cannot take you with me. Even if I wished to do so."

He set her on her feet, picked up the crutch and braced it under her arm. "You will go with me to the Eagle Clan, and follow my instructions."

She turned away. "They will kill me!"

"Yes."

She froze, making a choked sound.

"Unless you do as I say. Are you prepared to listen?"

"There is no choice."

They sat on the floor. He spoke carefully, so that she would understand in spite of his accent. Sunfather walked his long sky trail as they talked. Finally, Kokopelli asked, "Do you understand?"

"Yes." At last she knew what Kokopelli wanted. She could give it to him. "I will do as you say. But . . ."

His glance was quick. "But?"

"Only if you will return when the snows are gone, and take me to the Blue-eyed One."

He leaned back and regarded her silently. Blue eyes met his in a steady gaze.

"If you do not do as I say, they will kill you."

"They may kill me anyway."

She had courage; he admired that. "It is agreed. I will return when first flowers bloom." He had planned to do so anyhow for his trading.

"You will take me to the Blue-eyed One?"

Perhaps he could arrange his schedule so that he would arrive at the Chief's clan at a suitable trading time. Yes, he thought, it could be quite profitable.

"I will."

Solemnly, Kwani took what was left of the corn meal from her pouch and offered it to the Six Sacred Directions.

"You have heard our words, oh spirits. You have heard the promise of Kokopelli. Follow him, protect him." She paused, and caught a glimpse of his smug satisfaction. "If he betrays his promise, may worms consume his eyeballs and vultures pick his bones."

With a flourish, she tossed the last bit of meal to the Direction Above.

❖9❖

The vast green mesa, which would be known one day as Mesa Verde, lay silent under dimming stars. Ancient rivers and seas had clawed the land from north to south, gouging deep canyons which divided the one mesa into many. Kokopelli knew these canyons—inhospitable gorges resisting passage with huge boulders, thorny bushes, and treacherous footing. To travel from place to place, both canyons and mesas had to be crossed. Canyons were dead end; mesas ended in precipitous cliffs. Planning was essential.

He stood outside the cave, mentally charting the journey southward to the mesa where the Place of the Eagle Clan was recessed in a cave below the mesa's brim. The cliff city was accessible only by a treacherous path and small hand-holds cut into the cliff. How Kwani could reach the city was a problem he would solve when the time came.

He tasted the wind. It carried no message of rain. Good. Travel would be difficult enough without that.

"I am ready."

Kwani carried her pack, thong across her forehead, and braced herself steadily on the crutch. Her other hand held the spear.

He shook his head. No Toltec woman would touch a spear, let alone cherish one as this Anasazi did. He could not permit her to be seen in his company carrying a weapon. As though he needed her protection. "I will take that."

He reached for the spear, but she drew back. "No!" Kokopelli jerked the spear from her grasp.

Looking down his beak nose at her, he said, "You need no other protection in the company of Kokopelli."

"It is mine. It protects me."

"You forget our agreement. You are mine now. What is yours belongs to me. Do not forget again!"

In sullen silence, they left the cave heading south. Kokopelli strode ahead, pausing to wait for her, impatiently now and then.

By midmorning, Kwani was bone tired. *I hate him.* If I had my spear he would get it right in the chest! But what would happen to her without him? He had saved her life. And now she had agreed to his plan: he would assure her safety with the Eagle Clan if all that she made—blankets, belts, everything—belonged to him. She was his, as his knives and sandals were his, to be used at his convenience.

But she was not his mate.

It rankled. She had wanted him, he had made her want him . . .

Remembering, she burned with humiliation. It was last night, when they had finished planning. When the fire burned low. Lying on the blanket, she laid aside her robe. He pretended not to notice. She parted her legs.

"Kokopelli," she whispered.

He turned away. In his foreign tongue he spoke to the bird, who ruffled its feathers but did not reply. "My companion thinks this is not the time," Kokopelli said. "Unfortunately, I agree."

Now, as she hobbled after him and his abominable bird, Kwani swore she would never mate with him. Never. Not even if he flung himself at her feet and pleaded.

Visualizing the scene comforted her. He groveled and begged, but she turned away. "This is not the time, unfortunately." Ha!

Her pack had grown heavier; the carrying thong pressed deeply into her forehead. Secretly glad to be free of the spear, she used her hand to push aside brush and low-hanging limbs.

In a canyon jagged sandstone cliffs thrust strange formations against the cobalt sky. The coming and going of ancient seas had left the soil loose and rocky, with chaparral growth that jabbed her with sharp points.

I am tired. Why can't we stop to rest a while?

The prospect of facing a city of strange people in a strange environment filled her with foreboding. She was going to her doom and Kokopelli was to blame.

Who will be my protector in the cliff city? I shall have no one. No one.

Above, a jay screamed mockingly and hid in a tree. Kokopelli, some distance ahead, turned as Kwani dropped her pack and sank to the ground. He strode back impatiently.

"We cannot stop here! We have a long way yet to go."

"I must rest first."

He looked down at the round, brown face. It was smudged with sweat.

But her soft mouth was firm; black-fringed blue eyes met his with frank rebellion. A scratch followed the line of her bare shoulder. The small feet in their patched sandals were bruised and dirty. And her robe, clean that morning, was soiled and marked with sweat. She raised her arm to inspect the place that braced the crutch, and he saw the skin was raw and red. That—and the unconscious gesture of grace as she raised her arm—decided him.

He dropped his own pack by the tree. Lifting the macaw from his shoulder, he tossed it into the air. It circled above them, blue wings flashing, bright tail ashimmer, then hid itself among the tree's branches.

Leaning against the trunk, Kokopelli inspected the sky. In the distance, dark clouds billowed over the mesa. The wind had shifted to the north. He had wanted to arrive at the cliff cities unannounced, to give greater impact to what he would relate at the evening fire. But snow was on the way. Kwani could not climb the boulders and avoid thorns in snowfall.

He took his flute from his pack and began to play. The clear, sweet notes echoed in the canyons, and Kwani leaned against her pack and closed her eyes. It grew colder. She took the blanket from her pack and, wrapping herself in it, slept.

She woke with a start. Dogs barked nearby. Kokopelli still played, his fingers dancing on the reed. Kwani sat upright. A pack of dogs was on them, barking, sniffing, nosing them and their packs.

Kokopelli laid the flute aside and spoke to the dogs.

"Greetings, old friends."

Their tails wagging happily, they jumped on him until the hunters arrived, shouting the dogs away. Kokopelli stood as the hunters approached. He recognized Yatosha, the young Hunting Chief of the Eagle Clan. Yatosha raised both arms, and chanted greetings. Then the aged Clan Chief stepped forward, took Kokopelli's hand and breathed on it. Breath was the essence of life and to bestow it was a gesture of respect.

"We welcome you here."

Kokopelli bowed his head. "My spirit rejoices."

Courtesies exchanged, they gathered around Kokopelli and Kwani. They saw her blue eyes, and drew back.

"The witch!" one whispered.

Kokopelli explained, "We go to the Place of the Eagle Clan. But my servant"—with a brief nod at Kwani—"has broken her leg."

The Eagle Clan hunters drew away. They were squat, sturdy men with round faces and opaque black eyes. From properly flattened heads their hair hung in three long braids that swung as they talked.

"She is the witch of whom Maluku spoke! Did you not see the sky eyes?"

"She is the servant of Kokopelli. How could she be a witch?"

"Perhaps she has put a spell on Kokopelli."

"A spell on Kokopelli? That is impossible."

"But sky eyes—"

Yatosha, the Hunting Chief with the eyes of a predator, raised his hand for silence. His many bracelets of shell and polished stone and seeds jangled impressively with each motion of his arm. His braids were entwined with iridescent turkey feathers that fluttered in the breeze.

"I shall discuss this with Kokopelli."

He gestured to Kokopelli. Now is not the time, Kokopelli thought. But he stepped forward.

Yatosha spoke. "Honored one, the hunters fear that she of the sky eyes is a witch. The one cast from her clan by Maluku."

"Maluku is mistaken," Kokopelli replied calmly. "The sky-eyed one, my servant, is descended from Gods of the Rising Sun." He looked down his proud beak nose. "Only such a woman could be servant to Kokopelli."

The leader hesitated. Had the woman, indeed, put a spell on Kokopelli? He searched for words. "Will you consent to ease the hunters' fears?"

"At the evening fire I shall demonstrate my magic, proving that she of the sky eyes is not a witch." Kokopelli paused. "Provided, of course, we are able to reach the Place of the Eagle Clan before dark. My servant's broken leg makes her walk but slowly."

The hint was not lost on Yatosha. "My hunters will carry her. But first, they must be reassured of their safety." He jangled his bracelets. "They fear witches who ride the winds of the north." He sniffed the breeze. "Already, the wind—"

Not concealing his impatience, Kokopelli agreed. "It grows late. Inform your hunters I shall confer with spirits and will request of them that they speak."

Kwani, wrapped tightly in her blanket, gazed over their heads, pretending indifference. But her heart beat harder in anger as well as fear.

From his pack Kokopelli removed a gourd rattle with small copper bells at each end. Stepping back, he raised both arms, threw back his head, closed his eyes, and began chanting in his foreign tongue. The rattle hissed and rang in eerie emphasis.

There was a rustle among the leaves and the macaw flew from the tree and rested on Kokopelli's shoulder. It was as though the bird had magically materialized at Kokopelli's command. The hunters gazed in awe at the brilliant creature who eyed them with contempt.

Kokopelli continued his chant. At last, he lowered his arms and stood with eyes closed. The wind rose, stirring the leaves, bending the grasses, enveloping the hunters with a cold breath. Involuntarily, they shivered. Kokopelli seemed to awaken. He fixed Yatosha with a burning gaze; Yatosha shifted uncomfortably. Kokopelli strode forward. With a hissing and ringing of the rattle, he removed an object from Yatosha's ear. A small shell!

The hunters murmured and drew closer together. Yatosha rubbed his ear in astonishment. Kokopelli held up the shell in his outstretched hand, moving his arm from side to side so all might see what the spirits had brought forth.

He spoke to the shell. "It is said that my servant, the woman Kwani of the tribe of the Anasazi, is a witch. Is this true?"

No reply.

"I command you to answer, oh Spirit of Great Waters. Is this woman, my servant, a witch or is she not?"

"She is not."

The shell had spoken! Kwani thought that the voice sounded much like Kokopelli's. But his lips had not moved.

Again the shell spoke. "Your servant is child of gods who crossed the Great Waters of the Rising Sun. Those who accuse her of witchcraft shall never enter Sipapu."

Kokopelli closed his fingers. When he opened them the shell was gone—vanished into the spirit world.

The hunters stirred fearfully. To be denied entry to Sipapu meant their spirits would know no home, forever. Each came forward, took Kokopelli's hand and breathed on it, then stood before Kwani with hand over heart, the pledge of loyalty.

"Welcome to this place."

"My spirit rejoices," Kwani replied.

And, indeed, it did. She felt as she had when the cougar ran from her up the mountain.

Immediately, the hunters began to cut branches, removing the bark, until two parallel poles were joined by a platform covered with shredded juniper bark. Yatosha signaled. The hunters who held the poles at either end lowered the platform for Kwani.

"Servant of Kokopelli, it will honor us if you will permit us to carry you to the Place of the Eagle Clan."

Kwani nodded graciously. But the magical transition from witch to goddess was too heady for wisdom. "I am not a servant! My name is Kwani, and that is what I wish to be called."

Kokopelli's eyes darkened, and the faces of the hunters flushed red. Kwani ignored them. She seated herself like an empress and prepared to be lifted and carried regally to her destination.

A snowflake fell.

The twisting canyons slicing the vast tableland into many isolated mesas were often little more than wide ravines, choked with brush and boulders. Orange and red sandstone cliffs soared abruptly from the canyon floor. High, high, under the brow of a mesa, veiled by falling snow, a great, arched cave held the stone city, Place of the Eagle Clan.

To one side of the cave, a narrow walkway was gouged into the cliff around a rocky outcrop on the cliff's face; it led to the only access from above and below. From the canyon, the walkway could be reached by a tortuous trail up a steep slope. From above, a narrow path dropped from the mesa top to hand-holds cut into the cliff; the walkway was directly below. The cave city was impregnable, hidden from above by the bulging brow of the cliff, visible only from across the canyon or from the opposite mesa.

The floor of the cave sloped upward from front to back. Tier upon tier the city rose in cubicles upon irregular terraces like stepping stones, from floor to vaulted ceiling. Each cubicle was a home, entered by a small, keyhole-shaped door, or by a ladder from a hole in the roof. The roof of each home formed a porch for the home above it.

On these roofs and terraces, and within the open courtyard facing the city, community activities took place. A low wall in front of the cave separated the city from a steep, brush-covered slope below which the cliff plunged to the canyon floor. The slope was littered with debris: broken pottery, bones, worn-out sandals, corn cobs—whatever people no longer wanted—all glazed with the falling snow.

The city was boisterously alive. Children shouted and ran, ignoring the cold. Turkeys squawked and gobbled and protested winter confinement in the back of the cave, a confinement welcomed by the women who would no longer have to sweep up copious droppings. Dogs yapped. People sang, gossiped, and talked of the successful harvest, of corn and squash and beans, of seeds and venison and other game stored for winter in the highest back reaches of their cave city. This winter no one would starve.

Within the city, twenty-three kivas had been dug into the various levels of the cave's floor with circular walls enclosing the upper portions. These were deep, round ceremonial rooms entered from the roof by pole ladders.

With the first snow, preparations had begun for the important winter solstice ceremonies. Old men taught prayers, chants, and ceremonial procedures to boys who were expected to be letter-perfect; otherwise, the incantations would be useless. Men practiced chants and dance steps and each made corn meal offerings to the fetishes of their individual secret societies.

In each kiva, a fire blazed. It was cozy and warm, much more comfortable than in the cubicle homes. Because women owned the dwellings and everything in them, kivas were primarily a male sanctuary: a place to socialize or sleep, to weave, to make weapons, to gamble, and attend to the endless religious responsibilities, including the teaching of young boys.

Occasionally, the women were invited to participate in kiva ceremonies, or to observe the educational progress of their sons. During the oldest nights of the severe winters, women and children often slept in kivas with their men, close to the fire, surrounded by the thick stone walls embedded in Earthmother's protecting domain.

The busy sounds of the city blended with the singing, chanting, and throb of drums from the kivas of the Winter people, those of the clan responsible for the winter season ceremonials. The most important of all was drawing near, the ceremony to turn Sunfather back from his winter home; hour after hour, the canyon echoed with a pounding heartbeat, echoed by drums of other cliff cities nearby.

It was a time of preparation.

Tiopi brushed her long hair, admiring its sheen. Yatosha, her mate, said her hair was the most beautiful he had ever seen. And she was the most beautiful woman of all the clans of the Anasazi; Kokopelli said so, and who could know better?

She smiled, satisfied, remembering the envy of the other women when Kokopelli chose her to receive his sacred seed. Being chosen gave her enormous prestige, for his seed assured fertility and good fortune for the clan. It meant that she was of equal importance with Woshee, the clan matriarch, who sat in council with Chiefs. Only She Who Remembers was more honored. All other women in the clan were subservient to herself, Tiopi—and to Woshee, of course. Tiopi saw to it that they did not forget it.

Coals from a small fire smouldered in her cubicle dwelling. It was warm enough to have discarded her robe. She sat on a mat of woven reeds covered with soft fur, luxuriating in the feel of it against her bare body. As the mate of the Hunting Chief, she chose all the best skins. She wondered when he would return from hunting.

Thinking of Kokopelli had made her ready for mating. She stretched out on the mat, waiting for Yatosha to return from hunting and wishing for Kokopelli. Yatosha was a good enough mate, but Kokopelli . . . Soon he would come again and see that she was more beautiful than ever.

She laughed, gloating.

"Tiopi!"

It was Miko, one of the young girls of the clan, peering down through the roof opening.

Tiopi frowned. "Why do you intrude?"

"She Who Remembers wants her gruel." The face disappeared.

She had forgotten the cursed gruel. Hurriedly Tiopi dressed while she prepared the gruel with hot stones in a gourd pot. The Old One liked it cooked that way rather than in a pottery bowl over a fire; she said the spirits of the gourd and the corn were happy together and made the gruel more nourishing.

Tiopi stirred the gruel impatiently. She Who Remembers was very old and had no teeth; gruel was all she could eat. Although it was considered an honor to prepare it, Tiopi secretly regarded it as a tiresome chore.

It was time, long past time, for She Who Remembers to appoint a successor, one to learn the female secrets of the clan, what only women could know and remember, generation after generation.

She must choose me, Tiopi thought.

To become She Who Remembers would endow her with even more prestige than being chosen by Kokopelli. She would be consulted by the Chiefs of the clan's secret societies about things pertaining to the female aspect of nature—such as when the female rains, the gentle rains of fall, would come to end summer drought. Women would vie to be her handmaidens, to sit by her fire in long winter evenings and hear her stories of their ancestors, those ancient beings whose distant campfires flickered in the night sky.

Tiopi smiled, displaying teeth already worn from bits of the grinding stones inevitably left in the corn. Fingering her beautiful necklace made of burned and polished juniper seeds, she visualized instead the magnificent necklace of She Who Remembers, with the great shell pendant inlaid with turquoise in a sacred design. Not only was the necklace a symbol of prestige; it had in itself mysterious powers which only She Who Remembers could possess.

She will choose me, Tiopi thought. I am an important personage in the clan, as was my mother and my mother's mother. It is my right.

Impatiently, she poured the gruel into a bowl, and holding the hot bowl gingerly in one hand, she climbed the ladder to the roof, making her way to where She Who Remembers sat by the community fire in the courtyard.

The tiny frail figure was nearly hidden in the folds of a feather blanket that wrapped her from head to foot against the chill. Thin hands, twisted and gnarled, clutched the blanket around her. As Tiopi approached, one hand reached out; her mouth gaped wide in a toothless smile. She had long since lost all her teeth. Her nose and chin nearly touched. She Who Remembers was blind, but she knew Tiopi's footstep. She knew the gruel, prepared especially for her, was ready at last.

"I have been waiting."

"Forgive me, honored one, for taking so long." Tiopi said smoothly. *You have lived too long, old woman. Soon you will die and none will know the secrets. Choose me!*

Born so many seasons past that nobody remembered when, the old woman had had several names. But she was known only by her title, She Who Remembers. The web of wrinkles on her withered face did not obscure the serenity of her expression. She lived in a world of memory. Generations of women's tribal secrets were in her keeping. Now she lifted the bowl to her lips, recalling how she had prepared gruel as a handmaiden to her predecessor long ago, before years dried and twisted her like an old leaf.

Her predecessor, Lakatl, had been a big woman, strong, too, stronger than most men. But it was Lakatl's spiritual powers that had assured her of being chosen by *her* predecessor. Using tools of deer bone to peck out pictures of deer on the stone cliffs, Lakatl would Call the deer, chanting the sacred deer songs; and the deer would come. She would Call spirits from Sipapu to become Cloud People and bring rain; and rain would come. It was obvious she was Of The Gods and was qualified to become She Who Remembers.

When Lakatl chose *her* successor, she searched long for another who was Of The Gods. That was the essential, *and secret,* requirement.

Women were necessary to the continuation of life. The Anasazi was a matrilineal society, and She Who Remembers would be the living link with all women who had gone before. The mother of all mothers from time immemorial. By the powers of the necklace and the knowledge bestowed by the sacred stone at the altar in the House of the Sun, she would communicate with them. The spirits would impart secrets to her to be used wisely in teaching young girls what women, and only women, should know. Therefore, She Who Remembers must find a successor, who was Of The Gods.

Such evidence took various forms. Often the revelation was given only to one who was Of The Gods herself. When Lakatl found the young blind girl who could see without seeing, and who understood what people knew in their secret hearts, Lakatl sought a vision. The vision came. Her predecessor appeared to her, saying, "We of the spirit world request the blind one. She is Of The Gods."

And so it came to be. For many moons now the Old One had searched for her own successor. This Tiopi, standing there with resentment radiating from her spirit like heat from a fire, was the least qualified of all.

As she swallowed her gruel, a cry rose in the courtyard. "Kokopelli comes!"

"Tiopi, Tiopi, did you hear that Kokopelli comes?" Several young women rushed up.

"Yes, I heard." Her voice trembled with excitement.

"They say he brings a mate!"

Tiopi started as if stung. "A mate?"

"Yes. Beautiful. They carry her with poles, Okalake and Otoye. Imagine!"

Tiopi shrugged. "I do not believe it."

A sound, perhaps a chuckle, issued from the folds of the feather blanket. Miko—ripening like a sweet berry—leaned toward her. "Honored one, will he still choose one of us?" Her cheeks blushed pink.

"Kokopelli is Kokopelli." I pity these young ones, the Old One thought. She thanked the gods that the ravenous demands of her own womb were long stilled. And yet . . .

Tiopi did not wait for She Who Remembers to finish her gruel so the bowl might be cleansed and returned to its place of honor. Keeping her face expressionless, she hurriedly descended the ladder to her sanctuary.

Kokopelli with a mate! How could he take a mate on his endless travels? What wife would consent for him to sleep with a different woman every night? Even if the gods wished it! Kokopelli was on intimate terms with the gods. The woman must be a witch to have ensnared him. Yes! That was it!

Being *carried!* Tiopi angrily twisted her bracelets and sat down to think.

◆ 10 ◆

Snow ceased falling. Trees and bushes were frosted; flakes floated and twirled in the wind. Swaying on the litter carried by the hunters, Kwani brushed cold specks from her face. Going up and down banks, over and around boulders, and up a steep trail to the mesa top, she had to hang on with both hands to keep from sliding off. The crutch, tucked beneath her, had become increasingly uncomfortable. Her leg ached. Cold seeped into her bones.

They had become a procession led by Kokopelli who strode across the mesa, playing his flute, calling now and then in reply to greetings, his confident step setting his luxurious mantle swinging. His shining ear ornaments swayed gracefully and the turquoise beads on his cap were in constant motion. The bright feathers on his cap stirred in the wind as if they were alive. The brilliant macaw riding his shoulder was the final dramatic touch.

Yatosha, the Hunting Chief, followed, carrying Kwani's spear upright, as though it held a banner, with Kwani next, and then the other hunters, some with rabbits or other small game. They were joined by two of another clan with a deer hanging upside down from a pole.

Continuing southward on the mesa, they passed a number of deserted stone dwellings; gruesome stories of marauding tribes had been told by traders from distant places. Marauders, and the increasingly brutal winter storms had driven the people into caves among the cliffs. The caves were easily defended, and the dwellings within were protected from the elements.

Kwani noticed that all the trees had been cut. Only brush remained, and not much of that. Here and there were withered remains of bean and squash vines and the stubble of recently harvested cornfields.

Many cave dwellings perched like eagle's nests among the sandstone formations of the cliff walls. Some dwellings were only large enough for two or three people. Others could hold an entire clan. As they approached, the cliff dwellers called out greetings. Some clambered down long ladders or down foot-and-hand-holds cut into the cliff, to the canyon floor. Running along to where they could scale the mesa on the opposite side, many joined the procession, laughing, chattering, some with bowls of food for the coming feasting.

From cave to cave shouts relayed the news of Kokopelli's arrival. Runners sped through the canyon with details. The music of the flute, the barking of dogs, the whoop of children, and a babble of voices flooded the canyon with excitement. "Kokopelli comes! There will be feasting! There will be ceremonies! There will be stories and singing and dancing! Kokopelli comes!"

The procession slowed as a great cave came into view in the cliff beneath a mesa across the wide ravine. Kwani stared, awestruck. Never had she seen such a large and handsome city! There it was, hidden in the cliff. Buildings reached the cave's arched ceiling. And the kivas! She counted the openings in the floor of the cave where ladder poles protruded, not believing her eyes. Eight! Eight kivas! Imagine!

"Is that where we go?" she asked a hunter.

"No. That is the Place of the Wolf Clan. We go to the Eagle people."

Kwani was relieved. She would be intimidated by such magnificence. She wondered what sort of place belonged to the Eagle Clan. She hoped there would be room for her.

The Wolf people greeted them with glad cries. Many crossed the ravine to join them, carrying baskets of corn, bowls of meal and pine nuts, slabs of dried venison, gambling sticks and ceremonial objects—rattles and drums and pipes. Girls carried jars of water on their heads and babies on their backs.

It grew darker; snow fell again. Kwani wondered if the Eagle people would welcome her. She shivered with more than cold. She thanked the gods she was with Kokopelli. She lifted her chin. She was an important personage now.

The people of the Eagle Clan were in a frenzy of preparation. Girls feverishly ground more corn. The largest pots steamed over numerous fires, and enticing odors blended with the drifting fragrance of pinyon smoke. The Crier Chief, an old man who retained his honored post because of a deep, resonant voice and his admired manner of poetic elaboration, called reports as runners arrived with news.

"Kokopelli comes! He of the singing reed, he of the sacred seed, comes to assure the fertility and good fortune of our people. Prepare! Make ready the feasting, make ready the ceremonial fires!" And later,

"He has passed the place of the Wolf people. The Chiefs and elders will depart to greet him upon the mesa."

The welcoming committee lined up, each man dressed in his finest ceremonial robe. With a flurry of rattles and drums they left the walkway to climb the hand-holds and the narrow path to the mesa top.

Every woman, every girl, fingered the secret amulet known only to her which hung in a tiny pouch from a cord around her neck. "Make him choose me!" each one prayed, and smoothed her hair and rearranged her robe which was tied over one shoulder, leaving the other bare. It was cold, but no matter. Kokopelli liked pretty shoulders, bare arms.

Tiopi told herself, Kokopelli *will* choose me again! But fourteen times the moon had waxed and waned since the last time. She was older. The young girls, now blossoming . . .

She stood alone in the cubicle of her home. She relished the prestige of being Kokopelli's choice even more than the experience. Experience was momentary; prestige lasted. But discovering a witch was another way to acquire prestige. This woman Kokopelli brings, the one with sky eyes.

If Kokopelli does not choose me . . .

At last the flute was heard. The Eagle people were avid to witness Kokopelli's arrival and to see the woman he brought with him. The mesa above them could not be seen from the cave. Since only the official welcoming committee could properly meet Kokopelli upon the mesa, all who were able clambered down the steep, rocky trail to the canyon floor and peered up at the arriving procession.

"Look! Look! He comes!"

"A-a-a-i!"

There was a murmur of awe as Kokopelli appeared, the brilliant bird upon his shoulder and his fine mantle billowing in the wind. Behind him, Yatosha, proudly holding the spear, was followed by Kwani on the litter.

Women whispered, "She is carried!"

As hunters of the Wolf Clan appeared with the deer, shouts of recognition rang back and forth. These different clans of the same tribe, Anasazi, prided themselves on individuality, though basically their customs and beliefs were the same. Now the work of summer and of autumn's harvest was over; now was the time for celebrations and for ceremonials to appease the gods.

Kokopelli's arrival was a good omen. When he had not appeared in summer, at his usual time, there had been fear of some coming disaster.

But now he was here, and with a woman of sky eyes—surely an omen of special meaning!

The women straining to see Kwani, watching as the litter was gently set down, were astonished to see her reach for a crutch to pull herself upright. Kokopelli stood at the mesa's brim, playing his flute; she hobbled to him, and stood beside him as if she belonged there. One leg was swathed in wrappings.

"It is her leg!" Women smiled at one another. She was no sacred individual whose feet must not touch the earth. It was merely that she had broken her leg. A number of them had experienced the same. Maybe she was not even Kokopelli's woman! Some of the girls hurried back up the trail to smooth their hair, shake the snow from their garments, and adorn themselves anew.

Kwani gazed down into the canyon with amazement. Where was the pueblo? Women in the canyon were climbing a steep trail that disappeared under the mesa's brim. She peered over the edge and was not reassured. A narrow, very narrow trail curved down to hand-holds cut into stone. She bit her knuckles.

"Do not be afraid."

It was one of the hunters who had carried her. She had ridden with her back to him. His black eyes shimmered with life, and red-brown lips were firm. His hair was not black but dark brown, with turkey feathers entwined in the braids. His ear pendants were shiny black beads and a necklace of the same ended in a pendant identifying the Eagle Clan.

Softly, so others would not hear, he said, "My name is Okalake. I will help you."

His eyes said she was beautiful.

She smiled at him. "My name is Kwani."

Kokopelli was standing at regal attention, awaiting the welcoming party. If he noticed the handsome Okalake's interest in her, he gave no sign.

With a shrill flurry of drumbeats and rattles, the welcoming chiefs and elders appeared one by one, in single file, from beneath the mesa. The Medicine Chief stepped forward and raised both arms in a chant. When he had finished, he stepped forward, took Kokopelli's hand, and breathed on it.

"We welcome you to this place."

"My spirit rejoices."

One by one, the welcoming group repeated the courteous ceremony. Kwani stood, bracing herself upon her crutch. Her long, black hair was disheveled and weariness and pain shadowed her eyes. But she stood with dignity, ignoring curious glances. She kept telling herself, I am an important personage. Kokopelli brought me here.

At last, Kokopelli turned to her. "It is a narrow, twisting trail with a place of no trail at all, only hand-holds cut into the rock of the cliff. You will be fastened to the litter and lowered down."

The thought of being suspended like a spider from a web, swinging over the boulders far below, made her stomach contract in terror. But she said, "I am not afraid."

An elder waved a commanding arm. "Bring rope."

From his pack a hunter removed a coil of yucca twine rope. She was bound from under her arms to her feet as the hunter and Okalake wrapped the rope around and around her and the platform on which she lay.

"She looks like a papoose on a cradle board!"

Kwani looked up at Kokopelli. Her life would depend upon the hands of the one who carried her down the cliff. She saw herself dangling . . .

"Who is to carry me?"

With a finger Kokopelli summoned a hunter lumbering nearby.

"No!" she cried.

Kokopelli turned his head so abruptly that the turquoise beads on his cap jostled one another with a clicking sound. For a long mement he regarded her with hooded eyes.

"Carry her!" he commanded. The hunter stepped forward eagerly, grinning.

"No!" Kwani stared at the hunter coldly, and raised an imperious hand. The force of the icy blue gaze and the royal gesture made him hesitate.

Kokopelli's eyes glinted. A hint of admiration flicked, then was gone. Finally, looking down his beak nose, he said, "I grant permission for you to select the one to be so honored." Sarcasm gave his voice an edge. "Provided, of course, it is not I."

There was laughter. Kwani's cheeks flamed. She turned to Okalake. "You are the one I choose."

Whispers . . . Okalake was son of the Sun Chief—an influential member of the clan. His interest in Kwani was not unnoticed by the women.

But the elders and the Medicine Chief had drawn Kokopelli aside. The Medicine Chief, a gnarled ancient of forty-five, whose cheeks were marked with the black zigzag lines of his profession, spoke. "We have heard of a sky-eyed woman, a witch. Maluku—"

"I bring no witch. I shall have announcements at the evening fire."

The Medicine Chief was not satisfied. His small eyes slid maliciously to Kwani. "I am informed this woman is the one—"

The Elder Chief, short and squat, interrupted him. His face was stern, and his ear ornaments swung in agitation as he shook his head. "Kokopelli does not lie." He fingered the handsome bone necklace which was the symbol of his rank.

Kokopelli inclined his head graciously. "Maluku is mistaken. The honorable Medicine Chief has been misinformed. I shall discuss this at the fire." He bowed. "With your permission, of course."

The elders and Chiefs conferred briefly. "It is agreed," the Elder Chief said.

Ropes had been tied to the ends of the poles holding Kwani's litter. The ropes were coiled and placed on the litter until they would be needed. Kwani watched children, and women with babies on their backs and burdens on their heads, stride confidently over the mesa's brim, disappearing down the trail. Soon they would be climbing down the small hand-holds, slippery with recent snow. Surely, if women and children could do it, Okalake and the hunters could. But fear was a cold lump in her chest.

Okalake leaned over her. "You will be safe."

She tried to smile. She felt herself lifted, carried down the trail head first. The path was so narrow and steep that part of the litter was often suspended in space. She closed her eyes and prayed. Protect me, oh spirits. Save me, honored ancestors. She wished for her amulet, but it was with the medicine arrow in Kokopelli's pack.

When they stopped, the ropes were uncoiled and handed to men above and below them. Kwani looked over the edge of the litter; nothing but space and the canyon far, far below. Again, she closed her eyes.

Okalake said, "I shall remain here to hold the ropes. The man below will take you down."

In the canyon, people stood watching, among them Tiopi, her hands clenched, her mouth grim. As Okalake braced himself on the ledge, turning to speak to the men behind him who held the ropes, Tiopi commanded them in her thoughts to drop the woman suspended there, drop her and allow her to be crushed on the boulders below.

But the litter was being eased slowly, slowly down the cliff toward the lower ledge. Kwani clutched the poles. There had not been room to turn the litter around on the ledge. She hung head down in space. She closed her eyes and bit her lips as the litter bumped into the cliff again and again, jolting her so that she was certain the ropes would break. Once, she opened her eyes for a moment, and saw the small indentations cut into the cliff, worn smooth by generations of strong fingers. The litter twisted around a stony outthrust and she saw the boulders waiting below. She closed her eyes again and bit her lips. She was not about to scream like a frightened child.

Suddenly, it was over. Hands reached for her, pulled the litter to the ledge.

"You are safe."

She could not form the words "thank you." She was carried swiftly down a trail, around a bulge in the cliff, and into the vast, terraced courtyard of a cave city.

Kwani lay in the litter on the ground, looking up at a blur of faces staring down, eyes that looked into hers and drew back; faces alive with fear, curiosity, and suspicion.

·11·

Kwani stood beneath the jutting overhang of the cliff's brow, staring incredulously at the cave city towering tier upon tier before her. In the smoky haze of cooking fires, the city seemed to be an illusion, a tantalizing dream. The courtyard where she stood was a series of terraces from one side to the other, formed by the roofs of kivas below. Upon various other levels, round walls enclosed the upper part of many more kivas dug into the cave's floor. From the roofs of each one, ladders protruded like pointing fingers. Never had Kwani seen so many kivas, nor so many dwellings, buildings four stories high!

Women bent over cooking fires, and a ceremonial fire blazed in the courtyard. The city was aglow with firelight and redolent with the fragrance of juniper smoke and of food for the feasting. People were everywhere, hanging from windows, near the vaulted dome, crowding roofs and pathways. They ran up and down ladders, darted in and out of doors, laughed, talked, sang, and blew shrilly on clay flutes and bone whistles. More people arrived, and more. They pressed around her, gawking.

Kwani was overwhelmed. She turned for assurance to Kokopelli but he was not there. She was alone, a stranger among these people who dwelt like eagles among the cliffs, who stared and whispered behind their hands.

Huzipat, Chief of the Elders, raised one arm to her in greeting. He was a short, squat man with an ornate necklace dangling nearly to his navel.

"We welcome you to this place."

"My spirit rejoices." This was untrue. Her spirit felt threatened. Where was Kokopelli?

"Since Kokopelli requests that we accept you in our clan. We, the

60

elders and Chiefs, must confer with the gods." He turned to a dignified matron. "Take her to the keeping place." The matron's gray hair, dressed in cartwheel buns high over each ear, was entwined with blue feathers while more blue feathers dangled from each ear. She was gaunt but erect, and stepped with the surefooted grace of one who has spent a lifetime among cliffs and crags. Kwani followed her to the first ladder leading to the roof of the terrace above. She climbed awkwardly, pulling herself up by one hand, holding the crutch with the other, using only one foot to go from rung to rung. At the top the woman looked down. Her expression was stern, but not unkind.

"I will hold the crutch next time, so that you can use both hands."

The crowd murmured approval. Kwani was heartened. These people were, after all, Anasazi.

They crossed to another ladder leading to a third story. As Kwani began to climb again Okalake stepped from the crowd.

"I will take you."

Bending, he picked her up effortlessly, and ran up the ladder rungs as though they were steps. He reached down for the crutch the woman held up to him, and tucked it under Kwani's arm. "You will not remain long in the keeping place," he whispered, black eyes smiling into her own.

The acrid odor and the gobbling sound of turkeys grew near as the woman led Kwani to a small rear room. "You will remain here until you are accepted into the clan." A flick of pity touched her eyes.

Kwani stepped over the high doorsill and looked about her. It was a cubbyhole above the area where the turkeys were confined. During snows and storms of past winters the room had been used as a toilet; a putrid stench clung. Distant firelight shone faintly through the small, keyhole-shaped doorway. Curious children gathered to peer fearfully inside.

"My uncle says she is a witch!"

"Look at her eyes! Know what witches do with their eyes at night?" A gasp. "What?"

"They put them on a shelf and use owl's eyes instead. My uncle told me."

"Aye-e-e-e!"

Heads were abruptly withdrawn to be replaced by others.

A worn and soiled deerskin lay on the floor. Kwani snatched it up, shook out dust and bits of dried feces, and hung it from pegs over each side of the door. "Go away!" she shouted.

Giggles and murmurs. A corner of the deerskin was lifted, and bright eyes peered inside.

"Are you a witch?"

"No!"

She did not blame the children; they were but echoes of their elders. How long must she stay here? The indignity of being led through a gaping crowd into this dark and smelly place was insulting.

Kwani bit her lips in frustration. If she had her amulet upon her, this would not have happened. She had made a mistake to give it to the medicine arrow. Where was Kokopelli?

The deerskin still hung in place but the children were gone. She lifted a corner and looked outside. Visitors from other Anasazi clans sat elbow to elbow on the roofs, tier on tier, dangling their feet over the edges. Behind them, others stood, holding babies, baskets, jars, eating bowls. Women and girls ladling stews from large pots reminded Kwani how hungry she was.

Children ran up and down ladders, squealing. Dogs followed, yapping excitedly. Turkeys gobbled in alarm, and there was a constant buzz of talk and frequent explosions of laughter. From several kivas came drumbeats, chants, and songs, preparing for ceremonies to come.

As Kwani peered from behind the deerskin, she noticed one particularly beautiful woman nearby, wearing many necklaces and bracelets on each arm. One shoulder was bare; Kwani noticed how the necklaces were arranged to display the woman's neck and shoulders to best advantage. The woman turned from dipping stew and stabbed her with a glance so savage that Kwani reeled back behind the deerskin.

She hates me! Kwani thought. But why? I've never seen her before.

There was a sound at her door. A little girl's voice said, "I request permission to enter."

Kwani pulled the deerskin aside. A young girl, no more than eight or nine, offered a bowl of stew and a handsome pottery mug of water. An amulet on her necklace identified her as of the Wolf Clan. There was much visiting between clans and children were welcomed everywhere.

"Okalake gives you this," the girl said timidly.

"Thank you." Kwani smiled and accepted the food eagerly.

"He gives you also the bowl and the mug. They are yours."

"Tell Okalake I am grateful. My thanks to you as well. What is your name?"

"I have many names, but I like Ki-ki-ki, the bird song."

"I like it, too." Kwani pointed to the woman who had glanced at her so bitterly. "Tell me who that is."

"Tiopi. Mate of the Hunting Chief. Kokopelli chose her last time." The girl leaned forward, whispering. "She thinks Kokopelli will choose her again, but he won't."

"How do you know?"

"I just know."

"About Okalake—" It was improper to ask, but she had to know. "I am a stranger. Tell me about Okalake."

Ki-ki-ki pointed. Okalake stood high upon a roof near the top of the cave, watching them. The girl waved at him. "He is son of the Sun Chief." She said softly, "I will marry him when I am old enough. If he does not have a mate already."

"He has none, then?"

"Not yet." She gave Kwani a searching glance, wise for one so young. "You are Kokopelli's woman." It was a statement, not a question, and her voice quavered a little.

Kwani pretended not to notice, and looked away. Being young was painful, often. "He saved my life."

Ki-ki-ki smiled. "Kokopelli is—" She blushed.

"Is what?"

"You know. Everyone says . . . I leave you to eat now." She ran off.

Okalake still stood gazing down. Their glances locked. Kwani felt the impact. The deerskin made it too dark to see inside the room. She pulled it down and sat on the doorsill. As she ate, she glanced up now and then. But Okalake was gone.

The pottery mug was beautifully made, decorated with a black and white design. Kwani was used to drinking from a gourd cup. The bowl was handsome, too, with the same striking ornamentation. She wondered why Okalake would give the bowl and mug to her if, indeed, she were regarded as Kokopelli's woman.

She remembered Okalake's firm young lips, the warm dark eyes that spoke of intimacy and how he held her. Food and water had revived her; the pulse and excitement of the city were contagious. Her body spoke. It wished for a man. Kokopelli.

There was a sudden hush. The Chiefs and elders had gathered around the ceremonial fire. From the shadows, a bent figure, wrapped in a blanket, walked slowly, gropingly, toward the fire. The chiefs and elders made way. The figure sat down near the fire. The Crier Chief stepped forward.

"Hear, all people of the Eagle Clan. Hear, all welcome visitors. Kokopelli, he of the singing reed, he of the sacred seed, he who communes with gods is among us. He brings to us a woman from a distant clan, and requests that we accept her."

Children squealed, "There she is, up there!"

Everyone turned to stare as though they had not seen her already. Some climbed up or down ladders for a better look.

The Crier Chief continued. "It is first necessary for She Who Remembers to determine if this woman is worthy to be one of us, one of the Eagle Clan. If she approves, the Chiefs and elders will decide whether to accept her. If she does not approve, the woman must return to her own clan."

He bent to the seated figure in the blanket. There was a whispered conversation. He stepped forward and announced, "She Who Remembers is ready." Pointing dramatically, he called, "Woman, come forward."

Kwani rose. Her loosened hair flowed around her. Her robe, soiled and torn, nevertheless enhanced the beauty of her body as she stepped over the high doorsill to stand in dignity.

She looked about her; a blur of faces looked back.

Where was Kokopelli?

Or Okalake?

She hobbled to the first ladder, and hesitated. How could she climb down without looking ridiculous? With as much aplomb as she could muster, she held the crutch in one hand, faced the ladder, and eased herself down, one rung at a time.

A few children forgot their manners and tittered.

At the second ladder people offered to help her. But she refused. With head held high, she finally arrived to face the group at the ceremonial fire. In the dim light, the Medicine Chief's zigzag black lines from forehead to chin were fearsome. He took her arm and led her to the figure huddled in the blanket.

"Lie on your stomach until she tells you to rise," he commanded. "It is She Who Remembers."

Still holding her arm, he gave her a push. Kwani stared at the old face, nearly hidden in the blanket, whose eyes, enmeshed in wrinkles, looked at her but did not see her. From the face, from the entire shrouded figure, invisible light seemed to come.

"Come close to me." The withered lips curved into a toothless smile.

Kwani lay on her stomach with her head at the old woman's feet. She felt hands touching her, exploring her face, fingering her hair. There was a crooning sound. Kwani felt as though a tight knot were loosened, as though humiliation had never been, as though herbs were placed on a wound.

"Rise now," the old woman said.

Kwani sat up. She Who Remembers bent forward. Kwani saw the object Kokopelli wanted most of all, the secret thing he had ordered her to obtain for him. It was the most beautiful necklace Kwani had ever seen. From a long strand of brilliantly polished stone beads of many colors hung a pendant that caught Kwani's breath—a large scallop shell, the sacred shell from the Sunset Sea, inlaid with turquoise in a mystical pattern. It swung a little as She Who Remembers spoke.

"Why do you come?" The old voice was like wind in pine trees, rattling the cones.

"Kokopelli brings me here. Because my leg is broken."

"I must see it."

Bony hands reached out. Kwani had an eerie feeling that the hands did, indeed, have eyes. Twisted fingers, surprisingly strong, probed the bandage, the splint, the bones, and the flesh beneath.

"Who bound this?"

"Kokopelli."

"It heals. Soon you will walk as you did before. And then?"

"I wish to remain here until first flowers bloom."

"Why? Can you not return to your people?"

"I am Anasazi. You are my people."

She Who Remembers sat for a moment in silence. Finally she said, "Give me your hand."

Kwani placed her hand in the twisted one, and felt a surge of communication pass between them. The old woman held her hand for some time.

"You are afraid. Why?"

"People think I am a witch."

"Maluku says you are."

"But *I am not!*"

She Who Remembers shifted her position. "You say you wish to remain until first flowers bloom. Why only until then?"

"Kokopelli will come to take me to the Blue-eyed One. My eyes, also, are blue."

"He is of your blood?"

"Perhaps. I do not know. My mother—" She stopped, longing for her mother. "My mother told me to go to him."

The old woman nodded. "I remember your mother." She gestured a sign of blessing. "May her spirit reach Sipapu and find joy."

Kwani jerked upright. "My mother . . . my mother is in Sipapu?" Her voice cracked. "What happened to my mother?"

"You do not know?"

"Tell me!"

"Your mother took an arrow Maluku intended for you. She was killed unjustly."

Kwani gave a keening cry, and bent her face to the ground. The chiefs and elders were silent; the crowd, stirred uncomfortably at Kwani's wild grief. They knew that Kwani's mother had sacrificed more than her life; she had foregone eternity in Sipapu. They glanced furtively about. She might be among them right now.

The old woman reached both hands to Kwani and placed them on her head. "Your mother is near," she crooned, and her voice was like wind in the grasses. "Do you not sense her presence?"

Kwani raised her head. Tears were on the withered cheeks. For a moment, she forgot her own. For a moment, her mother's face looked at her from within the blanket.

"Yes," she whispered.

Abruptly, the old woman raised her arm. "I recommend this person to the chiefs and elders for membership in the Eagle Clan." She lowered her arm and gathered the blanket closely about her, disappearing into its folds.

Kwani was dismissed. She sat up, looking blindly about her, while small moans forced themselves from her throat.

The Chiefs and elders gathered in a tight group and whispered among themselves. The crowd watched breathlessly; such drama was a rare treat, to be savored over many a fire in nights to come. Kwani's hair had fallen over her face, and she looked like a witch in the firelight. Was she? But She Who Remembers had recommended her! They stirred uneasily.

The Medicine Chief pulled Kwani to her feet. He picked up the crutch and pushed it under her arm.

"You shall be questioned."

The face with zigzag lines and small eyes brimmed with venom. Kwani pulled herself upright.

"I do not choose to be questioned." Icicles dripped from her voice.

"Only witches refuse to answer." His eyes glittered.

"I am not a witch, this you know, all of you. I will not be intimidated."

The crowd gasped, and a woman's voice pierced the strained silence. "If you are not a witch, answer the questions!"

It was the beautiful woman with the bracelets, the one who had looked at her with such hatred. A cold finger touched Kwani's spine. Here was an enemy.

"Answer!" others cried.

Kwani faced them, eyes flaming with contempt. But her heart han.- mered and her mind shrieked, "Where is Kokopelli?"

The Medicine Chief and then the Chiefs and elders closed in about her.

"You refuse to answer, even though you do not know the questions?" The Medicine Chief's voice was bear fat oiling an arrow. "Or perhaps you know the questions? . . . the reason you refuse?"

Searing grief and anger overcame Kwani's fear. "You want to know if I am a witch. I tell you again I am not!"

A red flush had flamed beneath the zigzag marks. He grabbed her arm, the crutch clattering to the ground, then released her with a shove that sent her sprawling. Kwani fumbled for the crutch, but he kicked it aside.

There was a sudden sound like distant thunder. In the kiva beneath them, someone stomped on the sacred foot drum. Only those whom the gods selected were permitted to commune with it. The thunder beat rose to a crescendo, then ceased as a flute spoke in piercing command.

"Kokopelli!" The name flashed through the crowd.

The sound of the flute grew louder as its tip emerged from the kiva hole. Dancing fingers and Kokopelli's head followed, his ear ornaments glowing, turquoise beads swinging, bright feathers shining in the firelight. Still playing the flute he rose from the hole, an immortal spirit emerging from Sipapu.

The crowd sighed, entranced. How wonderful was Kokopelli!

Kwani pulled herself to her feet and stood with the others. The mood of Kokopelli's music changed. Now it sang of happiness . . . midsummer when corn grows tall and squash swells to fullness. It was gentle rain nourishing the ground; Sunfather's male power; Earthmother's pregnancy. Birth. Life. Wholeness, all as it should be.

The crowd relaxed. All was well. They settled back to enjoy Kokopelli's performance. He would bring them news, tell stories and ask riddles. And always, he had fine things to trade. Men took mental inventory of things they had to trade, wondering what rare treasures from exotic places they could buy from him. Women whispered, "Who will he select tonight?" Hoping secretly that it would be themselves. Children waited for the magic to begin; Kokopelli knew wonderful magic.

The flute sang a final happy note. For a moment, Kokopelli stood looking over the ampitheater formed by the city. Illuminated by firelight, and by an inner fire of his own, he was an arresting figure.

"I have brought you a woman." Kokopelli spoke at last. "I, Kokopelli, saved this woman's life, so that I might bring her to you." The lion eyes under heavy brows glowed. "You of the Eagle Clan, you of the Wolf Clan, the Turquoise Clan, the Coyote Clan—all of you—have heard how Maluku, Medicine Chief of the valley people of the north, proclaimed this woman to be a witch and drove her out to die."

There were sounds of assent. All eyes were trained on Kwani.

"You have heard it said that Maluku sent a medicine arrow to capture this woman's spirit. But her mother stepped in the arrow's path and gave up her own, instead."

Kwani flinched and turned her back, facing the darkness beyond the cave. Tears welled up, but were fought back; she would not let these people witness her pain.

Kokopelli's voice rose. "There is something you have not heard, something you do not know. I shall tell you." He paused to let their expectancy rise. "Maluku sent another arrow, one to kill witches. It refused to find her." Another pause, amid whispers. "It buried itself inside her pack!" Like magic, the arrow was suddenly in his hands and he held it overhead, turning from side to side so that all might see.

"Here it is. See it! See the sacred amulet it wears!"

The babble of excitement increased as Okalake rose from the kiva behind him holding the macaw, and handed the bird to Kokopelli. Kokopelli held the bird before him, eye to eye, and spoke rapidly in a foreign tongue. The bird cocked its head, and replied in the same strange language.

"My companion suggests that the arrow should speak. To tell you in its own voice whether this woman, Kwani, is a witch."

Babble climaxed into breathless silence.

Holding the arrow in one hand, arms outstretched, Kokopelli stood with eyes closed, head thrown back, silently commanding communion with the spirits. No one moved, no one made a sound. Then as if awakened he started, and held the arrow before him as though he had not seen it before. He spoke to it.

"Are you the arrow of Maluku?"

"I am."

The crowd gawked. The arrow had spoken! They shivered.

"Is your mission to find and to take the spirit of witches?"

"It is."

"Why did you not take the spirit of this woman Kwani?"

Silence.

The little eyes of the Medicine Chief glittered. Kokopelli's magic had limitations! Ha!

But the arrow was now speaking. "This woman Kwani is child of chiefs who rode the Great Waters of the East, Gods of the Rising Sun. I cannot take her spirit. She is not a witch."

There was a commotion. Kokopelli gestured angrily for silence.

"She is not a witch?"

"She is not."

"What is your desire that I do with you, arrow spirit?"

"Give me to the woman Kwani. I shall protect her. If any seek to harm her, it is they whose spirit I shall possess."

"I obey."

With a dramatic flourish Kokopelli strode to Kwani. He held the arrow high, then lowered it to Kwani's outstretched hand. "This will protect you until I return when first flowers bloom." He faced the Elder Chief. "Do you accept this woman, this child of Gods of the Rising Sun, as one of the Eagle Clan?"

There was a strained silence. The chief sputtered. Decision had been made not to accept her; but the testimony of the arrow put a new light on the situation. He turned to the others. "Is it your wish that we accept this woman into our clan?"

They shifted uncomfortably. Finally, one said timidly, "I do." "I, also," said another. The rest agreed,

All but the grim Medicine Chief. He stepped forward. "As Medicine Chief, it is I who determine the terms by which a new member may be accepted into the clan."

"That is so," Kokopelli replied.

The Medicine Chief turned to Kwani. "As Child of the Gods of the Rising Sun, I require you to create a vessel to hold my sacrifice to the gods during the Ceremony Before Planting. The vessel must be like none made before, holding that much water." He pointed to a jar standing tall as a child. "It must be light enough for me to carry with one finger, and must be of sacred design, more powerful than any I now possess." He paused, while his mind raced after more impossibilities. "Held to the fire, it will not burn. Thrown from the cliff, it will not break." Again his small eyes brimmed with venom.

"I accept," Kwani said.

The Medicine Chief's head snapped back. He stared at the small woman facing him defiantly, gripping the arrow with both hands.

"We shall see. You are now a member of the Eagle Clan, but only for the time being. If you fail, you will be an outcast. As you were before."

"I shall not fail."

But as she gazed over the whispering throng, she knew she needed the arrow's protection. She accepted the challenge because she had no alternative. How she would meet it, how she would create such a vessel, she had no idea.

From the folds of the blanket where the stooped figure sat, a cracked old voice said, "I welcome you to this place, my daughter."

Kwani kneeled before her. "My spirit rejoices, honored one."

The old woman reached out her hand and Kwani took it in her own. The Old One's spirit flowed into her.

"You were born for special things. Such people owe the gods, and may pay dearly. But the arrow will protect you. Kokopelli said so." She laughed a cackling, whispering laugh, like pebbles rattling in a gourd.

Kwani was taken aback and did not reply.

The Crier Chief rose, cleared his throat importantly, and raised an arm for silence.

"The Eagle Clan has a new member, Kwani, child of Gods of the Rising Sun, those blue-eyed ones from the Great Waters of the East." He paused to clear his throat. The situation was delicate and he needed time to think. "Kwani of the Eagle Clan possesses Maluku's medicine arrow, which refused to take her spirit. It has spoken, telling us that our clan member Kwani is not a witch. The arrow protects her. You have seen and heard. It is finished. The festivities of this happy occasion shall now begin." He sat down, wiping his brow.

With whoops of approval tension was released. The last bowl was licked clean, the last morsel of meat picked from bones and tossed later to the dogs who crunched contentedly. Women finished nursing their babies and replaced the shredded cedar bark diapering in the cradle boards with a fresh supply. Toddlers fell asleep in the arms of whoever was handy, while their older brothers and sisters crowded the front row, bright eyes missing nothing.

Cooking fires died to coals. Only the ceremonial fire blazed. Kwani sat beside She Who Remembers, the arrow held tightly in both hands. In the far shadows, a woman watched, fingering her bracelets, biting her lips.

As Kokopelli rose to stand again in firelight, Tiopi whispered fiercely, "Choose me!"

·12·

The hour was late. Cooking fires smouldered in ashes and the ceremonial fire burned low, fed now and again from a diminishing supply of juniper and pine logs. Cold seeped in. But still people huddled together, unwilling for the festivities to end. Soon there would be the contest for riddles and for love songs, with rich prizes bestowed by Kokopelli. And, finally, the choice of whom he would select to honor with his seed. Many bare shoulders glimmered in the cold.

Some of the older ones had taken burning branches to light pathways home. Others, including She Who Remembers, had long since gone to their beds. Children slept like puppies, curled up where they were, and babies slept snug in their cradle boards.

Kwani sat by the fire with Okalake at her side. He had taken the macaw to the kiva and returned with a blanket which he draped around her. To cover them both with the blanket would be announcing a relationship which did not exist. But it was obvious to everyone, especially the women, that such a relationship would be welcomed by Okalake. But as for Kwani, she had eyes only for Kokopelli, and there was whispered comment about this.

Kokopelli was finishing the news. Already, he had told of the drought creeping upon them: each year, more check dams had to be built to conserve water for precious crops, for drinking and cooking, and for mixing the building mortar as population increased and more homes were needed. Even the secret sacrifices of the Medicine Chiefs, their fasting and purification rituals and the rainmaking ceremonials did not increase the diminishing rainfall. There was barely enough.

Kokopelli continued, "I bring greetings from People of the River. They wish to trade salt for mugs and for pinyon nuts. They will meet at the Trading Place when Ceremonies Before Planting are completed."

71

There were murmurs of interest. Early spring was a good trading time. Mugs made by the Turquoise Clan were prized. Kwani wondered if the mug given to her by Okalake was one of these.

"Hunters have been seen in the north. They have also been seen in the northeast, and it is said they seek the mountain sheep."

Kwani remembered the hunters. Especially the one who traded Strongbow for the robe. Kokopelli still carried Strongbow at his side. Would he tell how it was obtained?

"Apaches ambushed a Ute near the place of his people and sent him to Sipapu."

Kwani held her breath.

"The chief of the People of the Rising Sun, those blue-eyed sons of the gods who dwell southeast of here, send greetings."

Kwani breathed more easily as people glanced at one another, and nodded. Now that Kwani was a member of the Eagle Clan, it was proper to receive greetings from a kinsman.

With a flourish, Kokopelli removed the crossbow and lifted it overhead. "This is their medicine bow—the bow of the gods. Observe its powers."

From the pouch at his side he took a two-pronged hook and strapped it to his waist. From the quiver came a strange arrow, different from any seen before. People watched in astonishment as he set the bow, fitted the arrow into a groove on the strange crossbar, and locked the arrow in place. He held the bow up for inspection.

"See how the arrow is captured—held to the bow until my touch chooses to release it." He pointed the arrow from one to another in the crowd. They shrank back, laughing nervously. He aimed at a tiny window near the ceiling where faces appeared.

"Stand aside!" he called. "The arrow will enter there."

The crowd gasped. Such accuracy was impossible!

Kokopelli raised the bow, sighted over his right thumb, and pressed the trigger. The arrow sped high and straight to the window, and disappeared inside. In a moment, a face appeared, and a hand was thrust outside, holding the arrow.

"Aye-e-e-e!"

Kokopelli stood in triumph, gazing over his hawk nose. "Tomorrow, I trade. Soon I leave for my home. But before I go I give this bow to the keeping of one of you until I return." His gaze swept the crowd. "Whoever protects this bow will, in turn, be protected by the medicine of the gods."

Holding the bow overhead, he intoned, "I entrust this bow to the only one qualified to commune with its sacred spirit!" He strode to the Medicine Chief sulking in the shadows. "I entrust this bow to your keeping. It is not to be used. But it is to be protected and included in ceremonies to which it is entitled. If my words are disobeyed—if the bow releases its power—the gods will take revenge such as only gods know." He paused. "Do you accept the responsibility?"

Hostility melted in the Chief's gratified smile. "Who else is as qualified as I?"

From his pouch, Kokopelli removed the rattle with the small copper bells. Shaking it, he swept the bow in circles overhead. "Medicine Bow of the gods, Medicine Bow of the sacred spirit, Medicine Bow of Those Who Walk The Sunrise Sea, I give you to the keeping of the Medicine Chief of the Eagle Clan." He permitted the rattle to hiss and to ring a blessing. He faced the Chief. "Guard this great man, guard this great clan, bring them good hunting, good rains, good medicine."

Kokopelli unfastened the belt holding the hook which Crooked Foot had carved, and the quiver holding the arrows Crooked Foot had made. With a final overhead flourish, he placed all in the outstretched hand of the Medicine Chief. "These arrows, this hook, are portions of the sacred bow. Protect and honor them as such until I return."

The Chief inclined his head in dignified acceptance. Never had the zigzag marks of his profession seemed so impressive. The Medicine Chiefs of the other clans gathered to inspect the bow, while other Chiefs and elders stood at a respectful distance, waiting their turn.

Kwani hid her face in the blanket. Crooked Foot's hook and arrows were as sacred as turkey droppings. As for the bow, she knew where it came from; it was not sacred either. Kokopelli must have excellent reasons for what he had done. She wondered what they were.

She looked for Kokopelli, but he had disappeared. She leaned toward Okalake who bent his head close to hers. "Where is Kokopelli?" she whispered.

"He goes to relieve himself." He grinned. "Maybe it will snow on his baby-maker."

She grinned back. "It has stopped snowing. But maybe he will get icicles."

They giggled.

Okalake said, "His baby-maker will be busy tonight. I wonder who he will choose?"

Kwani had been trying vainly not to think of this. She had not forgotten how Kokopelli had refused her; the hurt still lingered.

"Who do you think it will be?" she whispered.

"You."

Kwani's head popped from the blanket like a squirrel from its hole. "Me?"

"You are the most beautiful."

"You are kind to a newcomer." You are beautiful yourself, she thought, with those warm eyes encircled by bone like water in a smooth bowl. She thought briefly of what his loincloth concealed.

"Kokopelli returns," Okalake said. "Now we shall hear the riddles." He shifted his position closer. Kwani did not move away.

Kokopelli bowed ceremoniously to the Chiefs and elders. Dim firelight reflected his golden ornaments and the splendor of his multicolored mantle. Again, the rattle hissed and sang.

"Whoever guesses correctly this riddle will receive a bell like these upon my spirit talker."

There was a buzz of excitment. The rattle hushed.

> *He lurks beside the mountain pass,*
> *He hides within the avalanche,*
> *He makes his home amid the snowfields white.*

The rattle spoke.

> *He waits within the forest deep,*
> *He watches from the precipice,*
> *He seizes whom he will where-e're they are.*

The rattle spoke.

> *He hurls down rocks from mountain sides,*
> *He fells the tree that crashes down,*
> *He whispers to the serpent when to strike.*

The rattle spoke.

> *He guides the mountain lion's spring,*
> *He hides within the rushing stream,*
> *He seizes those who cross and drags them down.*

The rattle spoke.

> *He rides upon the wings of storm,*
> *He hurls the lightning's blinding flame,*
> *He hovers in the air above the home.*

The rattle spoke once more.

"Of whom do I speak?" Kokopelli asked.

There was silence, then murmurs. The Crier Chief's wrinkled face was alert. "The answer is He Who Seeks and Finds Us All. Death."

Kokopelli inclined his head. "That is correct."

The crowd applauded boisterously. Kokopelli took a small bell from his pouch. The old man held it between his thumb and forefinger and jingled it with delight—a clear, high, insistent little voice from far away.

Again, Kokopelli raised his hand for silence. "Whoever guesses this riddle will receive two scarlet feathers from my Bird-Who-Speaks."

Red feathers of the macaw were rare and highly prized, but to have them from Kokopelli's magic bird was a special achievement to be cherished. They hushed in anticipation.

The rattle sang in rhythm as Kokopelli chanted.

> *Across the land I wander far and wide, without a home,*
> *I wander over deserts bare and bleak, without a path,*
> *I cross the mountain white with snow, without a rest,*
> *I travel over mesas wide but cannot stop,*
> *I hurry onward through the night and cannot sleep,*
> *I move through canyons dark and forests deep, and there I weep.*
> *Who am I?*

The rattle hushed.

Ki-ki-ki raised her hand timidly. "Is it you, Kokopelli?"

He smiled. "No, little one."

"Is it spirit ancestors?" another asked.

"No."

Others called, "Is it Spider Grandmother?" "Brother Coyote?" "A witch?"

Each time he shook his head.

Okalake rose. "I know the answer. It is the wind."

"You speak correctly."

From his pouch, Kokopelli drew two feathers that glowed with scarlet brilliance, handing them to Okalake. People applauded and cheered.

Everyone likes him, Kwani thought. And so do I. Her eyes followed Okalake passing among his family and friends, showing them his prize.

The babble stilled as Kokopelli raised the flute to his lips. He played a few lingering notes, then chanted.

> *Does one live forever on earth?*
> *Not forever on earth, only a short while here.*
> *My melodies shall not die, nor my songs perish.*
> *They spread, they scatter.*

Again the flute sang, filling the cave with a torrent of tenderness. Melody soared and lingered, touched and caressed, speaking of secret, intimate things. Women leaned forward, lips parted; men listened with eyes half-closed. The flute's sweet song stole into dwellings where old ones slept, and they dreamed they were young and in love again, and it was spring.

Okalake reached for Kwani's hand, but she was transfixed. Kwani was beside him, but as far away as the Sacred Mountain. He withdrew his hand.

A final note lingered, and was stilled. Kokopelli replaced the flute inside his mantle, and called, "Who sings of love?"

A young man came forward. His name was Cayamo and he was fifteen, straight as a corn stalk and as beautiful. His gourd rattle filled with pebbles accompanied his song in syncopated rhythm.

> *Oh, that I might know your love,*
> *That you would yield yourself to me.*
> *That you might be my own.*
> *The shadows of the night lie in your eyes,*
> *The blackness of the raincloud is your hair,*
> *Your teeth are white as first spring flower's bloom,*
> *Your lips as red as crimson berries sweet,*
> *The singing of a bird is in your voice,*
> *Your step is swift and graceful as the deer's.*
> *Oh, that your beauty might be mine,*
> *To love, to fondle, to caress,*
> *But underneath your beauty lies—*
> *A heart as cold as stone.*

Loud applause and teasing met him as he finished. Some young girls looked at him with shining eyes. Several voices now called out, "Okalake." "Okalake sings well!" Until Kokopelli said, "Okalake, your people wish to hear your song."

"Chololo, will your play your flute for me if I sing my song?" Okalake nodded at a small boy seated nearby.

The boy beamed. "I play good!"

From inside his cloak he brought out a small wooden flute. Proudly he walked to the ceremonial fire at Okalake's side and faced the people.

"Play now," Okalake whispered.

With his arms raised so that his elbows stuck straight out, Chololo tilted his head back and played. A high trill was followed by a low, single musical note. Okalake's voice embraced it.

Oh lovely maid,
With moonlight in your eyes,
If single you should be
Come and give your love to me.

Ki-ki-ki gazed in wistful rapture, and women sighed and smiled.

Oh lovely maid
With sunshine in your smile,
If married you should be,
Stop not but go upon your way.

There were chuckles.

Oh lovely maid
With music in your voice,
If widow you should be,
Come, come to my arms for I will marry you.

He glanced at Kwani as he sang the last verse. She thought, your arms are inviting, Okalake. But I shall be Kokopelli's mate. If only . . . Will he choose me?

When the last singer had finished the last fine song, Kokopelli took a final treasure from his pouch. It was a pair of ear ornaments of glistening beads of abalone shell from a distant sea. "This prize goes to the singer who sang the finest song. The Chiefs and elders will decide who is to receive it," he said, to murmurs of envious admiration.

Male heads bent together in long consultation. Firelight grew dimmer and the cold more severe. The festivities were nearly over. Except for the announcement of whom Kokopelli would choose.

At last, the Elder Chief raised his hand. "We have decided. Cayamo and Okalake sang equally well. Therefore, the prize shall be divided between them. Each will receive one ear ornament."

It was a just decision and the crowd applauded.

Kokopelli intoned, "May the music of the sea from which these came be heard in the ears where these are worn." With a ceremonial bow, he presented an ornament to each.

Cayamo said, "I shall give this to the one who will be my bride."

People smiled approvingly, remembering a favorite proverb.

If you would win a woman's love, give her each day a gift.
If you would keep her love, give her each day two gifts.

Kwani rather expected Okalake to give his ornament to her, but he turned to Chololo who stood gazing up at him in a glow of hero worship. "Chololo, your music is what made my song good. The prize must go to you."

Okalake bent and looped the ornament over the boy's small ear. The dangling beads reached nearly to the boy's shoulder. Chololo flushed with joy and overwhelming pride, and stood so straight he nearly bent backward.

"I will always play good for you, Okalake. Your spirit speaks to my flute."

What a wise thing for a child to know, Kwani thought, and joined the others in congratulations.

The contests were over. Now the time had come. Kokopelli must choose.

Blankets that covered many chilly bare shoulders slipped down. Kokopelli stood looking them over. In the dim firelight he seemed, indeed, to be a god from another world, radiating the fire's reflections with golden ornaments, allowing the wind to play with his mantle so that its splendor flowed in ripples about him, moving as if to music unheard. He stood motionless, face impassive, eyes hidden in shadow.

Slowly, he turned and faced Kwani. There was a buzz, almost a rumble, of outrage and disappointment. Kokopelli said nothing. Only his eyes spoke. Kwani felt the force of his gaze penetrating her own, probing, searching. He was asking her something. But what? She cried silently, "Choose me!"

Abruptly, he turned away. "This night I do not choose."

With a sweep of his splendid mantle he whirled and descended into the kiva, ignoring a torrent of babble, women's outrage, and masculine laughter.

·13·

When Kokopelli disappeared into the kiva, Kwani faced the city alone. She stood straight and stony-faced, holding the medicine arrow to her chest, heedless of sly smiles and furtive glances.

Kokopelli did not choose any of you, either. With a cool stare she returned Tiopi's triumphant glare.

Okalake stepped forward and took her hand.

"Come. I take you to the house of my mother." Again, he swept her into his arms, and carried her lightly up the ladders. Stares and whispers followed them to a small house on a high level.

"He takes the sky-eyed one as a sister!"

"Sister?" Leers.

"One hopes Okalake remembers clan law. One does not mate with another of the same clan."

"But she is adopted . . ."

"Law is law."

Woshee was sleeping as Okalake removed the stone slab covering her doorway. She sat up abruptly.

"Who comes?"

Kwani recognized the voice. It was she who took her to the waiting place by the turkeys.

"It is I, my mother. I bring you a daughter."

Always Woshee had wished for many daughters and many sons. Her first two babies died. Then the beloved mate of her early youth was devoured by a bear. One child, Okalake, was left to her. But though she had taken other mates, including the current Sun Chief, her womb refused the seed of any but the first.

"Enter."

The bowl of sacred water waited in a niche by the door. Okalake stood

79

Kwani on her feet, then dipped his fingers into the bowl—apologies to
the house spirits for intrusion. Woshee was peering at Kwani in the
darkness.

"Who is it?" she asked.

"It is Kwani, child of the Gods of the Rising Sun, brought to us by
Kokopelli. I wish for this to be her home, my mother."

In the long silence Kwani thought, She does not want me here. She
is trying to find a polite way to refuse.

"Have you considered this well, my son?"

"I have. We shall be honored to have her here."

Another pause.

"Whom did Kokopelli choose?"

"He chose no one this night."

"No one?" Sharply. "That is not good. The clan—"

"Perhaps he will choose later, my mother."

"He departs for his home after trading!"

"Our people have multiplied. Already, there are too many to feed.
Perhaps he feels his seed is not needed for more."

"Fertility is essential! Why do you prattle? And why do you bring this
woman to my house?"

Kwani said, "Mother of Okalake, may I speak?"

"Speak."

"Okalake brings me here because I have no house. But I refuse his
generosity." She turned to go.

"Where will you stay?" Okalake's voice revealed his embarrassment.

"I shall make my home at the waiting place."

"With the turkeys? No!"

"Please take me there, Okalake. I cannot find my way in the darkness.
My pack is there—"

"Remain here until daylight," Woshee said. "It will be necessary to
clean the waiting place."

"I wish to go now."

"No." Okalake's voice was firm. "Stay here this night. Tomorrow my
mother will help you prepare the waiting place for your home. Do you
agree, my mother?"

"I do." Her voice revealed relief. She led Kwani to a mat in the corner.
"You may sleep here."

Okalake said, "I shall return in the morning." In farewell, he dipped
his fingers into the sacred water again.

From her mat Woshee removed a blanket and handed it to Kwani.

"I thank you, mother of Okalake."

"Sleep now." Woshee returned to her mat and lay down, sighing. But
Kwani could not sleep. Events of the day replayed themselves in her

mind. Again, she hung like a spider from a web, swinging over the rocky abyss; again she smelled the stench of the room that was to be her home. She remembered Kokopelli's searching gaze. Why did he not choose her? She hated him!

But her body refuted this, yearning.

She turned restlessly on the mat, pulling the blanket closer. Foreboding crouched on her chest like a predator as she recalled her rash promise to the Medicine Chief: to make a vessel never made before; one he could carry with one finger but which would hold much water; which would not burn when held to fire nor break when thrown from the cliff.

How can I make such a thing? And if I could, how could I complete it in time for Ceremonies Before Planting? Even if I did, would the Medicine Chief accept it?

No, he will never accept it.

She fingered the amulet on her medicine arrow. "Help me with all I must do," she whispered. "I shall feed you well when daylight comes." Exhaustion claimed her at last, and she slept.

A sound woke her. She sat up, peering through the darkness. Faint with distance, a long, sighing moan, like wind among the cliffs, came again.

Kwani gazed about her, trying to penetrate the darkness grown lighter by coming dawn. Woshee lay wrapped in her blanket. Insistently the moaning came, seeping through the cracks between the doorway and the stone slab covering it. Someone was in pain. Wrapping the blanket about her, Kwani fumbled in the darkness for her crutch, heaved the heavy stone slab aside, and stepped over the sill. The alien city hunched above and below her. She was on a small terrace formed by the roof of a room below which, in turn, stood upon the roof of another dwelling. Overhead, the great stone ceiling hung like a high, stone cloud.

A piercing sense of loneliness flooded her. Kokopelli . . . would he keep his promise and take her to the Blue-eyed One? No. She hated him . . . she wanted to hate him . . . but could not. She longed for him. In the marrow of her bones she knew Kokopelli would keep his word and return for her. He was a Toltec nobleman, mystic, wise, a superior being. But soon, too soon, he would depart, leaving her among hostile people. Her only friend here was Okalake, dear, boyish Okalake, who had swept her away from the gawking crowd. He was young and handsome, an important man in the tribe. And he wanted her.

But she wanted, needed, Kokopelli, and he had not chosen her. He had refused a mating. Remembering, her cheeks burned.

The muffled sound of a drum and of chanting rose from deep inside the earth—voices from Sipapu, infinitely awesome. Was it from there the moaning had come?

Silence around her and cold . . . and then again the moaning, a long sigh of pain in a voice worn thin with accumulation of years. It came from the room directly below. A ladder led from where Kwani stood to the roof terrace of the room below. She climbed down awkwardly, crutch in her hand. A hide covered the doorway.

For a long moment Kwani stood there, shivering, unwilling to intrude. Once more the cry came. Kwani could stand it no longer. It was as though her mother called to her for help.

"Please, may I come in?" she whispered at the door.

There was no answer.

Kwani lifted the hide and peered inside at a huddled figure lying close to a small bed of coals. It stirred.

"Have I your permission to enter?" Kwani asked softly.

Again, there was no answer, only a shuddering sigh like a child who has been weeping for a long time.

Kwani stepped over the doorsill. "It is I, Kwani. May I be of help to you?"

The shrouded figure on a thick mat of reeds and furs turned toward her.

"Leave. It is forbidden to enter without purification." It was She Who Remembers.

Kwani hesitated. She knew the Old One was in pain.

"Forgive me, honored one. I did not know. I wish to help—"

"You can do nothing. It is the price I pay for living long. Go now."

But an inner voice commanded her to stay. Kwani bit her knuckles with indecision.

"How may I purify myself, honored one?"

"You may ask in the morning. Go."

From other houses came the faint groans of those with abscessed teeth and aching bodies. Pain was expected in winter. But the quavering moans of She Who Remembers held urgency.

I don't know what to do.

"Stay," the inner voice said.

Spirits were speaking. What harm could come to her in this house? Did not Kokopelli say she was protected? And did not the revered one say that she, Kwani, was born for special things? Besides, the revered one was honored and feared. If she, Kwani, could ease the pain that twisted the fragile frame, would she not be honored, also?

Another thought crept unbidden into her mind. If I help her perhaps she will reward me. Perhaps the necklace . . . coveted by Kokopelli . . .

"Forgive me, honored one, but my spirit speaks and commands me to ease your pain. Will you allow me to purify myself twice in the morning, so that I may enter now?"

"You can do nothing."

"My own mother suffered much. I helped her." How I wish I could help her again! "Permit me to try."

"I must confer with the gods. Remain outside."

Kwani retreated. The cold wind of predawn penetrated her blanket and probed her bones, but triumph flowed warm in her veins. She Who Remembers had not refused.

It was a long time before the Old One called her back. "It is the winter, the night, that brings the most pain. If you wish to try to help me—"

"I will try."

Warming her hands close to the coals until they were nearly burned, Kwani slipped them under the old woman's blanket, massaging the skeleton-thin body, rewarming her hands at the coals from time to time.

"You have a good touch, my daughter."

"Do you have a piece of hide that will hold coals without burning through?"

"In the jar upon the shelf in the corner."

She found the jar in the darkness. Inside was a piece of buffalo hide, strong and tough.

"Is there water?"

"Aye. By the wall beneath the shelf."

Kwani thought, Because she is blind she knows this darkness as I know light. For the first time, she did not pity blindness.

"I shall need a few small reeds."

"Remove them from my mat."

Beneath the furs she found several small, brittle reeds. Carefully she broke them into bits. A gourd dipper lay beside the water jar, faintly visible in light from the coals. Kwani dipped a little water and poured it over the broken reeds; then placed them on the buffalo hide. With two small stones she lifted glowing coals to the dampened reeds, scraping the reeds over the coals. There was a soft hissing and a pungent odor.

"You are preparing a potion?" the old woman asked.

"No, honored one. I make a bundle to ease pain."

"Ah," she sighed. "That will be good."

While the reeds were still steaming, Kwani folded the hide over them. "Where does it hurt the most?"

"All over. But mostly in the hips."

Kwani lifted the blanket, tucking the warm bundle next to the bony body. "Now I shall lie beside you to keep you warm."

She curved her young body around the withered one. The warmth of the bundle served them both; the pungent odor was comforting. Often Kwani had lain with her mother this way. She whose spirit would never enter Sipapu . . . But it seemed somehow that She Who Remembers had taken the spirit of Kwani's mother into herself. A feeling of peace seeped into Kwani, and she slept.

She Who Remembers did not sleep, but lay quietly. The warmth of the bundle and the vitality of the young body beside her crept into her aching bones. As was her habit during long periods of isolation, she conversed with herself in her mind.

This young person, Kwani, does not know what she has done. How may I protect her, how may I justify her breaking sacred law? She is a stranger here; she could not know it is forbidden to enter my dwelling without the ritual of purification. Yes, but you permitted her to enter. But I was hurting, and now I am not hurting as much. She has the healing touch. Face it, old woman, your ancestors grow impatient for you to join them. You die a little each day; soon you will be gone. Why prolong your departure? Who is your successor? Why do you delay? You know well why I delay. There is no one, no one Of The Gods. Until now . . .

It is said that Kwani is kin to Gods of the Rising Sun. But those are not the gods of our people. Kwani is an outsider, not yet a member of our clan. If she is Of The Gods, it will be revealed. Age has ravaged your brain, ancient one. Age, and the fangs of winter. Ah, but that warmth feels good . . . good . . .

She slept.

In the kivas of the cliff cities, secret preparations for winter solstice ceremonials had been underway for weeks. Religious fervor was high. Within three days the final ceremonies would take place at the House of the Sun. Sun Chiefs of all clans would unite their powers for the awesome responsibility of bringing Sunfather from his southern house, to begin the long trek northward toward spring and summer. If they failed, winter with its cold, starvation, sickness, and death would be with them forever.

In the Place of the Eagle Clan, in the revered kiva of the Society of the Sun, the Sun Chief and Kokopelli communed with Sunfather's spirit. A fire blazed in the firepit of the deep, circular room; around it members of the Society sat elbow to elbow upon the floor, inhaling the sacred smoke clouds issuing from the pipe of the Sun Chief. He blew a small cloud upward between chants that grew more shrill and wavering as the night progressed. Each member communed with Sunfather through his own mediating spirit—a vision that appeared after he had partaken of the sacred plant brought by Kokopelli. The small, spongy growth in the shape of Sunfather's spherical form released the soul to commune with what was normally unseen.

Kokopelli had eaten but a small portion, enough to heighten awareness. He gazed about him with admiration. The circular room of uniformly cut stones was built below the surface, to be closer to Sipapu and the worlds from which all life had come. A vertical shaft with a tunnel opened into the kiva to allow air to enter. Between the firepit and the tunnel entrance, a stone slab, the deflector, prevented a draft on the fire. Giant pilasters supported the roof of heavy wooden planks. Between the pilasters, wide recesses held ornate bowls with lids for ceremonial objects, prayer sticks, masks, whistles and rattles, flutes and drums, and sacred objects whose use was known only to the Sun Chief.

On the opposite side of the firepit from the deflector, a small, circular hole permitted souls to enter and to leave Sipapu. There were many comings and goings as sacred plants and Kokopelli's magical plant were consumed. Soon members of the Society would appear to be in deep sleep. Kokopelli knew they would be eager to trade for more of the sun-shaped spirit plant.

This will be a profitable trip, he thought, but I must be on my way before the next storm. I shall stay for trading only.

Kwani.

She lurked in the secret places of his mind, disturbing his serenity. Nagging, that was it. Typically female. He frowned, unaccustomed to such harassment—this illogical compulsion to protect and possess a woman who flaunted her interest in another.

He had seen them together, how Okalake swept her into his arms, holding her close while Kwani smiled into his eyes. To choose Kwani after that would be unsuitable to the status and dignity of a Toltec nobleman, sorcerer, physician, scholar, bestower of the sacred seed, trader.

Yes, that was it. Trader. He was rich, and would be richer with the objects Kwani would have for him when he returned months from now.

Long months. During which Kwani would be with Okalake constantly. Okalake . . . handsome, possessive, young. Young!

This most recent journey from his homeland had been more exhausting than any before. Returning would be harder still. Time, the ultimate predator, stalked him. At home with his fountains and flowers, he could abide the Chichimecas, perhaps, if he had a wife to amuse him, to give him sons, to nourish his spirit with her beauty.

He visualized the lovely body, the smooth, warm skin with copper overtones, the brows like raven's wings hovering over the blue sea of her eyes. The sweet lips full with promise. Again he saw her fragile little feet and small hands, fine-boned. Remembering, ah yes, her response to his touch when he bathed her, and the silky feel of the sipapu beneath her sweet belly . . . His thrusting man part was now urgently erect.

Now was the time! He would bring her here while the souls of Society members left their bodies. Here, by the fire, surrounded by sacred smoke and spirits, they would unite.

The old Sun Chief lay prone upon the floor, mouth agape. Yatosha, the slack-jawed Hunting Chief, and the disheveled Medicine Chief lay beside him. The others were long gone into visions.

Kokopelli stepped over them and climbed the ladder to the roof, standing a moment, breathing deeply of the sharp, clean air. Wind had swept the sky of clouds; brilliant stars, Sunfather's children, gazed down at his pulsing desire.

In the kiva they had said that Okalake took Kwani to the home of his mother. Why had he not returned? Kokopelli nibbled a bit more of the sun plant he carried with him.

Okalake—ha! How the ignorant young one yearned for Kwani's sipapu. But it would be he, Kokopelli, who seeded her!

Swiftly, making no sound, Kokopelli climbed the ladders to Woshee's home. Outside the slab door he listened. Silence. He lifted the slab aside. There was a startled cry, and Woshee sat upright.

"Kokopelli!" She gasped. Had Kokopelli come for *her*?

"I come for Kwani." He searched the darkness. "Where is she?"

Woshee looked around in shocked surprise. "I do not know. She was here—"

Kokopelli grunted and stepped back outside, not bothering to replace the door. Anger, surprise, and something more surged in him. Okalake had taken her. He should have known! Well, every woman here was willing and eager for the one and only Kokopelli . . .

But the lovely body, the shining black cloud framing her face, the curving thighs, the sipapu moist with invitation . . . He groaned with desire. Where were they? He would find them, take her by force, if necessary.

But that would make him outcast here. Vast profits would be lost to him.

Tiopi! Of course. She would satisfy him, would slake his ravenous yearning.

Panther-quiet and quick, Kokopelli climbed to the roof of Tiopi's home, remembering with satisfaction how Yatosha, Tiopi's mate, lay in a stupor in the kiva. He descended the ladder. There was a sharp gasp of alarm, then a purring of triumphant welcome. Murmurs, soft rustling, groans of pleasure too great to be borne, filled the room, and drifted into the city, announcing that Kokopelli had chosen.

Tiopi. Again.

·14·

In the east, a faint radiance outlined the sacred mountain and was reflected in snow on the mesas. This was the hour of the Crier Chief.

Wrapping his winter blanket closely around his bent frame, the Crier Chief stood for a moment upon the roof of his house, pondering his announcements. Then, slowly and painfully, he pulled himself up the ladders to the highest point in the city, a ledge below the topmost window through which Kokopelli's arrow had sped the night before. This was the Crier Chief's pulpit, to commune with the gods, to call the people of the city to arise, and to instruct them in suitable conduct.

He rested a moment, panting more than usual. It is the winter, he thought. I cannot conquer cold as once I could.

Beyond the city, beyond the snowy mesas, the wavering outline of the holy mountain grew sharper. Cloud People had gone, running before the wind, bestowing precious moisture upon distant places. He would call them back to nourish the clan's fields once more. Much moisture was needed to quench Earthmother's desperate thirst after successive years of drought. Only the sacred dances and ceremonials and the building of check dams to hold meager rainfall—and, of course, his intercession with the Cloud People—had provided barely enough rain to sustain crops for a burgeoning population.

His responsibility was a solemn one. Standing as straight as he was able, he murmured his prayers softly, for the words were not for mortal ears but for Cloud People alone.

From a pouch at his side, he drew a packet of corn meal and tossed it to the Six Sacred Directions. Then, clearing his throat, he raised both arms and loudly sang his morning chant.

"All people, awake! Open your eyes! Arise! Become children of light—vigorous, active, and joyous. Hurry, clouds, from the four quar-

87

ters of the world. Come, snow, in plenty, that there may be water when summer comes. Cover the fields that they, after planting time, may yield abundantly. Let all hearts be glad."

He lowered his arms, and his voice reverted to its normal tone. "There will be trading before Kokopelli departs. Let all be ready to receive visitors from far places. Let women prepare food for our guests. Let firewood be brought and water jars filled. Let hunters return with much game for the feasting. Okalake, son of the Sun Chief, has been with them all this night; they go beyond the Sacred Mountain for game. May they return heavily laden and in safety."

He noted with satisfaction that the city stirred awake. Already children tumbled about, and small boys climbed the wall at the cliff's edge to urinate into the dump heap, competing with one another to make the finest arc.

"Today, Kwani, child of the Gods of the Rising Sun, will receive her first birth into the Eagle Clan, beginning the period of probation. She Who Remembers will instruct Kwani in suitable procedure—" He stopped abruptly, astonished to see Kwani emerge from the house of She Who Remembers. Surely, the honored one had not instructed Kwani already!

Saving his choicest announcement for last, he continued, "Kokopelli—he of the singing reed who brings the sun plant of the gods, he who converses with his bird and causes the arrow to speak, Kokopelli from beyond the great river and the mountains of the south—has traveled far to bestow his sacred seed upon our clan once more. Tiopi, mate of Yatosha, was chosen again to be so honored. Our people and our crops will be fruitful! Let all hearts be glad."

As the Crier Chief descended the ladder, Sunfather appeared in brilliant splendor. Simultaneously Kokopelli's flute sang a riotous welcome to the morning, flooding the canyon. People gawked and pointed. Kokopelli stood, stark naked, outside Tiopi's door. His thick black hair, usually wrapped in a knot and concealed by his jeweled cap, now hung loosly over his shoulders, making his nudity somehow more pronounced. He raised his flute skyward, shouting melodious laughter; his man part had swelled to astonishing proportions.

As the flute laughed, so did the people gathered on roofs and terraces. What a baby-maker had Kokopelli! After a busy night ("did you hear Tiopi cry out—how many times?") Kokopelli's man part was still hungry! Obviously, the clan's fertility and good fortune were assured. How wonderful was Kokopelli!

Secretly, men envied the organ thrusting upward to such heights. Women aching with longing pretended indifference. "Tiopi! Again. She will be impossible to live with. But look at Kwani!"

Outside the door of She Who Remembers, Kwani stood staring up at Kokopelli. Her face was scarlet and she leaned on her crutch with both hands as though she might fall. He laughs at me! Last night he went to that woman, Tiopi. Now he demonstrates how he still desires her, even after the long night. *I hate him!*

But seeing Kokopelli naked and aglow in morning light, head thrown back, flute raised in both strong arms, and muscular brown legs akimbo so that the great thrust jutted upward, made her body respond with ravenous desire. *I want him!*

I want him!

She stumbled back into the room, collapsing beside She Who Remembers. The wrinkled face was alert.

"Why does Kokopelli laugh?"

"I—I don't know." Kwani's voice cracked.

"Ah. He chose another. Who?"

"Tiopi."

"He is a fool." The Old One spat. "People laugh out there. Why?"

"Kokopelli . . . he is naked and . . . and his baby-maker—"

A snort. "And Tiopi?"

"I did not see her." Kwani clasped her hands around her knees and rocked back and forth. "Everyone thought he would choose me. Now he laughs, they all laugh . . ." An ache inside her spread until the largest pottery jar could not contain her misery.

She Who Remembers sat quietly for a moment and her face was suffused with understanding.

"Come closer, my daughter."

Kwani knelt beside the old woman.

"Give me your hand."

The hand was clasped in a bony grasp. Again, communication flowed between them, and Kwani felt her misery lessen. The old woman smiled with toothless gums.

"Do not concern yourself with Tiopi. What she seeks most she will not possess."

"What does she seek, honored one?"

"This."

She Who Remembers released Kwani's hand and reached inside the neckline of her garment to pull out her necklace. At that moment, Sunfather's light reached in through the open door, touching the polished stones and the great scallop shell inlaid with turquoise. The shell dangled, swaying, beckoning . . . Instinctively, Kwani reached out, but as though she sensed Kwani's gesture, the old woman drew back.

"No one may touch the sacred necklace but she who wears it. Tiopi believes she will be my succssor. Now that Kokopelli has chosen her twice, she will be certain. Ha!" The withered lips parted in a silent laugh. "It is well to learn disappointment when one is young, for the gods bestow it abundantly if one cheats death for long."

She leaned back upon her mat, pulling the blanket to her chin. Blind eyes stared impassively at the ceiling, and an expression of poignant sadness settled like mist upon her face. "I have waited long for one to follow me. I fear I shall enter Sipapu before I teach a successor all she should know." She rolled her head from side to side. "There is not enough time, never enough time, never enough." Kwani wanted to comfort the old one but did not know how. She Who Remembers mumbled, talking to herself or to those unseen. Outside were the sounds of the city awakening, of people talking and laughing, of children shouting and running about, the barking of dogs, the interminable noise of turkeys and the crunch of grinding stones upon the corn.

Kokopelli's flute was silent. Where is he? Kwani wondered. But she knew, she knew. The strong body with the great thrust . . . Kokopelli and Tiopi . . .

Kokopelli lay silent, sated at last. Beside him, Tiopi sprawled with legs still spread, mouth open and slack, eyes closed. Kokopelli rose, went to the water jar and splashed icy water over his body, cleansing himself. He glanced at Tiopi with disinterest. She had served her purpose. But although his man part was limp after repeated forays into Tiopi's sipapu, still he hungered.

All night long he had wished for Kwani, had imagined her vibrant body underneath his own, but knowing it was Okalake who had entered her. Repeatedly he asked himself, "Why did I not choose her?" He should have ignored his pride, forgotten Okalake. Now Kwani was lost to him, lost to one who lived close to her each day and who was young, yes, younger . . .

But I, Kokopelli, have always had any woman I wanted, at any time! Any woman but Kwani.

At the cave Kwani had desired him. She would desire him again! *He would have Kwani as his mate.* It was too late in the season to take her with him now, through high snows and treacherous passes. But he would return and take her away from these brutal canyons, these primitives, away from Okalake!

His spirit refreshed, he donned the fine cotton garment woven and embroidered by a Toltec woman who had loved him. (He had forgotten which one.) He wrapped his brilliant robe around him, bound his hair and fastened it with the golden pin, and pulled on his feathered cap—but not before inspecting it for crawling black specks. How good to return to civilization and to the luxuries today's trading would provide! Adjusting his golden necklace and great looped ear ornaments, he climbed the ladder to the roof entrance and strode into the morning.

Much later Tiopi awoke. For a while she lay there, triumphant and sated. Never before had Kokopelli chosen the same woman twice. Who could be of greater importance than herself? As for Kwani . . . Tiopi laughed, a purring laugh deep in her throat. She shifted on her soaked and redolent sleeping mat. It would be decimated into small pieces and buried with the crops to enhance their fertility.

What a man was Kokopelli! What stories she would tell at the grinding stones! The women would cease working to hear intimate details, never tiring of hearing them repeated.

Smiling, she stretched, jangling her bracelets, noting with satisfaction the beautiful new bracelet given her by Kokopelli. Every woman in the tribe would flock to see the token of her triumph; to hear how Kokopelli had caressed her, aroused her, possessed her, seeded her again and again. How many times? She tried to remember; but who would know if she added to the number in the telling?

As she cleansed herself at the water jar, she remembered uneasily the porridge for She Who Remembers. Already Sunfather was well on his morning path; the old woman would be hungry and waiting.

Let her wait. There is no way she can refuse to choose me as her successor now.

She stepped confidently through the roof door of her home. Yes, there they were, young ones, old ones, from her clan and others, gathered around a cooking fire on which her porridge bowl was already steaming, prepared for her alone.

Tiopi favored them with a smile. "Later," she said in response to eager questions.

She climbed back down into her dwelling to get the bowl for She Who Remembers. It was too late to bother cooking the gruel in a gourd with stones. She would take some of her own that was already cooked. The Old One would not know the difference.

At the door of She Who Remembers, Tiopi stopped short. The old woman was eating porridge from the bowl Okalake had given Kwani, and Kwani herself sat beside the Old One in what was obviously a companionable relationship.

"Ah, Tiopi." She Who Remembers paused in her eating. "You have been long delayed. I am fed."

"So I see." Tiopi speared Kwani with a venomous glance. "But Kokopelli—"

"We heard," Kwani said, returning Tiopi's glance with a spear of her own. "Congratulations."

"We will not detain you," She Who Remembers added, smacking her lips over the last mouthful.

Tiopi blushed furiously. She was dismissed! After her night of triumph! Kwani, yes, Kwani was to blame and would suffer the consequences. Tiopi made a silent gesture of spitting as she left.

She Who Remembers wiped her mouth with the back of her hand and sighed with pleasure. "You cook better than Tiopi, and she cooks well. Thank you, my daughter."

"I am honored to serve you."

"Yes. Well, let us proceed with instructions for your birth into the Eagle Clan. Ours is the only clan possessing this ceremony, so listen well.

"I am listening."

"The Medicine Chief will question you thoroughly about our clan structure. This is probably the same as that of your mother and your mother's mother, back to the beginning. As you know, each clan consists of a group of blood relatives descended from a mother's mother, so far back that the original mother is unknown. So in a sense we are all brothers and sisters." She paused. "This is why members of the same clan cannot marry."

"Even if a clan member is adopted from another clan?"

"It is sacred law."

Kwani pondered. Such a law meant that Okalake's interest in her was not serious. He was amusing himself. Well, let him! She didn't care!

But she did care.

She Who Remembers continued in singsong cadence having repeated the lesson countless times in her instructions to girl children when they reached the age of understanding. "Each clan manages its own affairs, which are not to be known or discussed with members of other clans. All of the clans together form a tribe. Important matters are decided by a group of delegates from each clan, who meet together in the kivas and talk and smoke and gamble and sing and make decisions and settle disputes. Is it the same in the clan of your mother?"

"It is."

"I must repeat, nevertheless." She shifted her position and Kwani saw that the bundle she made was still tucked close to the Old One's body.

"May I heat your bundle again?"

"No. You are not paying attention," she said sharply. "Listen carefully for the Medicine Chief will be eager to find you at fault." Settling herself again, she continued. "Men belong to the clan of their mothers. When they marry, they still belong to their own clan, so the wife belongs to one clan and the husband to another. Children belong to the clan of their mothers. Is this not the same as the clan from which you come?"

"Yes. Boy children are closer to their mother's brothers than they are to their fathers; their uncles teach them the important things."

"It is so. Men from other clans, the husbands, do not have as much authority as blood relatives do. However, they must share equally in the work and in sacred responsibilities, and seed good babies. That is the part they like best," she cackled. "As for women, we own our homes and everything in them including the crops stored here, which we use as need arises. Men own crops only while crops are in the field. Is it the same with your clan?"

"It is the same."

"Of course." She shifted her position to get more sunlight warming the room. "Each clan has its various Societies, responsible for hunting, ceremonials, healing, and so on, but all are dedicated to the welfare of the entire clan rather than to their own interests. But you already know these things. It is well to answer carefully when you are questioned by the Medicine Chief."

"What else must I know, honored one?"

"Sacred matters. Have you been taught how our tribe began?"

"I know of Sipapu where there is neither sorrow nor pain . . ."

"Who is our ancient father?"

"Payatyama."

"And our mother?"

"Sanashtyaya. When the world lived in the dark."

"That is correct. How many wombs did our people enter, and live in, and leave before reaching here?"

"Three."

"Good." This girl will be easy to teach, the Old One thought. "Who led us where we are now?"

"Masau'u and Cyoyaua his brother led our people here to this fourth world, which is round."

She Who Remembers concealed her surprise. Women were not supposed to know such things; only men were considered to be qualified for such knowledge. "Who told you this?"

"Wopio, my mate. Before he wished for the arrow to find me . . ." It had been long since she wept for Wopio or even thought of him. Remembering the days when they were lovers gave her a sudden pang.

"Do you grieve for Wopio?"

Kwani started. This Old One has powers, indeed, to see without seeing. Aloud, she said, "I miss having a man beside me, even Wopio. I want a baby . . . I lost my baby to Brother Coyote . . ."

"This I did not know, about the baby." She Who Remembers controlled her excitement. "Tell me about it."

"Brother Coyote saved me from the medicine arrow and from the

Apaches. I fell from the cliff and my baby was forced to be born before it was ready." Kwani clutched her abdomen, remembering. "My spirit left me, and when it returned my leg was broken. It was night, dark night, cold . . . But Brother Coyote was close to me, keeping me alive. And when I woke my baby was gone. Brother Coyote took it into himself so it would enter Sipapu with his spirit. Kokopelli found me and cared for me until he could bring me here."

She Who Remembers could control her excitement no longer. *It is as I suspected, as I hoped,* she told herself. *Brother Coyote gave the sign. Kwani is Of The Gods. I cannot reveal the secret until after the birthing, but I have found her. At last, at last.*

Her voice trembled. "You have been chosen, my daughter. It is a sign that you have powers of which you are unaware." Again invisible light radiated from the Old One as though a torch lit her spirit from some mysterious depth. Kwani felt enveloped by that light, as though she were on the brink of a magical revelation. Her own voice trembled as she said, "What powers?"

The old woman shook her head. "I cannot answer now. After you are born into our clan you must come to me at once. Have no fear of the Medicine Chief for you are protected by those who are stronger than he. Let us continue with the history of our people."

"I am ready!"

"The earth is round and flat, but it is also thick like a cake. The other three wombs are down below inside, one beneath the other. When our people came to this womb, the fourth world, it was cold and dark. Those Above saw that some of our people liked summer best, and some winter best. So Masau'u and his brother said to the men of our tribe, 'Go to where there is more light.' These, the summer people, went far southward, to the banks of a great river where it was light and warm. The others, the winter people, were sent south also but far around by the east, over the plains where the great buffalo are, where it is cold and dry. To both kinds of men, it was said, 'Come together in the mountains and live there in peace, each one getting food for himself and for others.' "

"I will remember."

Yes, you will remember, the old woman thought. She said, "Now you must learn the birthing song." She held out her hand, feeling the sun's rays so that she might judge the sun's position and know the time. "Soon you will be called. All women of the clan will unite to give you birth. As you are born, you sing this song." In a shrill, small voice like a child's reed flute, she sang:

Into the Eagle Clan I am born.
Into the Place of the Eagle Clan I am born.

My former clan I know no more.
My people of my former clan I know no more.
The spirits of my former clan know me no more.
Into the Eagle Clan I am born.
Into the Place of the Eagle Clan I am born.

"Now you sing it," She Who Remembers said.

It was a singsong chant, much like other chants but for the words, and Kwani sang it all the way through correctly.

The old woman nodded in satisfaction. "You are ready."

"But how am I to be born?"

"You will know when it is time."

She sighed deeply and lay back on her mat. "I will talk with my spirit now." She closed her eyes.

·15·

Kwani knelt on the stone floor of the courtyard facing the city, and the people gathered there—who missed not a word of the Medicine Chief's questions and Kwani's replies. News of Kokopelli's arrival had spread and already visitors had arrived for the trading. They sat with the others, agog at what was happening.

Kwani shifted to ease the pressure on her knees. She wished Okalake and Kokopelli were there, but Okalake had gone with the hunters to obtain game for the feasting, and Kokopelli remained in the kiva. But Cayamo, the singer of love songs, and Chololo, the flute player with the ear ornament dangling to his small shoulder, stood by smiling encouragement.

For a long time Kwani had knelt there. So far she had given no wrong answers, to the barely concealed frustration of the Medicine Chief. He stood on a higher ledge so that she had to look up to him. The freshly painted zigzag black marks from his brow glowed with lurid intensity. One hand held a gourd rattle adorned with secret symbols; in the other hand he held high the sacred bow entrusted by Kokopelli. Now he would demand answers he was certain Kwani could not supply.

He rattled his gourd with authority. "Whose brother brought us to the fourth world?"

"Masau'u's brother, Cyoyaua."

There was a murmur from roofs and terraces; few women knew the sacred names taught by old men to boys in the kivas.

The Medicine Chief scowled. She Who Remembers had taught this one well. Too well, perhaps. He would find out. He rattled the gourd again.

"Describe the shape of the fourth world."

Kwani sensed a trap. If she answered correctly, it would seem she had a witch's power to know what was known only by men of certain Secret Societies. Or that She Who Remembers had revealed untellable secrets. If she answered incorrectly, she would be sent alone again to the wilderness, to die.

She fingered her amulet praying to her mother's spirit and to the gods. I am afraid. Help me. Instruct me, honored ones. Tell me what to say.

The Medicine Chief smiled and his eyes glittered. "I wait for your answer."

There was a buzz among the crowd. No woman had been asked such a question before. It was unseemly, like expecting a woman to wear a man's robe or to urinate standing up. Could it be that Kwani was part man and part woman, a monstrosity? Was there a man part between her thighs, and was that why Kokopelli did not choose her after all?

"Is the answer unknown to you? Speak!"

Kwani's long hair, ceremonially washed by Woshee and still damp, clung to her cheeks. She brushed it back with both hands, closing her eyes in supplication to the spirits.

"Describe the shape of the fourth world!" His voice rang with malicious triumph.

Kwani begged of her mother's spirit. Tell me! Tell me!

There was a rustle of wings; the macaw flew out of the kiva, circled briefly, then lighted near to Kwani and waddled toward her.

This was her mother's answer! Instinctively, Kwani knew what to do. She held her hand outstretched, as Kokopelli did, and the bird clutched her fingers and climbed sideways to her shoulder.

The people gasped. "A-a-a-yee!"

The Medicine Chief's eyes bulged. This woman must really be a child of the gods after all. He felt a stab of fear.

Kwani turned to the bird, babbling what she hoped was an acceptable imitation of Kokopelli's foreign language. The bird eyed her scornfully, and replied in a guttural rasp.

"A-a-a-yee!"

Kwani rose and stood proudly. "Kokopelli's sacred bird speaks for me. He says the fourth world is round. That is my answer."

Fury and fear alternated between the Medicine Chief's black zigzags. "It is my duty to permit the women of the Eagle Clan to give you birth," he said, continuing with effort. "However, I remind you that until you make the vessel I require, your membership in this clan is temporary." He rattled the gourd in a wide gesture. "The vessel must be like none made before. It must hold as much water as the largest jar, yet light enough for me to carry with one finger. It must be of sacred design, more powerful than any I now possess; which held to the fire, will not burn; thrown from the cliff, will not break. It must be completed before Ceremonies Before Planting. And it is I, only I, who shall accept or reject it."

Holding the bow overhead, and with a final flourish of the rattle, the Medicine Chief strode away.

Kwani thought, no matter what I make he will never accept it. A knot twisted inside her. Maybe Kokopelli would return before Ceremonies Before Planting. Maybe . . .

Woshee stepped forward and faced the amphitheater of the city. Beside her Kwani stood with the bird still perched on her shoulder. Snow melted in Sunfather's afternoon warmth, and water dripped from the mesa above them, splashing into water jars lined up below, making a musical tinkle, *plink, plunk, plink.*

The mother of Okalake and wife of the Sun Chief was second in importance only to She Who Remembers. She stood erect, her gray hair rolled into large shiny coils high over each ear in squash blossom style, entwined with blue feathers. Blue feathers dangled from each ear. Her winter robe was secured at the waist with an ornate belt of dog and human hair, into which bits of blue feathers were woven. She spoke with austere dignity.

"The time has come for the women of the Eagle Clan to give birth to a new member. Kwani is her name. She has been brought to us by Kokopelli, and she speaks and is spoken to by Kokopelli's sacred bird. Her blood is that of the Gods of the Rising Sun, those who ride the great waters of the east. Kokopelli has said it. She comes from another clan to be reborn into ours. Women will prepare themselves."

Every woman and every girl who had experienced the moon flow that made her a woman lined up, front to back, across the courtyard. The line stretched all the way across and up over several terraces. The macaw flew from Kwani's shoulder and lighted on a roof as though to observe the proceedings.

Woshee said to Kwani. "I shall undress you. You will be born into the clan as you were born into the fourth world."

Men leaned forward and grinned in appreciation as Kwani's robe and undergarments were loosened and fell to the floor. She stood adorned only in total femininity. Her dark hair clung to her shoulders and around her breasts, framing each full swell. Women gazed in envy, especially Tiopi who bit her lips, scowling.

A man called, "Since she has no male pleasure part, I gladly volunteer mine."

Laughter.

Kwani ignored them and held her head high.

Woshee spread her legs, and gestured down between them. "Each of us will birth you. Crawl through and sing your birthing song. I am first. Sing now."

Kwani put the crutch aside; lately she had needed it less. As she kneeled and approached Woshee, she sang, "Into the Eagle Clan I am born," and crawled on her hands and knees between Woshee's legs. Woshee squatted and groaned loudly in birthing pain as Kwani passed beneath her. Then she said, "Now the others."

The long line of women and girls stood waiting, forming a tunnel with parted legs. As Kwani crawled through, each one squatted and groaned loudly. Kwani continued to sing.

> *Into the Place of the Eagle Clan I am born.*
> *My former clan I know no more.*
> *My brothers and sisters of my former clan I know no more.*
> *The spirits of my former clan know me no more.*
> *Into the Eagle Clan I am born.*
> *Into the Place of the Eagle Clan I am born.*

She had finished the song but there still was a long tunnel leading upward over the terraces.

"Keep singing!" someone whispered down to her.

> *Into the Eagle Clan I am born . . .*

She felt a warm trickle on her bare back. Urine. She glanced up. Tiopi smiled down at her and groaned so vigorously that more trickle came.

Kwani was outraged. She tried to continue singing, but the song caught in her throat.

"Sing!" someone hissed.

> *Into the Place of the Eagle Clan . . .*

The melody wavered and was lost. Titters sounded among the groans. Then, magically, the melody was reborn by a flute!

Kokopelli was watching!

Kwani crawled up a terrace and between the legs, some old and bony, some tender and young. Her voice picked up the melody, blending with the flute.

> *My former clan I know no more . . .*

At last it was over. Kwani rose, still feeling the dampness on her back. Woshee beckoned her to descend and Kwani obeyed, hardly noticing that she came without her crutch.

Woshee said, "Now you take the milk." She pulled her robe aside, exposing drooping breasts. "Suck."

Kwani obeyed. The nipples had a slightly sour taste.

"Now the others," Woshee said.

Already others, especially the young ones, stood exposed to Koko-pelli's gaze. Some were bared to the waist, and lower, as they turned a little this way and that, preening for him.

Kwani dutifully went through the motion of sucking from each breast. Occasionally, she got a mouthful of milk from a nursing mother; sometimes she had to lift a withered old breast in both hands to reach the nipple, while the aged one giggled.

When she reached Tiopi, Kwani stopped. "I do not drink from you."

"If you wish to stay in the clan . . . ?"

"And if I refuse?"

"I shall be delighted."

Kwani called to Woshee, "The milk of this woman will make me vomit."

"She is one of the clan. You must drink."

"If I refuse?"

"The birthing ceremony will be worthless. Drink!" she said urgently.

I must, Kwani thought. She bent to Tiopi's full breast.

"Kokopelli enjoyed it," Tiopi said.

Kwani touched her lips briefly to the nipples.

"You did not suck. Suck!"

"Very well." Kwani sucked in a nipple, and bit down hard.

Tiopi screamed and clutched her breast. A small red trickle oozed through her fingers.

"You bit me!"

"You wet on me!"

Tiopi swung at Kwani, knocking her sprawling. Kwani scrambled to her feet. Anger and humiliation exploded inside her. She leaped at Tiopi with a yell, grabbed her hair and jerked down the coiled rolls with such violence that Tiopi fell. Kwani straddled her, and banged Tiopi's head up and down against the stone floor while Tiopi clawed back.

There was an uproar as people laughed or jeered. Clan culture forbade men of the same clan to fight one another, but watching women fight was considered to be a spectator sport.

Snarling, Kwani and Tiopi rolled on the floor. Near the edge of a terrace, where a ladder reached to the floor six feet below, Tiopi was on Kwani, clawing her face, trying to gouge out her eyes. With a mighty effort, Kwani rolled to the terrace edge, turned, and shoved Tiopi over the edge. Tiopi grabbed for the ladder as she went down, but missed, and landed in a heap upon the stone floor where she lay, whimpering.

Kwani rose unsteadily. Scratches bled from her face and her breasts. Defiantly she let the blood dribble down her bare body. "The ceremony will continue," Woshee said in a clear voice.

But Kokopelli raised a hand. "Woshee, have I your permission to speak?"

They looked frankly into one another's eyes, acquaintances of long standing. "You may speak."

"Perhaps those who have yet to give the symbolic milk to the newborn member of the Eagle Clan would prefer not to have Kwani's blood smeared upon them. I therefore offer to take Kwani's place in finishing the ceremony. Is it agreed?"

An amused glint flickered in Woshee's eyes. She turned to the women still waiting.

"Is it agreed?"

"Yes! Oh, yes!"

Kokopelli strode with confident grace to the first woman in line, and squatted before her. Encircling her with his arms, he pulled her between his legs and sucked at each breast, teasing the nipples with his tongue until she gasped. Then he released her and motioned to the next to come forward. This was Miko, whose first moon flow had made her a woman and who had yet to take a mate. She approached shyly, offering her small breasts like flowers. Gently, Kokopelli pulled her to him and caressed the slender back and little thighs and buttocks. Smiling, he kissed each breast and held her tightly to him until she trembled.

"Kokopelli . . . oh, Kokopelli . . ."

He released her, smiling, and beckoned to the next, and the next. Kwani tried not to watch. Not to notice how his man part swelled until it seemed his garment would split. Not to see how women pressed themselves against him . . .

Tiopi whimpered, but no one paid attention. Every man, woman, and child saw only Kokopelli, giver of the sacred seed, seducing woman after woman, leaving them unfulfilled. Some of the women disappeared into their dwellings, their men following; others waited impatiently for their men to return from hunting and from the distant fields. Old men and those too young for mates watched avidly.

The barking of hunting dogs in the distance caused a sudden wild commotion among the dogs left behind. Yapping, they raced down the mountain to meet returning dogs and hunters with deer, rabbits, and a fat mountain sheep. Kokopelli and Kwani were forgotten. People crowded the edge of the cliff or clambered down the steep trail to help the hunters carry the heavy game.

Inspecting Kwani with a practiced and appreciative eye, Kokopelli said, "It seems that you need healing. Again." He looked down his nose and his mouth twitched.

"I shall make a poultice for the scratches. That one"—Kwani tossed her head in Tiopi's direction—"scratches like a dog after fleas. My wounds give little pain. Do not concern yourself."

Kokopelli restrained a smile. Tiopi was still whimpering.

Kwani said, "Why are you not with Tiopi? When one plants seeds, one hopes for harvest. She fell hard. I hope I have not interfered with your expectations." Blue eyes challenged him through a fringe of lashes.

His black brows met in a scowl. The independence of this Anasazi woman was too much.

How could he have considered taking her as mate?

He said, "I see you have discarded your crutch."

"So I have." Indifferently.

"It was I who made it for you, I who healed you, who saved your life, who brought you here to a new home, a new clan. Not only did I save your life, I saved your leg. You owe me for that, as well.

"So?"

"So remember our agreement. All you make is mine."

"With one exception."

"No exception." He stepped closer and whispered, "Remember the rest of our agreement, as well."

The necklace. He wanted the necklace of She Who Remembers, Kwani thought. But that necklace belongs to the Old One! I would never try to take it from her! Even though he made me promise.

She said, "I remind you I must make a vessel for the Medicine Chief before my membership in the clan is final. That, I cannot give you."

She wiped away a red trickle dripping on her stomach, pretending not to notice the urgency beneath his breechcloth. *It is not I whom he desires. He desires all women. To him we are a single body, a single flesh. He plays with us, he makes us hungry and leaves us hungry. It is a game to amuse himself. I hate him.*

But it had been long, long, since she had a man. His eyes were like the bird's eyes, piercing, mysterious; they cast spells. He nodded his head briefly.

"Very well. Make the vessel. In the end what I wish will be mine as you will see."

Hunting dogs and hunters bounded into the courtyard. There were shouts of welcome and loud rejoicing over the game; there would be plenty for the feasting. Amid the babble encircled by people surrounding them, Kwani and Kokopelli were as if alone, enclosed by an invisible wall. The men who had arrived stared avidly at Kwani, pressing closer to see her nakedness and her long hair falling like dark water, and the red scratches upon her cheeks and throat and her round breasts, and the dirt smeared upon her arms and upon her little round belly with the indentation like a sipapu in the center, and the dirt and bruises along the slope and swell of her buttocks and thighs, and each man thought he had never seen a more desirable woman. But she was a member of the Eagle Clan now, not to be possessed by any of them.

Okalake gazed at Kwani like a man starved, as though he could force her to turn to him and to him alone. He stepped forward, but was stopped by the invisible wall. He paled, and knots bulged in his jaw.

Kokopelli was oblivious even to Tiopi who came to stand beside him and tugged at his robe. He ran a finger down a scratch on Kwani's breast to the cactus fruit tip. He remembered its taste, different from any he had tasted that day. He bent to savor it again, pulling her to him.

She felt his man part thrusting hard against her. It had been long, long since she had a man. Desire surged through her—wildfire out of control. She clutched his head as his mouth took her breast and his hand caressed the other breast and he purred like an animal.

"Take me!" she whispered fiercely.

He swept her off her feet and into his arms and strode to a kiva.

"No!" Tiopi gasped, and Okalake stepped forward as though to snatch Kwani from Kokopelli's arms, but Kwani clung to Kokopelli and pressed her face against his chest; her long hair flowed over his arm and floated like a banner. When they reached the kiva, Kokopelli lowered her down the ladder, and followed.

The macaw flew down with a squawk, and lit on the floor near the kiva entrance.

Taking a woman for sex into a kiva defiled the sacred dwelling of spirits.

The Medicine Chief seethed, enraged. Even Kokopelli would not be permitted this. With a grunt of rage he approached the kiva. But the bird was there, guarding the entrance. It stared at him coldly with its fearsome eyes and spoke in its magic tongue. The Medicine Chief did not understand the words, but he feared their meaning.

The people murmured and looked at him, waiting for him to do something. The other Chiefs and the elders crowded around him.

"It is forbidden!" But they, too, were uneasy.

The Medicine Chief remembered how Kwani had held out her hand to the bird and it crawled to her shoulder. If he could get the bird away from the kiva . . . He approached the bird who cocked its head, and stared with its little black eyes. Hesitantly, the Medicine Chief extended his hand. The bird ignored him. He held the hand closer. With a quick jerk of its head, the bird bit him. Hard.

With a yelp of surprise and pain, the Medicine Chief jerked away his bleeding hand. Embarrassment fueled more fury and he shouted down into the kiva, "Kokopelli! It is forbidden! I, the Medicine Chief, demand that you return!"

No answer.

"Kokopelli! Return!"

Sounds from below made it plain there would be no return, not for a long time.

Kwani lay in a dreamlike haze, exhausted. How long had they been there? Kokopelli was propped up on one elbow, gazing down at her, his man part spent at last. Again and again she had felt its power deep inside her. His lovemaking, different from any experienced before, unleashed a response she did not know was possible. She was astonished at herself, her choked cries and writhing spasms, her frantic efforts to pull him closer, deeper.

How could the arrogant, downturned mouth create delirium, how hawk's eyes hold such tender fire? He was foreign, strange, and his odor, like no other, disturbingly compelling. Was that why she still feared him a little?

He leaned closer, golden ear ornaments swinging. "I shall not be with you again until first flowers bloom."

The resonance of his voice made her understand why animals used sound for seduction.

"You will return?"

"Of course." His lips twitched in a smile. "I choose you as my mate."

She looked at him, speechless.

He kissed her, the gentle kiss of one who has conquered and been fulfilled.

"I cannot take you with me now; it is too late in the season, too far to go." He removed a golden loop from his ear. "I give you this." He looped the ornament over her ear. "You shall have the other when first flowers bloom. Meanwhile, this will remind everyone"—he had almost said "Okalake"—"will remind them that you are mine and mine alone."

At last she found words. "I cannot be here without you. Take me with you!"

"I cannot." Seeing her stricken look, he added, "But I will tell you about my home, to be your home also, to think of while you await my return."

"Tell me."

"It is in a beautiful place, far south of here." He did not want to tell her how very far it was; that would come later. "My house is large and white with many rooms. You shall have a room for sleeping and a room for eating and a room for cooking that opens to an outside place with a fountain—"

"What is a fountain?"

"Like a big, very big bowl standing by itself up to here." He stood up to show her how high it was. "There is another bowl above it, to here . . . that is smaller, and still another, up here . . . even smaller. Water flows into the top bowl, overflows into the one underneath, then overflows again to the big one at the bottom. Water flows all the time. You will never have to go anywhere but there to fill your jar."

"Ah!"

"And you shall have a room only for sewing and making things, and talking to friends when they visit. Everywhere are flowers growing, and tall trees, and many birds come to drink and bathe in the fountain. And you, my love, will have a place to bathe, also. A little stream flows by my house and makes a pool under the trees . . ."

Kwani shook her head. It was more than she could visualize, a place for gods.

"Where will you be, Kokopelli?"

"With you." He smiled and kissed her again. "My sisters and brothers and cousins all have houses near my own. We have much land, fertile land, where corn grows high."

"Take me with you!"

"I cannot."

She knew it was final. Foreboding could not quench her joy as she drew him to her again. At last she would have all she longed for—a mate and protector, a home, children. Though Kokopelli was older, and her home among his people might seem strange at first—so many rooms!— who else had ever made her spirit soar? Or loved her so artfully?

"I am only yours forever, Kokopelli."

Upon the mesa, hidden by a boulder, Okalake crouched, staring blankly into distance, groaning with the pain of jealousy, ignoring the blindness of tears.

·16·

It was morning the day after Kwani's birthing. More traders had arrived and by sun-up, the city and the mesa above it were thronged.

She Who Remembers sat beside her door and listened. The many sounds translated themselves into images and she knew them all: the races and games with loud wagering and laughter, the chatter and clatter of women as they played and worked, the boisterous activity of children. Upon the mesa could be heard the endless haggling of barter where Kokopelli did business with clans of the cave cities and with traders from far places.

She drew her turkey feather blanket more closely around her and sipped from a mug of hot corn gruel. The warmth of the mug felt good in her hands and eased the pain in her twisted fingers, But nothing eased the trouble in her heart. Kwani had not come. Spirit calls from Sipapu grew stronger each day; soon she could deny them no longer. But there was no one made ready to take her place in the clan, in the tribe. Only she knew the secrets and remembered, only she possessed the sacred necklace and commanded its powers. What would become of them all with none to take her place, to teach the young girls?

Kwani had not come.

Kwani was Of The Gods, she was certain of it. If she could not reveal to Kwani the secret of being Of The Gods and tell her how to choose her own successor, and if she could not give Kwani the necklace and instruct her, who would become She Who Remembers?

What fearsome punishments would the gods bestow? She moaned and rocked to and fro.

Where is Kwani? She did not come to me after the birthing ceremony. She allowed herself to be seeded by Kokopelli. In a kiva! What sort of omen is this? You know

106

very well, Old One. It is ominous. Kokopelli or no, it defiled a sacred place. You are being stupid. Kwani and Kokopelli are chosen ones; they cannot defile. Be patient, Kwani will come. I have no time to be patient. I have no time. Kwani will come. Prepare.

Slowly, painfully, She Who Remembers stood and raised both hands overhead. Instantly, several women were at her side. "Summon the Sun Chief. At once."

"He is on the mesa, trading."

"Call to him."

The women went to the cliff's edge and called up in unison, "She Who Remembers summons the Sun Chief!"

Immediately, the call was returned. "The Sun Chief comes!"

He arrived, puffing slightly, wiping his wrinkled brow with the sleeve of his winter robe. His deeply set black eyes were concerned. "I am here."

"I must go to the House of the Sun."

"But it is not yet time for the ceremonies—"

"I do not go for the sun ceremonies, but for ceremonies of my own. Come closer."

As he leaned down, she drew his ear to her lips. "I do not wish anyone else to know. My time to enter Sipapu has come. I must go at once to the House of the Sun, the Gathering Place of the Gods."

He shook his graying head sadly and took her hand and breathed reverently on it. "It shall be. I am too old to carry you so I bestow the honor on my son." Again, he breathed on her hand and she heard his footsteps fade quickly away. Soon, Okalake's footsteps came running. He knelt with his back against her legs. "Lean forward and put your arms around my neck." Gently, he lifted the fragile body on his back and tucked her legs under his arms. She weighs no more than an empty basket, he thought.

The House of the Sun, the Anasazi's sacred temple, rose majestically upon the opposite mesa. Within its massive stone walls were sun-shaped rooms, a ceremonial plaza, and private chambers for those who, like the Sun Chief, communicated directly with gods. The temple had no roof; it was open to Sunfather's probing eye, to light and shadows cast by the moon, and to the awesome sweep of constellations. All clans of the community helped in the building of it, and all chiefs and holy men participated in ceremonies there.

She Who Remembers clung to Okalake through the rugged canyon across to the opposite cliff where the steep, narrow trail led up to the mesa. "I climb to the mesa now, but first I must bind you to me."

"There is no time to stop!" He felt her frail form tremble like a dry leaf before it falls.

"Forgive me, honored one, but I must use both hands in climbing the hand-holds and I cannot hold you."

"Make haste, then."

He set her down gently. With the strong, intricately braided belt that his mother had made for him of dog hair woven with yucca twine he secured her to his back. "Hold on to me as much as you are able, but do not be afraid if you cannot. You will not fall."

"I am not afraid. Climb now!"

The path was so steep he had to climb it like a ladder in places. Loose rock crumbled and slid under his sandals, but a lifetime spent among rocky cliffs gave him confidence. When he reached hand-holds cut into the cliff's face, he dug his fingers into the small crevices, slippery from melted snow, wiping each one with a corner of his robe as he went, hand over hand.

He could feel the thin arms around his neck and her legs dangling behind him. The wind, which had blown gently through the canyon, now came in sharp gusts as though the wind god challenged their puny endurance. The cold increased and so did the old one's trembling.

Okalake said, "We are nearly there."

He had almost reached the mesa when he felt her arms loosen, her weight shift. For an instant he teetered in the wind, while his hands clutched the shallow crevices and his feet fumbled for footing. His heart jerked with alarm. He refused to look down at the rocks far below, but stared up to the mesa's ledge only a few hand holds away, up into blue sky where Cloud People watched. They beckoned to him.

Like water rushing, strength flowed into his hands and arms and legs. One last reach, and he was over the ledge, safe on the mesa's grassy floor. He looked up to the Cloud People, his lips moving in a prayer of thanks.

"Untie me," She Who Remembers said faintly.

Okalake loosened the belt, lifted her gently and carried her to the temple.

A cloud covered the sun as they entered; the shadow passed over the holy place, drifted beyond the mesa, and into the distance.

"Take me to the Place of Remembering."

Across the plaza, and in a small room facing east he set her gently on her feet. She swayed but remained upright and said, "Bring Kwani here. Quickly."

"Bring Kwani here?" He gulped. It was against clan law, and Kwani . . .

"*Now.*" Her voice trembled with urgency.

"I go."

She Who Remembers went to a small stone altar at the end of the room, kneeling so that her head and arms rested upon it. Temple walls protected the room from wind; the altar was faintly warm. She pressed against the stone, seeking its strange and special powers from Earthmother's domain. It took longer than ever before. But at last she felt the mysterious force enter mind and body. She reached in the folds of her robe for a packet of corn pollen—the substance most sacred. Chanting a prayer, she tossed a pinch three times to each of the Six Directions. With hands that shook, she removed the necklace, and laid it upon the altar to receive the powers of the stone and be blessed by Sunfather's eye.

Again, she leaned forward and laid her head and outstretched arms on the altar. She touched the necklace, fingering the beads and the scallop shell with turquoise inlay in mystical design.

Like a seed that sprouts and gropes its way upward into the light of the fourth world, remembering grew.

Time is like constellations that swing in a great circle in the sky's vast bowl. There is no beginning, no end; all returns again and again, forever.

She pressed her face upon the stone. "Spirit of Earthmother, I have found one who is Of The Gods. She comes so that I may dedicate her to you." Her voice became fainter, as though of its own accord it chose to depart.

She struggled to speak again. "Teach her, for I cannot . . . It is too late . . . I have failed and Sipapu calls . . ." She moaned. She would be the first of an ancient line who had failed—and the last. The punishment would be too great to endure.

Desperately she clutched the necklace in both hands, as though to force its powers into a body that was disassociating itself.

"Kwani!" she cried in a voice shrill as an eagle's.

Only the wind replied from somewhere beyond the wall.

·17·

Kwani slept as one whose spirit roams from the body. She had ignored the hostile stares which greeted her as she left Kokopelli and emerged from the kiva, and had come to the waiting place which was now her home. She had collapsed on the floor, used her pack as a pillow, pulled her feather blanket over her, and surrendered to sleep.

Shadows shifted and grew long, dissolving into darkness. Hours passed. At last she dreamed.

Mother, where are you?
I am here, my daughter.
I cannot go to the Blue-eyed One until Kokopelli returns.
The wait will be long. Take care.
I am afraid. Enemies are in this place.
Listen to one who calls from Sipapu.
Wait! Do not leave me! Mother . . .

She woke to the morning call of the Crier Chief.

"Awake! Arise and be glad! Welcome visitors! We of the Eagle Clan invite you to remain for more trading. We invite you to share our feasting and games. Many valuable possessions changed hands yesterday. Cayamo, he who sings, won three fine feather blankets, two knives, and a cooking bowl."

The Crier Chief knew how the people loved gambling, especially during the long winter months. A fine necklace or blanket or choice flint from the south would have many different owners before the Ceremonies.

"Hopata of the Beaver Clan of the north won two bracelets, a thumb's length of salt, and ten arm's length of yucca twine. Someone else may win them today." He savored appreciative laughter from those on rooftops and terraces.

110

Hopata! Kwani jerked upright from her mat. She knew him, member of a clan near her own and friend of Wopio, her former mate. Did they know she was here?

The Crier Chief continued, "Those who seek mates from the Eagle Clan are advised to remember that Kokopelli seeded two—not one, but two—of our women. We will have many babies and our fields will have much corn. The gods are pleased with us. Consider these things in matrimonial transactions."

More laughter and approving comments.

"Soon Kokopelli departs for his home beyond the Great River of the South . . ." The people murmured in surprise; usually Kokopelli stayed several days at least. "Kokopelli thanks the people of this place for their hospitality and good trading. He is pleased with us, and assures us of the blessings of the gods. We will have good rains, good harvests, good fortune. Let all hearts be glad."

A buzz of pleasure was quieted by the Crier Chief's solemn mien. Raising both arms he intoned, "Kokopelli instructs me to inform you on a matter of great importance." He paused, to heighten suspense. "Kokopelli, he of the sacred seed, he of the magical bird and singing flute, he who communes with spirits and with gods . . . has chosen a mate."

"Who, who?" people called.

"She is the newest member of our clan. Kwani. Kokopelli cannot take her with him through the snows and high passes. But he will return when first flowers bloom to claim her, and to give each Chief of the Eagle Clan a valuable gift in payment for their protection of his mate until he returns."

Astonished silence. Followed by whispers and sly glances at Tiopi preening on her terrace. She flushed a furious crimson and disappeared into her dwelling.

"Kokopelli also instructs me to say that if harm comes to Kwani, if any Chief fails in his duty to protect her, the clouds will not let fall their rain, and evil spirits will dwell among us. That is all I am permitted to tell. The rest I cannot repeat. I have spoken."

In the waiting place Kwani rose and reached for her clothes which someone (Woshee?) had folded into a neat pile beside her mat. She was dishevelled, scratched, and dirty. She could not go outside looking this way. And Hopata . . .

I must go out there looking like who I am, *the mate of Kokopelli.* She fingered her golden ear ornament. From her water flask she sprinkled water on herself and rubbed with both hands, cleansing herself as best she could. The room was very cold and the water was icy; she shivered and dried herself with a portion of her blanket. She was brushing her long hair when she heard Okalake's voice at the door.

"Kwani! Come!"

She felt a twinge of sympathy for him. Dear Okalake. She hated to disappoint him.

"I cannot. I am mate of Kokopelli now."

"I know." Flatly. "She Who Remembers is at the House of the Sun and requests that I bring you."

"Oh." She was abashed. "I am not yet ready."

With an exclamation of impatience, he pushed the door covering aside. "The Old One enters Sipapu. She wants to see you before she goes. *Come!*" He snatched the brush from her hand and threw it to the floor. He pulled her over the sill.

"Hear, everyone!" Okalake cried. "She Who Remembers is at the House of the Sun and requests that I bring Kwani to her. Make way!" He lifted Kwani in his arms.

"Put me down! I can walk now."

But he ran down the ladders and through the crowd of gawking bystanders. There was a swirl of passing faces, staring in avid curiosity and awe. Among them, Kwani thought she glimpsed a face she had almost forgotten. Wopio.

Was it possible? Yes, Wopio had come to destroy her. But she had protectors now!

She clung to Okalake as he scrambled down the steep path and into the wide ravine, ignoring brush and cactus. At the cliffs of the opposite mesa, she climbed on his back, clutching him to keep from falling, until at last they were on the mesa.

He set her down. "Come this way." Kwani limped after him as he led her to the Place of Remembering he stopped abruptly at the entrance. She Who Remembers lay sprawled, her back against the altar stone. Her head was thrown back at a grotesque angle. Open eyes stared unseeing; and her twisted mouth was stretched wide in a silent, terrible cry.

Kwani's heart contracted; a sound was wrenched from her throat like that of an animal in a snare. She sank to her knees beside the frail body. With sickening guilt she remembered. She had not gone to the Old One after the birthing ceremony as She Who Remembers had requested. Now, it was too late.

She buried her head in the Old One's lap.

"Forgive me!"

The visitor tossed his gambling sticks, wagering a fine pair of fur foot coverings. He won, but there was not the usual chorus of congratulations and new challenges. Talk was of little else but Kokopelli's taking the sky-eyed outsider, Kwani, as mate. Then, when Okalake made his announcement and swept Kwani away to the House of the Sun, speculation was boundless.

Of all the people there, only Wopio and his friend Hopata knew that Kwani had been Wopio's mate. Wopio knew how much he had missed her. His second marriage had been a bitter disappointment; the girl was a wretched cook and had a sour disposition and they quarreled constantly. A baby girl died during its third moon. Wopio, hearing Kwani was with the Eagle Clan, had decided magnamimously to allow her to return to him. The Crier Chief's announcement left him shocked. It could not be! When the revered She Who Remembers summoned Kwani to the House of the Sun, and the handsome son of Eagle Clan's Sun Chief carried her past him and away, it was more than any man could be expected to endure.

What if Kwani refused him? Not likely, of course . . . but what if she did? He would be prepared, just in case.

Tiopi paced her room; banging her fists against the wall. That arrogant witch, that outsider, who pushed her, Tiopi, over the ledge! And mated with Kokopelli afterward! In a kiva! And now she was at the House of the Sun! A desecration even worse than mating in a kiva! There had been nothing but trouble since Kwani arrived. It was inconceivable that she should remain with the Eagle Clan until Kokopelli's return. Tiopi sobbed in her rage.

Kwani must be forced to go.

Kokopelli tied the last knots in the multicolored strings of his quipu, and reviewed his calculations. Satisfied, he rolled the quipu tightly, tied it with a leather thong, and stuffed it into his pack bulging with treasures. He could carry no more. It was time to depart.

The thought of leaving Kwani was deeply disturbing; he was surprised at how much. Was it possible to take her with him, after all? He pondered this. She still limped; her leg was not completely healed; she could never slog through the snows. No, it would be all he could do to keep himself and his bird alive.

He had seen Okalake carrying her across the ravine. Had She Who Remembers summoned Kwani to the House of the Sun to appoint her as successor? Why else would she call Kwani to the holy place? As the next She Who Remembers, Kwani would be safe here. That, at least, was reassuring.

And Kwani would have the necklace.

He glanced at the sun. The hour was late; he must go.

But he lingered. Perhaps Kwani would have his child, his son. He had sired many children in his travels. But they belonged to their mothers and to their tribes. This child would be his. His own son, at last.

He stood for a moment, looking over the ravine, but Kwani did not return. Shouldering his pack and taking his bird, Kokopelli headed for the trail. Few saw him go; they stared down into the ravine, watching as Okalake approached, carrying a limp figure with dangling arms and legs.

She Who Remembers!

A keening cry rose as from a single throat.

Kwani sat in the Place of Remembering. Alone, but not alone; spirits were there. She leaned against a wall and gazed at the stone altar where the necklace lay, its scallop shell pendant pointing toward her. Okalake had lifted the Old One tenderly and carried her away.

"I will send Kokopelli for you," he told her. But Kokopelli had not come.

Why did she send for me? Kwani asked herself. But she knew. *She was to be She Who Remembers* . . . a newcomer, an outsider, not yet completely a member of the clan in spite of her failure to come to the Old One after the birthing ceremony, in spite of everything. She Who Remembers intended to appoint Kwani as her successor. Why Kwani was certain of this, she could not say. But she *knew.*

The necklace lay upon the sacred stone, waiting.

Slowly, Kwani knelt before the altar. She lifted the necklace and held it reverently, then slipped it over her head and let the pendant find its resting place between her breasts. With both hands she pressed it against her and closed her eyes; it was as though she held the Old One to her.

Again, she saw the staring eyes, the open mouth grotesque in its silent scream. Whose name was it calling?

"Forgive me!"

Silence. It hung like a dark, heavy cloud.

From the distance came the wail of the mourning cry, rising, falling, fading away. Kwani echoed it, rocking back and forth, keening to the empty sky.

Shadows grew long. She was drained of tears. Wearily, she leaned upon the altar, resting her forehead against the stone. She stretched out both arms, palms down upon the smooth surface. Like a dream it came, rising from the stone's mysterious depths—a sense of *knowing.* Layers of consciousness dissolved one by one, until knowledge was exposed like a deep and shining pool.

I am She Who Remembers. This is what the Old One wished. Calm flooded her soul. The Old One's spirit was safe in Sipapu, for she had chosen one to follow her.

Time is like constellations that swing in a great circle in the sky's vast bowl. There is no beginning, no end; all returns again and again, forever.

It was as though the Old One had spoken. Kwani felt herself enfolded with serene power. She summoned the ancient past. *She remembered.*

When the people entered the fourth world into Sunfather's holy radiance, women were weak. Men were bigger and stronger. Many women died when hunters could find but little meat and there was enough but for a few, those few who were strongest. Women suffered most during late pregnancy when they were awkward and heavy or when they had small children to feed and protect.

Earthmother taught women to survive. She taught them to recognize plants and roots and seeds that were good food. When hunting was scarce, it was women who sustained the tribe with food gathering.

Women grew stronger and wiser; they learned guile. They bartered sex and their gathered food for protection for themselves and their children, and for meat. They developed a sixth sense—intuitive thinking. Unconsciously, they remembered wisdom stored in genes generation after generation, and no man, however strong, could best a woman skilled in hereditary remembering.

The great sky circle turned many times. Women forgot they knew how to remember. Knowledge lay hidden in a secret place, waiting to be summoned. Even when the knowledge was used, women did not know they had used it; the precious gift lay neglected and ignored.

Teachers were needed to instruct young girls so they would not forget, but there were none who could teach. Earthmother grieved. She said, "I will make a teacher." She took a grain of corn and made it grow strong. The ear became a head, the silk became hair, the leaves became arms, and the stalk divided at the bottom and became legs. The legs pulled themselves from the earth and walked, and She Who Remembers was created.

Earthmother said, "You must teach another and she must teach another, forever. You are to wear a symbol of your status, for you are one apart, a chosen person. This symbol will help you remember, so guard it well. You must chose a successor who is Of The Gods. If you fail, if there is none to follow you, I shall refuse to accept your body into my keeping and your spirit will roam homeless, seeking haven in Sipapu, never to enter. Women will forget they can remember, and the gifts I bestow will be as seeds drifting aimlessly in the wind."

Time is a great circle; there is no beginning, no end. All returns again and again, forever.

Kwani awoke as from a vision. She gazed at the stone with awe and clasped the necklace reverently. She felt as though she had emerged from a mystical womb, reborn.

Shadows were high on the wall; soon it would be dark. Kokopelli had not come; he had departed for his home, this she knew. She would return to the city alone.

At the brink of the mesa Kwani looked down, but she was no longer afraid. She climbed the hand-holds as if she were descending a ladder; carefully and surely her feet and hands searched and found the niches cut into stone. At last she reached the steep path to the ravine. She took the long trail home, the path of those who commune with gods.

∙18∙

Okalake stood on the terrace, holding She Who Remembers in his arms. People who saw the expression on the dead face had drawn back in alarm. What had happened that the honored one should die in such a manner?

It would be necessary to prepare the body for burial immediately. Spirits lingered after death for four days. If suitable ceremony were not observed, spirits would not go away but would wander accusingly among them forever.

Okalake lay the Old One upon the mat in her dwelling and stood looking down at her until he heard his father's voice at the door.

"Come to the kiva. We must decide."

"I should bring Kwani back."

"No!" Sharply. "Leave her there for now."

Okalake nodded. It must be determined who was to have the responsibility of burial. It had to be closest kin, but She Who Remembers had outlived all her children and many of her grandchildren. Because all members of the clan were related, the decision would be made among the chiefs, elders, and those who would succeed them. Okalake was son of a Chief.

The council was in the kiva of the Elder Chief. The Medicine Chief and the son chosen as his successor were already there, with others. They sat in solemn silence, waiting for all to arrive, waiting for someone to mention what was on the mind of all—who would be She Who Remembers now? They pondered the implications of Kwani being summoned to the House of the Sun and there were frowns and downcast eyes, but none spoke.

The Elder Chief placed another juniper bough on the sacred fire. The blaze illuminated his wizened, kindly face, shadowing his deep-set eyes. With a prayer, he tossed corn meal in the Six Sacred Directions.

"The spirit of She Who Remembers is among us," he said at last. "We welcome her presence and ask her to assist us to decide who will be honored in selecting her burial place." The discussion began. Kwani was not mentioned.

In the city, a pall had fallen. Kokopelli was gone. A spirit of the dead lingered there. Visitors departed, some with new mates, many with new objects in their packs, all with stories to relate endlessly over evening fires.

Two visitors remained: Hopata and Wopio.

Wearily, Kwani limped homeward. Her leg ached, and the wonder of her experience in the Place of Remembering was dissipated by foreboding. It seemed, now, that the remembering was a dream, a fantasy.

As she approached the city, only one small figure waited to greet her at the bottom of the steep trail to the cave. It was Ki-ki-ki, of a neighboring clan, who had brought Okalake's mug and bowl of food to the keeping place. The girl's round little face was alight with concern.

"Your leg . . . does it pain?"

"Yes, it pains." Kwani put her arm around the girl's shoulders. "Thank you for coming to meet me."

"I will help you up the trail." Admiring the necklace, she said timidly, "You are She Who Remembers now?"

"Yes."

Together they made their way slowly, watched by a group along the wall at the cliff's brink. As Kwani and Ki-ki-ki arrived at the courtyard, some of the women saw the necklace.

"She wears the necklace!"

Ki-ki-ki said, "Kwani is She Who Remembers now." Several women came to take Kwani's hand timidly and breathe on it. But others stood silent, black eyes expressionless. Men disappeared into kivas for discussion. Kwani turned to Ki-ki-ki.

"It is nearly dark. Your mother is waiting for you."

"May I come tomorrow?"

"No," Kwani smiled. "Not until four days have passed and the spirit of the revered one enters Sipapu."

The girl took Kwani's hand. Shyly, she breathed on it.

"I go now." As she ran down the trail, Tiopi pushed her way forward.

"Did She Who Remembers appoint you as her successor?"

Kwani paused. How could she explain what had happened at the Place of Remembering?

"She Who Remembers sent for me, but her spirit departed before I arrived. The necklace was upon the altar, and the spirit of the revered one told me it was mine. She Who Remembers appointed me as her successor."

"How could she appoint you if she was dead?" Tiopi cried, facing the gathering crowd.

"Her spirit spoke to mine." Kwani pressed the scallop shell to her and her voice was steady, although her knees trembled.

"Kwani." It was Woshee, standing at the door of the dwelling of the revered one. "Come."

Inside the Old One lay on her mat, a bowl of yucca suds stood at the head. The body was undressed for cleansing. Woshee said, "I heard what you told Tiopi. Is this true?" Woshee's dark eyes probed like a flint scraper.

"It is true, mother of Okalake."

Woshee held Kwani's gaze for a long time. "I believe you speak the truth. But you must not wear the necklace until four days have passed and the spirit of the revered one is no longer here." She knelt beside the withered body. "You may help me prepare her for burial. Then you will leave the necklace on the mat until her spirit is in Sipapu."

Kwani nodded speechlessly. The Old One's eyes were closed and the mouth no longer screamed. The spirit of She Who Remembers was at peace.

Prayer feathers were tucked into the hair and placed in both hands and at the feet. Woshee held a small square of white cotton, finely woven, above the dead face.

"You must repeat after me."

Kwani nodded.

"I give the cloud mask for your spirit to wear . . ."

"I give the cloud mask for your spirit to wear . . ."

"So you may return with the Cloud People and bring us rain."

"So you may return with the Cloud People and bring us rain."

Gently, Woshee placed the cotton square over the face. The stiffening body was arranged in fetal position, with knees drawn to the chest and arms wrapped around the legs, then tightly enfolded in a feather blanket and placed in a sitting position on the mat.

"The necklace," Woshee said.

Kwani removed the necklace, and laid it beside the shrouded figure.

Woshee stepped outside. "She is ready."

The Chiefs and elders stood waiting. They had decided. The Sun Chief, husband of Woshee and father of Okalake, stepped forward.

"I am the one. I go to find her burial place."

He turned and walked slowly away, head bowed, shoulders bent with years.

As the crowd began to disperse, Wopio and Hopata stepped from the shadows.

The Clan Chief looked them over. "Who are you?"

"I am Wopio of the Long Knife Clan of the north."

"You come to trade?"

"Yes."

"Trading is finished." The old Chief turned away.

"I come on a more important matter. This is my friend, Hopata of the Beaver Clan. He will tell you that what I say is true."

Wopio continued, "This woman, Kwani, returns from the House of the Sun with the necklace of She Who Remembers. Yet this woman has not even completed her initiation into your clan. How is this possible?"

Okalake, who had been standing with the Medicine Chief, strode forward. "Because she is child of the Gods of the Rising Sun."

"Because she has sky eyes, perhaps? Witches may have eyes of any color."

Okalake's voice was deadly low. "You accuse a member of this clan of witchcraft?"

Kwani climbed down the ladder to the courtyard. She stood regally straight, looking neither right nor left, and came to stand before Wopio. "Speak, Wopio, if you do not fear the truth."

Wopio gazed at the woman who seemed different from the one he had known. There was no cringing in her gaze, no supplication in her face.

"Your Medicine Chief wishes to know if I accuse you of witchcraft. What shall I tell him?"

"Tell him you accuse me as you have accused me before. When I was your mate."

There were gasps and whispers. Kwani was smiling in a way that made Wopio uncomfortable.

"I do not accuse you if you return to your people as my mate."

"These are my people, and I am mate of Kokopelli." She touched the golden ornament at her ear.

Wopio sneered. "Your mate leaves you."

"He will return. Now say what you came to say, then go."

"You refuse me?"

Again, she smiled. "Of course."

Okalake thrust his face close to Wopio's. "Go!"

"This is a matter for me to decide." It was the Medicine Chief, waving Okalake aside. "Do you accuse this woman of witchcraft?"

"I do. She brought the death spirit to our clan, just as she brought it here."

Tiopi elbowed her way to the front. "She wanted the necklace! She wanted to be She Who Remembers!"

"A-a-a-ye!" the people cried.

Kwani said to Wopio, "If I am a witch, why do you want me to return with you to your people?" Her voice was icy with contempt and she turned away. The people parted uneasily as she approached, and made way for her as she climbed the ladders to her dwelling.

"Chololo," Okalake called. The little flute player jumped down from the rooftop. The dangling ear ornament Okalake had given him swung wildly as he ran.

Okalake said softly, "Bring me my bow and arrows."

Aglow with importance, the boy ran off. Okalake turned to Wopio. "You have not answered. If Kwani is a witch, why do you want her as mate? Perhaps it is you who are a witch, perhaps it is you who brought the death spirit here."

"That is well spoken."

Kwani had returned to the terrace outside her door. In both hands she held the fearsome medicine arrow, the arrow sent by Maluku. "Take this, Okalake, and send it to Wopio's heart. If he is not a witch, the arrow will not find him. As it did not find me."

"No," Hopata cried. "Wopio is not the witch!"

But Okalake ran up the ladders and took the arrow from Kwani's hands. The Medicine Chief scowled, remembering acutely Kokopelli's warning about protecting Kwani. He recalled too the reward for her safety. He said loudly, "Only I, the Medicine Chief, may send the arrow. Give it to me!"

As Okalake descended the ladders, Chololo ran up, panting. Okalake's large hunting bow and his sheaf of arrows were clutched in both hands. He handed the bow and arrows to Okalake with the pride of an important mission accomplished.

Wopio and Hopata whispered together, looking uneasily at the people crowding about them with dark, silent faces and expressionless eyes. Those eyes could turn hostile in a moment.

The Medicine Chief held out his hand in a gesture of authority. "Give me the arrow."

Deliberately, Okalake turned his back, fitted the medicine arrow into his bow and aimed it at Wopio.

With a growl of rage, the Medicine Chief jerked the bow from Okalake's hand, but not before Wopio and Hopata turned and ran, followed by laughter and jeers.

Okalake said to the Medicine Chief, "I was not going to shoot the arrow. I wanted to frighten them. The medicine arrow may be sent by you only." He bowed politely.

His face saved, the Medicine Chief scowled in silence. But he was enormously relieved; he would not have to make a decision that would threaten his standing with Kokopelli.

Kwani came to the Chief and held out her hand for the arrow. Casually, as though the arrow were of no value and he had no use for it, the Chief gave it to her. Kwani held it to her chest and faced the people.

"Thank you, all of you." Her voice trembled. They had jeered at her enemy.

The Sun Chief had found the burial place. With ceremonial dignity, he entered the dwelling of She Who Remembers. Chanting the death prayer, he greeted the spirits and lifted the body in his arms. Still chanting, he carried the shrouded figure across the courtyard and down the path leading to the ravine. The Chiefs and elders followed in solemn single file. The Medicine Chief carried a prayer stick and the Clan Chief held a small bowl of water.

Halfway down the trail, the Sun Chief veered to the right and led the group along a difficult path to a tiny cave hidden by an overhang and brush. Kneeling, he laid the body in the cave while the others joined him in final chants beseeching the spirit of the dead to remain there and not follow them back. The prayer stick was placed at the head and the bowl of water at the feet, and the cave opening was sealed with rocks and what soil could be scraped from rocky crevices.

It was finished. She Who Remembers was no more.

But the death spirit must be prevented from returning to the city. Parallel lines were drawn from the burial place to the entrance of the city, and chunks of charcoal from the ceremonial fire were placed at four intervals to block the dreaded spirit's path. For four days, food would be brought to the grave. Only then would the spirit enter Sipapu and the people be at peace.

Kwani stood at the wall by the cliff's brink, watching. Black clouds swooped from the horizon; a storm was coming. The sound of the death chant echoed among the cliffs. She thought of Kokopelli alone in the wilderness. Would he make it safely home? *Would he return?*

Shivering, she turned away. A new ceremonial fire of juniper boughs burned in the courtyard to provide purifying smoke for the burial party when it returned. She approached the fire for warmth. The people parted, making way for her. Their faces were impassive, but Kwani sensed their feeling. They feared her.

To be feared was to be alone. Lonely. Isolation enveloped her in a cold breath. She wished for the necklace. But it remained where she had placed it, on the mat of one who was no more. Kwani huddled to the fire and tears stung her eyes.

She feared these, her people, who feared her.

·19·

"**I**t is time," Okalake said.

"Yes."

The Sun Chief and Okalake stood in sunset light below the cliff's brow and gazed intently at the horizon where it touched the opposite mesa. Each day, Sunfather had come closer to the point, indicated by cliff formations, beyond which he could not be permitted to go, or he would never return and the world would be doomed forever to endless night. Only the Sun Ceremonies would pursuade him to turn back to his northern home.

Sunfather unfurled scarlet and orange banners and sank in splendor behind the mesa. The Sun Chief turned to the people who waited and watched. For many years it had been his grave responsibility to determine when the Ceremonies would take place. Soon, the sacred duty would be Okalake's, for the old man's eyes grew dim and years lay heavily upon him. He raised both arms. It was the signal.

The Crier Chief was ready. He wore his finest robe and was already standing upon his platform.

"All people! Know the time has come for the Sun Ceremonies. Participants will assemble at the House of the Sun before dawn, taking medicine objects, sacred pollen, sacrificial corn, masks, ceremonial bowls, and prayer sticks. Let all women prepare the purifying potion and pray for the success of the Ceremonies."

The potion, an emetic of bark and roots, was put to boil. Soon a strong odor permeated the city. In the morning, mugs of the potion would be taken to ceremonial participants standing at the cliff's brink. They would drink and vomit over the edge into the rubble pile. If the emetic did not work, a long feather would be thrust down the throat

124

until the desired results were achieved. Internal purification was essential to the success of the Ceremonies.

After the men had retired to the kivas for final preparations, women, children, and those men and boys not participating in the Ceremonies gathered around the fires for their evening meal, the second and last of the day. Food was an important factor in the fight against the rigors of winter, and women spent long hours preparing meat, corn, bread, beans, and squash in various combinations, seasoned with dried fruits, roots, and berries gathered during the fall.

Woshee, as clan matriarch, was in charge of distributing provisions, with the help of several other older women. At Kwani's door she stood watching Kwani struggle to clean the stone walls encrusted with grime.

"It is cleaner than it has been in years. May I enter?"

Kwani wheeled around, and smiled radiantly. "Yes. Please come in."

Woshee came in and sat down. She sat easily for one so old, Kwani thought; she must be nearly forty. "I have no food to offer you," Kwani said, embarrassed.

"I know you do not have food. I invite you to eat at my fire tonight. Tomorrow I will give you your share of food from the storage bins."

"Thank you, mother of Okalake." Kwani had not realized how hungry she was.

"It is true I am mother of Okalake, Kwani. You may call Okalake son of Woshee if you like, but you are to call me Woshee."

Kwani flushed, realizing she had committed a social blunder. Woshee was an important personage.

Together, they stepped outside to encounter a group of chattering children who followed them. A small boy tugged at Kwani's robe.

"Was that really, truly, a medicine arrow to shoot witches?"

She smiled down at him. "Yes. Really and truly."

"A-a-a-a-ye!"

"Why do you go to the dwelling of Woshee?" a little girl asked.

Woshee said, "Because I have asked her to eat at my fire." She stopped and her dark eyes regarded each small face. "It is not proper to question. Go now."

They scampered to spread the news. But everyone had seen and heard and knew that Woshee invited Kwani to eat at her fire. It would be wise if they did likewise. Woshee was social leader of the clan.

Sitting in Woshee's immaculate dwelling, eating corn cake and venison stew, Kwani admired the bowls and other objects placed around the room. The only bowl she had was the one given her by Okalake.

Woshee seemed to read her mind. "You will be given bowls and baskets until you can make your own."

"I am grateful." A corner of her heart began to thaw. Everything would be all right, now that she was She Who Remembers. Three days had passed since the Old One was buried; tomorrow the necklace would be hers.

They had almost finished eating when Okalake and his father arrived. They had left their ceremonial garments in the kiva, but they still wore the painted designs on face and body; they looked fearsome and mysterious. They greeted only the spirits, and sat solemn and silent. In the morning, they would purify themselves, but now they must eat. It was not known how long it would take to turn Sunfather back.

Kwani whispered to Woshee, "May I help you?"

"No. It is best if you go now."

Kwani slipped outside. It was dark and cold, and the many small fires had burned to coals. Dogs and children lay together in companionable warmth. Old people dozed fitfully, pain in their bones and joints. Those with aching teeth moaned also, knowing that tomorrow the tooth must be tied to a leather thong, fastened to a stone, and the stone thrown over the cliff. But maybe the pain would lessen tomorrow . . .

Kwani pulled her feather blanket over her and closed her eyes, comforted by the warmth in her heart. She thought of She Who Remembers, shrouded in her hidden place. Each day people brought food to the grave. Tomorrow would be the last day before her spirit entered Sipapu. Did the Old One know that?

"Goodnight, revered one," Kwani whispered. She imagined she heard a reply, "Goodnight, my daughter."

She snuggled into her blanket and slept.

The fourth day dawned blue with clouds swelling over the Sacred Mountain. Women started the fires, and soon children huddled around them. A large jar of water heated over each fire; when it boiled, corn meal was stirred in to make a gruel for the children.

The Crier Chief made his announcements, reminding them that this was the fourth day, and at sunrise, the spirit of She Who Remembers would enter Sipapu. The period of mourning was over. The Sun Ceremonies would continue until success was assured and disaster was averted.

Men emerged from the kivas, purified themselves, and departed for the House of the Sun. The cold had driven deer and other game down from higher altitudes, and hunters left early, eager to find other game. The day had begun.

Kwani filled her bowl with water from one of the large community water jars in the courtyard and scrubbed herself clean. She took pains with her hair, brushing it and rolling it into a large bun over each ear. She hung the golden ornament on her ear, took a deep breath, and stepped outside.

She was astonished to find a group of women and girls there, with pots and bowls and baskets, some with food. They placed the vessels upon the terrace. A young girl stepped forward. It was Miko.

"My mother invites you to have porridge at our fire."

Another said, "Or at ours."

A woman bringing a bowl of corn said, "The bowls and pots and baskets are for you to use until you can make your own. The corn is from me."

"Oh." Kwani said, her heart overflowing. "Thank you!"

She put her arm around Miko who had her second moon flow. Miko wore her hair proudly in squash blossom style for she was a woman now. "I will go to your mother's fire."

When they had gone, the women and girls carried the vessels into Kwani's dwelling. They looked with interest at her belongings lined neatly against the wall. Like children, they opened her pack and took out everything, handing each item around so all might examine it. They exclaimed over her fine bone needles and flint knives. The spear was inspected with puzzlement. No woman they ever knew owned a spear. Why Kwani had one and where it came from—in fact, all her past—was a tantalizing mystery.

Speculation was endless about Kokopelli. Would he return for Kwani? They could hardly wait to hear all the intimate details of Kwani's experience with him in the kiva. Was it as fantastic as Tiopi claimed? The fight between Kwani and Tiopi was rehashed with relish and they talked endlessly of Kokopelli seeding both women. Would each bear his child? Kwani must tell everything at the evening fire.

While they talked and gossiped happily, Kwani was swallowing the last delicious bit of porridge from a mug. Miko's mother sat quietly, glancing shyly at Kwani from time to time. Occasionally, she smiled, revealing wide gaps between worn teeth. Wrinkles gooved her cheeks and brow, and her hands were misshapen in the joints. Kwani thought, She is not much older than I. Compassion surged in her.

"I thank you for the porridge. Will you and Miko come for porridge at my fire tomorrow?"

"I will come."

"So will I," Miko said eagerly. As though she could contain the question no longer, she blurted, "Will you talk at the evening fire and tell us about the medicine arrow and about Kokopelli and—"

"It is not for you to ask," her mother chided. To Kwani she said, "You are one of us now, one of the Eagle Clan. We want to know more about you. Will you talk at the evening fire?"

"Yes. Of course I will." Kwani was impatient to go for the necklace, but she remembered her manners. She took the twisted hand, breathed upon it, said a polite goodbye, and left.

Clouds swept over the mesa and a chill wind rose as Kwani made her way to the house of She Who Remembers. She walked with dignity despite her limp, and tried not to reveal her eagerness to hold the necklace. Her heart beat hard as she reached the door, pulled the curtain aside, and entered.

The necklace was not there.

·20·

"**K**wani, come forward."

The Crier Chief's deep, rich voice resounded through the cave where people had assembled upon roofs and terraces and thronged the courtyard to hear Kwani's story. She sat in the shadows, ramrod-straight and expressionless. She did not rise nor answer and the Chief cleared his throat importantly.

"Kwani, you may talk now." She remained silent.

"Why do you not answer?" he said loudly, flushing with irritation.

"Because you do not address me properly. I am She Who Remembers."

There was a stir in the crowd and whispered consultation among the Chiefs and elders. Kwani sat quietly, but she seethed inside. Who had taken the necklace? Could she remember without it? The necklace was hers; she must have it.

The Sun Chief rose. "I wish to speak."

"Speak." The Crier Chief appreciated the courtesy being shown to him by a Chief whose status was higher than his own.

The Sun Chief faced the people. "The revered one told me she was about to enter Sipapu and requested that I take her to the House of the Sun. Because my arms have lost their strength, I assigned the honor to my son. Okalake, you will tell what happened."

Slowly Okalake rose. He did not look at Kwani but gazed steadfastly at the people before him.

"I took the revered one to the Place of Remembering as she requested. Then she asked me to bring Kwani to her. I left her and returned with Kwani. The revered one was dead, and the necklace lay upon the altar." He paused, looking from face to face. "She Who Remembers knew she was about to enter Sipapu and that she had not yet appointed a successor. Why did she send for Kwani? Why did she remove the necklace and leave it upon the altar when she realized her spirit would depart before Kwani arrived? Consider these things."

Once more, the Sun Chief rose. "It was I who selected her burial place, I who laid her there, who brought her food. Her spirit speaks to me. She says that now Kwani is She Who Remembers." He gathered his robe about him, and sat down.

Tiopi cried, "I see no necklace!"

There was an uneasy silence, broken by the eerie gourd rattle of the Medicine Chief. The freshly painted black zigzags from brow to chin were embellished with scarlet dots around his mouth; the dots bobbed up and down impressively as he spoke.

"The necklace of She Who Remembers is in my Medicine Lodge. There it will remain until she who claims it has completed her initiation into the Eagle Clan."

He turned away, concealing a smug smile. It would be impossible for Kwani to create a vessel he would accept. Without the necklace, there would be no She Who Remembers. If it proved necessary—and expedient—for the clan to have a female with powers to challenge his own, this could be resolved after Kokopelli took Kwani away.

Kwani continued to sit with impassive dignity although she raged inwardly.

"I wish to speak."

It was Woshee. Deliberately, she climbed down the ladders and crossed the courtyard to stand beside the fire.

"It was the wish of She Who Remembers to appoint Kwani as her successor. It is also true that Kwani has not completed her initiation into the clan. Therefore, I assume responsibility for her. If she is negligent in her duties or disobeys the rules of the clan, I shall be punished with her, regardless of what that punishment may be."

"No!" the people cried.

Woshee signaled for silence. "I do this not for Kwani but for the one whose spirit is in Sipapu. Meanwhile, until Kwani completes her initiation, she is to be addressed as 'Esteemed One.' " She turned to Kwani. "You will speak now, Esteemed One."

Kwani hesitated. Okalake's mother was giving her a double responsibility—to avoid punishment for them both. How could she carry such a burden?

"I cannot . . . I cannot allow you to be punished for my wrongdoing."

"Then do no wrong," Woshee said gently.

"But—"

"We wait to hear your story."

"Yes! Speak!" the people cried.

Reassured by the warmth of Okalake's gaze, she came forward. The golden ear ornament quivered, betraying her nervousness. She told them of her birth, how her blue eyes caused suspicion, how Maluku drove her away, and his medicine arrow refused to find her. She told of the cougar, and finding Crooked Foot.

The cave city was totally silent, listening. Even the turkeys made no sound. People inched closer and children sat wide-eyed and breathless.

The fire died to coals, but people were too absorbed to notice. When she told how Brother Coyote found her and took her baby into himself and the spirit world, there was a great tremulous sigh. Then, when she told how she woke to find Kokopelli, how he cared for her and brought her here to the Eagle Clan, the people were spellbound. They whispered among themselves. There was no doubt about it; Kwani was a special being. No wonder the revered one had appointed her as successor.

Only Tiopi remained silent and aloof, eyes calculating, mouth grim.

❖ 21 ❖

Clouds concealed Sunfather's progress as the Sun Ceremonies continued day after day. Holy men grew hoarse with incantations; smoke rose constantly from sacrificial fires. Drumbeats echoed among the cliffs like the heartbeat of Earthmother herself, urging Sunfather to hear the prayers of his children. At last Sunfather appeared. He had turned back toward his northern home! Again, holy men were successful in their efforts. Never had they failed.

The people rejoiced. Days would grow longer now; soon the cruel sufferings of winter would end and it would be time for Ceremonies Before Planting.

Kwani walked alone upon the mesa. She had to get away from the city, from people, to think and to decide what to make for the Medicine Chief. The only thing that would hold enough water and not break when thrown from the cliff was a basket. But it had to be something never made before, something that would not burn when held to a fire . . .

She sat on a boulder, gazing over the valley from where she and Kokopelli had come. What if he did not return? If the Medicine Chief refused to accept her basket could she go alone into the wilderness and find her way, somehow, to the Blue-eyed One?

Remembering how boulders blocked passage, how brush clawed and scratched, remembering how swiftly Apaches appeared, how silently and patiently the cougar waited, Kwani cried aloud, "No! I cannot!"

She fingered her amulet, wishing it were the necklace and she was back at the House of the Sun. Often she returned there in her secret thoughts, remembering the wonder, the *knowing*.

"Tell me what to make!" she whispered.

The boulder's cold penetrated her blanket. She rose, shivering, looking for a sign, an omen, while thoughts thrashed about in her mind like birds in a snare.

What kind of basket has never been made before? A rustle in the brush made her stop short with alarm. A rabbit darted out, and hopped away.

The sign! She would make a basket like a rabbit! A seated rabbit with the head as a lid, long ears . . . and a bushy little tail at the bottom. She laughed, delighted with the idea. Surely, no such basket had been made before. Wet, it would not burn, and if she made it well enough, strong enough, it would not break when thrown from the cliff. She would make a handle, so it could be carried with one finger when empty. The rabbit was a bringer of good fortune; a basket in that shape would be ideal as a ceremonial container.

"Thank you," she told her amulet. "I shall feed you well tonight." She looked toward the opposite cliff where the House of the Sun rose upon the mesa, and raised her hand in reverent thanks. The spirits had given her a sign; she was one of them now, she was She Who Remembers.

Zashue, fourteen years old, eldest son of the Medicine Chief, sat with his father in the sacred Medicine Lodge adjoining their kiva. Zashue would be Medicine Chief when his father entered Sipapu. There was much he must learn. The Medicine Chief scowled at his son with his usual forbidding expression. But Zashue knew that he was the favorite son. He sat properly straight, eyes downcast, listening as his father spoke.

"You must not forget the source of a Medicine Chief's power, my son. Remember where it is in me so when my spirit leaves my body you may obtain the source for yourself."

He pulled his robe aside and pointed to a small, thin scar between the ribs on his left side. Beneath the skin was a grain of quartz crystal no larger than a seed, a magical substance passed from Medicine Chief to successor, generation after generation, and known to them only. When the Chief died, the successor removed the seed and inserted it into his own body, thereby acquiring the Medicine Chief's awesome powers.

"I shall do so, my father."

"Now, another matter." The Chief reached for the bow entrusted to him by Kokopelli. He handed it to Zashue who took it reverently, examining the strange crossbar and locking mechanism with intense interest.

"This bow also has powers. You have seen how fast and truly it finds its way. It is a sacred object."

Zashue nodded acknowledgment.

"Kokopelli says if we release its powers the gods will punish us.

However . . ." He stroked the bowstring. "However, it may well be that the powers of a Medicine Chief justify use of this bow for sacred purposes."

Zashue's black eyes sparkled. He loved bows even more than gambling. He combined them in the popular shooting-at-moving-targets game, where valuable objects were wagered. Tomorrow, a game was scheduled at the Place of the Wolf Clan down the valley. Participants would include the best bowmen within five days' traveling distance.

"My father . . ." How could he word his request to give the game sacred connotations? If he had that bow that flew so true, no challenger could best him. Much would be wagered and he would win it all. "My father," he began again, "perhaps the gods would welcome proof of the superiority of this bow in competition with those who doubt its powers. I request permission to display its sacred abilities—"

"No! Only I may use it." Observing his son's sullen glare, the Chief added, "You have much to learn. You would be wise to spend more time learning than gambling. I have spoken!"

Zashue turned away, fists tight. He was not accustomed to having his requests denied. Clan prestige was involved. Was not the welfare of the clan a sacred matter?

He strode through the city and down into the canyon to search for medicinal plants as his father expected, but his mind was not on plants. The bark of a distant fox rode the wind. A good omen? Would not the gods want him to preserve the prestige of his clan? One must obey the gods, of course. Smiling, he returned to the city and went to his mother's house for he was hungry and it was time for the main meal.

His mother placed a steaming bowl on the floor in the usual dining place. But his father and two younger brothers had not yet arrived.

"Welcome, my son," his mother said, thinking how much Zashue resembled his father: the same small eyes, close together, the same set of the mouth. She sighed. Men were difficult creatures but women needed them.

The Medicine Chief and Zashue's brothers arrived. They slipped off their winter robes, blankets with a hole cut in the center to be worn like ponchos. The mother placed a platter of thin corn cakes beside the bowl. "Eat now."

First the Chief took a small piece of meat from the pot and a bit of corn cake and threw them into the fire as offering to the gods. Then they ate, taking turns as they dipped the thin cakes into the hot stew, scooping it up and into the mouth quickly so that little spilled. Bones were gnawed and dropped back into the pot. When only thick liquid was left, the Chief lifted the pot. He drank from the brim, smacking his lips and then belching, as courtesy required.

His wife nodded approvingly. It was important to teach their sons the social niceties required by their position in the clan.

Now is the time, Zashue thought. I must leave before my father does. He rose. "I thank you, my mother. I go now."

His mother smiled. She had noticed his interest in a pretty girl across the canyon. His father and brothers were eating the rest of the corn cakes as Zashue bade them and the house spirits farewell.

It was warm in the kiva of the Medicine Chief. Zashue paused to place another log on the fire before entering the holy of holies, the Medicine Lodge, a small room adjoining the kiva. There was a sound and his heart jumped. His father was returning! But it was only dogs running by.

Quickly, Zashue searched in the semi-darkness for the bow. It was in its usual hidden place with the arrows and belted hook. He tied the hook around his waist under his blanket, slipping the arrows under the hook. The bow would be a problem to conceal. He tried to tuck it under his robe; the bulge was too noticeable. He took the feather blanket from his sleeping mat, and draped it over his shoulder so that the bow, tucked under his arm, was hidden. Everyone would think he was going somewhere to spend the night. His father would think he was with a girl. Ha! He would spend the night at the Place of the Wolf Clan to be ready for the contest tomorrow.

He descended into the ravine and walked toward the opposite cliff, as though he were going there. At a hidden place behind a small hill, he veered to the left, following a faint trail through the canyon. It would be difficult to climb the hand-holds to the Wolf Clan's city while keeping the bow concealed. But he wanted to make his wagers before his opponents knew he had the sacred bow. It was necessary to hide it. He slipped the bow into a crevice where it would be unseen and protected until he came for it, and climbed easily to the mesa.

The Wolf people greeted him warmly. Other contestants were already gathered. "Here, come by the fire," his friend Tonapa said.

Zashue squatted before the fire. "Who brought gambling sticks?"

A small leather bag of gaming pieces was emptied with a flourish. There were ten polished oval bones an inch long and three smaller circular ones, some etched with lines and designs, some plain. Two of the circular ones had a small hole partially drilled in the center of one face. It was a complicated and exciting game, with up to forty-four possible combinations in the lie of the bones alone, not counting their arrangement. Wagers were made. Soon the players were absorbed. There was the usual mention of the scarcity of rain; someone said they heard Apaches were seen in the southwest again; but attention was devoted to the complexities of the game. They played long into the night.

It was still dark when Zashue woke. The others slept soundly, curled in their blankets. Careful to make no sound, Zashue took his blanket and climbed from the kiva. He would practice with the bow privately before the contest so he might judge its powers accurately.

The moon hung low in a paling sky as he climbed down to where the bow was hidden. It was safe and dry, and he held the bow high overhead in exultation. He was alone in the valley with a magical weapon and he wanted to shout and sing; but he laughed quietly instead, and followed the trail to a clear place where he could see the arrow as it flew.

He fitted an arrow into the groove on the crossbar and locked it in place. He marvelled at the wonder of it. He held it up before him as he walked, aiming at a distant tree. He did not notice the rock in the path until he stumbled over it, and was flung forward with force upon the bow. He lay a moment, in panic. *Had he harmed the bow?*

He rose to his knees and examined the bow, running his fingers over it inch by inch. In the dim light of early dawn he could not see a crack; but his fingers found it, a hairline crack near the bowstring.

Zashue moaned. The gods had punished him; they made him kill the bow. What would happen when his father found out?

Maybe he could return home and replace the bow before his father learned of the theft. Maybe the crack would not be noticed. He ran toward home as quickly as he dared in the semi-darkness. Before he came in sight of home, he veered toward the opposite cliff so it would appear that he was returning from a night with a girl. He arrived at dawn as the Crier Chief was making his morning announcements.

The Medicine Chief sat quietly with the others, listening. Zashue held his arms as losely as he could without dropping the bow hidden by the blanket, and climbed down to the Chief's kiva. How could he atone for his crime? What would his father do if he discovered the truth?

What would Kokopelli do when he returned?

Zashue knelt before the altar, and prayed. If it was discovered that the bow was dead, he knew what he must do. He would blame a witch. The most likely suspect would be one who was different, one who had supernatural powers . . . an outsider.

The old crossbow lay in the sacred place far, far from its homeland. During the decades it had let fly arrows as many as autumn leaves—like them, stained red.

One more arrow would be spent. The final one.

❖ 22 ❖

The days of winter followed one another in a timeless blending of monotony, cold, and the inevitable illnesses caused by witches. There was much talk among the cave cities as to who the witch, or witches, might be. One who did anything unusual was suspect, so everyone made it a point to avoid being conspicuous in any way. Everyone but Kwani.

She sat outside her dwelling, working on a basket which certainly seemed like no basket made before except, perhaps, by a small child trying to learn how. Little girls tittered behind their hands; women glanced at it with disdain. The basket was lopsided and shapeless and made no sense at all. What possessed the one who called herself She Who Remembers to risk her reputation on such a pitable example of basketmaking?

The Medicine Chief delighted in the gossip. Privately, he took out the sacred bow and fondled it, thinking how he might be justified in using it to drive Kwani from the clan. He noticed that the bow seemed more weathered than when he held it last. But the old bow had seen many seasons; weathering was to be expected.

Tiopi was the center of many a giggling group commenting on the basketmaking efforts of the Esteemed One. Tiopi had anticipated this time of year when witches were known to be most active; she had plans for Kwani. Now the presumptuous outsider was playing into her hands in a way Tiopi had not dared to hope for. In addition, Okalake, son of Woshee who assumed responsibility for Kwani, was causing a scandal with his too obvious interest in Kwani. There he was, squatted beside her, examining the basket, the two of them talking earnestly. Maybe she could wander by . . .

Okalake was thinking he could drown in the blue depths of Kwani's eyes. He watched the lashes dipping upon her cheeks as she worked on the basket. He wanted to touch them. Instead, he touched the basket.

"Will the rabbit be standing upright, legs in the air?" he asked softly so no one else would hear. Kwani had told him the form the basket would take.

"Yes. I still have to figure out a way to attach the legs and feet—"

"Quiet, here comes Tiopi."

Without looking up, Kwani said matter-of-factly, "Did Zashue find the medicinal plants? I saw him searching."

"Yes. There will be more in a few moons."

"When first flowers bloom."

"And Kokopelli comes to take you away."

"Yes."

Tiopi passed, glancing at the basket with an amused smile. When she was gone, Okalake said, "I do not want you to go away."

Kwani looked up into his eyes and what she saw there aroused the latent hunger. But he was a member of the clan, her brother . . .

He whispered, "You are like first flowers blooming. You bloom here." He tapped his chest.

Her working fingers stumbled and tears welled up. It had been a long time since sweet words caressed her, too long a time since Kokopelli had gone. No word came from him. What if he did not return? Would she remain a childless woman bereft of a mate? Okalake was handsome, passionate, young, and he longed for her. They were not really related. *Woshee* . . .

Kwani looked away. "You must not . . ."

He bent closer. "I know a secret place, a small cave hidden behind a boulder—"

"We cannot." Her voice shook in spite of itself. "Leave now. People watch us."

"Yes," he sighed. "Always watching." He took her hand and breathed on it respectfully. "I go."

When he had gone, Ki-ki-ki darted from the shadows where she had lingered. Her round eyes were shiny with tears.

"It is you he loves," she whispered. "But I am the one who loves him most, and I am of another clan, and you are his *sister*—"

"Yes. I am his sister. That, and nothing more."

"He will be *my* mate," Ki-ki-ki said desperately.

Kwani looked into the troubled face, so tender and young, and at the small body where little breasts were only beginning to bud.

"You must become a woman first. But it will not be long," she added comfortingly.

"You are still mate of Kokopelli?"

"Of course."

"Will he return?"

"Yes."

"And take you away?"

"Yes. You know that."

"Then who will be She Who Remembers?"

Kwani was jolted; she hadn't thought of that. Of course she must find one who was Of The Gods. But even after the revelations she experienced at the House of the Sun, she felt unqualified to teach a successor until she had more experience—and until she had the necklace to help her with its special powers.

"I don't know yet. I must have the necklace before I decide."

Miko came running breathlessly, her hair flying and her eyes aglow. "Ki-ki-ki, come! I have taught my dog a trick!"

They ran off, laughing. Kwani looked after them, remembering how she laughed and played when she was young. Soon she would be an old woman, and she had no mate—not until Kokopelli returned, how many moons from now? Sometimes flowers bloomed later than at other times . . .

She shifted uncomfortably upon the menstrual pad she wore, woven of yucca fiber and layered with shredded cedar bark. She had hoped that Kokopelli's seed would grow. But it grew only in Tiopi, who never stopped telling of it.

"But he chose Kwani as mate," someone would say.

"Where is his child? She has the moon flow. And until Kokopelli returns how can she be mate to him?" Laughter. "My flow ceased after the following moon. Already I feel his life stirring here." A pat of the abdomen with a jangle of bracelets, chief of which was the one given to her by Kokopelli.

Kwani tossed her head, allowing the ear ornament to sway against her cheek. Yes, she thought, you have the child, but I shall have Kokopelli. And a white house with many rooms and a fountain for my water jar.

She bent to her work again, looking up now and then to watch Okalake as he sat in the courtyard teaching children the constellations. Pebbles of the proper size in proportion to one another were chosen and arranged according to seasons. Afternoon sun shone coldly upon them and the turkey feathers in Okalake's hair glistened with iridescence as he turned his head.

How handsome he is!

She wondered what it would be like to lie with him, to have him within her . . . Hunger welled and she muffled a moan. If only Woshee had not taken responsibility for her, assuming the same punishment, she would be tempted to go with him to the hidden place . . .

But no. She was mate of Kokopelli—who had refused to take her with him. What if he never returned? But of course he would, and take her to the Blue-eyed One.

Now that she was Kokopelli's mate, would she still need to find her kinsman? It was not necessary, but she would like to. Once she saw him and was with him a while she would know if they were kin; their spirits would recognize one another. She visualized how he must be. He would have blue eyes like hers, and shiny black braids, ornamented with shells . . . a fine, big man, maybe as tall as Kokopelli, handsome and gentle like Okalake, and equally protective . . .

Sometimes, she thought of Okalake at night as she huddled alone in her blanket in the cold darkness, remembering how he had swept her in his arms and how protected she felt there. Then she thought of Kokopelli and his masterful lovemaking, and her body hungered and she felt more lonely than ever. Kokopelli would give her what she longed for most—a home and children. Above all, security. It was a woman's need, a woman's right.

But how could she have a home, a family, and all the rest if she had to travel with him, wandering over vast distances most of the year? Even if he decided to settle down, did she want to make her home in a faraway, alien land?

She was troubled. She needed the powers the necklace would give her to know what she should do.

As the basket's rabbit form began to be recognizable, Kwani found herself surrounded by an incredulous and admiring audience.

"Look! A rabbit!"

"Is it for the Medicine Chief?"

"Yes."

"But will it hold water?"

"It will."

"Will you line it with pitch?"

"Only if it leaks," she laughed.

The change in status from inept to master basketmaker was heady stuff, and she worked with more of a flourish than was necessary. But something about her new self-confidence, the flash of her eyes, the lift of her chin, gave her a seductive air which was not lost on Tiopi nor the Medicine Chief, both of whom were secretly dismayed. A water basket shaped like a rabbit! Never had such a thing been made before. The people loved it! Kwani was the center of admiring attention. She was proving more of a challenge than they anticipated.

Tiopi watched her sullenly from a distance. She had hoped to plant a suspicion of witchcraft because of Kwani's unexplainable behavior, but now that the basket was taking shape and Kwani was admired—liked, even!—Tiopi knew she must be more adroit. She gazed over the city where she was born, where she grew up a favorite child and had ruled as an important personage, wife of Yatosha, the Hunting Chief, and the special one chosen by Kokopelli, certain to be successor to She Who Remembers. It used to be that when Tiopi walked through any of the cities among the cliffs, she was known and greeted as a person of importance. Since Kwani had come, and especially since the day they had had the fight, there was a subtle change. A look in the eye, a smile behind the hand. Now men gazed at Kwani the way they used to look at her. That special look that made a woman know she was desirable even though she already had a mate. If Tiopi and Kwani were together in a group, the men looked at Kwani first and longest. It was insufferable!

What if Kokopelli did not return? It was too late in the year for him to be traveling; a bear might have eaten him; or he could have perished in the snows. And now there was Kwani's basket so much admired. If it held water, the Medicine Chief could hardly refuse it. She sat down to think.

People crowded around as Kwani struggled to form the rabbit's head which would be the basket's lid. Woshee stopped one day and sat beside her.

"You are doing well, Esteemed One."

"Thank you, Woshee." Kwani glanced at the crowd around her, minutely inspecting her work, then bent again to her weaving. "But it is difficult . . . here . . ."

A look of understanding flashed in the older woman's eyes. She said casually, "I would be pleased if you might share my fire. Bring your basket if you like." She rose. "You will come now?"

Kwani smiled gratefully. "Yes."

The crowds parted respectfully as Kwani gathered her basket and materials and followed Woshee to her dwelling.

"Woshee has never asked me to share her fire," someone said. "Nor I," someone else said. Finally another woman declared, "I invite you all to my fire. Let us play a game. I shall wager my finest mug!"

Gossiping happily, the women crowded into a small dwelling. "Did you see how Tiopi looked when she saw Kwani's rabbit basket? Ha!"

"That's Tiopi. If her baby looks like Kokopelli, how can we live with her?"

"If we live with her now, we can live with her then."

"I suppose. But have you seen how Okalake looks at Kwani?"

"Of course. His man part tries to push out to look, too."

They giggled.

"Okalake should take a mate before his baby-maker gets him in trouble."

"And Woshee, too . . ."

The women grew silent. They liked and respected Woshee.
"It's too bad that Kwani came—"
"There has been trouble since."
"If Kokopelli comes—"
"*If* he comes—"
"He will take her away."
"It can't be too soon."
Heads nodded in unison. True, Kwani was a special person, daughter of the gods, mate of Kokopelli, beautiful and talented, liked by everybody now . . . They couldn't wait for her to leave.

Each day, Kwani had brought her basket makings to Woshee's dwelling and worked in the dim light, grateful for the privacy. The form of a rabbit's head took shape. All but the ears. She set out to find some yucca fiber for the ears because of its pliability.

She climbed the hand-holds to the mesa with ease. Although she still could not do as other women did, climbing hand-holds while carrying a jar of water or a loaded basket on the head—and a baby on the back—her fingers and toes found their places in the cliff's face with confidence. There was only an occasional twitch of pain in her leg; it was well and strong again, and as she strode on the mesa she felt a surge of well-being. After inspecting several yucca plants to choose the longest, strongest fibers, she took her flint scraper from a sack tied to her waist. She was so intent to cut choice leaves that she did not hear footsteps until Okalake was nearly beside her.

"Greetings, Esteemed One." He squatted beside her, smiling at her surprise.

"You should not be with me." But she had to bend low to hide her pleasure.

He watched with amusement as she sawed off the strong leaves at the base of the plant. "You have no knife? A scraper won't do the job right."

"I did not bring a knife." She felt ridiculous.

Taking a flint knife from its sheath, he nudged Kwani aside. His knife cut the leaves in a single, easy stroke until she had a bundle.

"I need no more. Thank you."

He moved closer, eyes glowing. Suddenly he pulled her to him, lying back so that she was on him, the bundle of leaves between them. With an exclamation he swept the leaves aside and she felt his heart pounding against her own. He pulled her close, so that his man part thrust hard against her.

Kwani groaned with desire. Her young body was ravenous for what he offered. It took all her willpower to pull away.

"Somebody will see . . . Woshee will be punished . . ."

At mention of his mother's name, Okalake released her. Perspiration glistened on him like dew. He sat upright and looked around to see who watched. There was no one.

"Come to my secret place."

Kwani looked at him, at the eyes burning bright, at the mouth alive with longing for her, at the strong young body beneath the robe. Her blood screamed demand for him. She began to tremble uncontrollably.

He saw, and his face was suffused with tenderness. "Come."

She gathered the yucca leaves, tied them in a bundle with a long leaf, and followed. At a steep trail down to the canyon, they paused to look again for observers. No one. Slipping and sliding on the rocky soil, they scrambled down. "We go that way." He indicated the north.

He turned and she followed, feeling she was a stranger, someone she had not known before, a person without reason or fear who was being manipulated by a force over which she had no control at all.

She realized this was the way she and Kokopelli had come—how long ago? Where was Kokopelli now? He had left her. This son of the Sun Chief, a member of her own clan, desired her, but it was forbidden. She must turn back and return; she must spare Woshee as well as herself and Okalake. But the stranger she had become followed as he led her away from the trail, through thorny brush. A huge boulder lay against the ruddy cliff from which it had fallen eons ago. The boulder seemed almost a part of the cliff, attached to it. How could one get behind it? Okalake climbed to the top.

"Come and see."

She laid her bundle on the ground and climbed after him. Between the cliff and the boulder was a small opening leading to a dim interior.

"The cave is there." He slid down and disappeared. After a moment, he called, "Now you come."

She slid down cautiously, inches at a time, astonished at what she was doing. At what she knew she was going to do.

He caught her as her feet dangled, and pulled her down. He held her as he had held her before, cradled against his chest. She heard his heart like a thunder drum, and her own beat a crazy rhythm as he laid her down.

It was a warm cave, small and snug and safe, smelling of dust and timelessness. Together they lay as one, timeless as rain, as yucca blossoming, enfolded by the ageless stone arms of the cliff.

Kwani returned greetings casually, crossed the courtyard, and climbed the ladders to her dwelling, thankful that she could do so now without being conspicuous. It was an hour since she had left Okalake. He had made love to her in a way that sated the hunger of her young body. But something was missing. There was a yearning, an empty place, a wound in her spirit that lingered.

Kokopelli. It was Kokopelli she wanted and needed . . . his arms, his voice, his sensual touch. She wanted his eyes beneath the fringe of turquoise beads to look at her; she wanted his flute to sing to her again and ease her heart. She missed the intriguing mysteries of him and the soul-satisfying security of his presence. She missed him so much it was an ache inside her—hidden away until now.

She would go with him anywhere. She didn't care if she had no home—not too much, anyway. It made no difference where they were, so long as Kokopelli was her mate.

Meanwhile, she must complete the basket. She wanted Kokopelli to see it and to be astonished and proud of her. She thought of the extra touches she would give it: painted eyes and nose, with a delicate, pale color inside the ears. And tiny claws on the feet! Smiling, she hurried the final steps to her door and pulled the curtain aside.

There was no basket. Strewn about the floor were the shredded remains. Only one little rabbit's foot was whole.

✦ 23 ✦

Kwani stood frozen, numb with shock. She picked up the little rabbit's foot. It had been ripped from the body. Bits and pieces of the basket were thrown everywhere; a part of the head lay upside down at her feet. She picked it up, too, remembering the hours of loving work that went into its creation.

Who had done this terrible thing? Had someone seen her with Okalake? But no; both of them had looked carefully and there was no one else at all. This was an act of aggression; someone hated her, and wanted her to fail.

From deep inside her anger boiled up and exploded in a scream. She scooped up an armful of shreds and stepped outside.

"Look! Look!" she yelled. "See the Medicine Chief's beautiful basket!"

She tossed the shreds into the air and went back for more. "Look what has been done! Who did this?"

There were astonished gasps from the gathering crowd. The Medicine Chief's basket!

"Who did this I want to know?" Her voice trembled with fury and she threw the shredded pieces at them. They drew back as if stung.

"Answer me!" she shouted. Her eyes were afire and her face contorted as though something inside was about to break through.

"Answer me!"

People shook their heads. Such an explosion of fury in a woman was unseemly and unnatural, especially for one who called herself She Who Remembers.

Kwani whirled and went back inside, grabbed her spear, and returned to face them. Balancing the spear expertly in her hand, she assumed a throwing stance. Her long hair fell about her and strands covered her contorted face. Her eyes blazed.

"This spear can kill." Her voice was deadly. "Tell me who destroyed my basket or I will throw this spear."

Women and children scurried for shelter, while men emerged from kivas with hunting bows. The Medicine Chief took the sacred bow from its hiding place and strapped the hook to his waist. What an opportunity! He would use the bow to save the life of one of the clan. What could be more just?

Yatosha and several other hunters drew their bows, aiming arrows at Kwani who stood like an avenging goddess confronting them with her weapon.

The Medicine Chief brandished his bow with the arrow locked in place ready to be released at a touch.

"If you throw that spear, you die!"

"Put down the spear!" the hunters cried.

For a moment, Kwani wavered. Then she slowly lowered the spear and gazed long at each hunter in turn.

She made them uneasy. There was an aura of magical power about her. Had she not communicated with Kokopelli's sacred bird? Was she not the chosen mate of Kokopelli? Did not She Who Remembers choose her as successor? They lowered their bows and did not look at one another.

Still grasping her spear, Kwani descended. The deadly point of the spear preceded her, and they stepped aside. She began to run, her face pale, her hair floating like smoke behind her. She reached the path to the ravine and stumbled and slid down in her haste to get away from them.

Only when she was out of sight of the city did she cry, wandering blindly through the brush, tears streaming, dragging the spear behind her like a toy.

The Chiefs sat in solemn semi-circle before the altar fire in the kiva. Juniper smoke wafted fragrantly, and firelight illuminated niches in the walls where prayer sticks, fetishes, flutes and rattles, and other sacred objects rested. The hour was late; the chiefs had been in consultation for a long time. The basket for the Medicine Chief's important ceremony had been destroyed. Bad trouble brewed.

The Medicine Chief was more than usually arrogant. It was not he who did it—although he was secretly pleased it had happened. He feared he was suspected because it might have been impossible for him to refuse the basket. Yatosha, mate of Tiopi, was silent. He knew how much Tiopi resented Kwani. Could it have been she who committed the crime? He lowered his eyes to hide his fear and anger.

For moons he had endured Tiopi's gloating that her womb had accepted Kokopelli's seed, when it had rejected his own. He had been subjected endlessly to her praise of Kokopelli's sexual superiority, his accomplishments, abilities, his achievements which made his own prestige and importance as Hunting Chief appear to be nothing. But for his position in the Eagle Clan, he would have left her long ago and returned to his mother's house and his own Turquoise Clan. But—and this gnawed at his spirit—he loved Tiopi. He moaned inwardly. He hoped Kokopelli had died in the snows, he and his accursed baby-maker.

Huzipat, Clan and Elder Chief, sat with his head bowed, his wizened face solemn. He was not unaware of Yatosha's humiliation since Kokopelli's last visit. He felt a pang of compassion for his young Hunting Chief and would not have blamed him if he accused Tiopi or even if he were somehow responsible for making Tiopi look guilty. A man must do what he must do to save face. He rubbed his ear and tugged at his ear ornament as though to extract wisdom from it.

The Chiefs and Elders sat in strained silence. Who among them had brought trouble to the clan? Huzipat raised his hand.

"One with bad feelings is among us. One of our people has done a wrong thing and has not confessed." Heads nodded in agreement.

He continued. "Therefore, we must ask help of the gods. We must fast and purify ourselves for three days and await a sign." He turned to the Medicine Chief. "Do you agree?"

"I agree."

"You will prepare the ceremony?"

The Medicine Chief nodded regally. "I will consult with the spirits of my Medicine Lodge."

The Elder Chief tugged at his ear ornament again, a habit of his when worry was on him. "Good. It is important to know who did this thing. Bad feelings should not be." He shook his head sadly. "It is not good for the clan."

Zashue, sitting beside his father, had been squirming in an effort to be silent. He raised his hand in the gesture-before-speaking.

The Elder Chief squinted at him. "You wish to speak?"

"Yes."

"Speak."

"Maybe the Esteemed One destroyed the basket herself."

There was a thud of silence. The men bowed their heads and clasped their hands. A gleam appeared in the Medicine Chief's eyes. He glanced at his son with pleased surprise. "Zashue speaks wisely."

"Wisely?" the Elder Chief said. "Why would the Esteemed One destroy what she had created? None like it was ever—"

"Because she knew it would not hold water and I could not accept it. She wanted blame placed on another—"

"And to cause trouble," Zashue added with an excellent imitation of his father's inflection.

The men looked at one another. Could it be possible? But no, Kwani's fury was genuine. Remembering it, they shifted uneasily. They must ask help of the gods.

Kwani did not know how long she had wandered aimlessly through the canyon. Now, she sat beneath a scraggly juniper and leaned against the trunk. Her arms and legs were scratched, and a small scratch bled on her cheek. She wiped the blood away, leaving a smudge.

Sunfather appeared from behind a cloud and the cloud floated away. The air carried a message of approaching spring; Earthmother was nearly ready to give birth. Soon it would be time for Ceremonies Before Planting. But there was no basket. Thoughts whirled in her mind like leaves before the wind.

It was Tiopi. *It had to be Tiopi.* But she would have been seen; people would know. Maybe they did know and wouldn't tell. Maybe they were glad Tiopi did it; they wanted her to be unable to complete her initiation and to be cast from the tribe. Perhaps all of the Eagle clan were secret enemies . . .

All but Okalake.

Kokopelli, why did you leave me? I would rather die by your side in the snows than to be cast away again, to die alone.

A cry rose in her throat. There were no tears; anger had dried them all. A breeze ran along the canyon, and the tree nodded as it passed. A field mouse peered at her from beneath a sage bush; its bright little eyes looked into hers before it darted away. Sunlight made the red sandstone of the opposite cliff vibrate with brilliance. And there was a swift flash of wings as a bird darted to and from its nest among the crags.

It was beautiful and peaceful but Kwani felt no peace. She rose, took the spear from where it lay and balanced it in her hand.

"I wanted to throw you," she said aloud.

But if she had, they would have sent their arrows and she would be dead. She wanted to *live.*

She squeezed the amulet tightly in its pouch around her neck. "Give me a sign!"

But the amulet gave no sign. She should return to the city, but she could not face them, not yet. Anger—yes, and fear—made her vulnerable. She could not match their wills with her own.

Sighing, she began to walk again, making her way more carefully, watching where she stepped. She did not see Brother Coyote until she was nearly to the place where he sat, smiling at her with his coyote smile.

Kwani stopped and stared. His reddish-brown coat shone in the sun as he sat on a little rise.

Her heart leaped. A sign!

"I greet you, Brother Coyote." She lowered her spear and bowed her head respectfully.

The coyote pointed his nose into the air as if to acknowledge her greeting, and loped away toward the opposite cliff. Kwani felt she should follow, and hurried after him. But soon he disappeared, and she was left facing the rugged formations and grotesque spires of the cliff.

Suddenly, she *knew*. She must return the way she came until she reached the climbing place to the House of the Sun. There she would learn what she must do.

"Thank you, Brother Coyote!" she called. Swiftly and carefully, Kwani followed the narrow path to the climbing place. She left the spear on the ground and pulled herself up by the hand-holds which she had used only once before.

The temple stood in empty meditation. But Kwani sensed the spirits there. "I greet you, honored ones. I request permission to enter."

Silence, peaceful and welcoming.

Slowly, Kwani crossed the open courtyard to the Place Of Remembering. Almost, she expected to see the Old One kneeling at the altar. But only her spirit was there.

"I greet you," Kwani whispered and her heart beat hard. She stood looking at the room as though she had not seen it before.

The walls, open to the sky, were of stones perfectly cut and fitted into one another. Opposite the doorway, a knee-high stone was set on edge, uncut except for the top which was smoothly finished and perfectly level. A tiny spider hung from a web dangling from one corner.

"Spider Grandmother?" Kwani whispered, approaching the altar. Spider Grandmother was an honored diety; some believed it was she who brought the people into the fourth world. Could this be she?

The spider hung motionless, clinging to the web which undulated slightly in the breeze. Reverently, Kwani knelt and walked slowly on her knees to the altar. She leaned down and bent to look at the spider.

"I greet you, honored one."

The spider ignored her. Careful not to disturb the web, Kwani stretched both arms upon the altar and leaned her cheek upon the stone. Closing her eyes, she willed herself to be receptive to the stone's powers and to the communication of spirits in this holy place.

She did not know how long she knelt there. Perhaps she slept and dreamed. But She Who Remembers came and knelt beside her and spoke.

"You are the one I chose. You will live as all the others have lived who were chosen—a stream entering the river of immortality. Your body will die but your spirit will live as mine lives and as all the others live who were She Who Remembers, and who will live when you are in Sipapu."

Kwani was overcome with awe. The Old One disappeared, and another came. It was her mother.

"Kwani . . ." The voice was tender.

"Mother!"

"Do not grieve. Do not permit anger to gnaw your spirit as a dog gnaws a bone."

"But my basket—"

"Make another."

"There is not time. Ceremonies Before Planting come—"

"There is time. You will see."

"The one who destroyed my basket could destroy again."

"Make one too sacred to destroy. That is your duty."

Kwani raised her head to look into her mother's face, but no one was there. Only the little spider moved in its web.

Kwani gazed around the empty room. "Mother!" she called, and felt her heart would burst. Had she dreamed?

Again she laid her cheek upon the stone, arms outstretched. Slowly her spirit calmed and peace entered her like a gentle spring rain. It did not matter who shredded her basket. She would make another, a better, more sacred one.

She sat up as if awakened from sleep. The small room was in shadow now, silent and infinitely serene. She whispered thanks to the powers of the altar and to the little spider—was it Spider Grandmother?—and bade the spirits grateful farewell.

Outside, the sky was cloudless; only the cold wind of winter lingered. Ceremonies Before Planting would take place in another moon; she must hurry to get her basket finished.

But what kind?

Kwani left the House of the Sun and walked slowly upon the mesa, searching for inspiration. The sky, the air, Sunfather's warm breath, the fragrance of sage and juniper flowed around her and into her, but inspiration did not come.

What could she create that would be too sacred to destroy? She asked her amulet, she pleaded with the spirits of tree and bush to tell her, but no answer came. She must seek the wisdom of Earthmother herself.

She found a place sheltered from the wind by a boulder, and lay down on her stomach. She pressed her lips to the soil, straining her entire body against the rocky ground, willing herself to become one with Earthmother.

"Speak to me, Sacred One."

Time passed. Shadows walked and grew long. Kwani lay beside the stone, absorbing the power that made grass grow, and made corn sprout and grow tall, that nurtured the tiniest seed and gave it life. The power entered her so that she was joined, as if through a common bloodstream, with everything that grew: every blade of grass, every leaf, even the little beetle scurrying by.

The shape of the basket began to form in her mind . . . round, like Sunfather, swelling gracefully from the base to a pregnant fullness, pregnant like Earthmother. The throat would be narrow, then widen again at the top to form a smaller circle, Moon Woman.

The design must be something that gives life . . .

Kokopelli! Kokopelli and his sacred bird!

With a cry, Kwani rose to her knees. A Sunfather, Earthmother, Moon Woman basket, with Kokopelli and his sacred bird, would be a holy thing. The Medicine Chief would not refuse it; no one would dare destroy it.

She gazed around her at her kinsmen, the trees, at the bushes and grasses and shrubs, her brothers and sisters. Her heart sang and her feet loved the place where she stood. She sang as she walked back to the city.

> *Beauty before me,*
> *Beauty behind me,*
> *Beauty above me,*
> *Beauty below me,*
> *I walk in beauty.*

Smoke from cooking fires was already floating from the cave and riding the breeze when Kwani arrived home. Smoke also drifted upward from kivas, and few men were about.

Kwani thought, the men are planning the Ceremony. But there was no sound of drums or of chanting. Strange. As Kwani entered the courtyard, the usual bustle of meal preparation and the noisy play of children slowed. Kwani was aglow, smiling! And she had no spear.

She called happy greetings and they responded uncertainly, glancing at one another. At her door she stopped in surprise. Woshee sat beside a neat pile of split saplings, more than enough to make the largest basket. Woshee stood with her usual dignity, but her eyes were troubled.

"I greet you, Esteemed One."

"My heart rejoices," Kwani replied truthfully. She stared at the materials for a new basket. "Did you bring these to me?"

Woshee shook her head so that the blue feathers entwined in her hair moved and fluttered like tiny birds about to take flight. She gestured over the city above and below them.

"All the women of the clan did this."

"Oh!" was all Kwani could say. She scooped an armful of saplings and turned and faced the women who had gathered and the others on rooftops and terraces.

"I thank all of you, and I shall make a basket better than before!"

Her heart filled. These were not enemies. They were her people. Her voice choked with emotion as she said, "I am sorry I acted as I did. Forgive me."

Only then did she realize she had forgotten her spear. She had left it at the base of the cliff where she climbed to the House of the Sun. She would get it tomorrow.

Woshee put her arm around Kwani. "Come and eat at my fire." At Woshee's house, Kwani accepted a corn cake and dipped it in the pot, scooping a mixture of corn and beans flavored with aromatic herbs.

"This is good," she said, eating greedily.

Woshee's dark eyes lingered thoughtfully on Kwani's face. She thought, Something happened to her today. She is not the same person that she was when she left in fury. She asked, "Where is your spear?"

"I forgot it, left it by the cliff where one climbs to the House of the Sun because I came back by another way."

"You were at the House of the Sun?"

"Yes."

"It is forbidden—"

"Brother Coyote sent me there."

Woshee sat back on her heels and stared. This girl would never cease to startle her. "Tell me about it."

It took several corn cakes before Kwani finished her story. She wiped her mouth with the back of her hand.

"I thank you, Woshee. My stomach is content." She belched delicately. "Will not the Sun Chief and Okalake eat also?"

"Okalake comes now."

Kwani turned as Okalake approached. He stopped in surprise when he saw her.

"I greet you, Esteemed One." He smiled.

"My heart rejoices." She smiled back.

He took his mother's hand and breathed on it. She wondered where he had been but she did not ask.

"Eat now," she said.

"Where is my father?" he asked Woshee.

"In council. They discuss the matter of what happened to the basket Kwani was making for the Medicine Chief."

"I shall go to be with them."

He took several more corn cakes and devoured them with big bites as though to vent his anger. He was nearly finished with his meal when Miko and her mother came and stood by the door. Miko showed signs of recent tears and her mother's face was grim. Politely they refused to come in to the fire.

"Miko has something to tell you," her mother said.

Miko sniffled and her mother nudged her. Finally, she said, "I know who destroyed the basket."

"Who?" Okalake asked sharply.

"It was one from another clan."

"Who?"

"I don't want to tell . . ."

Woshee said gently, "What clan, Miko?"

Miko hesitated. Her mother nudged her again. "The Wolf Clan," she said faintly, and tears rolled down both cheeks.

Quickly, Woshee reviewed in her mind every person from the Wolf Clan who had been there that day while Kwani was gone. There was only one remote possibility—a child—one who would be expected to run in and out of dwellings at will and whose going into Kwani's house would not be noticed or remembered.

Woshee came to Miko and put both hands on her shoulders. Miko hung her head and Woshee lifted the girl's chin and looked into her tearful eyes.

"It was Ki-ki-ki, wasn't it?"

Miko buried her face in her hands. "I don't want to tell!" she sobbed.

Her mother nodded. "That is who it was. Miko should have told you." She wiped tears from her own eyes and led Miko away.

Kwani swallowed hard. Poor little Ki-ki-ki, overcome with jealousy . . . A thought hit like a blow. *Had Ki-ki-ki seen her with Okalake?* Kwani glanced at him and knew he wondered the same thing. If the girl knew, she would tell others . . .

·24·

Okalake paused on the roof of the Medicine Chief's kiva, looking down into the dimness below while thoughts leaped through his mind like a hunted deer.

The welfare, the entire future of Kwani, Woshee, and himself rested on the word of a child. Would she tell?

I have caused this trouble.

It was love. Love for a blue-eyed woman with soft lips and a beautiful, ardent body. What would happen if the truth were known? No longer would he be his father's successor; never would he become Chief nor hold any position of responsibility in the tribe. Worse, much worse, was what would happen to Kwani and to his mother. Ostracized, cast away into the wilderness to die. Kwani might survive. But Woshee?

If they were cast from the tribe, he would go with them, take care of them. But shame would follow like a predator. Where could they go?

He loved these canyons, these crimson cliffs, this place where he was born and where he grew up learning the mysteries of the constellations to teach his own sons, learning to be the kind of man an Anasazi was expected to be. Honorable, modest, self-disciplined, active in the religious life of the clan, one who put the welfare of the clan above his own, skilled in farming and in hunting, trustworthy, dignified.

Self-disciplined. Honorable!

He gripped his amulet. "Guide me. Give me wisdom," he murmured, and stepped to the ladder and climbed down.

The elders and the Chiefs had been about to disband. Depression hung over them like smoke from an angry fire. Okalake sat down, folded his arms. After a suitable interval, he said, "I wish to speak."

The Elder Chief nodded. "Speak."

"The one who destroyed the basket is known."

There were sharp glances of surprise.

"Miko says it was the girl Ki-ki-ki of the Wolf Clan."

Exclamations of anger and surprise surged back and forth. Since the diminishing of the rains, relationships among clans was becoming strained. There were disagreements over farming areas. Hunting territories, too, were questioned. Game grew scarce as population increased and more animals were hunted.

Old Huzipat, the Clan and Elder Chief, sighed. "Why would the child do such a thing?"

The Medicine Chief said, "Perhaps she was instructed to do so by one of her clan."

Zashue gestured for speaking. "I believe there is another reason. If Ki-ki-ki did this, it was because she was jealous of Kwani."

Okalake lifted his head. "Why should she be jealous of my sister?"

"It is well known that Ki-ki-ki thinks she is in love with you, Okalake."

Okalake's voice hardened. "What has that to do with Kwani?" He turned to the others. "If Zashue means what he implies, he owes me and my sister an apology."

His gaze made Zashue squirm. "I only meant . . ."

"What did you mean, exactly?"

The Medicine Chief raised an imperious hand. "My son only repeats what is said in the kivas and around the cooking fires."

Okalake rose and his voice pierced like a lance. "Tell me what is said."

The Medicine Chief looked up at the young Sun-Chief-to-be, noting with relish the red stain in his cheeks.

"I shall tell you." He recrossed his legs and folded his arms, taking his time. "It is said that your interest in Kwani is more than brotherly." He smiled thinly.

The Sun Chief jerked his robe about him in anger. "It is unseemly gossip. My son is a good person, a true Anasazi; the Eagle Clan is proud he is one of them. You, all of you, know this. My son is kind to his sister as he is to his mother. If you permit those of the Wolf Clan to cause bad feelings among us, you are allowing yourselves to be manipulated to their benefit."

"My father speaks wisely," Okalake said, and sat down. His face was expressionless. But turmoil seethed inwardly, He must avoid Kwani from now on . . . if he could. *He must.*

The old Crier Chief cleared his throat. "Let us not be hasty in judgment—"

"Nor manipulated," the Sun Chief said.

Yatosha and the Medicine Chief, especially, were relieved that suspicion was now directed elsewhere. Trouble between clans was dangerous, more dangerous than fear of marauding attacks, which had forced them to retreat to inaccessible caves among the cliffs. Internal strife destroyed the brotherhood and mutual help needed for mutual security.

The Elder Chief said, "Let us meet with the Chiefs of the Wolf Clan." Heads nodded. It was a wise decision.

The meeting took place in the spacious kiva of Quolonquin, the Wolf Clan's Elder Chief. He was young to be Elder Chief, taller than most, and lean. A scar creased his cheek from nose to ear, giving him a twisted, one-sided expression, subtly ominous.

He passed his ornate hospitality pipe to the Elder Chief of the Eagle Clan, who puffed several times and handed it to the Medicine Chief. It was puffed and passed in turn to the others.

The aged Elder Chief of the Eagle Clan gazed thoughtfully at the altar fire, and said at last, "You have heard that the ceremonial basket being made for our Medicine Chief to be used in Ceremonies Before Planting was destroyed." He paused, and continued calmly, "It is said that the child Ki-ki-ki did this thing. We believe this is but a childish prank—"

"Who blames Ki-ki-ki?" Quolonquin asked sharply.

"Miko, of our clan, recently become a woman."

"She was a witness?"

The Elder Chief shifted uncomfortably. He did not know. Why had they not questioned Miko?

"Miko's mother also said it was Ki-ki-ki."

"She saw it happen?"

"We of the Eagle Clan do not lie."

There was an uneasy silence. The Crier Chief said, "It is not good to have misunderstanding between brothers. It is well known that girl children and women allow foolish emotions to overcome good sense. They do foolish things. Let us not permit the acts of females to loosen the important bonds of brotherhood."

There was silence again while the hospitality pipe made another round. Quolonquin turned to the young Chief-in-training who would be his successor.

"Bring Ki-ki-ki to me."

The young Chief nodded and climbed from the kiva. Soon he was back with Ki-ki-ki who looked frightened. When her gaze met Okalake's she looked away.

Quolonquin said, "The ceremonial basket being made for the Medicine Chief of the Eagle Clan was destroyed. It has been said that you did this thing."

She hunched her shoulders but did not speak.

"Did you destroy the basket? Answer, girl!"

"Yes," she whispered.

"Why?"

"Because Kwani is a witch."

Outraged murmurs came from the Eagle Clan. The Wolf Chiefs looked away, embarrassed.

Okalake said, "Come here, Ki-ki-ki."

She went hesitantly, and he pulled her down so that she was on her knees, facing him.

"My sister thinks well of you."

The girl bit her lips and a tear rolled down.

"You know she is not a witch. Why do you say she is?"

"Because . . . because she makes you love her!" she blurted. "You kiss!"

"Of course we kiss. People who love each other kiss, and she is my sister."

"Not really." The girl's mouth set in a hard little line.

The Elder Chief said, "She is mate of Kokopelli." He turned to the others. "She has admitted she destroyed the basket. Send her away."

The Medicine Chief interrupted. "Perhaps there are more reasons why the girl believes Kwani is a witch?"

Zashue, ever eager, said, "Tell us, Ki-ki-ki!"

The girl twisted her fingers and gazed about the kiva as though searching for an answer. "At night she takes out her eyes and puts them on a shelf and puts in owl's eyes instead." She glanced at Okalake triumphantly.

Okalake said, "You saw her do this?"

She nodded.

"When?"

"At night."

"What night?"

The Medicine Chief said, "What difference does it make what night it was? If she saw it, she saw it."

"The girl has been badgered enough," Quolonquin said. "Ki-ki-ki, you may go."

Okalake spoke. "Wait. I will not permit my sister to be accused of witchcraft, even by a child!"

"I am not sorry," Ki-ki-ki cried shrilly. "You are the one who will be sorry!" She ran toward the ladder. Okalake caught her by both arms.

He said, not too kindly, "Do you know what happens to those who lie?"

She struggled to be free but he held her fast.

"The gods punish liars, Ki-ki-ki. But worse, liars punish themselves because they cannot believe others." His voice grew more gentle. "When one loves, one wishes no harm to come to that person. Think about that."

He released her, but she did not go. Her small shoulders shook with sobs. "I want . . . I want . . ." She threw herself into Okalake's arms. "I want you to be my mate when I grow up!"

The men glanced at one another, and smiled. How typically female and foolish. She was jealous! They understood everything now.

Okalake wiped the girl's tears away and set her on her feet. "You may change your mind when you grow up."

She was glad to escape; her thin legs ran up the ladder. Okalake breathed in relief. If the girl had seen him with Kwani she would have said so . . . He fingered his amulet in gratitude.

Suitable farewells were spoken, and the men of the Eagle Clan departed. When they were gone, a Chief of the Wolf Clan said, "It is not seemly that they came as questioners because of an act by a child."

"A female child," an elder said.

They sat in silent agreement. "Perhaps they seek an excuse to take our farming plots for themselves?"

Another said, "Could it be the girl did see Kwani take out her eyes and put in the eyes of an owl?"

"Witches have brought much sickness to the tribe this year."

They glanced at one another uneasily.

Quolonquin said, "She is jealous. A jealous female will say anything."

They nodded, but kept secret opinions to themselves.

Kwani scrambled down the steep and narrow trail to the ravine. It was early morning, and clouds were pink and the air was cold and sweet. She wanted to sing, but the vast silence seemed too sacred to disturb. Ahead, a deer leaped up, disappearing through the brush. Kwani hoped she would encounter the buck when she had her spear again. If she could kill a deer, there would be venison for feasting, and she would scrape and tan the skin and make a new robe . . .

The Sacred Mountain shone pale in Sunfather's first light as Kwani reached the climbing place to the House of the Sun. The spear was not there. But surely, this was the spot where she had left it? She searched all around. The spear was gone. But now that she was mate of Kokopelli, she needed its protection no longer. Yet a nagging unease remained. Who had taken it? It had to be one from another tribe: such a weapon could not be concealed by one returning with it to the city. Perhaps boys playing had found it? Days later, when asked, she said she had discarded the spear. People, thinking she was ashamed at the way she had threatened them with it, considered this to be a noble act and forgave her former unseemly behavior.

Even Tiopi, big with child and reveling in her pregnancy, made it a point to demonstrate friendship.

"You may assist me with the birthing of Kokopelli's child," she said graciously.

Kwani nodded grimly and did not reply.

Now Kwani concentrated on her new basket. The round shape, conventional for hundreds of years, was easy to do. She spent many hours perfecting the graceful shape: the base swelling upward to pregnancy, then the slim throat that widened again at the top to form a perfect full-moon circle.

The weaving was not difficult; her fingers were intimate with the pliable strips. It was the design that took most of her thought. The base below Earthmother would be Sipapu, shown by a series of small semicircles joined in a curved line to resemble waves upon water. This would have double meaning, representing also the Great Water over which the Gods of the Rising Sun had come.

Earthmother and fertility would be represented by the pregnant shape and by Kokopelli and his sacred bird. Kokopelli would be on one side of the basket in a simple stick-figure design as he walked and played his flute. On the opposite side would be the bird in a simple line design showing its graceful form.

Above Earthmother would be the round opening of the basket in Moon Woman's form, with zigzag rain falling down the basket's narrow throat between sky and earth: rain that gave Earthmother her fertility.

It would be perfect.

Sometimes she took her materials to the canyon or the mesa to be close to Earthmother. Once, she glimpsed a tawny shape moving low in the distance. A cougar? But she did not see it again. Perhaps it was Brother Coyote, watching.

At last the basket was finished. It was tall and strong and beautiful. She tested it secretly, filling it from a distant spring, and it leaked not a drop. It was heavier than she had thought, because of its size, but a man could carry it, empty, with one finger. Filled with water it would not burn, and thrown from the cliff it would not break—she hoped. Though jagged rocks or thorns might pierce it if it were thrown with force from enough height. And if this happened, it would leak.

She prayed to the gods, fed her amulet and medicine arrow, and tried not to worry about what would happen. The basket would be presented to the Medicine Chief during a ceremony planned to take place within nine days.

It was during those nine days that Kwani realized her moon flow was long past due. At first, she ignored it, but when she could do so no longer she had to face the truth. She was pregnant. With Okalake's child.

·25·

K wani stirred restlessly on her sleeping mat, watching for pre-dawn light to slip under the curtain at her door. It was the seventh day before the Ceremonies, the day she must appear before the entire clan and present her basket to the Medicine Chief. The city was not yet awake. Even the turkeys were still.

She sat up and hugged her knees. Would he accept her basket? In the darkness her hands found it and cradled it. This was the child of her mind, her spirit, given to her by Earthmother. She caressed the sleek curves, fingering the place where designs made a subtle change in the surface. The design of Kokopelli . . . Loneliness and longing welled up in a flood. Would he return?

She cradled the basket in her arms. "You are beautiful," she crooned. "Beautiful and perfect. Earthmother's gift."

Involuntarily, she pressed her abdomen. Another gift was there. Oka-lake's. Soon it would be the third moon, swelling would begin. First flowers would not bloom until three more moons. Would Kokopelli arrive before the clan discovered her secret?

There was a rustle outside her door, and she clutched the basket to her chest as though it were a child. But there was a snuffling sound; a puddle of urine trickled on the floor beneath the curtain—a dog on its morning rounds.

"Go!" she hissed. She wiped the puddle with a handful of shredded cedar bark. The bundle of bark she had accumulated would no longer be needed for her moon flow, but it would be useful for the baby's diapering—as all mothers knew.

She thought of her first baby taken to the spirit world by Brother Coyote. Was it a boy or a girl? Were the eyes blue? A feeling of fierce protectiveness surged in her. She pressed both arms to her abdomen. This child would live!

Predawn. A baby cried, and another. Women left the warmth of their blankets to build cooking fires, and soon the comforting smell of juniper smoke began the new day. Young girls responsible for emptying the jars used as chamber pots carried them to the cliff and dumped the contents. Kwani carried her wide-mouth clay pot and emptied it with the others, watching with amusement as the little boys aimed their arcs high over the cliff. Perhaps hers would be a boy.

Returning, she saw Tiopi working at her cooking pot. Tiopi saw her and looked away, pretending she did not.

I don't care, Kwani thought. But she did care. She wanted no enemies; they were thorns festering in the spirit.

She washed her hair and dressed carefully in her best robe. With Kokopelli's golden ornament swinging at her ear she felt invincible. Wouldn't he be astonished to see himself and his bird in the basket's design! She smiled.

The hour of the Crier Chief grew near. The old man's bones protested the cold, but his spirit persevered. Slowly, he climbed to his place and gazed toward the Sacred Mountain.

"All people, awake and arise!" His rich voice rolled through the cave and echoed into the canyon. "Behold the dawn and welcome Sunfather's coming. He will appear to bless the happenings of this day, the seventh day before Ceremonies Before Planting, the day when she who is called Kwani will offer a special ceremonial vessel to the Medicine Chief and to the Eagle Clan. If the offering is accepted by the Medicine Chief and by all the Chiefs of our clan, Kwani will—"

Kwani listened in dismay. Her basket must be approved by all the Chiefs, not just the Medicine Chief! No one had told her that!

The Crier Chief's voice flowed on, but she did not hear it. Apprehension was cold in her veins. Was this a plot? Suddenly, she remembered her spear.

Who took my spear? Who has it now?

The Crier Chief's voice reentered her consciousness. ". . . will assemble after the morning meal, and she who is called Kwani will bring her offering to the Chiefs at that time. I have spoken."

All eyes turned toward Kwani who stood framed in her doorway. Her dark hair gleamed even in the dimness, and Kokopelli's golden ear ornament moved and swayed and reflected tiny lights from the fires. Her new robe became her and she stood in it with dignity, her face calm. Only the grip of her fingers into her palms betrayed tension.

* * *

The city was crowded with visiting clans from other caves. There was chanting from the kivas, and the sound of rattles, drums, and flutes. The various Societies of the Eagle Clan were proud of their ceremonial expertise and took the occasion to practice for Ceremonies Before Planting. A great shout from the thunder drum preceded the Medicine Chief emerging from his kiva, with other Chiefs in solemn file.

He was elaborately painted in ceremonial design, with the black zig-zag marks upon his face and mystical designs of brilliant colors upon his bare torso. A fine robe of the mountain sheep hung from his waist, fastened by a belt of intricately braided human hair with beads of shell from distant seas. A pouch adorned with feathers hung from his belt and a multiple-stringed necklace of shiny black beads—juniper seeds burned hard and polished—held the amulet which lay against his chest. Eagle feathers were entwined in the three thick braids of his hair; and great ornaments of the sacred blue stone hung from both ears. He was a splendid, fearsome sight, and he gloried in the knowledge of it. He strode majestically to the center of the community terrace, announcing his arrival with a hissing of the gourd rattle with a flourish, allowing its mystical voice to command silence. When the crowd's comments of awe and admiration quieted, he spoke.

For the benefit of the visitors he eloquently reviewed the story of Kwani's coming, of Kokopelli's visit and his magical bird, of Kokopelli's choosing Kwani as his mate and leaving her in the protection of the Eagle Clan. He spared no detail in re-telling how he, the Medicine Chief, was chosen by Kokopelli to keep and to honor the bow of the Gods of the Sunrise Sea until first flowers bloomed and Kokopelli returned for his bride.

All present knew each detail. But what had Kwani made for the Chief? Would he accept it? And what if he did not? They reveled in the suspense of it.

The Chief built to his climax. He swung his gourd rattle in great circles overhead as he chanted his challenge.

"I, the Medicine Chief of the Eagle Clan, demand that she who is called Kwani present to me a sacred vessel for Ceremonies Before Planting. I demand that this vessel be large enough to hold as much water as that jar." He thrust his rattle toward the community water jar standing nearby, shaking the rattle for emphasis. "I demand that it be like no vessel ever made before. It must be light enough for me to carry with one finger."

He extended his little finger. "Held to the fire, it will not burn, thrown from the cliff it will not break. I, the Medicine Chief of the Eagle Clan, demand this. If she who is called Kwani cannot fulfill these requirements, she will have failed in sacred duty and will be refused membership in our clan or in our tribe. No longer will she be welcome in the places of our people. She will go alone to the wilderness to seek forgiveness of the gods and enter Sipapu as the gods decree."

The crowd craned their necks. Did Kwani realize the impossibility of the Medicine Chief's demands? Had she gone away?

The Chief gave his rattle one final flourish and shouted, "Kwani, come forward!"

She did not appear.

Okalake stood with Woshee and his father and brothers on their roof terrace. His face tensed with anxiety. "Where is she?" he whispered to Woshee.

"In her dwelling."

"Why does she not come out?" Perspiration beaded his forehead.

The Medicine Chief shouted again. "I demand that she who is called Kwani appear before me." His voice shook with fury and embarrassment. He would teach her respect!

The Chief was about to shout again in a frenzy when the curtain of Kwani's doorway was pulled aside, and she stepped out. She carried a very large, gracefully shaped basket which she held with her forefinger.

The Chief's eyes glittered. A basket! This would be too easy. He watched as she descended the ladders from level to level as though they were broad steps, swinging the basket a little with her movements. She smiled as she approached him. She would lose that smile quickly. Ha!

Kwani stood before him. She held the basket high, dangling it from her finger, and turned so that all might see.

"I hold this by one finger," she said clearly, so that all might hear. "I assume the Medicine Chief might be able to do the same."

The crowd tittered. The Chief thrust out his hand. "Give it to me."

"Of course. But first, permit me to explain its form and tell how its meaning was revealed to me." She faced the city.

"I was in despair. I wished to obey the request of our Medicine Chief, but I did not know how. Brother Coyote sent me to the House of the Sun. Spider Grandmother was there at the Place of Remembering. She brought She Who Remembers to me. My mother came to me, also."

There were gasps and murmers. The zigzag marks on the face of the Chief seemed to undulate. "Give me the basket!"

"Of course," Kwani said politely. "As soon as I finish telling of Earthmother."

Earthmother! The deity most honored after Sunfather. The Chief blustered to conceal a small stab of fear.

"I demand the basket!"

Kwani turned to the Medicine Chief and her blue eyes were mocking.

There was something inside the basket he could not see, something which would reveal itself at the right time. She said, "You do not wish to hear of Earthmother?"

A voice from the crowd shouted, "We wish to hear!"

"Let her speak!" others cried.

"Very well," the Chief said with strained graciousness. He thrust his rattle at Kwani with a commanding gesture. "Speak!"

Kwani smiled again. "Of course." She turned to face the city. "I went to Earthmother, seeking wisdom. I prayed to learn what to create for the Ceremonies. I lay long upon Earthmother's lap, and at last she told me. This is the vessel I bring to the Eagle Clan."

She held the basket overhead. "See that it is round, like Sunfather. See that the base has small circles joined in a curved line. This is Sipapu, and also it is the Great Waters of the Gods of the Rising Sun."

The people stared raptly. Kwani followed the swell of the curve with her finger. "This is Earthmother, pregnant with life. And see where Kokopelli comes with his flute and his sacred seed."

She turned the basket so they might see the other side. "Kokopelli's bird comes, also."

"Ayee-e-e-e!" The crowd was entranced.

Kwani pointed to the round rim of the basket. "Moon Woman is here, above Earthmother, with rain falling between." She indicated the rain pattern upon the basket's slender throat. "Rain is a gift to Earthmother to help her give life to the planting." The people nodded acknowledgement of this truth.

Kwani held the basket again with one finger. "Therefore, I respectfully offer the Medicine Chief and all the Chiefs of the Eagle Clan a vessel which is Sunfather, Earthmother, Moon Woman, Kokopelli with his seed and his sacred bird, the rain gift, and Sipapu. Has any vessel like this been made before?"

"No!" they cried.

The Medicine Chief stood glowering. "Water! Fill it with water!"

At the community jar she nodded to a young man who stood gawking. "Please lift the jar and pour the water into my basket."

The jar was heavy, but he lifted it eagerly, and poured the water into the basket.

The Medicine Chief smiled widely. "Let us see if any man here can carry that with one finger."

"You did not say the vessel must be full. You said only that it must be light enough to carry with one finger. You saw me do so. You see also that the vessel does not leak."

The old Clan Chief stepped forward. "She speaks truly."

Okalake pushed his way through the crowd to the front. Kwani beckoned to him. "My brother, please carry the basket to the fire. Let us see if it will burn."

The Medicine Chief growled. "It is wet!"

"You did not say the vessel could not be wet. You said only that it must not burn when held to the fire."

"True! True!" the people cried, enjoying it.

Okalake lifted the basket. As he did so, the feathered shaft of Kwani's sacred medicine arrow bobbed to the surface. Kwani held the arrow overhead. "The spirit of my medicine arrow protects my basket as it protects me."

"We shall see!" the Medicine Chief cried. Seizing the basket he strode to the cliff. With a mighty heave he threw it over the edge. The precious water gushed out, staining the cliff's red flanks, falling, falling with the basket to the rocks below.

A sullen murmur rose, like the sound of a distant storm. Women who walked far to carry water and who climbed hand-holds with babies on their backs and jars on their heads, who horded every vital drop, were not pleased. But the desecration, the insult to the sacred spirits of the vessel shocked and angered the people the most. They crowded the cliff's edge, gazing down at the basket which lay in a crevice, partially concealed.

"You destroyed it! You killed Sunfather's, Earthmother's, Moon Woman's, Kokopelli's sacred vessel!" someone cried. Others took up the chant, "You killed it! You killed it!" The chant grew louder as the crowd drew closer to the Medicine Chief.

Kwani watched in astonishment. They had turned against the Medicine Chief! But it was he and only he who could assure her final membership in the clan, and give her the necklace. Until the necklace was hers, she could not be fully accepted as She Who Remembers. She stepped to the side of the Chief and raised her hand.

"My basket is strong," she called. She held the medicine arrow overhead. "The spirit of my medicine arrow protects it. My basket is not dead. Send one to see!"

"I go!" Okalake shouted. He was followed by Yatosha, the Hunting Chief and mate of Tiopi, and by Cayamo, the singer, and little Chololo who leaped after his hero like a young mountain ram, bounding from rock to rock. They reached and pulled the basket up from where it lay, top up, at the cliff's base, wedged between stones and brush. Okalake inspected it.

"It is wounded but not dead," he called up. "There is water in its belly."

"Ayee-e-e-e!" People gazed at Kwani with respect and wonder and awe at her powers.

Kwani breathed a deep sigh. She had not been at all sure that her basket was not dead. Water made the basket heavy, and the rocks were sharp below. She wondered how badly the basket was damaged. Could she repair it?

The Medicine Chief stood in stoic silence, raging in his heart. No one, no female, no outsider could be allowed to have medicine this strong. The moment when the people turned against him . . . *Him!* . . . A cold finger poked at his heart. Yet this blue-eyed woman so different from the others had turned away their anger. To prove again how right she was, how powerful was her medicine! It could not and would not be endured.

Okalake and the others returned in triumphant procession. He shook the basket overhead, back and forth, so that the water sloshed inside.

"Earthmother holds her water!" he laughed, and people laughed with him. The ugly mood of moments before was gone. "There is no damage; it does not leak. However"—he indicated a handle torn at one side—"one handle is torn loose." Carefully, he lifted a portion of the rim encircling the basket's mouth. "Look. Moon Woman is wounded." He thrust the basket at the Medicine Chief, who took it with obvious reluctance.

Kwani leaned close to look. "The damage is not serious. I can repair it."

It was the opening the Medicine Chief needed. He thrust the basket at her with a gesture of contempt.

"Then repair it, and I will decide whether or not to accept it."

Fear coiled like a serpent in his belly. Never before had he met with the humiliation the blue-eyes outsider had inflicted on him. He must seek the intercession of the gods. Never would he approve that woman's basket. Never!

The Medicine Chief retreated to his kiva, seething with rage and bitter shame. Spread before him on a mat were a bowl of corn meal ground very fine, a small jar of the holy of holies, corn pollen, six prayer sticks with eagle feathers, and his fetish, a small figure of a bear carved from stone wrapped around its midsection with a string of yucca twine upon which were strung polished bits of shell. A small pouch of finely woven cotten from beyond the River of the South held the last of the sacred sun plant brought by Kokopelli. Beside him lay the magical bow entrusted to him. He had fed and honored it faithfully as Kokopelli required.

He sat for some time before these objects of powerful medicine, giving them time to calm his spirit and remove the pain of his shame. She who was responsible was now repairing her basket. Tonight, at the evening fire, he must make a decision. He would refuse the basket, of course. But how could he do so and keep the good will and respect of his people?

He rocked back and forth, chanting prayers, but the givers of wisdom offered no solution. There was one thing left to do. He must seek a vision.

He had saved the last bit of sun plant for Ceremonies Before Planting, but he needed it now. It was bitter and dry. But he ate it all.

Colors. Deep blue, red, black, swirling. Blue deer running across the mesa and beyond, into the sky. A fearsome sky, dark, boiling. Thunder drums booming. A loud cry. (His?) Clouds coming close, close, and dissolving.

She Who Remembers stood before him, tall, tall as the trees of the forests of the north. She wore her burial robe, and in her eyes was a terrible light. She spoke; and her voice was storm winds among the cliffs.

"You dishonor me. You dishonor my successor whom I have chosen to receive my necklace."

"No!" the Chief cried.

The face of She Who Remembers became disembodied and floated slowly toward him, filling the place where he was so that all he could see was the gigantic, wavering face with terrible eyes.

"You have taken that which is not yours. You have my necklace. Give it to me."

The Chief thrust a shaking hand into the pouch at his waist and removed the necklace. He offered it to the terrible face. The great mouth opened wider and wider until there was nothing but blackness, but the voice continued.

"I am within my successor. Give the necklace to her. Return it or Sipapu will be denied you, and vultures will pick your bones."

The blackness receded; the voice faded away. He still held the necklace in his outstretched hand. It was evening. He could hear the sounds of the city above him and smell the odor of food and of cooking fires. He was hungry, but he did not leave. He was shaken at what the vision had revealed. He must approve the basket. It was the only way Kwani could become a member of the clan and be qualified to receive the necklace.

He rocked back and forth, chanting prayers for wisdom.

The evening meal was over; it was the time of the evening fire. Visitors were reluctant to return home until the Medicine Chief emerged from his kiva to approve or refuse the basket which stood in mystic magnificence in the center of the courtyard. Kwani had repaired it during the day, and no matter how closely the basket was examined, the faint evidence of repair detracted not at all from its beauty. The designs of Kokopelli and his bird were particularly noted by every woman there who determined to incorporate similar designs in their next pottery creations. All the Chiefs of the Eagle Clan were seated in a semicircle before the fire, all but the Medicine Chief.

Kwani sat beside her basket, smiling at those who came to inspect it and remark on its beauty and workmanship. Tiopi, impassive in the shadows, hands across her swollen abdomen, reminded herself that soon Kwani would be gone. All she had to do was wait.

Kwani turned to the old Clan Chief. "Why does the Medicine Chief not come?"

"He confers with the spirits of his Medicine Lodge and with the gods."

Zashue had been striding about importantly, striking poses of his father. One day he would be Medicine Chief, honored and feared by these people. He paused at Kwani's side and gave her an imperious glance.

"My father speaks with gods. He will appear when it is time. Do you fear his decision?"

"No."

"You would be wise to do so!"

"He comes," people shouted.

Slowly the Medicine Chief emerged. He wore the mantle of One Who Has Communed With Gods. In his left hand was the gourd rattle and his right hand held the necklace of She Who Remembers. Red circles were painted around each eye and around his mouth, for he had seen and spoken with deities. He chanted and shook his rattle in rhythm as he approached the semicircle of Chiefs.

"The sacred sun plant has granted me a vision. She Who Remembers came to me. I have spoken with her."

A sound rose from the people like a rustle of leaves.

"The vessel prepared for me by the woman called Kwani is not worthy. I cannot accept it. But it is the wish of She Who Remembers that her successor be given the necklace." He held it dangling from his outstretched arm. "It is necessary that the basket be approved and that the woman called Kwani become a member of the Eagle Clan so that the necklace may be hers. I will not do this. The responsibility is yours."

He thrust the necklace at the stunned Clan Chief. Without a glance at Kwani, the Medicine Chief turned and disappeared into his kiva.

There was a clamor of confusion and of solemn comments. The Chiefs of the Eagle Clan drew close in conference. Visiting Chiefs stood at respectful distances, waiting to be summoned for advice, if necessary. Kwani's heart raced. Now was the turning point, the crucial moment. Her future, even her life, rested on the decision being made.

At last, the Clan Chief rose; the other chiefs rose with him. He raised his hand in gesture-before-speaking and the crowd quieted.

"We of the Eagle Clan accept the vessel made by she who is called Kwani. The wish of She Who Remembers is honored."

He came to Kwani who rose as he approached. They stood facing one another for a tense moment. Then the old Chief smiled and Kwani smiled back, joy warming her smile so that all who saw it smiled too. The Chief held the necklace with both hands and placed it around Kwani's neck.

"You are now one of us. You are now She Who Remembers."

Kwani bowed her head. "I accept the honor."

But as the great shell lay against her breast, she realized for the first time that she was untrained and totally unprepared for the responsibilities that were now hers.

It would be like stumbling blindfolded along a narrow path—with rocks waiting below.

·26·

Zashue lay on his stomach at the edge of the mesa, gazing down at a large boulder at the foot of the cliff. Between the cliff and the boulder was a shadow. An opening to a hidden cave? He wondered if it might be a den. Cougars, perhaps? Or coyotes? It might even be the den of a bear.

He reached for his bow. Ever since he failed to appear for the moving-targets game with the Wolf Clan, he had been ridiculed unmercifully. Killing a cougar or a bear would prove what a future Medicine Chief could do.

He fitted the arrow in his bow, threw down a handful of pebbles, and and waited for something to appear. Nothing.

He threw down a rock. Not even a field mouse appeared.

He would investigate. Slipping and sliding in haste, he made his way to the canyon floor and headed back to the hidden cave.

Suddenly he stopped, astonished. He got on hands and knees to examine faint tracks leading to the boulder. They were unmistakably those of a man and a woman who wore yucca fiber Anasazi sandals. A trysting place for lovers! He snickered. Perhaps they were inside now!

Quietly, he climbed the boulder and peered into the dim interior. It was empty—or was it? Something glimmered on the floor against the back wall. He eased himself down into the cave. The rough rock of the ceiling sloped downward so that he had to crawl on hands and knees to the back. He groped with one hand. A spear! Kwani's spear!

His small eyes sparkled in triumph. Kwani had hidden her spear here and claimed she lost it! It was she who came to this place with a lover—and Zashue had a good idea who that lover might be. He could hardly wait to tell his father.

He started to take the spear with him. But if Kwani and her lover

171

discovered the spear was gone, they would know someone had found their secret cave. Better to leave it and catch them in the act! He replaced the spear visualizing his triumph when those two who had broken a tribal law—the mating of brother and sister—were exposed.

He climbed out and sat on the boulder, thinking. Perhaps it would be better to remain silent for now and watch for them to come. He would hide under a bush where he could see up and down the canyon, and not be seen. When they came, he would run to get the Medicine Chief and together, father and son, they would confront the guilty ones.

But what would happen when Kokopelli returned and found his mate gone, driven away? Punishment would be terrible. He, Zashue, would be blamed for telling what he had discovered. His future as Medicine Chief would be endangered.

No. He would wait for others to discover what was going on. Surely they would, in time.

It was the third moon since Sunfather turned north toward his summer home. Days were often blustery; sometimes it snowed again, and bitter cold still lingered. But now and then, Sunfather's faint warmth pushed winter back briefly with promise of spring. Women spread blankets and robes upon roofs to air, and swept out the debris of winter from their houses. There was planning of how they would redecorate their homes with white clay and red ochre, and talk of repairing walls and maybe adding another room.

On the rare warmer days, chipmunks and squirrels came out to sun on warming rocks, and people did the same. They thronged the courtyard and terraces, soaking up the tentative warmth, while they discussed the Ceremonies Before Planting due in three days.

Gaunt old men whose arthritic bones had forced them to forsake dancing long ago, vowed that this year they would dance during the Ceremonies. And yes, they would plant a crop, too, for who had more experience than they? They retold of the miraculous crops of years past. They would do it all again, for who knew Earthmother's needs better?

Old women flexed gnarled fingers, dreaming of pots and bowls they would make again, yes, even now, and ordered daughters and nieces and granddaughters to fetch the clay from the best places. For the day, turkeys roamed the canyon at will, feasting on delectable new bugs. The toms, however, wasted little time eating. They cocked their heads back, unfurled magnificent tail fains, puffed out their chests, wagged their scarlet wattles, and let loose with rousing gobbles intended to drive every hen mad with desire.

Kwani was moving to the home of She Who Remembers, for it was hers now. She knelt on the floor to roll her sleeping mat to carry it to her new home when the doorway darkened; someone stood there. Women of the tribe had been helping her move; even Tiopi had carried out the bowl of cedar bark. But it was Okalake reaching down for her. He kissed her hard.

"No! Someone will see!" She struggled to be free, although she had no wish at all to be free.

"Come to the hideaway cave."

"No." She wanted to say yes-yes-yes!

"Come tonight. Moon Woman will show the way."

"I cannot." But it had been long, too long . . . If only the risk were not so great . . .

He picked her up and held her in his arms so that she looked into the warm, dark eyes. Almost she told him . . . But she did not let herself; he might inadvertently betray the knowledge that he would be a father, and endanger them all. She would wait for Kokopelli to take her and her secret away.

"Beautiful," he whispered. "You are beautiful."

Steps outside. Okalake set her down, lifted the rolled sleeping mat, and carried it out, almost colliding with Zashue who was walking by.

Miko and her mother entered. After the respectful formalities, Miko said shyly, "I want to help, also." Since her experience with Ki-ki-ki, she was growing up. She did not yet have a mate, but it would not be long, Kwani thought. The girl was becoming a beauty—sturdy, but well formed, with a sweetly curved mouth and large eyes that shone with intelligence.

As the three of them carried the rest of Kwani's belongings to her new home, Miko said, "When will you teach us the remembering?"

Kwani paused before answering. She felt she could not teach, not yet. But she must.

"The day after tomorrow." That would give her a day to prepare. "You and the other girls are to come here after the morning meal. But first you are to wash your hair and you are to bring meal to honor the spirits of my dwelling. You will tell the others?"

"I will tell them."

"Sandals must be left outside the door."

Miko nodded. Such a procedure was expected; this was the dwelling of She Who Remembers.

That night Kwani lay awake a long time. What would she tell the young girls? How could she be She Who Remembers with no training, no experience?

She must go again to the Place of Remembering.

It was not yet dawn when she climbed the hand-holds to the House of the Sun. The wind blew bitter cold from peaks still snow-covered. Ravens, nesting in the cliff, squawked and swooped at her. At the mesa top she paused to calm her spirit and ease the beating of her heart before entering the abode of gods.

The Place of Remembering was dim in predawn light. From the doorway the altar could barely be seen, but Kwani sensed its presence, its mystical powers. Reverently she offered pollen to the Six Sacred Directions.

"I respectfully request permission to enter," she said to the unseen spirits.

No sign came. Her own spirit bade her approach the altar stone. She knelt there, pressing her forehead upon the smooth, cold surface, reaching out both arms on the altar as though to embrace its ancient wisdom. She opened her mind, her very spirit, to receive it. Slowly it came—the serene, inner knowledge. It was as though she had always had it, but did not know that she did until her spirit opened to receive it.

She saw it again as in a dream: that women were weak when they entered the fourth world, and how they became stronger. She saw again how they bartered sex and gathered food for protection and for meat, how women forgot to remember, and how She Who Remembers was created. And now it was her awesome responsibility to be the latest in a long line going back to the beginning of time, when She Who Remembers was created.

Time is a great circle; there is no beginning, no end. All returns again and again, forever.

Kwani walked on the mesa, to think and decide how she would teach and what she would say to the young girls who would come so eagerly to learn the things that only women are to know.

She looked across the canyon at the Place of the Eagle Clan. The city stared back like a giant eye from under the mesa's brow. Elsewhere among the cliffs in the twisting canyons were other cities, other clans, a network of interrelated families that joined in the ceremonial life reaffirming ties to the land and to the spirit world. Communication among the clans was constant. If suspicions of witchcraft or a violation of clan law surfaced again in the Eagle Clan, the other clans would know, would participate . . .

But I am She Who Remembers now. Honored, esteemed. No one would dare . . .

Kwani looked about her, seeking communication and comfort from trees, shrubs, grasses, birds, and animals unseen—all things created by Masau'u. Their spirits would speak to hers if she allowed her own spirit to be receptive. She touched a stem of sage and fingered the leaves.

"Speak to me," she whispered.

She touched the rocky soil, sliding both hands over it, fingering the pebbles, seeking reassurance. She lay down, pressing her whole body to the ground.

"Earthmother, give courage to your daughter, for I am She Who Remembers now."

Her spirit calmed. She rose and clasped the necklace in both hands, allowing its power to envelop her.

"Miko, tell how Earthmother created the first who was She Who Remembers."

Miko looked up. The door was closed and the only light was from a small bed of smouldering coals. The room was not large and the girls were bunched together, overlapping one another like puppies.

Miko said, "I . . . I don't know, honored one."

Kwani was surprised. She assumed the Old One had told them. Was it a secret only She Who Remembers should know? She thought, I must do it my way now.

"Very well, I shall tell you. But all of you must remember that everything spoken in this room is secret. Never tell others, especially men and boys. Is that understood?"

"Yes!" they chorused, eyes bright. They loved secrets, especially from boys.

Kwani began the story of how Earthmother nourished the seed of corn and made it grow tall, and how the stalk became a woman who pulled herself from the ground and walked. The girls listened breathlessly. When Kwani was through, one of them said, "Tell us from the beginning."

Miko said, "Yes, when women were weak."

One said, "Miko knows because she is oldest."

Another added, "The Old One told her."

Kwani smiled. "Miko, you tell the story. Come and sit beside me."

Miko extracted herself from a tangle of arms and legs and sat next to Kwani. Although Miko had had her moon flow, she still seemed like a child. The fragrance of her freshly washed hair and young body and the vulnerability of her little bare feet gave Kwani a warm maternal feeling. She put her arm around Miko and said, "Tell the story now."

"It was a long time ago when our people first came to the fourth world," Miko began. "Men were strong and big. They were the hunters and had all the meat they wanted, and they didn't like to share. They only gave women what was left over and sometimes there wasn't any to give. Women were smaller and they were weak, especially when they had babies in their stomachs and couldn't run fast or fight for some of the meat. So Earthmother taught them how to find good plants and roots and seeds and flowers to eat so they wouldn't be hungry any more."

"My mother is teaching me," a little girl said. "I know where berries are."

"I know where to find pinyon nuts," another said.

"Everybody knows that. All you have to do is find the tree, and that's easy!"

"It is not!"

"There is to be no arguing in my dwelling. And it is rude to interrupt. Miko, continue." Kwani smiled inwardly. Children were children, but she had to be as She Who Remembers was supposed to be, whether she wanted to or not.

"When the women found good things to eat and learned to cook them, the men wanted some. So the women asked Earthmother what to do and Earthmother said, 'Trade your good things for what the men can give you.' 'Do you mean their meat?' the women asked, and Earthmother said, 'More than that. Men can give you protection, you and your children. They can provide a dwelling. Trade yourselves and the food of your gathering for what men will give you.' "

Miko paused and looked up at Kwani. "Is this correct, Esteemed One?"

"It is."

"Shall I tell more?"

"Yes." She thought, there is something about this girl, something special.

"And so the trade was made, and now men share meat with us and we share what we gather with them, and they protect us."

"You told that well, Miko." Kwani looked around at the group. "Are there questions?"

"Why must this be secret?"

Kwani smiled. This was an intelligent child. "Because men don't like to know they have been manipulated to do something, especially for women. They want to think that all they do is their own idea. Remember also that the most important thing to the clan—to all of our people—is that we continue to exist. And to do that, we must have babies. Only we can birth babies, and this is why women need protection, why we crave it.

"Men can go hunting and get killed or they can fight and die in wars or in other ways, and the clan will still live if women are protected and safe and keep on having babies. Even if every man died but one, that one man could seed many babies and the clan would live. But if every woman died but one, she could not have babies fast enough to keep the clan alive. The clan would die no matter how many men there were. So we, all of us, and our babies are more important and necessary to the clan than the men are. Men know this even if they don't like to acknowledge it, because they want to be best and most important at everything . . ."

Kwani paused. It was almost as though the words came from a mysterious source. The necklace? She clasped it to her, and continued.

"Because men are bigger and stronger and can do harm to us, we must know how to protect ourselves and our children. Earthmother created She Who Remembers to help us remember what we have always known—but forget, sometimes, that we know. The secrets are inside us, deep inside, born with us when we are born." She rose. "There is more. I will tell you about it next time."

For a moment longer the girls sat gazing up at her solemnly, faces alive with awed understanding, then they rose and bid respectful farewell to Kwani and to the spirit of the dwelling. Kwani stood looking after them. What I saw in my vision at the Place of Remembering is true, it is what the Old One taught. Perhaps she speaks to me through Miko. Is she telling me that Miko should be my successor?

My successor. I must choose her and train her as best I can before Kokopelli comes to take me away.

But would Kokopelli still want her, pregnant with Okalake's child? Soon the pregnancy would show. What if Kokopelli did not come before then?

What if he did not come at all?

◆ 27 ◆

"**M**y daughter says that She Who Remembers teaches well."

"But not as well as the Old One."

"She does not have the training."

"Or the experience. The Old One taught our girls for . . . how many years?"

"She taught me when I was a girl, and she was old then. At least forty moons, maybe more."

Thinking of how ancient the Old One must have been when Sipapu called made them silent with awe. The three of them sat side by side at the grinding stones working in unison to a happy tune Chololo played on his small flute. They leaned forward, necklaces swinging, newly washed hair rolled high over each ear as they rubbed the mano stones back and forth on the metates.

Corn was ground in three phases. The first girl ground it coarsely, then passed it to the second who ground it finer, and, in turn, passed it to the third whose special mano ground it to its final form. Sometimes, they sang in harmony to the tune being played, but now they gossiped furtively.

"Kokopelli does not come."

"No."

"If he does not return, She Who Remembers will have no mate."

"Unless . . ."

Significant glances.

"But it is forbidden."

They looked around quickly to see if they were overheard. The sound of Chololo's flute would drown out their voices.

"There she is now."

178

They looked to where Kwani had come out of her dwelling to stand in the sunshine.

"She still wears a winter robe."

Again, glances.

Kwani saw them looking at her, and smiled at them. She knew they had probably been talking about her; she wondered what they said. As She Who Remembers, Kwani was greeted now with utmost respect. She had established her own requirements for rituals, especially in regard to granting permission to enter her dwelling. Visitors must not only have freshly washed hair, still damp, clean garments, and sandals left outside the door, but corn meal must be brought and offered to the spirits before entering, and suitable prayers recited.

She had been teaching for several weeks and was pleased with the response. She wished there might be a way she could teach something to everyone and experience the same rapport with all the members of the clan. Although they were scrupulous in their proper relationship with her, Kwani sensed secret undercurrents.

As her self-esteem had increased, her fear of the Medicine Chief lessened. She was routinely polite but made little effort to conceal her disinterest in his magical powers and her confidence in her own. Also, her fear about discovery of her pregnancy grew less. Let them think what they wish, she told herself. I am She Who Remembers. But caution enough remained to keep her away from the hideaway cave, and although she had discarded her heaviest winter robe, she still wore a concealing garment of soft deerskin.

There were shouts from the courtyard as boys played the corncob game. They lay on their backs, grasped a corncob with their toes, and threw it backward over their heads to see who could throw it the greatest distance. Even the little boys gambled for a bow or an assortment of polished stones.

Smiling, she walked to the courtyard and sat down to watch. The smallest boys had trouble grasping the cob with their toes and had to use both feet. One little fellow did a complete backward somersault as he threw the cob, and this initiated a new element to the game. The bigger boys added a somersault to game requirements amid much laughter and hooting at the hilarious results. One little boy could not do the somersault and shamefacedly left the game.

Kwani saw his humiliation. "Come and sit by me and tell me the rules. I do not know this game."

He came, grateful to save face. With grave authority he explained how the cob must be grasped, thrown, and the distance measured. "The one who throws the farthest wins all that is wagered."

"I see." She looked down at the round little face with hair askew over his forehead. "Did you know that I tell stories?"

"To girls. For the remembering."

"I have boy stories, too." She didn't, but she would invent some if he wanted to hear. She knew so well how he felt and her heart went out to him.

"What are the stories about?"

"It's a surprise. I will tell you tonight at the evening fire."

He jumped up and ran back to the group and told them, to astonished silence. Such stories were to be told in kivas, and by men only!

Kwani sat by the community fire in the courtyard, facing the small boys who waited curiously. Beyond, in the shadows, sat older boys, pretending not to be interested. The Chiefs and Elders remained in their kivas. Telling boy's stories! It was sacrilegious.

Other fires blazed on roofs and terraces where people sat watching. Word had spread that She Who Remembers would tell boy stories.

"It is improper."

"For men only to tell. In the kivas."

"But she is She Who Remembers. Perhaps the spirits have told her to do this."

"Perhaps . . ."

But they shook their heads.

Kwani smiled at the group in the firelight. "I shall tell the story of one who deserted his people. Do you know what happens when one turns away from his own people?"

"The gods punish him?" one small boy asked shyly.

"You speak wisely," Kwani said with respect, and the boy ducked his head to hide his pride.

"His name was Eagle Boy. He had a cage with eagles in it so the men of his clan would have the feathers for the sacred ceremonies."

The boys nodded. Eagle feathers were essential; caged eagles were not uncommon among the pueblos.

"Eagle Boy cared well for his eagles, especially the female. The bird was so beautiful that Eagle Boy fell in love with her. One day he said, 'If I open the cage and let you fly away, will you take me with you and be my mate?' "

" 'Yes,' she said."

"So Eagle Boy opened the cage. The bird grasped him in her strong talons and they flew high, high, until they came to the great opening in the sky. They flew through it, up and up, past the endless cliffs, until they came out on the other side of Sky World. They flew to the very top of

Turquoise Mountain, so blue that the sun shining on it makes the sky blue."

"Ay!" the boys breathed.

"All the other eagles were there. Eagle Boy and his beautiful mate were given the mating feast, and the eagles gave Eagle Boy an eagle garment so he could fly, too."

Kwani was carried away with the magic of the story as she saw it in her mind. She gestured, using both hands to illustrate the eagles flying. The older boys moved closer and conversation around the other fires ceased as people watched and listened.

"The eagles said to Eagle Boy, 'Do not fly beyond those distant mountains. It is forbidden.' Eagle Boy loved to fly. He flew far . . . far . . . The feeling of being an eagle was wonderful!"

"Ay!" the boys sighed.

"But one day when he was flying, feeling like the strongest, most powerful eagle that ever lived, he said to himself, 'Why should I not see what is beyond the mountains? Who can harm me as I fly on my strong wings?' So he flew over the mountain ridges. And behold! Rising up from the plains beyond was a great city, with high stone walls and towers and many dwellings with windows and fine terraces, and the largest kiva Eagle Boy had ever seen. The ladder pointed up at him, inviting him to enter. It was evening; firelight shone from the windows and terraces. Smoke rose from many fires, and people were walking about and some were eating and some were dancing.

"The Clan Chief came to greet him, saying, 'We invite you to enter our kiva.' So Eagle Boy climbed down the ladder into the great kiva. There were many fine paintings and many wonderful ceremonial objects in niches around the walls. But nobody else was there."

Kwani paused, looking around as though searching for someone in a kiva. There was breathless silence.

"Then a dead woman, a corpse, fell through the kiva opening. Then another. They had been dead so long that they smelled of rotten flesh." Kwani covered her nose with her hand.

"Aye-e-e-e!" The cry came from all who had been listening, and not only the boys.

"Then, all of a sudden, both women came to life! They were beautiful young maidens with smooth, plump arms and big, black eyes. They danced toward him. They laughed and smiled and sang, 'We are dead, dead, dead!' as though it were the happiest thing in the world to be dead."

There were shocked murmurs. The little boys huddled together.

" 'Come, dance with us, laugh with us,' they sang, and Eagle Boy danced and laughed more than he ever had before. 'Spend the night here with us,' the maidens sang, laughing, and they pulled him down to the sleeping mat with soft furs and they lay beside him and put their arms around him."

Kwani looked solemnly at the small faces in the flickering firelight. "At last, Eagle Boy went to sleep. And then . . ." Again she paused dramatically, ". . . and then he woke in the morning and thought it was lighter than it should be in a kiva. So he looked up and he saw that the timbers were rotted and falling, and the roof was gone. He sat up, and then he saw . . . *them* . . ."

She lowered her voice and gazed into each wide-eyed face. "Bones and rotted fingers fell from him where arms of the maidens had been. All around were bits of rotting bodies, hands and feet, and over there"—Kwani pointed—"was a head, with one dead eye staring at him—"

"Aye-e-e-e! Aye-e-e-e!"

"Eagle Boy climbed out of the kiva *fast.* Around him were only crumbled ruins of a city long dead. Only the wind made things move . . . pieces of sandal and bits of garments and other things inching through the grasses . . ." She moved her hands the way a snake moves. "He flew quickly back to the Turquoise Mountain. The eagles were very angry. 'Why did you go where it was forbidden? You are no longer one of us,' they said. And they took away his eagle garment and he could no longer fly. His mate was even more angry. 'Why did you become enamored of Death? However beautiful? Who would dance and take joy in Death? You are no longer my mate.' She grasped him with her strong talons and flew down, down through the sky opening, and far, far to the cliffs and canyons where his people were. When she was high above the place of his pueblo . . . she dropped him."

Kwani pointed dramatically to a nearby place in the courtyard, and people turned to stare, visualizing.

"His head broke open like a pottery jar. His brains spilled out, and broken bones poked themselves from his body—"

There was a great, shuddering sigh. "Aye-e-e-e!"

Kwani rose. "So now you know what happened to Eagle Boy because he deserted his own people. When you are men you will mate with those of other clans and go to live with them. But you will remember that always you are Anasazi, born of the Eagle Clan, and here is where your spirit will enter Sipapu."

There were impressed murmurs through the city. Obviously She Who Remembers had been chosen to be a Storyteller as well.

Okalake stepped from the shadows. "I listened, honored one. It was a good story and one the boys should know. Will you tell another?"

"Yes. But at another time, my brother."

Tiopi sat with a group and as Kwani passed to her dwelling, she said loudly, "What will happen if you leave your people and go with Kokopelli—or is he Anasazi now?"

Laughter.

Kwani ignored them and entered her own doorway. Why hadn't she thought of that? She might be kin to the Blue-eyed One, but she was born Anasazi. If Kokopelli took her away she would be forsaking her own people. Forever.

·28·

The Sun Chief stood with Okalake, watching the sun set at the point of Ceremonies Before Planting. Everyone in the canyons and upon the mesas knew it was time for the Ceremonies, but it was necessary for each clan's Sun Chief to formally verify the time. It would dishonor Sunfather not to do so.

"Tomorrow are the dances," the Chief said. "We begin." He noted again the unhappiness in Okalake's eyes. My son yearns for what he cannot possess, he thought. It was sad—and dangerous. He touched his son's arm. "There are things we must discuss. Come to your mother's home."

Okalake followed him silently. Woshee had prepared Okalake's favorite delicacy, the paper-thin blue corn cakes to be rolled and dipped into spicy sauce made from roots and plants that Woshee gathered at special times of the year and stored in a basket within a stone-lined and covered hole in the floor.

After suitable greetings, the three of them sat on the handsome mats Woshee had made and dipped the cakes into the steaming pot before them. For a time, they talked of trivial things.

Finally, the Sun Chief said, "I hear that Kwani speaks with the young girls as though she has always been She Who Remembers. What does she say?" His eyes twinkled.

Woshee smiled. "She tells them how to get a husband. Perhaps she should follow her own advice."

"Um," the Chief nodded, his mouth full.

Okalake looked at the floor, face impassive. "Kwani has a mate. Kokopelli."

"If he returns," Woshee said.

The Chief nodded. "I hear nothing of him from the runners and the

184

traders from distant places. No one knows where he went after he left the canyon. It is strange."

"He will return," Okalake said.

Woshee glanced at him. "How do you know?"

"He is Kokopelli."

"Yes," the Chief said, grateful for an opening to what must be discussed. "Even if Kwani were not one of the Eagle Clan, she cannot marry here or anywhere. She is mate of Kokopelli."

Okalake gave his father a quick look. Did he know? But his father's face was blank and calm as he wiped his mouth with the back of his hand, and belched in loud appreciation of his wife's cooking.

The Chief turned to his son. "Speaking of marriage, it is long past time for you to take a mate. When Ceremonies are over, I shall excuse you from work on the land. You may visit other clans as you choose and find someone to share your sleeping mat."

Okalake pretended to be busy dipping a cake into what was left of the sauce. Woshee occupied herself with cleaning up. Her feelings ran too deep to risk blurting them out in an unguarded moment.

The Chief continued, "I hear there are two very beautiful girls at the Place of the Serpent Clan who seek mates. It is said they cook well and make fine things."

Okalake shook his head. "I am not ready."

"But we are. I am old. Sipapu calls. Soon you must assume my duties, and you must have sons of your own to teach as I have taught you. There is talk, not good talk, about why you do not marry." Lovingly he put his hand on his son's shoulder. "What must be, must be. She is your sister."

Okalake turned away and shame burned in him. His father knew! How?

The Chief did not remove his hand from his son's shoulder. "You are young and life runs strong in you. We cannot change the life force but we can decide what is wise to do."

"What do you mean?" Okalake's voice was strangely muffled. "Of course she is my sister. I know that."

"Your love for her, your desire for her, you wear like a garment which anyone can see. You must leave us, go to the house of she whom you take as mate, and return only when I am in Sipapu and you must become Sun Chief. You must do this. For Kwani, for yourself, for your mother and me, for the entire clan. It is necessary."

Okalake bowed his head. The truth pierced him like an arrow. He wanted to sob as he did when he was a boy and fell and gashed himself on the rocks. He rose. Unspoken words of love passed between himself and his mother and father.

"I shall do so," he said.

When he had gone, Woshee came and sat beside her husband. "I am afraid for him."

The Chief looked into his wife's face. He took both her hands and breathed upon them. "He honors us, Woshee."

"Have you heard the whispers about Kwani?"

"Men do not listen to the gossip of women."

"But men gossip among themselves, do they not?"

He chuckled. "I suppose so. What is being said about her?"

"She is the only one who has not removed all her winter garments. She still wears the deerskin robe although it is too warm. Why?"

He shrugged. Women would always mystify him. "Maybe she thinks it gives her dignity, now that she is She Who Remembers."

"She is not using her menstrual belt. I see it when I visit her. Tiopi visits also—courtesy requires it—and she says Kwani is not using cedar bark, either. She carried the bowl of bark when Kwani moved. None has been used since."

"But it has been only a few days." *Women.*

"True. But the menstrual belt has not been used for three moons. I have been watching . . ."

Alarm flashed in the Chief's eyes. "What are you saying, woman?"

"I fear that Kwani is pregnant."

"She mated with Kokopelli!" His voice had a shaky edge.

"Tiopi did, also. See how big she is. Kwani has missed her moon flow only for three moons. No, it is not Kokopelli's child she carries."

"Then whose?" But he knew. His stomach contracted.

Suddenly, she began to cry, great shaking sobs. "I fear for him!"

"And I fear for you. Why did you take their punishment on yourself also?"

"I knew, I knew from the beginning that Okalake wanted her. But she wanted only Kokopelli. I thought Okalake would not endanger me . . ." She threw herself into the chief's arms, clinging to him. "I never had a daughter, I liked her, I wanted to protect her, like my own—" Sobs shook her body.

He tried to comfort her. Through tears of his own he said, "Okalake will go away. He will be with another clan, another mate—"

"But he will be punished just the same. You know he will!"

"Only if it is proven that he mated with one of his own clan. Who can prove it?"

Woshee clasped both hands over her mouth, swallowing her sobs. "We must speak quietly. Someone may be listening." She tiptoed to the doorway and looked out. "I've seen that young Zashue following Kwani, watching whenever Okalake came near. Always sneaking about. He is up to something."

"Do you think he knows?"

"If he did he would be shouting it from the Crier Chief's platform. But he may suspect something."

"We must warn Kwani."

"Since she has become She Who Remembers she has been striding about like the Medicine Chief, giving orders. People resent it." She shook her head. "The Old One made a mistake in appointing her; Kwani has not been trained enough to know how to act, what to do and what not to do . . . I don't understand why the Old One did this thing."

"Perhaps she saw in Kwani that which we cannot see. The Old One was wise."

"Perhaps . . ."

Zashue lay on his stomach in his concealed place on the mesa, watching the canyon and the boulder below. Nothing moved but the wind. It was pleasantly warm and the fragrance of sage and juniper comforted his senses. He grew sleepy, and dozed.

He awoke with a start. Something had moved nearby. Cautiously, he raised his head. It was a cougar, heavy with cubs. She paused a moment, lifting her nose to the wind, and although Zashue was downwind, he froze. The animal was too close for him to risk drawing his bow; the sound would alert her. In her fright and pregnancy she might be upon him in an instant.

The head turned and the long tail twitched. Then she padded swiftly away.

Zashue sighed with relief. He fingered his amulet and murmured a prayer of thanks. Glancing at the lengthening shadows, he rose to hurry home. The gods were pleased with him; had they not protected him from the cougar? Sooner or later he would see who came to the hidden cave.

He ran through the canyon, nimbly avoiding thorns and brambles. He jerked to a sudden stop. In his path, beneath a pinyon pine, lay a dead owl. He kicked it aside. Owls were demon spirits, companions of witches.

Witches! He peered all around to be sure no one was watching, then picked three feathers from the owl's tail. They could not harm him, for his medicine was too strong; not only was he son of the Medicine Chief with access to magic, but soon he would be Medicine Chief himself, with the powerful seed of rock crystal between his ribs. He tucked the feathers securely under his belt. Owl's feathers would be useful if Kokopelli did not return.

* * *

Okalake knelt in the kiva of the Sun Society. On the kiva altar were two prayer sticks, the most important he had ever made. For their powers to become effective, he must recite the Prayer Stick Chant accurately. One mistake would nullify his efforts. Placing both hands on the prayer skin mat, he chanted, closing his eyes and rocking to and fro.

> *Seeking yonder along the river courses*
> *The ones who are our fathers,*
> *Male willow,*
> *Female willow,*
> *Four times cutting the straight young shoots,*
> *To my house*
> *I brought my road.*
> *This day*
> *With my warm human hands*
> *I took hold of them.*
> *I gave my prayer sticks human form.*
> *With the striped cloud tail*
> *Of the one who is my grandfather,*
> *The male turkey,*
> *With eagle's thin cloud tail,*
> *With the striped cloud wings*
> *And massed cloud tails*
> *Of all the birds of summer,*
> *With these four times I gave my prayer sticks human form.*
> *With the flesh of the one who is my mother,*
> *Cotton woman,*
> *Even a poorly made cotton thread,*
> *Four times encircling them and tying it about their bodies,*
> *I gave my prayer sticks human form.*
> *With the flesh of the one who is our mother,*
> *Black paint woman,*
> *Four times covering them with flesh*
> *I gave my prayer sticks human form.*

It was finished. Now the prayer sticks were ready to perform their task. One would go into the home of his mother, and the other into the home of She Who Remembers, to protect them while he was gone.

·29·

H*o-á-á! Heiti-na! Ho-á-á! Heiti-na!*
The chant echoed among the cliffs and in the canyons. The dances were under way. Young men who had married and gone to other clans had returned to dance the important Corn Dance and ensure fertility for their own clans. Old men communed with the spirit of the drums, giving them voice, and chanted raptly, beseeching the gods.

Ho-á-á! Heiti-na! Ho-á-á! Heiti-na!
Men and women, side by side, encircled the courtyard in time to the rhythm. Men stomped, echoing the drums, and women stepped more lightly with the chanting.

Each man wore a deerskin around his waist and a fox skin fastened to the back which swung as he danced. Below each knee a band of buckskin held bunches of deer hooves and pendants of polished bone to shake in rhythm with the gourd rattle he carried in his right hand. The left hand held a tuft of hawk feathers that fluttered with each swing of an arm. A band of skunk fur encircled the ankles, and long strings of polished seeds and bone, or shell and stone, hung upon bare chests. Ear pendants of turquoise and feathers hung low, swinging. Braids had been unwound and the masses of dark hair hung free, swaying with the steps of the dance.

Ho-á-á! Heitni-na!
Women wore light cotton mantles draped loosely and tied over one shoulder, allowing the other to be bare. Proudly they wore their tall, flat headdresses made of hide, scraped and flattened, from which white feathers fluttered. The headdresses were painted the color of young cornstalks, embellished with sacred designs in red and yellow. Sprigs of spruce twigs in each hand wagged as the dancers stepped in rhythm.

Hu-hu-hu-hu! Hu-hu-hu-hu! Hu-hu-hu-hu!

189

As the dancers circled, the Medicine Chief rose majestically from his kiva, carrying the basket Kwani had made. He danced to the center of the courtyard and set the basket down, dancing around it. It held three perfect ears of corn, and other objects known only to him.

Abruptly, the chanting and drumming ceased; a distant drum called in a different rhythm. Now, singers emerged from another kiva—twelve men with clay-whitened faces, singing the sacred Corn Song. They were led by Okalake, followed by an aged drummer who wore an eagle's feather behind each ear. They advanced in time to their singing, gesticulating to indicate the planting, the growth, the harvesting of corn, and the sacrifice of corn to the gods.

The Medicine Chief took up the song. The other drummers joined in as the singers circled the basket, surrounded by the dancing couples who changed places, men by men, women by women, moving back and forth. Every roof, every wall, every terrace was crowded with spectators watching devoutly. The Ceremonies would determine the success of the planting—whether or not starvation would be avoided for another year.

Of all the performers, Okalake was the most outstanding. There was almost a desperation in the ardor of his singing, the strength of his pounding steps, and the eloquence of his gestures. It was as though he were doing it for the first time—or the last.

The Medicine Chief drew the three perfect ears of corn from the basket and held them overhead. The husks were tied together by red and yellow cords, each tipped with white feathers representing clouds. Dancing in rhythm, he offered the corn to the Six Sacred Directions, then replaced the corn in the basket.

The beat of the drums ceased; the song and dancing ended. It was time for intermission.

The performers gathered in groups or mingled with spectators. Exercise and the warming sun made the clay on faces melt and run down chins and necks, and there was a crowd around the water jug as mugs were passed for drinking. Children resumed their play in the courtyard while women and girl dancers rested, enjoying envious glances at their ornate headdresses and their beautiful necklaces, bracelets, rings, and ear ornaments. Babies nursed. Women gossiped. Old men related their extraordinary participation in wonderful dances of long ago, while old women criticized the costumes of the dancers and singers who were not as good as they used to be. The sun rose higher, the sky shimmered, and the red cliffs, with sharp black shadows in every crevice, towered over all.

Okalake knelt before the altar in his kiva, praying to the sacred fetishes and to the gods to protect his people, especially Kwani, while he was away. Beside him were his pack and traveling clothes; he would place the prayer sticks where they belonged and leave while people watched the Ceremonies.

Hiding the prayer sticks under his breechcloth, he sauntered to the home of his mother who, with Kwani, sat in back of the cave with a group of women, talking and nibbling pine nuts. He placed a prayer stick against the wall inside the doorway; the other was left inside the doorway of Kwani's new home. At the kiva he washed the clay from his face with water from the bathing bowl, and changed his clothes. He was ready to go.

Footsteps descended the ladder and his father entered. He glanced at his son without concealing his affection. "What were you leaving in your mother's home and in the home of She Who Remembers?"

Okalake smiled. His father missed little.

"Prayer sticks."

"Ah." The Sun Chief nodded. "That is good."

"I request permission to leave now."

"Your part in the Ceremonies is ended." Neither wanted the ordeal of goodbyes. Okalake breathed on his father's hand, shouldered his pack and climbed from the kiva. People were crowding to watch the next performers come running and stumbling into the courtyard with hoots and yells. These were the Delight Makers, six clowns, one of whom was Zashue. No one paid attention as Okalake left the city, pausing now and again for a backward glance at the place and the people he loved.

The clowns, naked but for flapping breechcloths, were thickly covered with white clay and ornamented with horizontal black stripes painted on around torso, arms, and legs. Black circles outlined eyes and mouth, and their hair was gathered in knots upon the top of their heads, with protruding corn husks. Deer hooves dangled and rattled from each wrist; bone pendants encircled each leg below the knee.

The Delight Makers began a loud and ribald conversation, sparing no opportunity for obscene remarks accompanied by exaggerated gestures, all greeted with howls of laughter.

The leader was a favored person in the clan. He was short and squat, with small eyes that seemed to have been punched into his round, pudgy face at random, so one eye was a bit higher than the other. He had a short, bumpy nose and wide mouth with a gap in his front teeth through which he could whistle piercingly, to the envy of all. With every obscene remark he whistled, flapped his elbows like wings, and kicked the clown next to him so that the fellow sprawled with a great show of grotesque suffering. One rolled on his stomach and pounded his hands and kicked his feet; another grabbed his legs and dragged him around the courtyard to approving yells. From roofs and terraces corn cakes were thrown down to performers and devoured on the spot.

Finally the Delight Makers scattered and climbed up the ladders and into dwellings from which they emerged with whatever they fancied to enhance their antics. One brought out a metate and mano, set them down, and gave an exaggerated imitation of a woman grinding corn. Another tossed everything out the door, in a hilarious housecleaning. One grabbed a bundle of reeds and squatted as though giving it birth; another snatched the bundle and held it like a baby, pretending to nurse.

The commotion gave Zashue the opportunity for which he waited. He and his father chafed under Kwani's attitude of superiority. Her magical powers were a threat to the prestige of the Medicine Chief. It was intolerable. If Kokopelli did not return and take her away . . .

Owl's feathers, the possessions of witches, would rid them of her if it could be proven they were hers. The three feathers concealed at his waist made him uncomfortable. Discovered on him, their consequences could be disastrous. He had to place them so that it would be assumed they belonged to Kwani.

While attention was riveted on the other clowns, Zashue scampered up to the place where Kwani used to live, and stepped inside. He covered the doorway, knelt in the darkness in a far corner. He scratched and clawed a small hole in the floor, while his heart pounded for fear someone might enter. He took the three feathers and dropped them into the hole, covered them, and stomped the dirt down. If it became necessary, he would see that the feathers were discovered at an opportune time.

He stepped outside, making a comical grimace as though annoyed because nothing was there for him to take. He ran down the ladders and into another house where he took a cooking pot outside and pretended to urinate into it, to the joyful howls of bystanders.

Kwani turned away. The Delight Makers were part of the Ceremonies Before Planting of every clan. Usually she enjoyed them as much as anybody. But today seemed to be different. Perhaps it was concern for her swelling belly. Soon other women would wear little but an ornamental, fringed belt looped between the legs and tied around the waist with fringes dangling. Pregnancy would be impossible to conceal.

Again there was a great whoop of laughter, and Kwani turned to watch the leader of the Delight Makers being readied for his highlight performance, one talked about and awaited eagerly from year to year. A giant penis of buckskin was fitted over his own and fastened with thongs between his legs and around his waist. There were ribald calls from the crowd, and much laughter as he waggled it with a leer.

Assuming an arrogant stance, he looked down his nose in unmistakable imitation of Kokopelli.

"Come mate with me!" he shouted to the girls in Kokopelli's Toltec accent.

The girls giggled, but none came. This was part of the performance, to deny him. He ran up the ladders and confronted Kwani.

The giant penis wiggled. "Come mate with me! Come mate with me!"

Kwani laughed as she was expected to do. But under her breath she hissed, "You go too far!"

The penis thrust closer. "Come, little sister," he crooned with a leer. "Mate!"

Kwani froze, but only for a moment. Slapping the giant penis aside she came face to face with the clown who involuntarily stepped backward and nearly tumbled over the edge of the roof terrace.

Kwani's voice was low, but it carried all the way to the courtyard. "Do you presume to insult the mate of Kokopelli? Do you dare to insult She Who Remembers?"

"I am Delight Maker. I delight," he blustered.

"I shall inform Kokopelli that you do not delight *me*. The gods shall know that I—"

"I amuse only," he interrupted, retreating. His pudgy face assumed a look of ludicrous mock embarrassment; he made his way back down the ladders with exaggerated clumsiness. There was relieved laughter. The leader meant no insult; he was delighting only. The clowns resumed their performance.

But Kwani had a sick feeling in her stomach. Where was Okalake? How could he allow what had happened? She needed him, his protection, his comforting presence. She needed *him*. Where was he?

The leader was strutting around the courtyard with movements that grew increasingly suggestive. To the cheers of onlookers, he fell to his knees while the giant penis pumped and pumped in symbolic mating with Earthmother.

This, after all, was what the Ceremonies were for—to ensure fertility for the planting. He whistled in rhythm, louder and louder, until the pumping ceased; he sprawled on his back, waving arms and legs wildly in the air. Two clowns ran and lifted him, and carried him to his kiva. They swung him back and forth as though to throw him in, then changed their minds and lowered him down the ladder head first.

"More! More!" the crowd yelled.

But the performance of the Delight Makers was over for another year, to be reviewed and discussed endlessly, especially the confrontation between the leader and She Who Remembers. Already, there were many whispers behind hands.

Where was Okalake? Kwani searched the entire city from where she stood, but he was not there. She felt a sudden overwhelming longing for him. Perhaps, while everyone was watching the Ceremonies, they could slip away to the hideaway cave unnoticed . . . She walked through the city, looking for him, but he had gone.

The Ceremonies were over. Ribaldry had lasted long into the night; many a young man had proven his own virility with a young woman as eager as he. Miko had found a young man she liked and was aglow, relating the details of the experience to all who would listen.

It turned cold suddenly; a few flakes fell. There would be a light snowfall, then the sun would shine again and the snow would melt, sinking into the soil, preparing it to receive the seed of the planting. So it was, so it had always been, the endless turning of the time circle.

As Okalake followed the trails southeast, he encountered small cairns here and there, conical piles of stones which were shrines to Masau'u. He added another stone to the pile. Masau'u was god of the underworld from where all people had traveled to reach the upper, fourth world, and to which they returned after death. Therefore, Masau'u was god of both life and death, and of travelers here upon this fourth world. Because traveling was often dangerous, and the farther one went from his own pueblo the more dangerous it became, homage to Masau'u was important.

Okalake had been noting how centuries of farming had depleted fertility in many places. New land must be cleared, and new dams built. Not only had winters grown colder in recent years, but rainfall had diminished alarmingly. It was becoming more difficult to provide enough water for crops to feed a growing population.

The Great City in the canyon to the southeast, built in a half circle where many, many people used to live—was it true it was nearly deserted as farmers were forced farther and farther southward in search of new land? He wanted to see the city and to see the Sun Circles again on the giant butte that soared in remote majesty from the canyon floor. He knew his solar calculations were correct but he wanted the pleasure of having them verified by the wisdom of the ancient ones who used the sunlight of noonday, rather than that of sunrise or sunset, as a sunspear marking.

He wished also to verify again his calculations as to when first flowers would bloom—the time he had left with Kwani. Only after she was gone would he take a mate, only then. He would lie with eager girls of other clans to slake his manhood hunger, but none would become his mate until Kokopelli took Kwani away. Meanwhile, he would return to his hideaway cave, waiting for Kwani to come to him—if she would. Then he would hold her again, oh yes, and love her again. And he would return the spear he had kept for safekeeping. If she did not come, he would watch for her on the mesa or in the canyon. His heartbeat quickened, thinking of it.

"Ho! Okalake!"

It was the Chief of the tiny Fox Clan, a group of eight or ten who lived in a cliff so high and inaccessible that access was by rope ladder only. The Chief had discovered the small cave while hunting one day and had himself lowered from the mesa top by rope to explore it.

"Ho!" Okalake called, waving.

The ladder began to dangle as it was lowered. "Come to our fire!"

"I cannot come now, but I thank you. I shall come another time."

The ladder was pulled up again. "Come before the next moon. My mate gives me another son."

"Good! Good! I shall come for the naming ceremony."

There were shouted greetings and invitations as Okalake made his way through the canyons, following trails centuries old, some of them originally game trails. Okalake noted with dismay how parched the land was, even after recent rains and snowfall. Moisture did not go deep enough to nourish Earthmother as she required. Too many trees had been cut; none remained of the tall ones that used to be. Only scraggly trees and brush were left, and even those had to be cleared to find soil rich enough to nourish the planting. It was ominous. Perhaps some day his people, also, must leave . . . He loved these canyons, these soaring cliffs, these fragrant mesas. He loved the undulating line of the mountains across the horizon, crests still streaked with snow. He stopped to gaze, allowing his spirit freedom.

Some small boys with bows and arrows came quietly around a bend, sharp-eyed and alert.

"We greet you, Okalake."

"My spirit rejoices, young hunters."

"Have you seen a rabbit?"

"No, but there are rabbits about. See?" He pointed to a small cluster of little, round, black balls drying in the sun.

"We know rabbits are about," the leader said with dignity, not deigning to look where Okalake pointed.

Okalake restrained a smile. "Of course. It was unnecessary for me to say that. Good luck with your hunting."

He had gone only a short distance before the boys were on hands and knees, examining the scat intently to determine how old it was. Okalake knew they would do that and did not look back. It seemed only a few moons ago that he had done the same, when he was a child . . . long ago.

Occasionally he stopped to talk with farmers already removing brush with their strong digging sticks or cutting juniper trees with stone axes, in preparation for planting.

As daylight waned he accepted an invitation from the Badger Clan, famous for the excellence of their women's cooking. He sat with the family of the Clan Chief at their fire, admiring the handsome blankets hanging from pegs and the bowls and mugs of intricate black and white design.

"Do you go for trading?" the Chief asked.

"No. I go to the Great City in the Canyon."

"Ah." The Chief nodded. "The last time I was there few people remained. Whom do you seek?"

"No one. I go to consult the Sun Circles and will also visit the city while I am near. Is the Sun Chief still there?"

"He believes it is his duty to remain, to continue with his duties. He is old. Sipapu will welcome him soon."

His wife nodded. "It is the witches."

"Witches were everywhere there, bringing fevers and weakness and hard coughing. Many departed for the south. Witches were everywhere active this winter, more so than usual."

They sat in silence, pondering the mysteries of the inevitable.

A young woman entered carrying a round, flat basket holding thin blue corn cakes. She was pretty, with round, full breasts and a small waist swelling to inviting proportions below. Something about her reminded him of Kwani: he experienced a sudden arousal.

They rolled the cakes and dipped them into a tasty stew of mountain sheep seasoned with new herbs. Okalake was hungry and ate ravenously, managing a satisfactory rumbling belch afterward.

The girl smiled at him, her dark eyes glancing briefly into his with a look that was unmistakable. This was not unnoticed by her father who belched politely, wiped his mouth with the back of his hand, and said casually, "It is said that you do not have a mate."

"No."

"That is surprising," his wife said. "Why not?"

Okalake shifted uncomfortably. "There is no one . . ."

The woman waved an imperious hand at her daughter. "Our guest has had a long journey and must rest. Find a comfortable mat and take him to the storage room."

The girl rose, smiling. She took a mat from a pile in a corner, and led Okalake from the room, through the crowd of people gathered at cooking fires who greeted him as they passed and smiled behind their hands. Okalake followed as the girl climbed ladders to the storage room, a long, low-ceilinged crevice at top in back of the cave where food was stored. At this season of the year it was sufficiently empty to allow two people to enter, provided they did so on hands and knees.

The girl carried the mat to the darkest recess, lay down on it, and pulled her robe aside. The pale curves of her ripe body glowed. Lost in darkness, in surging passion as the eager young body responded to his, Okalake listened to a chant in his brain like a heartbeat: Kwani . . . Kwani . . . Kwani.

It was not quite dawn when Okalake left, pausing at the home of his host, as was his right, to put corn cake and dried meat into his backpack, and to fill his small water jug at the community jar. He was careful to be quiet as he stepped over sleepers and around dozing dogs. Soon he was heading southeast again to the long, wide canyon where the Great City lay. Refreshed and renewed, he began to run, an easy lope.

"Ho! Ho!" he called out to no one, and laughed at himself.

It was late in the day when he approached the curved walls from the north. The half-moon-shaped city faced south and its back was turned to him; the city inside the walls was concealed but for three-and four-story buildings clustered around the perimeter. No dogs came barking to greet him, no welcoming people, no curious children appeared. No drums, no flutes, no shouts or laughter, no sound at all came from within the city's tall walls.

Sick at heart, Okalake followed the curve of the walls to where the circle was cut in half, as walls faced south in a straight line. At the entrance, he stopped to smell, to look, and to listen. It was silent; the great plaza was empty. Tall buildings stared at him with empty windows; stones had crumbled and fallen here and there, and weeds grew between them.

Grieving, Okalake raised an arm in spontaneous greeting and farewell. He remembered when his father brought him here as a boy; a giant metropolis then, powerful and wealthy, with the greatest and most respected Sun Chief of the Anasazi nation. He was an imposing man, tall and muscular, with strong arms that lifted Okalake high so that he might see throught the small corner window which allowed sunlight to enter and illuminate the altar of the Sun Chief's lodge when it was time to turn Sunfather back to his northern home.

"Ho!" Okalake called, but there was no answer. Occasionally, he saw a jar left standing in a corner, or frayed sandals or broken arrows or other things left behind.

He was nearly at the Chief's doorway when instinct spoke a warning. He stood silent, all senses immediately alert, straining to hear, to see, to smell danger. Nothing. Then he glanced down to the stone walk covered with dust, and froze. A footprint was there; he recognized the moccasin that made it. Apache.

He jumped into shadow against the wall, pulling his flint knife from its sheath. His eyes scanned every window, every shadow, every crevice where an enemy might hide.

Cautiously, he peered inside the Chief's chamber. The old man had been dead for a long time; the bones were nearly clean. They lay in grotesque disarray, with only a shredded undergarment thrown aside. Someone had stripped the skeleton of clothing and vandalized the sacred room. Prayer sticks and mats were shredded, fetishes were strewn about and bowls were broken, but blankets and other valuables were gone. Apache footprints told the story.

Okalake squatted to examine the tracks. They were recent, made by the same man during the last few days. Apaches seldom traveled far alone. Where was he now, and where were the others? Okalake searched every room, every kiva; only spirits were there. He returned outside and found moccasin tracks leading toward the Great River of the South. Good. They would be camping by the river soon, several days away.

It was nearly sunset as Okalake followed the canyon eastward to where it forked like a river. In the center of that split, an enormous butte soared to the darkening sky. The top was round, like a kiva, and surrounded by cliffs leading to sloping banks—a majestic, holy place. He would climb it in the morning.

Exhausted, he laid his head on his pack. The stars were hidden intermittently by drifting clouds. Which of those distant campfires was that of the great Sun Chief whose bones lay scattered in the empty city? Okalake chose one and spoke to it respectfully.

"Revered One, I have not forgotten you. I go to the Sun Circles and will return to honor your bones with proper burial and put your spirit at peace."

The cold dawn woke him. He drank sparingly from his jug, and ate a bit of venison. The trail to the place of the Sun Circles followed a steep bank, then curved around the top to a point near the summit.

He felt renewed and totally alive as he breathed the cool air deeply and began the climb. Now and then he paused to gaze over the canyon; it was vast and empty. Nothing moved but the wind in fragrant brush and grasses, or a dancing whirl of dust. He reached the cliff walls that formed a natural circle and followed a dim, precipitous trail to the sun watcher's station near the summit.

At last, it was there—the sacred place. Three massive slabs stood on end, leaning against the cliff's wall. Behind the slabs were the Sun Circles, hidden except for one who knew they were there.

Okalake tossed corn meal to the Six Sacred Directions, chanting a prayer. Then he knelt and looked behind the slabs. Carved into the rock were two spirals: the larger one just behind the slabs, the smaller one below and to the left of the larger.

The edges of the slabs directed the sunlight, allowing a narrow shaft, the sunspear, to appear on the wall and slide down on the spirals in such a way that the Sun Chief knew exactly when Sunfather should be returned to the north, and when he reached the halfway mark between his northern and southern homes; when he should be returned from north to south; and when all important events and ceremonies should take place.

By observing the position of the sunspear in relation to the spirals, Okalake estimated the days until first flowers bloomed. His calculations had been correct.

Elated at his success, he climbed to the summit and gazed into hazy distance. The sky was blue, so blue that wings of a soaring hawk sliced the blueness. Beyond, far away, a mountain curved and beckoned. Surrounded by beauty, by infinity, his spirit soared and he sang:

My heart flies to the mountain
Like a bird to its distant nest.

He did not hear the movement behind him nor see the Apache arrow that pierced him through.

❖30❖

Woshee poked her bone needle through the rabbit skin that would be a robe for a baby. Infants were always being born into one clan or another, and she liked to have gifts ready for the birthing ceremony. She pulled the thread of yucca twine through the skin, and paused, looking across the city to the canyon where Okalake had gone six days ago.

Communication between clans was constant, and everyone knew by now that Okalake had spent the night with the Chief's daughter at the Place of the Badger Clan, and had said he was going to the Great City and to see the Sun Circles. No one had seen him since. Did he change his mind and go elsewhere? If so, where?

Apaches were said to be traveling south. But Apaches were known to reverse direction and to turn back for sudden raids. There was stockpiling of arrows and gathering of stones suitable for throwing down upon enemies. Sentinels were posted up and down the canyons. But the Apaches continued their swift march south; people breathed easier. Anasazi were farmers, not warriors, but they could fight fiercely to protect their families and their homes.

Perhaps Okalake had gone eastward for trading, and would seek a mate on his return. It was not like him to take a mate from a clan far distant from the home he loved. He would be back.

But foreboding wafted like a cold breeze. Her womb gave fruit but once; her entire being rested in her only child. Again she concentrated on the bone needle. Who would wear this tiny robe next winter? If Okalake's mate got pregnant right away . . . She counted on her fingers. Yes, the robe would be useful then, in cold weather. She worked with new interest. A garment for a potential grandchild!

Kwani. The thought came unbidden. What if . . .

Laying her work aside, she climbed down to Kwani's dwelling. She was sitting outside, preparing clay to make a pottery jar, and did not notice Woshee standing at a distance, watching.

Kwani was spreading the blue-gray clay in the sun, to dry thoroughly. She would grind it in her metate and mix it with finely ground bits of broken pottery for temper to keep the jar from shrinking and cracking as it dried. She picked out the stones and foreign particles. Woshee noted again the natural grace of Kwani's movements, the long hair neatly dressed in squash blossom coils, the thick, dark lashes hiding the blue eyes as she looked down at her work. Woshee inspected the round face as though she were seeing it for the first time. There was allure in the smooth cheeks, the small nose, the seductively curving mouth. The sweet curves of her body . . . It was not difficult to understand why Okalake . . .

Kwani suddenly sat upright and clasped her hand to her abdomen, smiling. She feels life, Woshee thought. With a sharp pang of mixed feelings she returned to her sewing. Her hands trembled as she worked. Was this why Okalake had gone to who knew where? Because Kwani carried his child and he wanted to avoid confrontation? But she would be punished along with Kwani . . . Okalake would not leave them unprotected.

The prayer sticks. They were for protection. Did he deliberately leave her and Kwani to face consequences alone? A knot tightened in her stomach. If Kwani had not come, Okalake would have a mate by now. He would not be gone without explanation all this time. Someone else would be She Who Remembers.

Tiopi, probably. Since her pregnancy, Tiopi had mellowed. She had outlined her left hand over her doorway five times—one for each moon of pregnancy so far—and filled in the outlines with red ochre. The hand was a sacred symbol. When nine hands were lined up overhead, Kokopelli's child would be born. The row of crimson symbols would remain to remind all who entered that Tiopi nurtured the sacred seed in this place.

Controlling her trembling fingers, Woshee completed the tiny robe, and walked with her usual dignity to where Kwani was still bent over the clay.

"I greet you, Esteemed One," Woshee said.

Kwani looked up with a smile of pleasure to see the woman she most admired and for whom she had a warm affection. "I am making a jar for Kokopelli to trade." She noticed the small fur robe in Woshee's hand. A quick look flicked in her eyes, and was gone.

Woshee held up the little garment for Kwani to see, saying softly, so others would not hear, "See what I have made for my grandchild." She leaned closer. "We must talk. Come to my fire."

Kwani followed Woshee up the terraces and the ladders. Her knees felt weak. Woshee knew! Did others know? Was that why Okalake had gone?

Inside her dwelling Woshee pulled the door curtain closed before they sat.

"I know you carry Okalake's child," she said.

Kwani stared at her with a stricken gaze. How could she have endangered this woman who had befriended her, this mother of Okalake? And endangered her unborn child! She would deny it.

"No!"

"Whose child, then?"

Kwani turned away in panic. What could she say?

"Answer me, Kwani."

"I cannot."

"You must. The child—"

"It was the basket. The spirits of the basket entered me," Kwani blurted in sudden inspiration. "Earthmother, Moon Woman, Kokopelli. Their spirits entered me and now I shall have a Spirit Child."

Woshee smiled grimly. "And why have you kept this wondrous miracle a secret?"

"I am waiting for Kokopelli. He will announce the coming birth of the Spirit Child." She hugged her arms, carried away with her idea.

"M-m-m-m." Woshee studied Kwani's flushed face. "You are She Who Remembers, so perhaps you will be believed."

"You do not believe me?"

"No."

Blue eyes turned away from dark ones. There was no deceiving Woshee. "I cannot endanger you, or my baby, or Okalake. Yes, it is Okalake's child." Kwani's voice broke. "I must make people believe it is a Spirit Child. Help me!"

Running footsteps outside stopped at the door. "Kwani! Kwani, are you in there?"

"Who is it?" Woshee asked.

"It is I, Ki-ki-ki. I have a surprise!"

Woshee whispered, "We can't turn her away, it will seem suspicious."

Kwani pulled the curtain aside and stepped over the door sill. "Look!" Ki-ki-ki was so excited she forgot the formalities. She held out both hands cupped together. "Guess what I have!"

Kwani smiled in spite of herself. "I cannot guess. Tell me."

Slowly, Ki-ki-ki opened her hands. She held a flower, a globe mallow the color of a summer sunset. "See! The first flower! I found it in the canyon. Kokopelli is coming!" She jumped up and down. "Kokopelli will come and take you away and I shall be mate of Okalake!"

Woshee stepped outside. "Okalake has gone to find a mate and will not be back," she said gently.

"Oh." The girl's face crumpled. "I thought . . . everybody says he has gone for trading . . ." She threw the flower down and ran away.

Kwani picked up the flower and cupped its rosy glow in her hand. *Kokopelli* . . .

"Let us make plans," Woshee said. Together they stepped back inside.

Grass grew green, leaves budded on bare trees and shrubs, and flowers bloomed, but Kokopelli did not come. Birds returned, and canyons carried the rich, earthy smell of damp leaf mold and plants growing, but there was no word of Okalake. The exuberance of spring was shadowed; all was not well. Woshee grew thin, and dark shadows ringed her eyes. The Sun Chief smiled seldom. Where was Okalake?

Yatosha was consulted. Would he and his hunters go south and east in their search for game, and learn what they could of Okalake?

Yatosha agreed, but some of the hunters were not pleased. There were no mountain sheep in the wide canyons; they hungered for the rich meat and their mates wanted the skins and furs for next winter's robes. As for Okalake . . . they shrugged. He had found a woman somewhere. But they would go, and search. Preparations were made for their departure; they would be gone for several days or until they had all the game they could carry home.

It grew warmer; although it was still cool in the morning and evening and during the night, the days were hot. Children ran naked, reveling in it. Men wore breechcloths only, and women brought out the woven belts and small aprons they had made during the winter and wore them with pride. Only Kwani still wore a light robe.

"What is she hiding?" some asked.

"She Who Remembers is not as we are. She is different."

"Perhaps she feels it is more seemly to wear a robe."

"Kwani does not care about what is seemly."

"I think Kwani is pregnant," someone said.

There was shocked silence, although the possibility had been whispered for weeks.

"Who was it?"

Silence. Everyone knew who it probably was.

As though it were an afterthought, another said, "I wonder when Okalake will return from trading?"

"Woshee says he goes to seek a mate. He may not return until it is time for him to become Sun Chief."

"By then, Kokopelli will have taken Kwani away."

They nodded, thinking how that would solve everything.

Another moon passed and Kokopelli did not come.

Yatosha and the hunters had returned with game, but with no word of Okalake; the Sun Chief invited Yatosha into his kiva for conference.

"Did you visit the Great City?"

"We stopped there, but the city is empty. Bad spirits abound; the hunters refused to enter."

"Tracks?"

"Old ones. Apache. They passed that way heading south. We did not linger."

The Sun Chief turned away abruptly to conceal his fear. "I request a meeting of the Chiefs and elders. Okalake must be found."

They sat in a semicircle in the Lodge of the Medicine Chief, solemn-faced, facing the altar before which a small fire burned. Spread before the Medicine Chief were his objects of strong medicine, but none so strong as the small stone shaped like Motsni, Masau'u's bird. At Masau'u's bidding, his bird flew everywhere, over mesas and mountains and rivers, seeking those travelers whom Masau'u chose to assist. The Medicine Chief had discovered the stone on the bank of a distant river when he was a boy; it was Masau'u himself who sent it to tell that boy he would become a powerful Medicine Chief one day.

The ceremonial pipe was passed. As each Chief or elder blew a small cloud to ascend to Masau'u, the Medicine Chief chanted a prayer, beseeching Masau'u to send Motsni to find Okalake. The pipe made the rounds with many small clouds ascending. The Medicine Chief finished the prayer with a final flourish of the rattle. For a time, all sat in silence.

At last the Sun Chief spoke. "All of us must do what we can to pursuade Masau'u to send Motsni to find my son. I shall go alone to search for him. I request a gathering of all the clan for a Calling Ceremony to bring the spirit of Masau'u to us so suitable sacrifices may be made and our request granted."

There was a stunned silence. Calling ceremonies were usually conducted to lure game for hunters. To call Masau'u, the god of Death as well as of Life, was dangerous. What if he took the Caller back with him to Sipapu?

The Medicine Chief scowled. "Is my medicine not sufficient that a Calling Ceremony is necessary?" His face flushed darkly.

Huzipat, Clan and Elder Chief, said in a reasonable tone, "Our Sun

Chief departs to search for Okalake. Both require Masau'u's assistance, and the more prayers and homage which are offered to him, the more likely he will be to hear. All know the powers of your medicine"—he bowed respectfully to the Medicine Chief—"but it is expedient to involve all members of the clan. I agree with the Sun Chief that a Calling Ceremony take place."

Whoever did the actual Calling would be in gravest danger! "If my medicine is not powerful enough, then my Calling would not be powerful enough." The Medicine Chief smiled grimly. "Whom do you propose to do this Calling?"

They gazed down at their hands in uncomfortable silence. They were acutely aware of the dangers. To name one to do the Calling might be sentencing him to Sipapu.

Yatosha spoke. "I have heard good things about the teaching of She Who Remembers, and about her story of Eagle Boy. It was felt that she brought the spirits among us and that the spirits were gratified. I suggest that She Who Remembers call the spirit of Masau'u at the ceremonial fire and that the Calling Ceremony be prepared."

The men gazed at him with pleased surprise. Even the Medicine Chief nodded agreement. It was the ideal solution. To call game or spirits, it was necessary for the Caller to relate all that was known about them during the Ceremony. This made the game or spirits *want* to come. Who could tell about Masau'u better than a Storyteller? Besides, if Masau'u did take Kwani with him to Sipapu, Kokopelli could not blame the clan for his mate's death.

The Medicine Chief said, "I shall inform She Who Remembers of the honor we bestow."

They nodded silently.

Only the old Sun Chief bent his head in troubled silence.

·31·

$\mathbf{K}$wani and the Medicine Chief stood on the terrace outside her door.

She said, "I know of calling the game but I know nothing of calling spirits." She stared, astonished.

He returned her stare with an imperial gaze. "You know the story of Masau'u, do you not?"

"Yes."

"You will be allowed to reveal all you know about Masau'u. However, you will not be permitted to participate in other events of the Calling Ceremony."

"I am not sure I care to participate at all. It is not the duty of She Who Remembers." She turned away.

"You wish for Okalake to return, I presume?" He restrained the sarcasm, but it was evident, nevertheless.

"Of course."

"The Sun Chief goes to find him. You would like for him to return safely?"

"Naturally. But—"

"Then you can hardly refuse to participate. Unless, of course, you have reasons for not wanting Okalake, and his father, of course, to return." He smiled widely.

Kwani whirled to face him. People had gathered, pretending not to listen, but edging closer.

She said, "I will confer with the spirits of my necklace and the medicine arrow to decide whether or not to participate in the Calling Ceremony. However"—she raised her voice slightly for the benefit of the bystanders—if I do decide to participate, it will be because of what the spirits tell me to do, and not because the Medicine Chief needs me to accomplish for him what he is unable to do on his own."

She turned and entered her doorway, yanking the curtain behind her.

It was only too true that she cared—too much—whether or not Okalake returned; and cared a great deal for Sun Chief's safety, as well. But regardless of the Medicine Chief, she knew she would agree to be the Caller for the ceremony. Anything to bring Okalake and his father safely home.

Yatosha could feel the trembling of the rabbit in his pack. The animal was small but well formed, suitable for the sacrifice. It had been caught in a snare; there were no marks anywhere on it. Yatosha's duty as Hunting Chief was to provide an animal whose blood would sanctify the sacrificial corn. He glanced at the sun; the day was nearly spent.

Preparations for the Calling Ceremony were underway when he arrived home. Preliminary ceremonies would take place in the kiva of the Medicine Chief with only the Chiefs and Elders present. The sacrifices and the calling would be held in the courtyard where everyone in the city could attend. Yatosha was the last of the Chiefs to arrive.

"You have the animal?"

Yatosha opened the bag and dumped the rabbit upon the floor. It stood frozen in fear, then hopped uncertainly into the shadows.

The Medicine Chief nodded. "It is suitable." Taking his spirit rattle, he began the Chant-Before-Sacrifice to appease the spirit of the rabbit for taking its life. The aged drummer added his beat, chanting raptly, accompanied by the chants of the others gathered there.

The rabbit huddled silently against the wall.

Kwani stood in the dimness of her dwelling, clutching the medicine arrow with one hand, pressing the scallop shell to her with the other. Closing her eyes, she commanded the unseen.

"Make me wise. Make me strong. Make me unafraid to call the spirit of Masau'u."

She stood there for some time, but she was still afraid.

"Kwani."

It was Woshee. The two women stood looking at one another in silent communication. "You are afraid?" Woshee whispered.

"Yes."

Woshee nodded. Suddenly she pulled Kwani to her in shaken embrace. "Help them find Okalake!" Her voice choked with tears. "My mate goes to search . . ."

"I know. I will try."

As they stepped out into the darkness, the courtyard was crowded. People sat around an altar before which a fire blazed. The Sun Chief sat with the other Chiefs and Elders in a semicircle before the altar, a waist-high pile of large rocks in a stepping-stone arrangement. On each step was a perfect ear of corn. The top held a prayer stick, eagle feathers, and a bowl of water from a sacred spring. Firelight made eerie, wrinkled patterns on the rocks.

To one side sat the musicians, instruments ready. On the other side was the Medicine Chief in his ceremonial robe of deerskin adorned with turquoise beads and shells, and painted with bright colors in a mystical design. His face was freshly painted with the usual black zig-zag stripes. In addition, a scarlet line undulating like a serpent crossed his brow, swooping down to encircle one eye—the mark of one who would make a blood sacrifice. The encircled eye seemed to gleam from a secret place.

A sweep of the Medicine Chief's spirit rattle was the signal to begin.

The drummer beat a slow, pulsing rhythm, gradually increasing to crescendo, and stopped. Silence. Firelight flickered against the rocks, darkness enfolded them like the darkness of Sipapu where Masau'u, the Skeleton Man, awaited.

Woshee touched Kwani. "Speak now."

Kwani opened her mouth to begin, but her voice would not come. She tried again.

"It was a long time ago. Before people entered the Fourth World. It was dark . . . cold and dark . . ." Her voice grew stronger. "The people were unhappy. They quarreled among themselves, they wanted to travel up to another world. They feared Masau'u, who was made from nothing and came from nowhere. No one had ever seen him." She looked around, peering into the shadows, as though searching for Masau'u. "People were tired of the dark, of the cold. It was said that Masau'u had a fire, a fine fire, where he sat and warmed himself. If they found Masau'u, he might give them fire."

The drummer began to rock back and forth, chanting softly, "Masau'u . . . Masau'u . . ." His hands stroked the drum, making it echo in a whisper.

"And then they heard it! She paused, as though listening. "They heard footsteps up there." She pointed upward; everyone gazed up at the great, arched dome and the starlit sky beyond.

"Masau'u, Masau'u," the drum whispered.

"They said, 'We must send someone to see who walks up there.' Four brave men went, but returned, frightened. Then four others left, to find their way in the darkness."

Rattles hissed and echoed with the drum, and people began to sway with the beat.

"They became lost and did not know where to go. And then Motsni, Masau'u's bird, found them. 'Follow me,' Motsni said. They could not see Motsni in the darkness, only the sound of his wings. Masau'u sent him."

"*Masau'u, Masau'u . . .*" The people moaned, swaying to and fro. Flutes joined, like faint spirit voices.

"They followed the sound of the wings, and came to the Fourth World. There, far away in the distance"—Kwani pointed to the opposite mesa shrouded in darkness—"they saw a fire, and someone was seated there with his back to them."

"*Masau'u . . .*" the flutes sang.

"Motsni flew away. They were there alone, with the Skeleton Man sitting far away, over there, by his fire." Kwani rose, turning to face the altar. "They knew, they had been told, that Masau'u could not see in daylight. Everywhere he went, he carried a torch." She leaned down and picked up a burning branch, holding it overhead like a torch. "His magical fire!"

"*Masau'u, Masau'u.*" The people's moan was louder. The drum moaned with them and the rattles hissed in echo.

Kwani dropped the branch back into the fire, but remained standing. In the firelight she seemed to be one from another world, a spirit being.

"The men were afraid. But they went closer to him as he sat by the fire, facing away from them. His head was big, bigger than any squash. There was no hair on it!"

The flute gave a startled trill.

"The men came to where the fire was, so they could see his face. And they saw him!" She stared at the altar as though transfixed. "He wore fine garments, and many necklaces of turquoise, and turquoise orna-ments at each ear. But his *face . . .* " She covered her eyes with both hands as though the sight were too much to endure. "His face was hideous. Covered with blood!"

"*Masau'u . . . Masau'u . . . Masau'u . . .*"

Some of the men had risen and were swaying together in time with the voices of the drum and flute and rattles.

"The Skeleton Man said, 'Why are you here? No one has come here before.' The men said, 'It is cold and dark where we are. We want to come to this, the Fourth World. We want fire.' Masau'u did not an-swer—he changed his face! He became a most handsome god."

"*Masau'u!*" the people chanted. More men joined those who were standing; they shuffled in a swaying dance around the altar.

The drummer lifted his rapturous face and cried, "Come, Masau'u!" The people echoed, "Come, come, come, Masau'u!"

"And then," Kwani continued, "the four men said, 'Why was your other face bleeding?' and Masau'u replied, 'I was hunting and grew weary and sat down to rest. I slept. Rabbit hunters found me early in the morning, in daylight . . . I could not see . . . I stumbled into a tall rock and cut my face. I turned and stumbled to another, and then another, and the rocks cut my face each time and it bled. So now I require blood in your sacrifices to me.' "

"Come, Masau'u . . . come."

"The men said, 'If we give you blood sacrifice, will you send Motsni to show our people the way to the Fourth World?' And Skeleton Man said, 'I do not bargain with you. Return to where you were.' His face changed again to the hideous one. The men were frightened, for Masau'u's eyes were like the burning coals in his fire. They feared to be consumed by those eyes. They ran back into the darkness. Motsni came to show them the way back. They could not see him, only the sound of his wings . . ."

There was a hushed silence. The drum, the flutes, the chanting, even the rattles quieted as if by a mysterious signal. There came a sudden quick, quiet, rush of sound in the darkness outside, the sound of a bird's wings.

"Motsni!"

"Masau'u . . . Masau'u . . . Masau'u . . ." they moaned in terror and awe.

Kwani felt suddenly drained. She sat down and wrapped her robe around her. Was it an owl that flew by? Or was it . . . could it be . . . Motsni?

Again the thunder drum spoke from the kiva. The dancers sat down. The Medicine Chief strode forward. He raised both hands overhead.

"The sacrifice! Masau'u awaits the sacrifice!"

Slowly a hideous head emerged from the kiva—the bloody mask of the Skeleton Man.

"Aye-e-e-e!" Children sobbed and clung to their mothers.

The masked figure emerged carrying a rabbit by the ears. Zashue, for it was he, approached the altar as the drum cried out and rattles snarled. The Medicine Chief stood waiting, flint knife in hand. Zashue handed the rabbit to his father. The rabbit did not struggle; its small body was limp and its eyes glazed with terror.

The Chief held the rabbit in one outstretched hand. Then, with one quick slice of his knife, he ripped the furry belly from throat to tail. As blood gushed, the Chief thrust his face to the rabbit's nose to breathe the dying breath, thereby inhaling the animal's spirit into himself.

Again, the flutes sang out as the Chief held the bleeding body over each ear of corn, bathing it in scarlet. When each ear had been sanctified, he tossed the rabbit into the flames. Chanting, he took each ear of corn, offered it to the Six Directions, and threw it into the fire.

More wood was added, and more, until the fire blazed high. There was a smell of burning fur, burning flesh, and burning corn. The Medicine Chief and the masked figure loomed eerily by the altar, chanting the Sacrifice Song and shaking their spirit rattles. Drum and flutes took up the cry; people moaned, "Masau'u . . ."

There was a sudden long, shrill scream. A woman, eyes wild, pointed into the darkness beyond the cave. They turned to stare toward the opposite mesa where a light flickered. Like a torch. It wavered, disappeared.

"Aye-e-e-e-e! Masau'u! He has come!"

They gazed in frightened awe at Kwani, expecting her to vanish or to fall dead. She had Called Masau'u, and Masau'u had sent his bird and had appeared himself. Would he take She Who Remembers back with him?

People strained to see into the darkness. But the light did not come again. Kwani sat wrapped in her robe. She did not look up when the Medicine Chief approached, the terrible masked figure beside him. Or when they stood over her, shaking their hissing and snarling rattles.

When Kwani raised her eyes to meet those of the Medicine Chief, the one encircled in red gleamed, and the serpentine mark on his forehead seemed to squirm in the firelight. Something in the Chief's eyes made her sharply aware . . . of danger.

The Chief came and bent over her. Only his rattle spoke. But power, a terrible, evil power, flowed from him, enveloping her. With a surge of overwhelming fear, Kwani realized the Medicine Chief was willing her to die. She rose, faced him, tried to fight back with her own spirit. But his power was too great. She felt her spirit weakening.

He stepped closer, and the red encircled eye bored into her. "Masau'u is taking you! Go!"

Desperately Kwani summoned her own power. From some mysterious depth it came. Of its own accord her mouth opened and a sound emerged—high, weird, powerful—not a cry, not singing, but a chilling combination of both. She reached out both hands as though to push the Chief away; he stepped backward.

"Go!" he cried again. "Masau'u . . ."

Again Kwani stepped forward, arms outstretched, and the harrowing sound grew stronger. Again the Chief stepped backward toward the altar fire. He stumbled and fell. His head hit a stone on the altar; he twisted to escape the flames but he fell into the fire where the rabbit smouldered.

A shocked silence was followed by an uproar. The Chief's hair was ablaze when he was pulled from the fire. Dazed from the blow and the burns he stared at Kwani who knelt beside him, shocked. Her face seemed to waver and dissolve into that of another, a terrible stranger.

"Take her away!" he cried hoarsely. He tried to sit up. "She's a witch, a witch!" He fell back unconscious.

"A witch!" Tiopi's voice.

Kwani rose, Woshee at her side. Woshee said, "The Medicine Chief has injured his head; he does not know what he is saying" Her voice was calm and assured. "Take him to the home of his mate until his spirit returns. She will care for the burns."

Zashue removed the mask and laid it aside. Kneeling beside his father he looked up at Kwani with hatred.

"My father knows well what he says."

Kwani walked away. The silent, staring crowd parted, backed away as she approached. Never had they heard such a sound as she had made. Never had they seen what they witnessed that night. This outsider, She Who Remembers, had powers, frightening powers, which no woman, no *natural* woman, possessed.

◆ 32 ◆

The Medicine Chief lay on his sleeping mat, and stared at the ceiling. For days he had lain there. The burns were healing. But only much time could give him back his long braids. No amount of time could heal his shame. He ventured outside only at night when the city slept so none could see the frizzled remains of his hair or the burns the witch had inflicted upon him.

Remembering the sound Kwani made . . . how she pushed him into the fire—yes, she *pushed* him even though he avoided her touch; she pushed him with her witch's power—remembering that night, over and over, seared him deeper inside than where the flames had reached.

Twisting as he fell, he had managed to land only at the fire's edge, so that his body escaped the flames from the waist down. But he was badly burned on the back of his neck and head, and on one hand and arm where the robe had not covered him. His beautiful robe . . . ruined.

He touched his hair with his unburned hand. A tangled frizz. He groaned in despair and shame.

He sat up. "Zashue!" he called.

"Zashue is not here." His mate carried his charred ceremonial robe from which she had been removing the tiny shells and turquoise beads.

"Where is he?"

"Why do you not go to find him?" She was weary of having her mate in her dwelling all day and all night, day after day. It was unseemly.

"Look at me, woman. Should the Medicine Chief of the Eagle Clan appear like this?"

Her face softened. "I shall make you a fine cap, better than Koko-pelli's. See, there is enough left of the robe to make a cap, and I have shells and beads."

213

"Make it then." He lay down again on the mat, wincing at the pressure on the burned places.

Zashue had returned. "You called for me, father?" He suppressed a desire to laugh at his father's appearance.

"Yes." He waved his mate outside. "I wish to speak with my son."

When she had gone, the Chief asked, "What are people saying about the Calling Ceremony?"

How much should he tell? "Everybody knows about the Calling of Masau'u and Motsni. Runners have carried the news everywhere. Other clans want to make pilgrimages here, to pay homage to our clan, for we are the only ones to have achieved this."

"Yes. But . . . but what about me . . . falling into the fire . . . ?"

He resembled a ceremonial clown with his hair like that and poultices on the burns on his face, Zashue thought. If he told the truth—that people were laughing—his father might be enraged enough to storm out and reassume his duties to assert his importance. As it was, Zashue was taking his place, and relishing it. Perhaps if he soothed his father's spirit, he would relax and allow the healing to take its time, until his hair grew . . . while Zashue's own importance increased.

"It was Masau'u's gift of his sacred fire. They say he chose you, father, to receive it, knowing you were strong enough to withstand the burns. You have greatly honored the Eagle Clan. The Medicine Chiefs of other clans wished to present you with gifts," he lied, "but you have refused to see anyone."

"They wish to see what I look like with burned-off hair!"

Zashue could not restrain his smile. "I heard my mother say she would make you a cap more beautiful than Kokopelli's." He had a thought. "Remember that when Masau'u was first seen, he had no hair at all. Maybe Masau'u was making you like himself?"

The Chief jerked upright. He had not thought of that! His admirable son already possessed a Medicine Chief's wisdom!

"Yes! It was Masau'u! Tell your mother to make haste with the cap."

The mother was outside, bent over the charred robe. "I have spoken with my father," Zashue said, assuming his father's tone of voice. "Burns on the scalp are slow to heal. It would not be wise to slow the healing further with a cap."

The old woman gave her son a knowing glance. "I shall make the cap. He will know when to wear it."

The Sun Chief departed secure in the knowledge that all that could be done to assure his safety and success had been done. Days grew warmer. Houses were repaired, walls were plastered and decorated. Men spent all day in the fields with planting sticks and seeds, and boys too young to plant carried pouches of stones to throw at maurading crows. Some awed visitors from other clans came to pay their respects to those Masau'u had chosen to honor—and to see the Caller. Would she call game for them? She Who Remembers remained polite but aloof.

Zashue's father finally reappeared, in a fine new robe suitable for a holy man, wearing a handsome cap adorned with shells and turquoise beads. Visitors were invited to hear how he, the Medicine Chief, had been chosen by Masau'u to be tonsured like himself. The Chief's fame spread.

Zashue retreated into sullen frustration, his only consolation being that Kwani's part was seen as an instrument of Masau'u's to honor the Medicine Chief—placing honor where it belonged, to a Medicine Chief rather than to a witch.

As days grew longer, women searched the mesas and canyons for new herbs, roots, and tender young shoots. They spent many hours making new pots, cups, and bowls. Many were broken during winter when hands were numb and awkward.

Kwani sat in her usual place outside her door, preparing to make a jar. Working with her hands would help her to think. The events of the Calling Ceremony were heavy upon her mind. She had summoned a power she did not know she possessed! She must use that power to help her with the problem of her pregnancy; It could not be concealed much longer.

The clay and temper had been mixed, one part of temper to two parts of clay, and water was added until there was a thick, heavy paste that did not stick to her hands. She was ready to begin the actual construction. But she sat looking over the activity of the city. Only Woshee was truly her friend. Those others with whom she had lived all these moons showed polite faces, spoke pleasant words, but their spirits did not talk to hers.

It is because I am different.

But it was more than her accursed eyes. There was a difference inside. She was kin to the Blue-eyed One, not to these. These people had loved the Old One. They did not love her and never would; they feared her.

"I greet you, Esteemed One." It was Woshee, coming to visit.

"My spirit rejoices. Here, sit beside me."

Kwani pinched a small piece of paste and rolled it with her palm upon a smooth stone to make a thin rope smaller than her little finger. Being busy would make it unnecessary to speak and she did not trust herself with words right now. Woshee watched silently for a while. Then she said, "If Kokopelli does not come soon we must make the announcement."

Kwani picked up the rope of clay which was several inches long and strong enough so it did not break when she held it. She spread it before her. "He will come."

"There is too much talk. It is not good."

"What do they say?"

"That you are pregnant."

"Well, so I am."

Beginning at one end, she began to coil the rope of clay around and around on itself. As one coil encircled another, she pinched the two together with her thumb and forefinger, giving the construction a rippled effect. Woshee watched approvingly as the jar took shape.

"I think it is time to tell them now."

"I wish to wait for Kokopelli."

Woshee did not conceal her exasperation. "He may be long delayed. He may not come at all. Talk about you is not good; for you, for me, for the Sun Chief. For the entire clan. I cannot allow you to harm either yourself or us."

Kwani rolled another rope of clay and her hands were not as steady as before. "Kokopelli will come."

"First flowers have bloomed and faded; your belly swells. It is time to announce your pregnancy. Tonight, at evening fire."

Kwani's hands dropped to her lap. Blue eyes searched Woshee's in desperation. "Where is Okalake?"

"I do not know. It has been long . . . too long."

The two women gazed at one another, sharing despair.

Kwani said, "I will come tonight." She would summon her power . . . somehow.

Woshee nodded. "It is time." Tears were in her voice.

The fire burned high. Everyone in the city was gathered, waiting. Kwani sat beside the Crier Chief, huddled under a blanket even though it was warm enough so that a blanket was not needed. Stories had been told, planting had been discussed, songs sung, and old jokes retold. There was much talk of where Okalake had gone and when the Sun Chief would return with news. The Crier Chief had promised an announcement that day. People grew impatient.

The Crier Chief rose slowly, easing his painful joints.

"We all know that Kokopelli, he of the sacred seed and the magic bird, is not among us. First flowers have bloomed and gone. But there has been no word of him. Therefore his mate, She Who Remembers, wishes to make an announcement which she was saving for Kokopelli to make when he came. She wants us to know because she is one of us now."

He turned to Kwani who rose with calm authority, clasping her blan-

ket about her. Her hair was freshly washed and coiled high over each
ear, entwined with crimson cords she had made to ornament clothes for
the baby. Her eyes seemed more deeply blue than ever before as she
stood looking from one to another and then beyond them all, as to those
unseen. Mystical power enveloped her like a radiance.

Softly she began to sing, gliding into rhythmic cadence, swaying with
the words as though to music.

> *"The Old One chose me*
> *to be her successor,*
> *to be She Who Remembers.*
> *She came to me*
> *at the Place of Remembering*
> *and gave me the powers,*
> *the powers of her spirit."*

Again, the song, stronger.

> *My mother came*
> *to the Place of Remembering.*
> *My mother told me*
> *to make again*
> *a basket, a sacred basket,*
> *for the one that was destroyed.*

The song rose high and clear. As she swayed, the people began to
sway also.

> *I sought Earthmother,*
> *I lay upon her breast.*
> *She told me,*
> *Earthmother told me*
> *to make a basket*
> *to enfold her spirit*
> *and that of Sunfather,*
> *Moon Woman,*
> *Kokopelli,*
> *and his sacred bird.*

The wordless song soared triumphantly, and ceased. Kwani's eyes
glowed as from hidden fires as she cried, "I obeyed her! I obeyed
Earthmother and she rewarded me!"

She flung the blanket aside and stood naked but for a belt looped between her legs and around her swollen waist. Upon her belly was painted the stick design of Kokopelli which adorned the basket. Above, between this and the shell pendant, was the bird. Around one full breast, grown fuller with pregnancy, was the yellow circle of Moon Woman; Sunfather's crimson rays encircled the other.

Kwani turned this way and that so all might see.

"Behold Earthmother's gift! A Spirit Child!"

"Aye-e-e-e!" They stared at her with awe. A Spirit Child! Could it be? After all, she was She Who Remembers! A Caller with mystical power!

"When will be the birthing?" someone asked.

"During the Harvest Moon."

They nodded. It was an appropriate time. Only Zashue noticed the fury in Tiopi's face. He smiled.

❖ 33 ❖

Kwani was smoothing her jar with a curved piece of dried gourd rind when she decided the jar should become a pitcher. There were many jars available, but fewer pitchers. Kokopelli might like one for trading. The clay was still pliable, so she indented the jar a third of the way up, expanded the bottom part a bit, and made a pouring lip at the top. A strong handle would make it a fine pitcher. She would dry it in the sun, then gather white clay from under the mesa's brim and mix it with water to make a white covering. She would polish it with a smooth stone and decorate it beautifully with black paint made from boiled beeweed. Then her pitcher would join other vessels in a shallow pit for firing. Hers would be the best. Kokopelli would be pleased.

When was he coming? Corn and squash and beans were planted. There was no rain. But if none came, there would be ceremonies and dances and Kokopelli would use his magic to bring the Cloud People, and rain would come. Surely, it would come.

The baby inside her moved, and she thought of Okalake. The Sun Chief had been gone long, tracking Okalake as people told him where they had seen his son last. The last word known was that the Sun Chief was going to the Great City.

"It is dangerous there," some said.

"The evil spirits made Earthmother unproductive. That is why people left."

"Witches."

"The cold. They had no caves to keep ice and sleet and snow and wind away."

"Apaches!"

"Yes, Apaches."

Tiopi watched from a distance. Kwani continued to wear her painted designs and Tiopi was scornful. Kokopelli on Kwani's abdomen! It was not Kokopelli's child she carried. Such a design should be on the body from whence Kokopelli's child would come. In three more moons.

Tiopi was sick at the thought of Kwani giving birth to any so-called Spirit Child when a child from Kokopelli's sacred seed was about to be born. Perhaps the Medicine Chief could find a way . . . or Zashue . . .

Meanwhile, Zashue sat with his father in the Medicine Lodge, watching with some anxiety as the Chief brought out the bow entrusted to him by Kokopelli. If Kokopelli did not return, the bow was his.

"Permit me to hold the bow, my father." In the dim light of the Lodge, the hairline crack could not be seen. But it might be felt.

The Chief handed the bow to his son. "It may be yours one day."

"If Kokopelli does not return?"

"Yes."

"I do not think he is coming."

They sat in silence for a time, contemplating a bitter future with She Who Remembers challenging their prestige. Finally, the Chief said, "Has there been word of the Sun Chief?"

"No."

"Prowling animals may have found Okalake while he slept."

"Bears, perhaps."

If Okalake did not return, Okalake's parents might blame Kwani. An intriguing thought.

Zashue said, "If Okalake does not come back—"

The Chief nodded. "It will be best for us."

Kwani stirred a pot of porridge over her fire. She planned to take some to Woshee, who had prepared no food for herself since the Sun Chief left. Woshee had grown even thinner. Fear lay only half-hidden in her dark eyes as she looked down the canyon for her mate and her son.

Kwani placed a bowl of hot porridge on the circular mat used to carry loads on the head. She adjusted them expertly, and made her way to Woshee's dwelling. Woshee lay on her sleeping mat though it was past noon, and Kwani saw with a flood of concern how wan she was.

"I greet you, Woshee."

"My spirit rejoices—and so does my stomach. I was hungry but did not feel like cooking."

Kwani set the bowl down and watched as Woshee ate. Again the baby moved inside her. "Here, Woshee, feel your grandchild." She took the thin hand and placed it on her abdomen. The baby kicked and Woshee smiled, "He is strong."

"It may be a girl."

"No. It is Okalake's son." Fear clouded her eyes. "If Okalake does not come . . ." She bit her lip. Making an effort to be cheerful, she said, "When the boy is older he will be a Sun Chief also."

Kwani thought, it may be a girl, but she said, "Of course he will. Okalake will teach him." Woshee smiled. "Finish the porridge."

Woshee ate it all. "It was good, thank you. I shall dress now and be ready for evening fire tonight."

"Good." Kwani took Woshee's hand and breathed on it. She was surprised at how dear its owner had become to her.

A distant roll of thunder sent Kwani hurrying outside to see clouds hung over the horizon, great billowing thunderheads promising rain. People crowded the cliff's edge, gazing thankfully.

But rain did not come. Clouds hung low, thunder boomed, echoing and re-echoing among the cliffs. Wind whooshed through the canyons with a growling whine. A tantalizing curtain of rain drifted in the distance but passed them by.

It was a bad omen. Foreboding seeped through the city like a fog. Only children laughed as they ran free in the canyon and on the mesa, shouting above the barking of their dogs. It was their commotion that obscured the sounds of an arriving procession.

They approached from the south, a long line of men and women of various clans, led by a stooped figure walking with effort. Behind him, on a platform supported by poles, a figure was being carried by two men.

The children saw them. "People come, people come!" They saw who was the leader, and who was being carried, and they stopped short, staring.

Kwani rushed with the others in the city to see who was coming. Some ran down the path to welcome them, and stopped in their tracks.

The Sun Chief led the procession, for surely it was he, bent and looking incredibly old, with white streaks in his hair and crevices on his face that were not there before. He did not speak, but stumbled blindly.

Behind him, upon the platform, lay what was left of Okalake. Rats had found him. An Apache arrow protruded from the base of his skull. His mouth was stretched wide in a grotesque silent scream, revealing maggots squirming inside. The eyes had been devoured; and holes in his garment revealed where the rats had been.

A groan of horror rose. Woshee gripped the edge of the wall, standing immobile, gazing blankly, as the procession climbed the steep path to the city. Those around her parted in silence as she turned to meet the oncoming ones. The Sun Chief saw her and came to her. He tried to protect her from seeing and he put both hands on her shoulders. He raised his ravaged face to look into her eyes.

"Okalake . . ." He swallowed, and tried to continue. Tears streamed, and he could not.

Woshee tore from his grasp and ran to Okalake's side. She gazed down, gave a great gasp and a wild, keening cry. She turned and ran across the courtyard, arms stretched before her, eyes wide and staring. Screaming and screaming, she ran up and down ladders, across terraces, and down to the courtyard again. Her hair loosened and blew behind her as she fled, arms outstretched, eyes staring at a horror still seen.

Kwani wept in stricken anguish. One glance at the figure on the platform was all she had been able to endure. She tried to stumble up to her dwelling, but Woshee saw her and threw herself on Kwani in an insane fury.

"It was you! He went away because of you! You killed him! *You took his seed and you killed him!*" The stricken eyes rolled upward suddenly and she crumpled.

Some lifted Woshee and carried her to her home. Others stood silent, staring at Kwani with rigid, impenetrable faces. She retreated to her dwelling and pulled the stone slab door closed. Sobbing, she sank to her mat and lay in a shuddering heap. What she had seen . . . No, it could not be Okalake, dear Okalake . . . and that wild creature mad with grief could not be her loved and trusted friend.

Woshee had told them!

Outside was a sound like gathering thunder. People were massing outside her door.

"Come out!"

The baby moved more forcibly than ever before. Kwani said, "Do not be afraid." She pulled the stone door slab aside, and stepped out.

"You killed him!" People crowded close.

"It was not I who sent the arrow. Okalake is in Sipapu, but he is also here." Kwani placed her hand over her abdomen. "It is true. Earthmother's gift, my Spirit Child, is Okalake's also. If you harm me, you harm his child, all that Woshee and the Sun Chief have left. Their grandchild."

She walked among them, looking from one sullen face to another. "I am Anasazi, but I am not of the blood of this clan. Okalake did no wrong to mate with me, nor I with him, regardless of what clan law may be. In your hearts, you know this is true. Do not make Woshee suffer more, do not burden the Sun Chief with greater sorrow. Allow Okalake to live again in his child. Let it be born in peace as Earthmother desires."

Huzipat, the Clan and Elder Chief, seemed also to have aged more. He gazed into the face of his friend, the Sun Chief.

"Your grandchild will be born. You will have your son again." He put an arm around his friend; the two old men went to be with Woshee.

The Clan Chief had spoken. People retreated slowly, though faces were grim. The Medicine Chief chanted incantations over Okalake, shaking his spirit rattle.

Kwani retreated inside her dwelling and pulled the stone slab closed again. Alone in the semi-darkness she began to tremble violently.

I must stay here, the baby must be born here. Why does Kokopelli not come?

She thought of what lay on the platform, and nausea rose with her terrible grief. She remembered Woshee running, screaming, accusing; agonized pity mingled with foreboding. Would people really believe she was responsible for Okalake's death? She pressed the necklace to her, demanding to know.

Yes, they would believe.

With wrenching fear, Kwani knew what she must do.

Tiopi searched for Zashue among the people standing in solemn groups on the platform, around the figure covered with the finest feather blanket the clan could provide. The Medicine Chief assured Okalake's spirit a safe haven in Sipapu with his chants and magic incantations. She found Zashue among those who had come from other clans; he was asking them where they had found Okalake.

"Zashue."

He turned impatiently. "What is it?"

"I must speak with you."

"Don't you see I am engaged in conversation with friends?"

"I see also that you do not wish to discuss a matter of importance to you and to the clan." She turned away.

"Wait." He approached her belligerently, as the son of a Medicine Chief should. "What can be more important than what has happened to Okalake?"

"Perhaps . . ." She leaned closer. "Perhaps a conversation about Kwani."

"Ah."

They looked at one another in silence for a moment. Tiopi smiled thinly. "Kwani admits her crime, yet she continues to flaunt her authority. It is an insult to the clan, to the Medicine Chief, and to you—"

"I will go with you to your dwelling."

They made their way through the sorrowing crowd. Inside Tiopi's home, in semi-darkness, the two sat close together, speaking in whispers.

Tiopi said, "Kokopelli is not coming. We must find a way to make Kwani leave."

Zashue's small eyes gleamed. He could hardly believe his good fortune. Tiopi was playing right into his hands, making everything easy.

"There is a way."

"How?"

"We shall prove that she is a witch and used her powers to kill Okalake so that he could never divulge their secret."

Tiopi drew back. "Do not be stupid. It has been proven she is not a witch. People tried, but failed."

Zashue drew himself up with commendable dignity. "The son of the Medicine Chief is not stupid. We shall not fail."

"Convince me."

"Owl's feathers. Three owl's feathers are buried in the place by the turkeys where Kwani used to be."

Tiopi regarded Zashue with surprise and something like respect. "Where in the room are they?"

"In a corner. If you might have occasion to go in there . . . ?"

"I might do that." She smiled. "Go now."

"But first . . ." He glanced at her bracelets. "A small present would be seemly, would it not?"

"It would not!"

He shrugged. There was no harm in trying.

Hours dragged sadly to the time of the evening fire. Woshee lay on her mat in a coma while the Medicine Chief, with Zashue beside him, sought to return her spirit to her with the sacred cloud from his pipe and with ritual incantations. The Sun Chief, withered and bent, slumped in a corner. Occasionally, he moaned softly, rocking to and fro.

Around the fire, people gathered in groups. Discussion was hushed and angry, touched with fear. Because Okalake broke clan law, he suffered terrible punishment. Woshee's spirit had forsaken her and refused to return. Yet the outsider was to blame for it. She was at this moment hiding in her dwelling unpunished. What fury of the gods would strike the clan now?

Huzipat, the Clan Chief pointed out, "Remember what Kokopelli said, if harm comes to She Who Remembers, terrible punishment will befall all of us."

"Let Kokopelli take her away!"

"If he comes!" another spoke up.

"What if he does not return?"

"What if he is in Sipapu?"

Huzipat warned, "His spirit will return in vengeance if we harm his mate. We must be prudent. If we protect her, good fortune comes to us. That was his promise."

There were sullen mutterings.

"We have protected her and disaster befalls us!"

"Apaches. Breaking the law brought Apaches!"

"They are in the south."

"Perhaps."

They peered into the darkness beyond the cave and gathered closer to the fire.

"I wish to speak." Tiopi strode to the fire. Firelight playing on her swollen abdomen reminded them all whose seed she bore. "I have heard the voice of Kokopelli," she said.

"Speak, then," the old Chief said.

People crowded close, fell silent. She placed her hand on her abdomen.

"Kokopelli has spoken to me through his child. He is not coming, because he has had a vision. He sees owl's feathers."

"Aye-e-e-e!"

"He sees owl's feathers in the place where Kwani lived, the place by the turkeys. He refuses her as mate."

"You lie, Tiopi."

Kwani stood on a terrace above them. She wore strong sandals and a robe for traveling. A heavy basket was on her back fastened by a thong around her forehead, and she held the medicine arrow in both hands.

"It is I who have seen a vision. The Old One came to me. She says I must leave and take Okalake's child to safety, for there are those of you who would harm me and my child. She tells me Kokopelli *will* come and find me, and pass judgment on you all."

"Witch!" Tiopi shouted. "Owl's feathers!"

Kwani said, "I know nothing of owl's feathers. If a witch is among you, it is one who wishes to harm the clan by harming me." She held the medicine arrow before her. "My medicine arrow will take me to Kokopelli." Her voice wavered. "I long to stay, to give Woshee and the Sun Chief their grandchild, to give Okalake back to you. But I must leave this place."

The Clan Chief stepped forward and his wise old face was creased with troubled concern. "Do not go in darkness. Wait until dawn."

"My medicine arrow will protect me."

She climbed awkwardly with her burden down the ladders and made her way through the city, followed by threatening growls. Thoughts whirled through her mind like leaves in a storm.

These are enemies. It is good that I leave this place . . . But I am afraid to go alone . . . No, not alone, you have Okalake's child to protect. Walk carefully, do not fall . . . But it is dark! . . . No matter, watch each step. Go down the canyon to the hideaway cave. You will be safe there until morning. Then go to the place where Kokopelli found you for he may pass that way again . . . But that is where I lost my first baby . . . The spirit of the Old One goes with you . . . How dark it is! They say Apaches can see in the dark . . .

Back in the city, there was an uproar. Owl's feathers! Were they actually where Tiopi said they were? Who would go to see? Only the Medicine Chief would be immune to contamination, and he was still with Woshee.

"Send Zashue!" Tiopi cried. "He has the powers, he will be safe."

"Yes! Zashue!"

With an air of modest reluctance, Zashue climbed to the small dwelling. People huddled in frightened groups. It was incredible that the Old One could have chosen a witch as successor. But what if it were true? Could a witch cast a spell on holy ones like the Old One?

Waiting became unbearable. Some crowded outside the doorway and held burning torches so Zashue could see as he searched the room, inch by inch, chanting prayers. At last he began to dig, first one place and then another, while onlookers commented admiringly on his professionalism. What a fine Medicine Chief he would make!

The chanting ceased abruptly. Zashue bent over a hole he had dug, and stared down. Slowly, he lifted out three owl's feathers.

"I have found them," he announced solemnly.

"Aiii! Aye-e-e-e! He has found them!"

They shuddered and moved closer together as Zashue stepped outside, holding the feathers in his outstretched hand. Bystanders made way as he climbed down to the fire. He stood in the firelight, holding the feathers overhead.

"Behold! Three owl's feathers! A witch buried these. A witch caused Okalake's death so he could not reveal a terrible secret!"

The blanketed figure on the platform seemed to stir, but it was only the wind tugging at the covering.

"A witch caused Woshee's spirit to forsake her; perhaps it hovers here. A witch caused the death of our revered Old One so that she who is evil might become her successor."

Women sobbed, and children cried out in terror. Men fingered their amulets and glanced furtively about. What spirits lurked beyond the shadows?

Zashue stepped to the fire and tossed the feathers into the flames. Two sizzled and curled; but the third rose with the updraft, fluttered, hovered, and drifted through the cave opening into darkness.

A howl rose with it. "Look! The feather follows the witch!"

"After her! After the witch!" Tiopi shouted, and gave her mate a push.

The Medicine Chief's rattle sounded imperatively over the uproar as he emerged from Woshee's dwelling. "Woshee's spirit awaits Sipapu. Woshee is dead. Bury her beside her son."

For a moment there was stunned silence. The Sun Chief's heartbroken moaning rose faintly. An echoing moan rose from those who had loved Woshee and from those who were overwhelmed with fear. Then a cold rage for vengeance swept them like a strong wind, blowing fear away.

"Kill the witch!"

"Find her! Destroy the witch!"

Yatosha said with cold certainty, "I and the hunters will follow. But not tonight. She will leave tracks like a buffalo. We shall wait until dawn. I promise you our arrows will find her."

The Medicine Chief frowned. Important decisions had been made while he was performing sacred and profane duties, decisions involving matters in which he was the ultimate authority.

"You forget, Yatosha. Your arrows will not kill a witch." His voice was withering. "I remind you that I and only I have the bow and arrow which must be used, the bow and arrow entrusted to me by Kokopelli."

People glanced at one another, nodding. Kokopelli's magical bow!

Zashue thought of the bow's hairline crack, and did not speak. He would leave before dawn, retrieve Kwani's spear, and kill her with her own weapon. He would succeed where his father was certain to fail!

·34·

Walking as quickly as she dared in the starlit darkness, Kwani stumbled over rocks or slipped on loose gravel, but she did not fall. It was cool and the air was sweet with sage and juniper. A half moon rose; and, far away, Brother Coyote sang to the moon, his voice echoing from canyon to canyon, lonely and free.

I, too, am free! Kwani thought. Fear was gone, and grief was dissipated in resolve. She must go where Kokopelli would look for her.

The moon rose higher and a night bird called. It was beautiful there in the canyon with the great cliffs soaring on either side, and the stars piercing the sky to let pinpricks of bright light through.

This is how it will be when I travel with Kokopelli, she thought, and her heart lifted. For the first time, she realized how hard it had been to live with the Eagle Clan—always fighting witchcraft taunts, or raised high and lonely above others. She wanted only to be loved and protected by a mate, to have children, to be a *woman*. And yes, she wanted more than that. She wanted to see what the world was like; she wanted adventure!

This was not an Anasazi heritage. Anasazi women wanted only home, family, and clan. Distant places were regarded with distrust. Only now did Kwani realize how pervasive was her heritage from a remote ancestor, those blue-eyed ones, the explorers.

It was a revelation. She stopped to rest on a large rock and to think about the implications of her discovery. Her dual heritage was the real reason she was different. The color of her eyes was only what showed; she was different inside.

They fear me as they fear unknown places. And because they fear me, they will try to destroy me.

There was a rustle and whispering all about as a breeze passed through. Fear pinched her heart again. *Are they following me?* She remembered the glances like thrown spears. She hurried on, and stumbled on a twisted root.

Be careful, she told herself. The hideaway place was not far away. In the morning she would follow the canyon to the place where Kokopelli had found her. She could watch the canyon unseen and know when he came.

She strode with strength and resolve. The baby stirred.

"You will be safe, little one. You have a protector; you will travel far and see great things. Be content."

The tall boulder against the cliff was there, reflecting moonlight. It took much effort to climb with her burden, but at last she reached the top and slid down into the cave's black depths. She lay on the floor, enveloped in the dry, dusty smell, embraced by remembrance, drifting into exhausted sleep.

It was not yet dawn when she awoke startled. There was a sound outside as though something, someone, was climbing the boulder. She jerked upright, and listened. Yes! The sound came again.

She reached for the medicine arrow tucked into her pack, seeking its magic. But her hand grasped something else instead, something cold and hard. Her spear!

Stung by surprise and fear, she balanced it anew in her hand. It was as though Okalake had come to protect her!

A head poked down. Someone lay on his stomach to peer inside. Instantly Kwani knew who it was. Zashue!

He saw her and laughed. At such close quarters, any arrow could kill its prey, even a witch! He drew back, and a drawn bow and arrow pointed at her heart.

With all her strength, Kwani threw the spear. There was a sharp cry as Zashue fell from the boulder.

I hit him!

Quickly, she climbed to the entrance and looked down. Zashue was struggling to dislodge the spear which had gone through his cheek from nose to ear. Blood gushed as he jerked the point of the spear through, tearing his flesh further. He tried to stop the bleeding with both hands.

Kwani slid down the boulder and seized her spear. His bow lay nearby. She grabbed that, too. Assuming a throwing stance, she confronted Zashue who rose and backed away, holding his torn cheek; it flapped as he tried to speak through bloody lips.

"You tried to kill me." Ice froze in her voice. "Now I shall kill you."

"No!" He turned and stumbled away. "No! No!"

As she looked at the boy's disfigured, bleeding face, Kwani suddenly remembered the mutilated face upon the platform, and she could not throw the spear. Enough was enough.

She watched him go. He would be horribly marked for life. She threw his arrow aside and stood holding the spear. Okalake had found it, had put it in the secret place for her, had saved her life. She had his prayer stick for protection, her medicine arrow, her necklace, her amulet, and the spirit of the Old One to watch over her. She needed the heavy spear no longer, and threw it down.

Weary, she returned to the cave, shouldered her pack, and climbed out again. It had grown lighter. She could see Zashue as he ran down the canyon. He would tell his people—*his* people, not hers—where she was. He tried to kill her. Would they not try to do so, also?

Cold certainty gave her strength and she began to run. Then she realized she was leaving tracks. It would be no problem for them to follow her, no time at all to overtake her. Where could she go to hide? Panting, glancing this way and that, she clutched the shell at her breast. "Help me! Tell me where to go!"

A sound behind her. Were they coming?

She began to run again, searching for a climbing place to the mesa. The sound came closer. Dogs! Yatosha and his hunters and dogs were tracking her. She pushed along against the cliff, hands searching for foot-holds not seen in the dim light.

An indentation! She reached for another. The holds were ancient, not used for years, and crumbling. But fear gave her strength. Her fingers clawed and her feet clung and she climbed. Higher and higher she went, while loose soil crumbled behind her. She was afraid to look down, afraid to see the hunters, knowing if she could see them, they could see her. One hand slipped and a hold gave way. She swayed and reached desperately for another. It held. She pulled higher, higher, reaching for the mesa brim. With a final exhausting effort, she pulled herself over and lay trembling, her heart thudding.

The sounds grew close. From a concealing bush she peered down. The hunters came running. Yatosha had found her spear and carried it triumphantly. Dogs reached the climbing place and tried to climb, barking madly. With them, brandishing Strongbow, was the Medicine Chief. He had met Zashue back in the canyon and had pulled his son's bloody hands from the torn face; Zashue's jaw was exposed, and several teeth ripped away.

Zashue pointed behind him. "Kwani. Spear." was all he could say.

"Go to your mother until I return." He brandished his bow at the hunters. "Kill the witch! Kill her!"

With an answering shout the hunters ran, led by the Chief and Yatosha. There had been excitement when they found the spear and Zashue's arrow near the cave. But the dogs ran swiftly ahead, intent on the trail, and the hunters followed.

The Medicine Chief gripped his bow. He had not yet fitted the arrow in the bow; he would do it at leisure when the witch was taken. Then he would send the arrow where death would be certain but long in coming. He would avenge his son, himself, and the clan.

At the climbing place one of the dogs managed to claw himself up for a short way and fell back, feet thrashing the air.

Yatosha said, "If she climbed here, so can we."

"No!" The Medicine Chief elbowed his way through the hunters. "It would take too long. I must climb here, for my magical bow must follow the witch's footsteps. The rest of you go up the canyon a short way where the path leads to the mesa. You and the dogs will be on the mesa by the time I reach the top. Go! Don't stand there doing nothing while the witch escapes."

Yatosha and the hunters called the dogs and ran up the canyon. The Chief grunted with satisfaction. Now he could confront Kwani alone.

He began to climb, amazed that Kwani had managed so difficult an ascent. He was a big man, and heavy, and the holds were weathered. Several times he nearly fell. But if a female could do it, so could he. His strong fingers dug into the cliff's face, and his feet felt their way with a lifetime of experience. But he was panting and unsteady when he reached the top.

He squatted to rest. There was a time when such a climb would have tired him but little, if at all. He was growing old. And his successor, his son, bleeding and torn, would wear the witch's scar forever, no matter how carefully the flesh was sewn back together. His wounded son . . .

Enraged, the Chief rose, clutching the bow. Almost, he fitted the arrow. But no, he would corner the witch first. It was daylight now. He could see the tracks clearly. He followed swiftly, head down, noting where the trail led into the trees. She would be hiding there. Running easily, he reached the first thick clump of pines, and stopped. Was that a movement ahead? He must nearly be upon her. He gripped his bow. He would corner her and wait for the others to come and witness his triumph.

Quietly, with all the cunning at his command, he approached.

Too late, he saw the cougar with three cubs passing in the shadows. In his surprise, he stepped on a twig. The cougar whirled with a snarl. The Chief fumbled for the arrow and fitted it into the bow while the cougar crouched, tail twitching, ears laid back, fangs shining white.

As the Chief pulled the bowstring, the bow snapped with a loud crack. In the same instant, the cougar was upon him, claws unsheathed.

When Kwani reached the trees she had to stop again to rest. Pregnancy and carrying a pack slowed her down. The fainter barking of the dogs showed they were going away. Then she remembered there was a good climbing place up the canyon. The Medicine Chief and the hunters would be on the mesa momentarily. Frantic, she ran through the trees. Where to go? Where to hide?

A terrible, piercing scream stopped her. Only trees and brush and shadows could be seen. *Who screamed? Why?*

Then she knew! The hunters following her had encountered Apaches. Apache hid in ambush; someone had received an arrow. Just as Okalake did—and as she might! Terrified, she ran blindly, recklessly, stumbled into a shallow gully, picked herself up, and ran through a clearing toward another wooded spot. Her breath came in wheezing gasps, and her heart pounded like a crazed thing.

Yatosha and the hunters heard the scream and stopped abruptly. Yatosha whispered, "Wasn't that the voice of the Medicine Chief?"

"We can't be sure."

"It sounded like it," another said.

The dogs set up a sudden wild clamor. A cougar and three cubs had dashed across a gully. In frenzied pursuit, one of the dogs caught a cub; at its squeal the cougar whirled and dropped the dog with one swipe. The other dogs were upon her and she slashed at them with lightening power.

Yatosha threw the spear in a long arc. The cougar fell; hunters' arrows finished her, and then the cubs, one by one. A dog was dead and several were wounded, some badly.

"Find the Chief!" Yatosha cried.

It did not take long. He lay gashed open, the broken bow beside him. Cougar tracks were red with his blood.

Stunned, overwhelmed by this final proof of the witch's power, some of the hunters turned to go back. Yatosha lanced them with scorn.

"Witch or not, she has only a woman's weak body! Kill her before her powers destroy us all!"

They urged the dogs on.

Kwani heard the dogs. They had found her tracks! Where were the Apaches? In panic, she slid into shallow gully where a dead limb leaned against a tall tree. Panting with the effort, she pulled herself up the limb to the tree. She pushed the limb away to fall splintering to the ground, and inched her way up to the branches. At least, the dogs would not get her. She climbed as high as she could and crouched among the leaves, trying to still her thundering heart.

She wrapped her arms around a limb, pressing her cheek, her entire body against the rough bark, willing the tree's strength and serenity to flow into her. Up among the branches, surrounded by leaves, she forced her spirit to seek the powers that the Old One bequeathed to her, the powers of She Who Remembers.

Know who you are! she told herself. Stop cowering. Think!

The scallop shell dug into her as she clung. Slowly, her heart quieted. The spirit of the Old One spoke.

They fear you, not only because you are different, but because you are a woman. Men fear their need of women and powers women possess. You are feared also for the powers I have given you. Be strong. Show no fear.

The barking came closer; Kwani heard the shouts of the hunters.

Kwani answered the Old One. "They think I am a witch. Because of owl's feathers. What feathers?"

Knowledge rose like water in a spring. Someone had found owl's feathers and wanted to prove they belonged to her. Who? The Medicine Chief? But he also feared Kokopelli and she was Kokopelli's mate.

Who had reason not to fear Kokopelli! Who would benefit the most from her death? Tiopi? . . . who wanted to be She Who Remembers? Who longed to be mate of Kokopelli whose seed she had twice received?

Yes! Tiopi, mate of Yatosha, whose dogs and hunters were nearly at the gully!

Be strong. Show no fear.

Kwani removed her medicine arrow from her pack. Okalake's prayer stick was in that pack; it, too, protected her. Let the dogs and hunters come, she told herself. I am ready.

The dogs leaped into the gully, baying, circling the tree, trying to jump to where she clung among the leaves. Yatosha and the hunters gazed in astonishment up into the tree where Kwani clung, dark hair streaming, eyes flashing defiance as she clutched her medicine arrow. How had she managed to get up there? They drew their arrows.

"Crows!" Kwani's insult was piercing. "Tiopi knows well that I am not a witch. She makes stupid fools of you all."

Yatosha's arm was raised to signal the arrows, but it paused in mid-air.

"Tiopi wants to be She Who Remembers. She wants to be mate of Kokopelli. She would have you kill me and kill Okalake's child, your next Sun Chief. And you do exactly as she wishes. Crows!" She spat at them like a treed cougar. As she crouched among the branches above them it seemed that, indeed, the spirit of the cougar had entered her.

Yatosha lowered his arm. Could it be true? Had Tiopi made a fool of him again? Of them all? They had lost their Medicine Chief, and Zashue was wounded; Okalake was dead, Woshee dead, and the Sun Chief near Sipapu. A string of deaths and disaster for the clan. Had the Old One chosen Kwani to give them a new Sun Chief as well as to be She Who Remembers? He struggled with indecision.

"Owl's feathers!" a hunter cried.

Yatosha could not argue with evidence he had seen with his own eyes. Again, he raised his arm, signaling for arrows; bows twanged in unison.

Kwani was ready. As Yatosha signaled, she dropped to lower branches, and arrows hissed above her.

There was a distant sound. Hunters lifted their bows. The sound came again. Yatosha shouted, "Wait!"

Silence; and again the sound. A flute, high and sweet and powerful with authority.

Kokopelli.

·35·

Kokopelli! Yatosha paled, and the hunters exclaimed in frantic dismay. What could they tell him, how could they justify an attempt on the life of his mate? The dogs, hearing the flute, ran to welcome Kokopelli as always. Yatosha clenched his fist—why had he listened to Tiopi? What if Kwani was not a witch, after all? Disaster came on disaster; what had the clan done to so offend the gods? Kwani was right, Tiopi had made fools of them, just as Kwani claimed.

Kwani too had heard the flute. She leaned back with an enormous sigh. "Thank you, thank you!" she whispered to the spirit of the Old One. Kokopelli! Joy raced through her. She tried to smooth her hair, to rearrange her robe which had been torn in the climbing.

The hunters drew away from Yatosha and talked, gesticulating, arguing.

The sound of the flute grew closer.

"Come down!" Yatosha called to Kwani. His hunters babbled to one another, glancing at him, and he knew what they were saying and could not blame them. "Come down!" he called again.

Kwani clung to the branch. Let Kokopelli see where they had driven her; let him see the arrows bristling above her!

The flute sang, "I am coming!" and it laughed as it sang.

"Come down, come down!" Yatosha demanded shrilly.

"No."

The flute sang closer. Yatosha stood in a frenzy of uncertainty as his hunters left to greet Kokopelli. He followed them at last.

The flute was stilled. The hunters must have met Kokopelli. What were they telling him? Kwani peered through the branches, waiting to see them return, straining for a glimpse of Kokopelli. Time passed. Then three of the hunters ran by. They passed without glancing up, their faces stiff with fright. They raced for the climbing place down to the canyon.

Kwani clung to the branch where she sat. The hunters ran as if they were chased. Apaches? But Kokopelli was friend of all tribes, all animals. Nor did he ever carry a weapon. An ambush? Anxiously she climbed higher for a better view. From her pack she pulled the ear ornament he had given her, and fastened it to her ear. She brushed leaves from her hair. She wished her robe had not been torn and soiled; she wished she looked better.

Again the flute sounded, and a procession appeared. Leading was Kokopelli, splendid in his mantle of glowing colors and intricate design. He wore a different headdress, one with tall, green feathers that undulated regally as he moved. No bird rode his shoulder. Great, shining ornaments lay on his bare brown chest. His strong legs were also bare except for sandals with thongs wrapped nearly to his knees. A short, embroidered garment encircled his waist.

How handsome he was! Desire, too long denied, surged in a flood.

The hunters plodded behind Kokopelli like whipped dogs except for Yatosha who marched with head high. Kwani, leaning out for a better look, nearly toppled from the branch, and the medicine arrow fell to the ground. Jaw agape, she stared.

Bringing up the rear was a giant of a man, so large that he made the hunters look puny. Great muscled arms and legs protruded from a garment of bright blue, with short sleeves, and a shiny scarlet band at the square neckline and around the bottom which reached to mid-thigh. A leather belt held a large buckle glinting in the sun. It held also a scabbard for a sword with an ornate, glittering handle.

The arms, the massive thighs, all of his body that she could see was a strange color—as though dye had been washed from the skin, bleaching it to a warm tan color. His cheeks and chin were covered with curly hair of an extraordinary shade, like autumn leaves. A mat of hair the same color protruded from beneath his pointed cap, that was hard and shiny and had a strip that came down the front between his eyes to cover his nose.

A bow hung on his back and a large quiver of arrows swung at his side beside the sword. One huge hand held a fearsome ax with a long handle. The giant swung it easily as he walked.

The dogs returned and ran yapping around the tree. Kokopelli stopped and gestured the hunters aside, and the giant stranger came to stand beside him. As he looked up at Kwani, she saw his eyes were blue, a clear, deep blue. Her heart leaped. Her kinsman!

The man's blue eyes sparkled amusement. He called in a strange accent, "Ho, small bird!"

"I greet you," Kwani said politely.

Kokopelli looked up at her and his eyes smiled. But the downturned lips were grim as he picked up her medicine arrow and examined it speculatively. He studied the arrows above her, and turned to Yatosha standing close by, face expressionless.

"You have told me, your hunters have told me, that Okalake died, Woshee died, the Medicine Chief died, and Zashue was wounded because my mate is a witch." His eyes scorched them. "How can you not realize that disaster comes because you have not honored and protected my mate? Did I not warn you that punishment would be yours if you failed?"

The hunters glanced at one another, and hung their heads. Only Yatosha stood rigid and defiant. Kokopelli thrust the medicine arrow toward him.

"You heard this arrow speak once. Now you shall hear it again."

From inside his mantle he brought the spirit rattle with copper bells. Holding the arrow outstretched, he passed the rattle above it, allowing the rattle's voice to hiss and sing. Back and forth he moved it over the arrow, then closed his eyes as though beseeching the arrow's spirit to speak.

Yatosha watched with dread in his eyes. The giant watched in tolerant amusement. At last, Kokopelli's eyes opened; he spoke to the arrow.

"These people of the Eagle Clan do not believe when you tell them my mate is not a witch. They have tried to destroy her. Should they be punished?"

"Yes."

The arrow spoke! The hunters murmured in fear.

"What shall their punishment be?" The rattle hissed.

"They must return to their city, and inform their people that you, Kokopelli, will never trade with them again, nor bring to them your sacred seed."

Again the rattle hissed; again the arrow spoke.

"Never again will you go to a place where Anasazi dwell. The tribe, the clan, their homes, their fields, are cursed forever."

"Aiii! Aye-eee!" The hunters moaned, covering their faces with their hands.

"The arrow has spoken."

Kokopelli handed the arrow to the giant, who tucked it into his pack. The rattle was returned to its secret place in the mantle.

To Yatosha Kokopelli said, "You may inform your mate and all your people I shall not bring my seed to them again. The gods have spoken."

Yatosha's lips curled. "My mate carries your seed. The child will be born after three moons. Your seed remains."

Kokopelli looked down his nose. "She carries my seed as do countless others from here to Tenochtitlán!" He waved an arm to the tree where Kwani leaned over a limb. "She will carry my seed, also."

"She carries the seed of Okalake."

Kokopelli's sharp glance sought her. "This is so?"

"First flowers bloomed and died, and you did not come . . ."

The Blue-eyed One threw back his head and laughed, and his voice boomed like a thunder drum. "Kokopelli traveled to bring me with him," he said in his thick accent. "It took long."

Kokopelli did not laugh. He gestured Yatosha and the hunters away. "Go! Tell your people what the spirit of the arrow revealed to you."

Some of the hunters hurried away. Yatosha confronted Kokopelli with a frozen gaze. "My hunters and I go or we stay as we choose."

The Blue-eyed One swung his ax around and around overhead. It made a whooshing sound.

"I take from him his head. Ya?"

A hunter raised his bow. The ax flew through the air, and the hunter's hand fell to the ground still clutching the bow. Blood gushed from his arm. The men turned in fury to the giant to be confronted with a drawn bow of awesome proportions and a cold blue gaze equally deadly.

Kokopelli said, "Is this not enough?"

"We choose to go," a hunter said at last, and turned away. Others followed, seeking to help the wounded man stop the blood flow.

Yatosha faced Kokopelli, and his face was smooth and hard as a stone. "I shall remember this day." He turned abruptly to follow his hunters.

The Blue-eyed One watched him go, pulling a handful of grass to wipe the ax blade. "I will remember that one. It is revenge he wants."

"We shall not return here," Kokopelli said. He came back to the tree and looked up at Kwani, and his lips parted in a sudden smile. "It seems I must rescue you again. How did you get up there?"

She pointed to the dead limb. "It was leaning against the tree. I pushed it down when I got up here."

"And how do you propose to get down, foolish one?"

The vibrance of his voice left tender echoes which made her suddenly feel weak.

"I . . . I don't know."

The Blue-eyed One strode to stand beneath the tree. He stretched his arms wide and smiled up at her. "Jump. I catch."

Kwani shook her head. She could not bring herself to jump into space, great arms outstretched or no.

"I fix." The giant heaved back the ax and gave it a swing that cut a huge chunk from the trunk and shook the tree so violently that Kwani nearly fell.

"No!" Kwani cried. "Stop!"

"I cut tree, you come down hard."

"No, no! I'll jump!"

Laughing, he stretched wide his arms again, and she jumped. He caught her and held her in his arms as though she were a child or a puppy, looking at her with eyes as blue as her own. She was surprised to see how young he was; she thought he would be as old as Kokopelli or even older. Something in those blue eyes made her self-conscious.

"Put me down."

He smiled. "Eyes like mine." He patted her stomach. "Baby have blue eyes too, maybe? If Kokopelli does not want, I keep." He bounced her up and down a little as though she were a baby. "We have many more, maybe?" The thunder drum laugh boomed again.

"I am mate of Kokopelli!" She tried to sound angry.

Kokopelli watched with his inscrutable gaze. He had brought Thorvald with him as a partner of sorts. He wondered, briefly, if his decision was wise. But of course. His decisions were always wise.

"Put her down, Thorvald."

Upon her feet, Kwani swayed momentarily but Kokopelli caught her and held her to him. Her heart beat crazily. "I greet you," she whispered, feeling she should say something to welcome him.

"Can you hear my heart rejoicing?"

She looked at him. "Where is your bird?"

"He died in the snows." No point in telling her how he had nearly died, too, before he reached Thorvald's camp, and how Thorvald cared for him until his strength returned and he could travel southward for winter trading.

"I am sorry about the bird," Kwani said.

He held her away from him and looked down his nose. "I do not grieve when I have you, foolish one." He reached into his pack and brought out the other ear ornament to match the one she wore. He fastened it to her ear.

"Now you are my mate," he said, glancing briefly at Thorvald. His eyes lingered on the necklace, and he looked at her abdomen. "I will take you to Thorvald's camp where the child will be born. Then we shall go to my home which will be your home also."

Home! Beautiful word! And a fountain for her water jar!

Kwani said, "My pack is up in the tree."

More swings of the ax toppled the tree and Thorvald retrieved the pack, holding it between thumb and forefinger as though it were a delicate object, a female thing. He tucked it into his own pack. "I like to carry."

Side by side, they walked from dappled shadows into the sunlit sweep of the mesa. Beyond and beyond, blue distance beckoned.

Kwani strode between them as though she would never tire. The golden ear ornaments swung gently, caressing each cheek. She had a mate. Soon, she would have a child and a home. She had not one protector, but two, both of whom smiled at her with their eyes.

She felt beautiful. She felt like a woman.

Kokopelli raised the flute to his lips.

> *Does one live forever on earth?*
> *Not forever on earth, only a short while here.*
> *My melodies shall not die, nor my songs perish.*
> *They spread, they scatter.*

·36·

Zashue knelt beside his father who lay in the sacred Medicine Lodge, awaiting burial. Blood from the Chief's terrible wounds had been washed away, and gashes inflicted by claws and fangs of the cougar were concealed by the finest robe the Eagle Clan could provide.

Zashue chanted the death prayers, gazing at his father's ravaged face. His own face was savagely torn—a great, jagged wound. Blood still oozed where pieces of flesh were sewn back together by his mother. No cougar was responsible for this. It was the blue-eyed outsider, the witch, whose spear attacked him and mutilated him forever. Yes, Kwani, who pretended to be She Who Remembers, and who killed his father and Okalake and Woshee, and who, at this moment, was far away, traveling with Kokopelli and her supposed kinsman, the Blue-eyed One.

It was too much to bear.

He held his hand to his throbbing face where a poultice had been applied to prevent infection and hasten healing, but his face was aflame and pain pounded with each heartbeat. From above came the keening of the clan.

A breath of air entered and touched the feathers in the Chief's hair. The feathers responded, coming alive. Zashue bowed his head respectfully; his father's spirit wished to speak with him.

"Speak, my father."

"You are Medicine Chief now. Assume your duties as the gods require."

Zashue nodded. It was as though he heard his father's voice. He climbed the ladder to the kiva's opening and looked out over the courtyard; there was something he must do unobserved. From other kivas came chanting and drums in preparation for the burial ceremony. No one came his way.

241

He climbed back down and returned to his father. He lifted the burial robe, exposing the open chest and gaping abdomen. Taking his father's flint knife, which was to be buried with him, Zashue held it in readiness and listened intently. Was anyone about to descend into the kiva?

No. He and his father were alone.

He forced himself to push the slimy body contents aside so that he might find the place. Yes, there it was, between the ribs where his father said it would be—a small grain of rock crystal no longer than a seed. Extracting it with the knife, he held it in his hand. This was the secret of a Medicine Chief's power, known only to him and to his successors.

The power! His now. At last!

Again he listened. No one came. Taking the knife, he held it between two lower ribs and slit the skin. He pushed the seed of crystal into his body as far as he could, and pressed his hand over the small wound to stop its bleeding.

He sat back on his heels, gazing around the kiva, the finest of all in all the cave cities among the high cliffs and mesas. His, now.

He replaced the burial robe and regarded the silent figure with respect.

His father had been feared. So would he be. He, Zashue, new Medicine Chief of the Eagle Clan, would be feared by all. Again he touched his torn face. Since the magic was inserted into his body, the pain seem diminished. Already he felt the power! His eyes glittered. He would accomplish great deeds. He would avenge his people.

The witch would not go unpunished.

·PART· II·

The White Buffalo

·37·

Kwani lay looking up at the stars. Perhaps that very bright one was Okalake's campfire. But it hurt too much to think of . . . what had happened to him. She turned on her side toward Kokopelli and Thorvald. Kokopelli's brilliant cloak and cap with its tall green feathers lay beside his pack; the golden pins holding his hair in a knot on top of his head reflected starlight. Kwani heard his breathing, deep and slow, and her blood responded to the rhythm. She moved closer to inhale the scent of him; she had not realized how much she had missed it during the long months he had been away.

Now he was here. The gods had sent him in time to save her from the dogs and the hunters. This was their first night together again, the first night of a new beginning, a new life. She yearned to be in his arms. But he slept as though his spirit wandered in dreams.

Thorvald slept close by, with great arms outstretched. Never had she seen arms like that, nor such legs, or giant chest. He had removed a strange garment of interlocking links, made of something hard and black. The blue tunic was rolled in a bundle under his head. He wore only a short, white garment enfolding each massive leg from waist to mid-thigh.

His chest and legs were covered with fine hair, the color of that on his head. Kwani wondered if it might feel like fur; she was curious to touch it. His bulging pack lay beside him with his weapons and the shiny helmet with a nose guard that thrust down between his eyes like a beak.

The mass of hair released from the helmet made his head seem even larger, and each breath stirred the hair growing between his upper lip and his nose. Kwani had never seen a man with hair on his body or hiding his cheeks and hanging from his chin. It was like an animal's—

245

intimidating with its implication of animal power and ferocity. She wondered if all her kinspeople grew hair on their faces and bodies.

She visualized women with hair on their cheeks and chins and on their breasts. She was glad her skin was soft and smooth and pleasing to Kokopelli. She lay close to him, but he had kissed her only briefly before falling asleep.

Okalake's star glimmered. Was his spirit speaking? From a distance came Brother Coyote's song, wavering, rising, falling, dying away. It was as though both Okalake and Brother Coyote reached out to her.

They had stopped to camp when it grew dark, ate corn cake and dried venison, and had talked of the journey ahead.

"We go to Thorvald's camp," Kokopelli said. "His men are building a boat to sail down the rivers to the gulf. They will take us south to the shore nearest my home before they head north on the Sunrise Sea. We will travel inland to Tula." He gazed toward the southern stars. "It will be good to be in Tula again."

"Ja." Thorvald's voice rumbled like a thunder drum. "It is good to go home."

"I have never been in a boat. Is that where the baby will be born?" Kwani hoped women would be with them. Women needed women during a birthing.

"Perhaps," Kokopelli said. "It depends on what happens during our journey. Maybe the child will be born before we get there."

He played his flute softly for a while. Kwani thought he was telling her something, but she did not know what it was. She sat in silence, listening, thinking of riding on water and going to a strange land to be among strange people. But she was not afraid. She had a mate who would protect and cherish her always.

"Where is Thorvald's camp?"

Thorvald jerked a large thumb toward the east.

"But if Kokopelli's home lies south, why do we go east?"

Kokopelli smiled. "A sensible question. But it is easier to ride than to walk, is it not? It would be closer to go directly south from here. But there are rugged mountains and great deserts with no water. And tribes which are hostile even to me. The longest way is the best." He glanced at Thorvald. "If the boat is still there when we reach camp."

"Ha!" Thorvald snorted. "My men wait for me. They want to be paid." His big fist thumped his chest. "I am navigator. They wait."

Now Thorvald and Kokopelli slept under the rising moon. But Kwani could not sleep with the wonder of looking at them and thinking about the new life she would face in Kokopelli's homeland. Her Toltec dwelling would be in a great pueblo with many kivas, surrounded by fertile fields of corn and squash and beans, and by green forests. As She Who

Remembers she would be honored by all, invited to sit with the chiefs and elders in council. Many young girls would come to her to learn the secrets and the wisdom of the ancients. She would be part of an important family.

She saw herself kneeling at the grinding stones with Kokopelli's mother and his sisters and aunts, singing the corn grinding song while a young boy played the flute. She visualized also the many sons and daughters of her own, all of them strong and beautiful.

This was her heart's desire. And it would all come true because she was mate of Kokopelli. Meanwhile, wonderful adventures awaited. Kokopelli had said they would visit many pueblos on their journey, beginning tomorrow.

The baby moved and kicked, and Kwani felt a pressure that told her she must go to squat in the bushes. She rose quietly and walked a short way into the brush. For an instant she thought she saw a movement, but it did not come again.

Kokopelli watched her go. He had wakened at once when she stood up, but he lay motionless, observing. What defenseless creatures women were, big-bellied with child. He was glad to be male, glad to be Kokopelli, bestower of sacred seed. There were many pueblos along the river, all eager to trade, eager for the sacred seed to assure good fortune and fertility.

Kwani rose and was silhouetted against the moon. Even in pregnancy she was graceful in movement. Kokopelli felt a surge of tenderness. When she lay down with a sigh, facing him, he reached out and pulled her close. He kissed her small nose and her eyes and warm mouth and felt his passion rise with her quick response.

"I want to!" she whispered.

He glanced at Thorvald who lay motionless, eyes closed. But Kokopelli was not deceived; he knew Thorvald's trick of feigning sleep until an enemy was nearly upon him, when one swing of the ax would sever an arm or leg or a head in a wild gush of blood. Kokopelli knew Thorvald was awake and watching. He had no intention of giving Thorvald the satisfaction of observing Kwani's lovemaking. No, that was for himself alone.

"Please!" she whispered, caressing him.

"Thorvald—"

She lifted her chin in a gesture he knew well. "Ignore him."

Her caresses grew more pursuasive and his urgency more demanding.

"Now!" She pulled him closer and he felt the warmth of her and the beating of her heart.

He entered as forcibly and as deeply as he dared. She must not have a miscarriage again, not now when they had so far to go to reach his distant homeland. He was uncomfortably conscious of Thorvald's secret gaze. He resented being watched; it made him feel like an animal in casual copulation. But since there was no withdrawing now, he would demonstrate his legendary expertise. Thorvald would learn how a Toltec made love.

Kwani's response astonished him. It had been only a matter of hours since he had found her cowering in a tree surrounded by hunters and yapping dogs. An ordinary woman would be cowering still. But not this woman, this Kwani . . . Ah, how sweet the cries, the moans, the warm flooding . . .

Thorvald smiled inwardly. What an uninhibited little Skraeling Kwani was! Of all the primitives he had encountered since the shipwreck stranded him in this distant land, blue-eyed Kwani was most like his own people.

The passionate sounds increased. Thorvald felt an urgency of his own. Kokopelli was adept, but it took a Northman to truly satisfy a woman . . . a woman like Kwani. He wanted her, and had from the moment he saw her among the leaves and branches like a treed cat. He wanted to hold her again.

Kwani was not like the other Skraelings, squat primitives who knew nothing of metal or the wheel, and who used only stone for tools and other implements. His people had learned of the wheel and of bronze long ago. They now enjoyed the luxuries of enlightened times—the benefits made possible by that magical discovery, iron. He thought of his fine home an ocean away, his horses and good wagon, fine clothes of silk and wool and linen embroidered and embellished and lined with finest furs.

Much was lost in the shipwreck, but more was at home. He wished he had some of his gold jewelry to wear as Kokopelli wore his. He thought of his jewel chest at home filled with bracelets and rings and buckles and necklaces and clasps of silver and gold, ornately inlaid with enamel in brilliant colors. How beautiful they would look against Kwani's tawny skin! His urgency increased.

More moans . . . sounds . . .

He must assume control, put his mind to other things. His time with Kwani would come.

The shipwreck. Much was lost, including his men—in Valhalla now. Only himself, two of his men, and three thralls—his slaves—made it to shore. Skraelings were there in a canoe, but his own good ax took their heads, and the canoe took them up the rivers to where his ancestors had gone before and left inscriptions on stone. He, too, would leave word of his coming, for he was descendant of heroes of the Sagas. It was his duty, his destiny, to explore, to find new lands for Viking colonization.

Kwani cried out and Kokopelli groaned in crescendo. Thorvald sat up and grasped his ax.

Not now, not now. Keep control. Your time will come.

He lay down again. He had offered to accompany Kokopelli as burden bearer and partner of sorts. Traveling with him, seeing the land, learning how to deal with Skraelings—different tribes had different names but to him they were all Skraelings—taught him much his people must know for future exploration. Now he would return home to relate his discoveries and to plan colonization. He, too, would be immortalized in the Sagas.

Kokopelli and Kwani lay side by side now. The odor of their mating wafted to him. It was too much. He rose and strode away among the trees to spill his own seed on the ground.

The pueblo rose in a cluster of squares from the canyon floor, bright in afternoon sunlight. Imposing buildings of several stories huddled together like chiefs in conference. Buildings were of stone and heavy wooden beams hauled from distant mountains. Doors were larger at top than at bottom—to permit burden bearers to enter, perhaps—and ladders protruded from rooftops. A figure waved from a roof.

"They see us," Thorvald said.

"Of course." Kokopelli's fingers danced upon his flute. Soon the rooftops were crowded, and people and dogs came running.

Kwani smoothed her hair and her soiled robe. She wished she looked better. "Do they know I am your mate?"

If Kokopelli heard, he gave no sign. His flute sang, "There will be fun and feasting and wonderful happenings because Kokopelli comes!"

A welcoming party met them, six men bearing staffs indicating their authority and positions in the clan. They were Pueblos but of a different tribe, much like the Anasazi except that their heads were not flattened in the back.

"Greetings, Kokopelli. We welcome you."

"My spirit rejoices."

Each man came to take Kokopelli's hand and breathe on it. Children and several women and older men stood at a distance, watching. The women looked sharply at Kwani, smiled the woman's smile at Kokopelli, and glanced at Thorvald with lowered lashes.

Thorvald towered over them all, bright cap shining in the sun, bright hair glistening beneath the cap, and great chest bulging under the blue tunic. One huge hand rested easily on the ornate hilt of his sword. The other carried an awesome ax.

Kokopelli said, "I bring you Thorvald, son of the Gods of the Sunrise Sea, and She Who Remembers, my mate."

His mate! Women stared at Kwani with an impenetrable gaze. She Who Remembers was not what they expected, so young, so beautiful. And the necklace! They had heard of its powers.

"We welcome you."

"My spirit rejoices," Kwani replied.

"Mine, also," Thorvald said.

A naked little boy came to touch Thorvald's ax and stare up at him. "Why is hair growing on your face?"

"To keep it warm when the wind is cold."

"Oh." He gazed at the ax. "What do you do with that?"

"I take off the heads." He laughed his booming laugh.

The boy backed away and his mother called him to her. "Do not be afraid," she whispered. "He makes big noise only."

Cooking fires were blazing in the pueblo; the fragrance of pinyon smoke and rich aromas from simmering pots greeted them like old friends. The Clan Chief met them in the courtyard. He was bent and thin, with a long face and graying hair, and he carried his head to one side as though pushed there by an invisible force. But his smile was young and he still had some of his teeth.

"Welcome! Come, eat."

They were led to the fire by Towanki, mate of the Clan Chief. She reminded Kwani of Woshee with her air of dignity and quiet authority. She wore no blue feathers, but her dark hair was in two braids twined with yucca cords dyed red and yellow.

They sat on deer skins spread on the ground around a pot. Beside it was a basket of round, flat corn cakes to be dipped into the pot to scoop up the beans flavored with herbs.

"Eat," Towanki said, and sat at a distance, hands folded.

Kokopelli bowed thanks with a courteous flourish. They sat around the fire and each took a corn cake, threw a bit into the flames as offering to the gods, and dipped into the pot. Kwani was hungry and ate greedily. The beans were delicious and she smiled approval at her hostess who smiled back.

The men ate even more greedily, while people crowded in the background, watching. Only the children came close, staring and whispering among themselves.

When it was time for the announcements, Kokopelli rose. "We thank you for your gracious welcome and for your generous hospitality." Kwani noticed his glance searching among the women. "We shall reward you. There will be good trading all this day. This night, She Who Remembers will do a Storytelling."

Kwani was taken back. He had not mentioned this to her. He continued, "I will tell the news at the evening fire. Thorvald, son of the

Gods of the Sunrise Sea, will tell of his journey, of his shipwreck, and will demonstrate his markmanship with the bow."

There were comments of approval, and excited speculation. A group of women were whispering among themselves, arguing. One was pushed forward. "Ask, ask," they told her. She shook her head, blushed and giggled. They pushed her again. "Ask him."

Hesitantly she stepped forward and faced Kokopelli. "We wish to know if you will choose . . . Now that you have a mate . . ." Her voice trailed off.

"Certainly. How could I deny this pueblo good fortune?"

Kwani was thunderstruck. He would mate with another woman? Her expression remained impassive; only her eyes sparked fire. She turned to Thorvald and he followed a distance away. She said, "I will not stay here. Take me away."

"Why?"

"You know why. If you will not take me I will go alone."

His eyes searched hers. "Wait here."

Kokopelli was conversing with the Chiefs. Thorvald spoke with him briefly, and Kokopelli strode to where she stood. His amber eyes burned into hers.

"You are mate of Kokopelli; you remain with me." He raised his hand, and for a moment Kwani thought he would strike her. But it was a gesture of emphasis. *"Always."*

"While you mate with another? *Always?*"

"Foolish one." He lowered his voice, curbing furious impatience. "It is necessary. Customary, expected. It is business. As my mate you are privileged to share the wealth I shall obtain here this day in the trading. The trading! Consider that before you presume to shame us all."

She flushed crimson and her eyes flamed. "It is I who am shamed. I am your mate. I refuse to share your seed."

She turned her back and gazed toward distant mountains, seeking to control her rage. Strangers stood about, watching and listening. Kokopelli sought to humble her, to cause her to lose face—before the entire pueblo! She pressed the scallop shell of the necklace to her with both hands, willing it to calm her spirit. She would not permit Kokopelli to humiliate her. She would not! With all her inner strength, she called to the spirits of those who were She Who Remembers before her, silently pleading for their ancient wisdom.

Kokopelli stood with his arrogant stance, looking down his nose. She met his gaze with steady intensity. A look flickered in his eyes, and vanished.

Suddenly, she *knew*. It was if she could see beyond his eyes into a secret place. His spirit, his true self, was revealed.

He is afraid.

It was a revelation.

She looked at his face as though for the first time. The high, sloping forehead, black brows crouched over lion-colored eyes, the haughty beak of a nose, downturned, sensuous lips, the black dots ornamenting the lower half of his face—it was the same face she first saw bending over her in the cave. But not the same. There was a subtle difference. Lines creased his face, lines that were not there before; there was a tightness around his eyes, tension around his mouth. Something had happened to him during the long months he was gone. It had aged him.

He fears he is growing old and he wants women, many women, to prove it is not so!

She turned to Thorvald. "Take me away."

For a moment, the two men looked at one another in wordless understanding. Finally, Thorvald said, "I will take her to the next pueblo and stay until you come."

Kokopelli's downturned lips were grim. "Perhaps I do not need a mate."

He reached inside his mantle for the flute and raised it to his lips. A laughing torrent of sound cascaded as he walked back to the people waiting for him with smiles.

"We go," Thorvald said. Kwani walked beside him as they turned their backs to the pueblo and entered the blue afternoon.

·38·

Kokopelli's decision burned like a coal in Kwani's chest. She wanted no other man. Why did he need other women to satisfy him? If he loved her, would he want someone else? Business or no? She suspected it was Kokopelli himself who originated the idea of his "sacred seed" bringing fertility and good fortune. It gave him an opportunity to enjoy a different woman at every pueblo. She swallowed a lump in her throat.

Thorvald strode beside her, scanning the land, alert to any movement. At least she had him, the Blue-eyed One. She had not exactly expected his huge size and his body hair and thunder-drum voice, and she had caught a predatory look in his glance. But she felt secure in his presence, and was comforted. She would ask him about his people, his homeland, when they reached the pueblo and sat at the evening fire.

Thorvald stopped abruptly. "Look!"

Two runners approached from behind. They seemed to be pursuing something and kicking it before them. "They race. They make a ball with roots and rabbit fur, for speed. They kick ball and follow, and run all day. Kick ball, run, kick ball, run. The one who returns to the pueblo first gets"—he tried to remember the right word in Anasazi—"good things . . . blanket, necklace, food."

"What pueblo are they from?"

"Where we go, I think."

The runners sped past them at a distance. Thorvald and Kwani had left the river and were in a sandy arroyo in a desert canyon. It was hot; sweat ran down Thorvald's face and dripped from his beard to evaporate in the dry wind. He had removed his helmet and tunic and stuffed them in his pack. He still carried Kwani's pack in his own. She had offered to take it, but he said, "I will carry."

They walked in silence. The canyon was a wide, shallow valley, streaked with polychrome colors. In spots it was rose and ochre, in others palest green or marked by dark layers. The wash flowed with windblown sand that rose in little dancing swirls. Hawks rode the updraft, circling.

Kwani was tired; one sandal was worn thin. Thorvald glanced at her from time to time, but they did not speak.

Dark clouds billowed over distant mesas. The desert wind changed; there was a hint of coolness. Thorvald stopped to inspect the clouds and sense the wind with his navigator's instinct.

"A storm comes." He pointed to the clouds.

"I want to rest a while."

"No." He tasted the wind. "We must find pueblo before night comes."

"Where is it?"

He pointed southeast.

She removed the sandal. "See how thin this is? My feet hurt." She flopped down on the sand, rubbing her foot.

Thorvald threw her an oblique glance. He was unaccustomed to being challenged by any woman, let alone a Skraeling. He was tempted to stride away and leave her there. She was, after all, Kokopelli's woman and Kokopelli's responsibility! However, if his objectives—to explore, to colonize this bleak and burning land—were to be achieved, he needed Kokopelli. It would not be wise to antagonize him. Not yet. Besides, Kwani . . .

She stretched out, using both hands as a pillow, and closed her eyes against the glare of the sky. Her sandal lay beside her and her bare, dirty little foot lay helplessly exposed. For a moment, the dark lashes trembled on her cheek and her eyes opened to stare into his. Her blue eyes.

Swiftly he bent and scooped her up. From either side of the nose guard, eyes bluer than hers mocked her.

"I will walk! Put me down!"

"Stop squirming, Skraeling. We go faster this way." He plopped the sandal on her chest.

"My name is not Skraeling," Kwani said hotly. The hair dangling from his chin touched her forehead and she brushed it away. It smelled sweaty and so did he.

He strode rapidly, and she swayed with his long stride. The ground passed swiftly beneath her, and Kwani had to admit it was a relief not to have to walk. She relaxed against his chest, and felt his grip tighten imperceptibly.

Clouds rose fast, casting shadows, dark ships that sailed the valley floor. Gray curtains of rain fell on distant mesas, obliterating them. Thunder rumbled.

"Thor," he said respectfully. "It is for him I am named."

"Who is Thor?"

He glanced down at her with disdain. "In my land, even a baby knows who is Thor." Again thunder rumbled. "Hear? Thor pounds his hammer."

Kwani remained politely silent. She was not about to question his word. Something about this kinsman (were they really kin?) gave her pause.

Lightning flashed nearby, and thunder crashed above them. Rain began to fall in huge drops—too heavily to see into distance. Again, lightning hissed and flashed, and wind pushed them with a giant fist. From a distance came a strange sound, an ominous muttering.

Thorvald began to run and she clung to him, her arms around his neck, her face buried in his sweaty beard. His bow and heavy pack bounced as he ran. A hill loomed ahead. But the sandy, rocky soil was loose and the uneven ground, studded with cactus and brush and small boulders, made running difficult. Thorvald slid as he tried to climb; Kwani could hear his breath laboring and his heart pounding as he struggled to outrace whatever was overtaking them.

"What is it?" she cried.

"Water."

He climbed the hill just as the flash flood swept by with a guttural growl. Brush, dead branches, and drowned creatures swept by—lizards, mice, and the broken body of a badger with its head bashed in. They swirled, tumbled, and disappeared in muddy oblivion.

Thorvald set her down and climbed higher; she followed him. At a shallow cave with an overhang, they heard a warning buzz; several rattlesnakes were coiled inside, and one slithered away as they reached it.

Thorvald raised his ax.

"No!" Kwani cried. They could be sacred beings in serpent form. To kill them would bring fury of the gods.

But the great ax swung once, twice, and only pieces of snakes were left. Kwani watched in horror as Thorvald kicked the bleeding bits down the bank. Surely the gods would take terrible revenge! She must beg forgiveness.

She stood erect, her eyes closed, straining for communication with the angry deities, then began to chant, a singsong supplication.

The Northman, the Blue-eyed One,
is a stranger here. Forgive him!
Forgive him for he did not know
your sacredness, your holy being,
dwells in serpent form.
Forgive him! Forgive us both
for he is my kinsman.

She stopped, confronted by doubt. *Was he really kin?*

Inside the cave, she sank to the floor, avoiding the bloody place where the snakes had been. Her sandal was washed away in the flood. She wanted to cry, to open her mouth wide and howl, but she bit her lips and huddled in her drenched robe, refusing to look up at Thorvald who stood over her. Rain poured from the overhang like a waterfall, isolating them within the cave.

Suddenly, tears forced themselves free. She tried to hold them back, but they gushed, and she sobbed in weakness and discomfort and anxiety and for everything that had happened in the past and for what might be in the future, and for what else she did not know.

Thorvald snorted in disgust. "You should be happy. You could be dead. Maybe you want to go back down there, ja?"

He towered over her, ax in hand. It dangled before her eyes, swinging a little so that it was inches from her face; the sharp edge was bloody red. Kwani visualized herself chopped in pieces, rolling down the hill to the water. It would be easy for him, and who would know? The flood would wash it all away. Nausea, and a sick feeling of fear welled up in her.

Thorvald saw her staring at the ax, and he turned away. Shocked, she gazed after him. Had he been threatening her with that bloody weapon? Doubt began to grow like a fungus. Who was this man, really?

He yanked off his soaked clothes, and draped them on rocky outthrusts of the cave's wall. He strode about in animal self-confidence, showing off his magnificence. Again Kwani was astonished by the hair on his body. Her people were smooth and clean, not hairy like dogs. His chest was shaggy all the way down to his man part which was surrounded by a curly mass. She was surprised also to see that although his body was much larger than Kokopelli's, his man part was the same size. It was beginning to swell.

Did he expect to mate with her? No kinsman of hers would violate the most ancient of taboos. She was alarmed at what he might do if she refused. Her mind scrabbled for a solution.

This is a dangerous man. If I do not acknowledge it he will be forced to demonstrate it. He saved me from the water. I must speak of it. I must thank him. I must make him want to protect me.

"You are right, Thorvald. I could be dead, but you saved me. You are courageous. And strong." She rose and gazed at him trustingly. "I am grateful for your protection."

His eyes glinted. "Take off your wet clothes, Skraeling."

She spoke gently. "My name is Kwani."

"You are Skraeling. Take off clothes."

Slowly, she removed her soaked garments and stood naked. She put both hands on her abdomen. "You saved my baby, also."

He lifted her with one sweep of his arm and held her a moment. He bent and rubbed his beard against her belly.

"I give baby a brother," he laughed. He inspected her appreciatively. Again he rubbed his beard on her belly. "You welcome new father, ja?" He took a rosy nipple into his mouth and sucked lustily. His hair was against her face, and she tugged at it, He raised his head.

"I steal milk from baby?" He chuckled and carried her to a corner of the cave.

She held him off. "I am mate of Kokopelli."

"Kokopelli mates with another. Every pueblo, another. Now you mate with me."

"But my baby . . . it will come soon."

"Did baby hurt last night when you mated with Kokopelli? Ha!"

She looked pointedly at his man part, swollen to maximum size. "But he is not as big as you," she lied.

He smiled in gratification. "I mate with many women, Skraeling. I know how."

"I do not want to mate with you."

"But *I* want." He straddled her.

"I will tell Kokopelli."

"Not if my ax makes you silent."

"Kokopelli would know." She pushed him away.

"If he does not like, I take his head." He drew a finger across his throat.

Kwani stared at him, and at the overhang above. She remembered another overhang where a cougar crouched. Now the man of cougar color bent over her, upthrust ready; this time it was he who had the spear. Slyly she said, "Wait! Women of the next pueblo will be honored to mate with you. You will not have to use your ax to make a woman mate with you there."

That stung. He sat back on his heels, eyes hooded. Never before had it been necessary to threaten a woman with his ax to make her accept him. If he raped her, and if she told Kokopelli . . . But of course, one blow of the ax and he could bury her and nobody would know; he would say she was drowned in the flood and swept away. But he did not want to kill her. He wanted to mate with her. Often.

He would wait. His time would come.

She sensed his indecision. "I shall make another sandal now. If I hurry we can leave before dark. See, the rain has stopped." She reached for his pack which contained her own.

"No! Do not touch my pack!"

Taking his ax, he strode outside and returned, carrying an entire yucca plant cut at the root. He threw it on the floor.

"I need my knife to slit the leaves."

With a muttered curse, he jerked her pack from his, tossed it at her, and strode outside.

Kwani stared after him. Could this be the protector she had waited for, longed for? This man was a predator. He had threatened her with his bloody ax, trying to force a mating. She had trusted and believed in him—and allowed herself to be brutally betrayed. She wanted to scream with anger and humiliation, but she choked back the cry and clutched the shell to her naked breast.

Never, never again would she believe in a man until she saw behind his eyes into the place where his spirit dwelled, and knew his secret heart, his true self.

Thorvald sat outside under the overhang. The waters were already receding; it was as if the flood had never been. He took his wet clothes and hers outside to dry in the hot sun. If the sandal was finished before dark, they could leave. But he was not sure how far away the pueblo was. He was uneasy about traveling this terrain at night, even with a moon. Last night something had moved in the shadows. Or was it his imagination?

Remembering last night, he clenched a fist. He was ten times the man Kokopelli was; why should Kokopelli be the one to possess Kwani? One day *he* would take her, and make her glad to be taken! But Kwani was not like any other woman he had known. He felt, somehow, that she had bested him, and in his bones he knew she would do as she said she would and tell Kokopelli.

He was anxious to get back to his camp.

The boat his men were building would be finished soon. He knew his two men and the thralls were anxious to sail. They would wait for his return, because only then would they be paid; but unease nagged at him. If the men left without him he would be stranded here in this primitive land, far from his beloved northland, his two buxom wives, his children (seven at last count) and his home and his horse and wagon and fine clothes and jewels and his drinking horn, never empty.

He thought of the camp far southeast, where two rivers converged in the green hills, and where his ancestors had come centuries before, leaving inscriptions on stone. How little had they really discovered, how little did they realize the vastness, the incredible variety of this land!

What stories he would tell when he returned home! Ballads would be sung about him in years to come in the great halls of his homeland. He saw himself in the honored High Seat in the dining hall of the king.

It had been wise to persuade Kokopelli to let him become a partner of sorts. This way he could acquire important information for king and homeland—and accumulate wealth for himself at the same time. Turquoise! Turquoise was rare in his homeland. He was surprised and envious at the amount of turquoise Kokopelli took in his trading.

A coyote chased a rabbit down the sandy wash, and trotted out of sight with the rabbit clamped in his jaws. Thorvald admired the coyote; he pursued what he wanted until he got it. I shall do likewise, Thorvald thought. I shall acquire Kokopelli's wealth—and his mate as well. He imagined the stunned surprise of people at home when he returned after all this time with riches, great deeds to relate, and with yet another wife the like of which Northmen had never seen. Kwani.

Thus fortified, he could forget the real, the secret reason he had sought immortality in distant exploration rather than conquest and plunder closer to the luxuries and comforts of home. He had come far to forget his secret; but it haunted him still.

Kokopelli lay on the mat beside the woman he had chosen. He burned with mortification. How could he explain what had never before happened? In the middle of his mating when she cried out for him, his man part collapsed. It took all his efforts and her frantic caresses to make him a man again.

But he knew the problem. Kwani. She and Thorvald were alone together . . . he had not handled the situation well. He had thought of little else. The trading was meager; this village and the others along the river were poor. Why had he insisted on trading here?

He rose and pulled on his clothes while the girl watched. People of these northern tribes could yank down an invisible curtain between their emotions and the outside world. One could never know what was behind that curtain. One thing was certain; he could not allow anything like this to happen again; he would become an object of derision. He must devise a way to avoid such disaster.

The girl's gaze did not falter. He said, "I shall give you a gift."

Fumbling in his pack, he drew out a bracelet cut in a single piece from a shell. "I give you this because you are the final one to be chosen by Kokopelli. No other woman is so honored."

He slipped the bracelet over her hand; it shone pearly white against her skin. "This is for all to know that you are the last to be chosen by Kokopelli. The gods have spoken," he intoned grandly. "From this day, and forever, the powers of my seed shall be in my flute. Wherever my flute sings, there shall fertility and good fortune be." Her expression did not change.

He flung his cloak about him and strode outside. What an inspired idea! Using the gods as an excuse! Of course, he might wish to choose again . . . now and then. He would make suitable sacrifice to the gods afterward. Meanwhile, his flute would become as sacred as he, with no possible disaster.

It was dark and the hour was late, too late to travel. A fire still burned in the courtyard, and a group of hunters sat around it, re-telling hunting experiences, and marveling at the good rain. Perhaps the long drought was over. At last.

Kokopelli joined them to announce the revelation bestowed by the gods. By this time tomorrow, every pueblo along the river and beyond would know that the gods had bestowed the powers of Kokopelli's seed on his flute.

Later, as he lay in the kiva of the Clan Chief, Kokopelli could not sleep. Outside, the voices of spadefoot toads sounded in the night; they had emerged from the sand after the rain, and croaked incessantly. Where were Thorvald and Kwani? What were they doing? He climbed the ladder to stare into the darkness. The toads taunted him, telling him and one another that Kwani, his mate, lay with someone else. A young man. Strong, virile. *Young.*

Unease gnawed in his belly.

·39·

Morning light framed the cave opening as Kwani woke. Her sandal was finished, but it had been too late to leave though their clothes were dried. Thorvald had slept outside, his ax and bow beside him. She rose and stepped out. Thorvald was on his hands and knees, inspecting the damp soil a distance away.

She sat beneath the overhang and gazed across the canyon. Cliffs rose steeply on either side of the wash; beyond, the desert canyon undulated between the mesas. Here and there, tortured rock formations thrust from the canyon floor to soar in mysterious isolation, lone abodes of what must surely be formidable spirits.

"Kwani!" Thorvald strode to the cave. "We leave now." He stuffed her pack into his and strode down the hill, not bothering to see if she followed. Hurriedly, she glanced in the cave to see if anything was left. The morning sun illuminated a spot on the wall that had been in dark shadow before. Kwani gasped, and stared.

Pecked into the wall was the sacred figure of the Horned Serpent, surrounded by other deities. The cave was a holy place, dedicated to the serpent god! That was why the snakes were there—the ones Thorvald chopped to bits.

She stood frozen. *What would be their terrible revenge?* She wanted to stay and offer chants and a sacrifice. But Thorvald walked swiftly away along the canyon floor. She ran after him.

"The cave was a holy place! The Horned Serpent was on the wall. That is why the snakes were there."

Thorvald paid no attention. His expression was grim, his eyes alert. Occasionally, he looked behind him. "Forget snakes. It is not snakes who follow."

261

She remembered how he bent to inspect the ground. Footprints! She swallowed. "Who do you think it is?"

"An enemy. Who hides."

"*Who?*"

"It is Anasazi. Your enemy."

She stopped and stared. "But the Medicine Chief is dead."

"Was he your only enemy?"

"Tiopi . . ."

He snorted. "The tracks are not woman's." He gave her a look. "Did you refuse another man? He may be your enemy."

She returned his look. "Do you mean you may be my enemy also?" She lifted her chin and stared him down.

"No, but I am Northman. He is Skraeling."

She flashed him a furious glance. "I mated with the father of my baby. He was the only one besides Kokopelli—"

"So nobody else wanted you, eh?"

She yearned to scream in outrage, to claw his hairy face. Instead, she smiled. "You are not the first."

She was saying that he still desired her! Well, she was right. He laughed his booming laugh, and slapped her round behind.

The man followed as closely as he dared. In this wide canyon, concealment was difficult in daylight, but he did not know where Kwani and the man were headed, and he could not lose them. Too much depended on fulfilling his objective.

He squatted behind a rabbit bush, watching from a distance until they disappeared behind a tall upthrust. When he was sure he would not be seen, he followed swiftly and silently.

Kokopelli walked rapidly. He knew this desert canyon and respected it. The air was fresh after rain, pungent with the scent of sage, sumac, and countless other bushy shrubs, many with thorns, some with flowers, and all known intimately to the people of the area. He glanced at the sun and increased his pace. Thorvald and Kwani were on their way east to the next pueblo. Now he could do what he must do alone at a secret place.

He headed south for the Great City built long ago by the pochteca, Toltec traders like himself, who supervised construction by local artisans and taught them much. At one time, the city was renowned for its splendor and importance. People of many tribes came from great distances to trade and participate in games, gambling, feasting, and ceremonials. But that was long ago. Before rains ceased and sickness and starvation came, driving people away. Now they believed the city was cursed by evil spirits. Only his old friend, the ancient Sun Chief, lingered there.

Kokopelli reached one of several arrow-straight roads that radiated from the Great City; thousands of sandaled feet had worn the road into the canyon floor. He wished he had lived in the days of pochteca glory. As a trader he might have been partner of a king, traveling with a retinue of criers, servants, and musicians. He saw himself in kingly garments, carrying an ornate staff and a jeweled fan of brilliant colors, while burden-bearers bent under the bounty of his trading.

Musicians would have announced his coming, while criers chanted of marvels for sale: live macaws in cages, shells from distant seas, salt in leather pouches, fine flint, fine obsidian, copper bells, bright beads, and magical substances to heal or to cast spells.

Ahead, the city walls shone in the sun. Kokopelli paused at a shrine to Masau'u and added a stone to the pile. Taking his flute, he began to play. If the old Chief were still alive, he would be welcomed. What stories they would trade!

He entered the city, noting again the perfectly aligned, perfectly designed stone walls. He wandered through empty passageways, up and down ladders from room to room until he came to the lodge of his friend.

He stood in the doorway, staring in shock. A rat scurried away from scattered bones. Only a few scraps of clothing, broken pots, and other discarded objects lay about. A crude and savage desecration.

He bent to examine faint footprints. Apache. And Anasazi! There was no mistake. The Apache footprints were older, barely visible. The Anasazi were more recent, maybe several weeks ago. An Anasazi would not have done this. It had to be Apache. But if the Anasazi came later, why did he not give suitable burial to the sacred bones of a Sun Chief?

"I shall give you rest, Old One."

With his buffalo bone digging implement he scooped out the stones of the flooring and dug up the soil to make a shallow grave. Gently, he placed the bones in it, arranging them in proper order. He replaced the soil and stamped it down, chanting a death prayer, and fitted the stones of the flooring back where they were.

"Rest now, old Chief."

Back through deserted rooms and along hallways he at last reached the great kiva, a long, rectangular room of splendid proportions, with great stone pillars and walls with built-in niches and seating areas, and a pit for the thunder drum. He had paid the Chief well to store his valuables in this one of his secret hiding places.

The empty thunder drum pit had a stone slab floor. Kokopelli heaved it aside. There it was intact—a large pottery jar with a lid. He lifted the lid and reached in. It was all there, the bright chunks of turquoise, and ornate turquoise jewelry including long strings of the precious stone. A fortune. And one he would see that his burden-bearer knew nothing about.

He had his suspicions about Thorvald. True, Thorvald had saved him from the snows. He had agreed when Thorvald offered to accompany him on his journeys to trade and to explore while his boat was being built. In these dangerous times when travel was not as safe as it used to be, Thorvald and his weapons would serve as a necessary bodyguard against wandering tribes from distant places, tribes who knew nothing about Kokopelli and his skills and magic. But Thorvald's weapons could be used against him, Kokopelli. He had seen the gleam of avarice in Thorvald's eyes when Kokopelli had re-arranged the contents of his pack.

Kokopelli unrolled the quipu from his pack. He had acquired it in trade far southeast of his homeland, and found it to be remarkably useful. It was a thick fringe as long as his arm, and of many colors. Each string of the fringe had knots of different sizes at various intervals, representing inventory, places, dates, and other information.

The string of palest green, the color of new leaves, was the string for the hiding place in the Great City. He added a small knot, indicating removal, joined by two others close together, giving the date. Now he must specify the turquoise addition to his pack. He found the purple string of many knots listing additions and removals, tied the large knot showing the addition of turquoise, rolled the quipu tightly, and tied it with a thong.

The contents of the jar went into a buckskin bag he had brought for the purpose; he tucked the bag and the quipu far down into his pack, then replaced the jar and the stone slab. He might need to use this secret place in the future if he decided to become a trader again. Who knew what the gods decreed?

He should be on his way; but he sat on the stone floor, remembering. The snows . . . . It had been too late in the season to attempt the high passes. He remembered how he staggered through the drifts, trying to keep the macaw alive under his cloak, then burying the limp form in its shroud of bright feathers. Weakness had seeped into him . . . He fell asleep, and woke in Thorvald's camp. Thorvald had been out hunting, and found him—nearly dead. He had never fully recovered. His bones ached where they had never ached before. He felt old.

He had lingered to save Kwani's life and take her from the Eagle Clan. He should have remained with the clan through the winter. But he wanted the trading; he wanted more wealth for himself. And for Kwani, his love.

Yes, he loved her in spite of her maddening independence. Those blue eyes of hers probed his soul. Did she believe that being She Who Remembers of the Eagle Clan made her Kokopelli's equal, rather than his mate? Ha! When they reached Tula, she would learn her place. There would be no She Who Remembers there.

But he loved her—in spite of Okalake's child, in spite of everything. She had grown in his consciousness, appeared in his dreams, haunted him with her beauty, her spirit. Yet, it was the manifestation of that spirit which irritated him sometimes when she ignored her status and assumed equality, even superiority. Anger surged in him, recalling how she defied him and left with Thorvald.

He would not leave her alone with the Northman again.

Kwani trudged resentfully after Thorvald. It was hot, and she was hungry and apprehensive in this vast, empty canyon where distant mesas reached to an empty horizon. An eagle rode air currents high in the blue. Great wings bore him effortlessly wherever he wished to go. She envied him. It would be days, weeks perhaps, before they reached Thorvald's camp. Even farther to Kokopelli's home.

Kokopelli. Did he mean it when he said he did not need a mate? What if he abandoned her? She would be alone with this Northman who strode ahead of her, swinging his fearsome weapon with each step. She suspected he would have no reluctance to abandon her, also. All her life, Kwani had longed for love, for security, a home, and children. She believed that at last they would be hers. Now, she wondered. Fear nudged her heart.

They passed several crumbling villages, long deserted.

"Have you come this way before?" she asked. She hoped Thorvald knew where he was going.

"Of course," he snorted. "It is trading route of Kokopelli. We came this way to get you."

Kokopelli had traveled a great distance to bring the Blue-eyed One to her. He had saved her life, made her love him. Of course he would not leave her. Perhaps when they reached his home in Tula (wherever that was) and he was with his family in familiar surroundings . . . It would be all right then. Of course it would.

Sunfather soared higher; heat grew intense. The canyon colors—rust, gold, green, gray—faded in Sunfather's glare. Even the wind was still.

"Where is the Great City?"

He gestured to the right. "Far that way. We do not go there."

"When will we reach the pueblo where we are going?"

He glanced at the sun. "Soon."

"You walk so fast. Please go slower."

He shot her a cool glance. "No."

She stopped, and turned to gaze again at the eagle soaring over the mesas, and commanded her spirit to soar with him. When her spirit was free, her weariness would lessen.

Thorvald turned impatiently. "Come."

She stood immobile, watching the eagle.

"Come!" he said again.

She ignored him, and continued to stand gazing into distance, communing with the soaring bird, willing her spirit to soar with it.

"I say come." He grabbed her arm and spun her around.

She jerked her arm away and blazed up at him. "I go and I come as I choose."

He swung his ax back and forth, meeting her gaze with a blue blaze of his own. "I am Thorvald, I am Northman of Sunrise Sea. I say come, you come."

His big hand gripped her arm and he pushed her ahead of him. She stumbled and nearly fell, and struggled to free her arm.

"Let me go!"

Suddenly he laughed and released his grip. It was impossible not to be amused by this small female who dared to challenge him.

Puffs of smoke rose in the distance. Signals. They were being observed from distant mesas. Nearby was a scraggly juniper tree offering meager shade. Kwani walked to it and sat down.

Thorvald muttered impatiently in his foreign tongue. "We do not stop now."

Kwani gave him an imperial gaze and did not reply.

He leaned over her. "No stop!"

She pointed to the puffs of smoke, faint smudges against the sky. "We are seen. Watchers tell the pueblo we are coming. When you arrive, inform the Clan Chief that She Who Remembers is here, awaiting him." She held out her hand. "Give me my pack."

His blue eyes darkened. He looked at the distant signals and back to her, then removed her pack from his and threw it on the ground. "I leave you, Skraeling. For vultures."

"Inform the Chief to bring bearers. I shall not walk further."

He snorted and walked away. She smiled grimly. He had killed the snakes in their holy place; the gods would take revenge. She ate a bit of dried venison from her pack, inching back against the tree trunk. Its low branches drooped comfortingly over her to the ground, and gave her a feeling of protection.

Embraced by the tree, surrounded by infinite silence, by distance, she felt released from an invisible grip. Thorvald diminished her, forced her to fight back. It was contrary to her basic female nature to fight with a man; the man should be fighting others, protecting her.

How could Kokopelli want Thorvald as a partner? The two men were so different from one another, and yet in a way the same. By choosing to mate with others, Kokopelli also diminished her.

The baby moved and kicked. Kwani wrapped both arms over it and rocked back and forth. Okalake's child. Dear Okalake, who always made her feel that she was loved.

She peered through the branches and thought she saw a movement in the distance. A man moved, approaching. It must be Kokopelli! She tidied her tangled hair with her brush of pine needles fastened with a leather thong. The man was still too far away for her to be certain.

But he did not have the strong gait of Kokopelli. Though there was something familiar about him.

She cowered against the tree's trunk. She would not be seen unless he came close. He stopped, staring at the horizon. Kwani thought, He sees the smoke signals. Then he ran to a tall clump of rabbit bush and hunkered down in its shadow. *Who was he?*

She had seen him somewhere before . . .

Hours passed while the man still hid behind the tall bush. Kwani grew stiff in her cramped position but she was afraid to move and reveal her presence. Where was Kokopelli? Surely, he would come this way.

A kangaroo rat hopped by, with a snake slithering after it. An earth-colored lizard passed, its tail zigzagging behind. Insects droned, and a hot wind rose, but the man still hid in the shadows. Who had walked like that, stood like that with his head at such an angle? She felt a chill of foreboding. Maybe Thorvald would not send help; he himself might not return. Where was Kokopelli?

She was alone, unprotected, in this empty canyon. Alone but for one who waited in ambush nearby. She began to tremble and tried to control it; trembling would make the leaves quiver. She closed her eyes and pressed the shell pendant to her.

"Help me, ancient ones!"

Slowly, she saw again the altar in the House of the Sun. Again she felt the mystical surge of awareness flowing into her as she laid her arms and face against the sacred stone. Silent voices whispered.

You are She Who Remembers, chosen of the gods, and protected by us, your sisters. But you have much to learn, much to endure . . .

The voices faded away.

"Why?" Kwani whispered. She clutched the shell with both hands, willing the voices to return, but they were gone.

She peered through the branches at the rabbit bush. Was there a movement? She couldn't be sure. She ached all over from her cramped position. Then the pure sound came. The flute!

Kokopelli! With a surge of joy and relief, she watched him come. He had discarded his multicolored garments in the heat, and was naked but for his embroidered breechcloth and the gleaming oraments. The headdress of tall green feathers swayed, and his strong, brown legs were crisscrossed from knee to ankle by leather thongs fastening his sandals.

She would surprise him! When Kokopelli was about to pass her, Kwani called, "Ho, Kokopelli!"

He stopped as if stung, and stared about him. She laughed and crawled from under the tree. "I greet you."

He stared at her with an impenetrable expression. "Why are you here? Where is Thorvald?"

"I tired of walking and wanted to wait for you." She was piqued that he did not seem to be happy to see her.

"So he left you here alone." His voice had a strange undertone.

"I asked him to send men with a litter to carry me the rest of the way." His expression did not change, and she said, "There was a storm and waters flooded the wash. He carried me across and up to a cave—"

A spark flashed in his eyes. "You spent the night in a cave?"

"Yes."

"Did he . . . did you mate?"

Surpressed anger in his voice—he was jealous! She took her time to answer. "Why do you ask since you were mating with another at the time?"

His amber eyes probed hers like torches. "Did you mate!"

She relished his jealousy. Let him wonder! She turned away without reply.

He grabbed her arm. *"Did you?"*

"He wanted to." She tried to jerk her arm free, but he held it in a vise grip; she felt the vibration of fury in his fingers. She had better tell the truth. "He has hair on his body all the way from his neck down to here." She pointed. "I could not. Besides, his blue eyes . . . I thought he might be my kinsman."

"Ha!" He released his grip with a gesture of contempt. "You mated with Okalake, your brother."

"He was *not* my brother, as well you know. And why should you care whether or not I mate with anyone else at all since you choose to mate with others?" In spite of herself, her voice quavered.

He assumed the stance she knew so well. "I am Kokopelli. It is my obligation to bestow my seed. It is business. However"—his gaze softened and he took her face between his hands and looked down into her eyes—"it will no longer be necessary. The gods have spoken and given the powers of my seed to my flute. Whenever I play, there will my powers be. So you see"—he bent lower and the amber eyes glowed beneath his dark brows—"from now on I shall mate with you only."

He folded her in his arms and her resentment melted in the warmth of his embrace. "Kiss me," she whispered.

His response made her weak, and she wanted to lie with him right there. But he released her and nodded toward the distant mesa. "We are expected at the next pueblo. The watchers—"

"Wait! A man is hiding over there, in the shadows behind the rabbit bush."

He swung around swiftly. "Where?"

"Over there."

Kokopelli strode angrily to where she had pointed. She ran after him. "Wait! Thorvald saw tracks and said an enemy was following us."

"We shall see."

They reached the tall bush where the man had been hiding. Only shadows were there.

Kwani wiped perspiration from her face. Steep cliffs blocked their passage like giant upraised hands. They had turned eastward to where the cliffs plunged from the mesa to the canyon floor. Kokopelli carried her pack; but the baby seemed an enormous weight. To put one foot in front of the other was an impossible effort.

"How do we get up there?"

"Follow me."

They approached the base of a cliff. Kwani thought, I cannot climb hand-holds now! But she was astonished to see steps cut into the stone. She stopped to rest halfway up.

Kokopelli watched her with concern. He knew her strength was nearly spent. Anger at Thorvald roiled in him. Where was he? Where was the litter Kwani needed? Perhaps it had been a stupid mistake to allow the Northman to accompany him. Thorvald had been eager. Too eager, maybe. It would be wise to be cautious.

On the mesa trees offered welcoming shade. Kokopelli spread a blanket. Almost instantly, Kwani was asleep. Kokopelli lay down beside her. He was more tired than he wanted to admit. Age was betraying him; and there were more mountains and plains still to travel to reach Thorvald's camp. He longed to be at home with his house and flowers and singing stream, and to have his family, his own people, about him. Kwani would nourish his soul with her beauty, and enrich his life with their children. Their sons.

He watched her as she slept. Her dark lashes lay against her cheeks.

Her swollen abdomen seemed almost grotesque in the slender body. There was a movement in it as the baby kicked.

Okalake's child.

This pregnancy was a more serious inconvenience than he had anticipated. He reviewed his medical lore for ways of disposing of it. Roots ... seeds ... bark ... certain leaves and blossoms. But would miscarriage solve the problem? What if it made her weaker? What if she died? No. The pregnancy must run its natural course. He could dispose of the baby, Okalake's baby, afterward.

He wondered about the man in hiding. He had seen no footprints, but the wind could have smudged them. Were they being followed? If so, by whom? And why?

Suddenly, he knew! He remembered his confrontation with Yatosha, Hunting Chief of the Eagle Clan, when he and Thorvald discovered Kwani treed by dogs. The hatred in Yatosha's eyes ... Yes, here was an enemy. An efficient tracker, skilled in killing.

He peered about him with unaccustomed uneasiness. Was Yatosha hiding among the trees? They were safe for now. He and Kwani had been watched from the lookout; it was known they were there. Yatosha must have been observed, also. So he could not kill them until they left the pueblo to continue their journey. By then, they would be prepared and waiting for him.

Kwani sighed and stirred in her sleep. A squirrel sat on a limb, watching. Kokopelli spoke to him mentally, "Greetings, my friend." The squirrel chirped acknowledgment and scurried away. Kokopelli drifted into sleep.

Footsteps woke him. Thorvald was standing over him, smiling widely. Several Chiefs stood looking down at them with inscrutable expressions as Kwani woke.

Thorvald's bow and ax and sword were welcome sights. Kokopelli recognized two of the Chiefs with whom he had traded in the past. They were Pueblo, but shorter than the Anasazi, and wore their hair in two braids. Their ear ornaments were obsidian and turquoise, and they wore many necklaces of shell and bone and animal claws. Their only clothing was a fringed breechcloth tied with a fringed belt, and woven yucca fiber sandals. Each carried a bow and quiver of arrows. A sheathed knife was at each belt.

Kokopelli made the sign of greeting. To Thorvald he said, "Why did you abandon her?"

"She would not walk. I gave them salt and tobacco. They come to carry her." His smile had a hint of mockery.

Kokopelli swallowed his anger. Such a gift was necessary, and he had not been there to agree or to disagree. The men lowered the litter; it was draped with a bearskin, and Kwani sat upon it with deliberate dignity. They walked in single file, while Kokopelli played his flute and the men walked in rhythm to the melody.

Kwani experienced mixed feelings. It was good to be carried; she was more tired than she had ever been. But the people at this pueblo had probably heard of her scandalous behavior at the Place of the Eagle Clan. What would their reaction be? Well, it didn't matter. She was mate of Kokopelli, she was She Who Remembers, and both Kokopelli and Thorvald were with her. Thorvald with his ax and bow and sword . . . No, she was not afraid.

But who was following them, skulking behind, hiding in the shadows?

From where she sat on the litter Kwani could see over the mesa's brim. Her eyes searched the canyon uneasily.

"Kokopelli."

He turned, questioning.

"I think I saw something moving down there."

He strode to the mesa's brim, followed by Thorvald. There was a brief consultation, as they scanned the terrain, and returned.

"A coyote," Thorvald said.

Kokopelli leaned close to Kwani. "It is Yatosha."

She shook her head. She knew Yatosha well. It was not he.

They did not notice the Chiefs exchanging glances.

· 40 ·

Sunfather was low on the horizon when the pueblo appeared. Stone buildings clustered in an irregular arrangement, with as many as a hundred rooms. Smoke rose from cooking fires, muffled drumbeats sounded, and people moved about. But no one approached to greet them.

"Who are these people?"

"Keresen. The Raven Clan."

Kwani knew that the Keresen, like the Anasazi, were one of a number of Pueblo tribes. They did not all speak the same language, but they shared a common culture; they were farmers, fine potters, and expert builders in stone. She had never met a Keresen, and was curious. But the farther she got from her home among the Anasazi, the more she felt she was a stranger in a strange land.

Kokopelli began to play a new melody, a happy announcement. As Kwani listened, something deep within her responded, and she began to sing with it, a wordless song, high and sweet. The men kept step with the melody, and Kokopelli nodded his head in rhythm so that the tall, green feathers of his headdress bowed and rippled in splendor. One of the Chiefs began to chant with the rhythm. "Hu-hu-hu-hu!" The others joined in. Even Thorvald caught the spirit and added his own deep voice, chanting words in his native tongue.

Dogs came running, barking, jumping on those they knew. Children followed, squealing, and marched along with the Chiefs, delightedly, chanting "Hu-hu-hu-hu!"

People were gathered in the courtyard and upon roofs. The sound of the flute, the singing, the chanting, and the astonishing sight of a pregnant woman singing as she was carried on a litter caused excited comment.

"Hear how she sings!"

"It is She Who Remembers, the Storyteller who—"

"When will the baby come? Can you tell?"

"In another moon, it looks like."

"It is she who calls the spirit of Masau'u and Motsni!"

"Beautiful!" a man said.

"Mate of Kokopelli," a woman replied pointedly.

"Some say she is a witch."

But the young girls and many of the women had eyes only for Thorvald.

"Like a bull buffalo," one whispered.

"That chest! Those arms. Did you ever see such arms?"

Others watched only Kokopelli.

"Did you hear that his flute carries his powers now?"

"I shall miss his choosing."

"Yes, I know." Sigh. Wistfully, "Maybe the gods will speak again."

As the procession arrived, the old Clan Chief raised his hand in welcome. Bones protruded under his papery skin, and a network of fine lines crisscrossed his red-brown face. Eagle feathers were in his hair, which was still dark as a young man's. He stood in silent dignity, suitably arrayed in a cotton mantle flung over his chest which was bare but for a necklace of bear claws. At his waist was a short, fringed, deerskin apron, ornamented with dyed porcupine quills, tied with a fringed belt. A small design of a bear paw was tattooed under his left eye.

"You are welcome here, Kokopelli," the Clan Chief said.

"My spirit rejoices."

There was no breath-of-life bestowed here, but Kokopelli raised his right hand at the elbow, holding two fingers upward close together, then brought his hand to his heart.

The old Chief acknowledged the greeting of warm friendship. "Come."

The litter was lowered and Kwani stepped down. Kokopelli whispered, "There will be a smoke in the kiva but I shall be with you afterward."

"Please obtain a new robe for me. I did not have time to pack."

"As my mate, your status is such that you need nothing more." He turned away. "However, I shall see what is available."

The village was a cluster of squares, one upon the other, two- and three-stories high, facing a courtyard where a ladder protruded from a kiva. An old woman stood waiting.

"This is my mate, Wakoni," the Chief said to Kwani. "Go with her."

Kwani followed the old woman through the crowd. Little girls followed like turkey chicks after a mother hen, and gazed up at her in awe.

Wakoni led Kwani up two ladders and to a rooftop where ears of corn tied in a bundle dangled from a protruding beam.

"Welcome to my dwelling."

Each paused at the entrance to dip fingers into a bowl of water from a sacred spring, and sprinkle it in offering to the spirits. Inside, it was dim and cool. In one corner, a baking stone stood beneath an opening in the roof. The stone was a fine-grained rectangular slab, smoothly hewn and polished, resting on four stones, one at each corner. A handsome bowl stood nearby.

Wakoni noticed Kwani's glance. "You are hungry."

Kwani nodded, smiling, and patted her abdomen. "Both of us."

Wakoni laughed; her withered breasts bobbed as though they laughed with her. She wore only the fringed apron tied at the waist with a finely woven cotton belt. Her hair was in two long braids and she smoothed whisps from her forehead with both hands.

"I shall make piki bread for both of you." Her eyes sparkled as she reached for the bowl.

Kwani thought, She is old, but her spirit does not know that. She said, "Where shall I put my pack?"

Wakoni gestured to a corner. "Over there. Unroll the sleeping mat and rest now."

It was good to be in this cool, pleasant room with Wakoni. Kwani watched the old woman adding twigs to smouldering coals under the baking stone. She blew the fire to a steady blaze. "We did not think Kokopelli would take a mate."

Kwani smiled but did not reply. Wakoni put corn meal into the bowl, added a bit of ashes and enough water to make a thin gruel, and stirred the mixture with her hand.

"Kokopelli takes you to his home? Far away?"

"Yes. A fine house with many rooms. And a fountain."

Wakoni paused in her stirring. "What is a fountain?"

"It is three big bowls, one over the other. Water fills the top bowl and spills down to the others and never stops. I shall always have water for my jar."

"Aye-e-e! Where does the water come from?"

Kwani paused to think. "He said there is a stream nearby."

"How does water get from the stream to the fountain?"

Kwani had no idea. "It is his magic."

Magic indeed! Wakoni spat on the baking stone to see if it was hot enough. Satisfied, she swabbed it with a fistful of corn husks tied with a thong and dipped into a small bowl of mountain sheep fat. "His home is far away."

"Yes." Lately, Kwani had been wondering just how far away it was. She didn't like travelling as much as she thought she would.

"The baby will be born before you get there."

Kwani nodded.

The thought had occurred to her but she tried to ignore it. If her baby was born in a wilderness with no women to help, no clan to welcome her child, no one to conduct the birthing ceremony afterward . . .

You have much to learn, much to endure.

Wakoni spread a small quantity of the batter with a quick, sweeping motion of her hand. In a few seconds it was cooked and she lifted one corner gingerly, peeled it off, and placed it in a shallow basket.

While the second sheet cooked, she laid the first on top of it to absorb the heat. Top sheets were removed while each layer was spread, and then put back on top for extra cooking.

Kwani watched with admiration. It took much practice to achieve such skill. Wakoni folded the paper-thin sheets into fours, stacked them neatly in the basket, and brought the basket to Kwani.

"Here, eat."

Kwani propped herself on an elbow and ate eagerly. "Good!" she smiled. Wakoni squatted beside her companionably. She was silent for a while, and then she said, "I am old, and the old ones know many things. Thorvald's people are not our people, not Pueblo. Nor is Kokopelli. Your baby must be born Pueblo."

"But—"

"Wait here with us for the baby. I will help you." She peered at Kwani kindly. "I help many babies to be born."

"You are kind and I am grateful. But Kokopelli will not want to stay . . ."

Suddenly, Kwani remembered the story of Eagle Boy who left his people to become an eagle like his mate. She, too, would be leaving her own people. To become Toltec, taking her baby away.

A chill touched her heart.

Thorvald sat in the kiva with Kokopelli and the Chiefs while the ingredients for smoking were spread before them. The Clan Chief passed a basket of clean, smooth corn husks with other baskets of tobacco and purslane, a fleshy leafed herb. Each took a husk from the basket, creased it with his fingers and teeth, and cut it to a convenient size with his thumb nail. Thorvald managed to do this, but was embarrassed by his awkwardness. If the others noticed, they gave no sign. They took a pinch of tobacco and a leaf or two of purslane, mashed them into the palm of the left hand with the right thumb, then dampened the slip of corn husk in the mouth, drew it between their teeth to make it flexible, placed a pinch of the tobacco mixture in the middle of the slip, and rolled it tightly to about the length of the little finger. They licked the outer edge, pinched the roll together, and folded up and pinched the ends. When all but Thorvald had finished, they sat silently, ignoring his clumsy efforts, although the eyes of several glinted with secret amusement.

Thorvald finally made the roll stay pinched together. Now it was time for the fire stick. The youngest man present reached for a long slender rod which lay with its point smouldering in the fire, and touched the burning point to the tip of each man's roll, beginning with that of the Clan Chief.

The Chief blew a puff to each of the Six Directions, paused in brief contemplation, and said, "We are honored to have Kokopelli and his mate and Thorvald among us."

"We are honored to be here," Kokopelli replied.

No more was said while the men coughed and hacked and puffed. Thorvald fumed with impatience. These endless preliminaries which Skraelings always indulged in were a waste of time. Why could they not come to the point and get down to business at once? Besides, he wanted to get back to the dark-eyed girl who had welcomed him so ardently when he came to arrange for the litter. He had given her a gift of salt (although Kokopelli did not know it yet) and she was willing and eager for him to come again. He felt a tightening in his loins, thinking of her.

The tobacco was finished and the remainder of the roll thrown into the fire. Thorvald thought, now they will discuss the weather, the crops, the weather, the crops. How can I get away?

Kokopelli sensed his impatience and guessed the reason. He said to Thorvald, "My mate requires a new robe. Perhaps we have something suitable to trade for one?"

Thorvald rose, bowed ceremoniously, and climbed from the kiva. There were smiles as he left. Kokopelli said, "My partner has been long without a woman, and yours are beautiful."

The weather and crops were discussed at length, and gambling sticks brought out. Several women carried down steaming bowls of corn and beans cooked together, and rabbits roasted on a spit. They were thanked profusely and admired as they climbed back up the ladder.

The Warrior Chief spoke. He was a young man, squat and muscular, with the eyes of a hawk. "It is said that your mate is a Storyteller who Calls the spirits of Masau'u and Motsni."

"Yes."

"Some say she is a witch."

"So they do." Kokopelli tossed the gambling sticks casually.

There was a strained silence. The lie of the sticks was examined, more wagers made. The Warrior Chief spoke again. "You are taking your mate to your home beyond the Great River of the South. Witches are acceptable in your homeland?"

Kokopelli stared at him coldly. "Witches are unacceptable everywhere. As are those who violate rules of hospitality, insult guests, repeat lies, and demonstrate ignorance of spiritual gifts bestowed by the gods. He glanced at the others who sat with heads bowed in embarrassment. "Perhaps it is jealousy that makes some speak as they do."

The Warrior Chief rose. "It is you who insult us, Kokopelli. You are no longer welcome here."

Kokopelli rose also, and looked down his nose at the short Chief. "Do you speak for the entire pueblo?"

"He does not," the Clan Chief said. "You are welcome here always, Kokopelli. However . . ." He paused and glanced away. "However, it is true that words have been spoken of your mate which are disturbing to us."

"Lies."

"Undoubtedly. But spoken, nevertheless, and once heard, repeated. Our people are uneasy."

"Who has spoken these lies?"

The old Chief looked down at his hands and did not reply. The others gazed stonily ahead, faces expressionless.

"I think I know. Someone from the Eagle Clan is spreading untruths, someone who seeks revenge because my curse is on them for mistreating my mate."

"Because she is a witch?" the Warrior Chief said. His hawk eyes flicked a malicious gleam.

Kokopelli spoke slowly. "Disaster befalls the Eagle Clan, as all know well. *It can befall this clan, also.* I will not allow my mate to be wounded by poisonous tongues. Think well before you endanger yourself and your people." He flung his cloak about him and strode to the ladder.

"The trading—"

"Never. We leave at first dawn. I shall not return here."

He climbed the ladder and stepped into the night.

Thorvald lay beside the dark-eyed girl who had, indeed, welcomed him again. He was unable to sleep; his bed mate snored with surprising vigor considering the delicate mouth and pretty nose. At least she had satisfied his man hunger; for that he owed her a gift. He had already given her salt. But Kokopelli wanted his mate to have a new robe.

The girl's robe hung from a peg on the wall. It was a nice one, he supposed, as far as a Skraeling was concerned, and Kwani was about the same size as this girl whose name he had already forgotten.

Quietly he dressed, and tucked the robe into his pack. He would tell Kokopelli he traded salt for it; how could the Toltec object? As for the girl, he had given her salt and a fine baby; surely a fair trade.

He strode into the night to sleep under the stars.

Wakoni sat watching Kwani as she slept. Sunfather had long since slipped below the horizon to journey underground to his house in the east. Kwani murmured in her sleep. She is talking to spirits, Wakoni thought. She is not a witch; witches do not become pregnant. Witches do not call the spirits of Masau'u or Motsni. I know these things. It is said by the Watchers that she and Kokopelli and the pale bear of a man with them are being tracked.

She shook her head. She wondered about the pale bear and his strange and fearsome weapons. Did he know that Sho-Kotl, the girl who had welcomed him to her sleeping mat, had weapons of her own? Eldest daughter of the Medicine Woman, Sho-Kotl was renowned also for her ability to cast spells. Already she was an important personage in the clan; one day she would be Medicine Woman herself. Truly the pale bear had been honored. Wakoni hoped he had rewarded Sho-Kotl accordingly. Otherwise, she and the Medicine Woman and the entire clan would lose face; The Warrior Chief would be required to do what he liked to do most—take revenge.

She sighed. It took little for men to justify their use of hunting skills on one another.

·41·

K wani slept and dreamed. She was wandering on the mesa when an eagle swooped down and landed on a rock close to where the mesa's brim plunged to the rocks far below. It was the largest eagle she had ever seen, and as she stood gazing, the eagle's head began to waver like a reflection in water. It became the head of a man with a beak nose, piercing eyes, an arrogant stare and tilt of the head. Kokopelli!

"Come closer." It was Kokopelli's voice, compelling, hypnotic.

She approached the mesa's brim. A feeling of danger, of foreboding, made her hesitate.

"Closer," the eagle commanded. His voice caressed her; his amber eyes willed her to obey.

Helplessly, she stepped closer. The eagle waited, great wings ready to unfold. Kwani stared at his talons clutching the rock where he stood, and she knew those talons could clutch her and swoop into empty space. And drop her.

"Closer," he crooned, flexing his wings.

It seemed to grow darker as Kwani moved toward the brim.

"Stop!" a silent voice commanded. An unseen force made her turn. A white form emerged from the mesa's misty darkness. Kwani stared in awe. It was the fabled White Buffalo, chief of all buffalo, a Spirit Being.

"Come to me," it said.

"No!" Kokopelli's voice spoke sharply. "You are *my* mate."

"You are She Who Remembers," the White Buffalo said. "I await you. Come to me . . ."

Kwani woke, shivering. Was she being warned that Kokopelli lured her to destruction—to be carried away like Eagle Boy? To die, abandoned?

She searched her spirit, her innermost knowledge, for recognition of the dream's meaning. She whispered. "Tell me!" But there was no reply.

It was time to go. Leaving the pueblo, Kwani followed Kokopelli and Thorvald along the trail. It was barely light enough to see. She had to watch carefully to keep from stumbling. The dream was still with her, an unseen presence with a hand on her shoulder, holding her back.

Kokopelli asked, "Have you seen any signs of a tracker?"

"No. But he may be too far behind to see," Thorvald said. He looked in every direction. "Maybe he is not following us now." He tugged at the garment of interlocking iron rings under his blue tunic. "This is too hot to wear, but it kills arrows."

"Do you have a robe for my mate?"

"Yes."

Kokopelli eyed him sharply. "What did you trade for it?"

"Salt."

Kokopelli frowned. "I must make calculations on my quipu before more is lost. Who did you trade with for it?"

Thorvald shrugged. "I don't remember her name, but she snores." They laughed.

Kwani was irritated. These men had no manners. Any Pueblo knew better than to laugh without covering the mouth with the hand, and it was rude to laugh without sharing the reason why. An insistent voice in her head said, *"These men are not your people."*

Sunfather rose from his house in the east and the coolness of early morning began to dissipate. They climbed down a steep trail to enter the floor of the canyon. When they could see into unobstructed distance, Thorvald removed his blue tunic, and pulled off the one of iron links.

"This sun cooks me like meat in an oven if I leave this on." He removed his helmet, also, stuffing the helmet and the iron tunic into his pack. "What do we give at the next pueblo?"

"We amuse only."

"Ja?" He was surprised and gratified. So far, nothing he had obtained in his own trading had been given away. But he assumed it would be expected eventually; he had no intention of complying.

Kokopelli said, "I play the flute. You demonstrate your markmanship. Kwani sings and tells a story." He gestured grandly. "They await our arrival."

"They know we are coming?" Kwani asked, surprised.

"Of course. Always they know." He pointed to a distant upthrust like a rocky tower. "Someone is up there, watching." He pointed to the opposite mesa. "And there, also. And there. A lizard cannot move in this canyon without being seen."

"Then one who follows us will be seen, also."

"Only if he travels during daylight."

Thorvald said, "Maybe I backtrack and surprise him one night?"

"No, Thorvald!" Kwani said. "Do not leave us unprotected."

"I do not protect you?" Kokopelli asked sharply. His cheeks flushed red.

Kwani realized her mistake at once. She said respectfully, "You protect us with your magic. But would not the ax and sword and bow be useful also if we are attacked?"

"My sword grows hungry," Thorvald said.

Kokopelli stared at them with disdain. "People worship those who entertain them only a little less than they worship their gods. We shall not be attacked."

He strode on and they followed in silence. Hours passed. They stopped only to eat and to drink, and continued eastward toward where the land rose, humped above the canyon. It grew warmer, and warmer still. Sawtoothed crests of distant mountains wobbled in the heat waves rising from the sunbaked ground.

Thorvald said, "I wish for my horse."

"What is that?" Kwani asked.

"Like a big dog or a big deer. No antlers. I sit on the back and it takes me wherever I want to go."

"Aye-e-e-e! You ride on the back of a deer or a big dog?" She wasn't at all sure she believed him.

Thorvald shook his head in frustration. He wanted to go home. He was weary of this burning land, these Skraelings with their primitive gods and endless rituals. The amount of turquoise he had acquired in trading thus far might be enough for his mandatory gift to the king. But nothing would be left for him.

He wondered if Kokopelli had more hidden away. Once they had stopped at hidden caves where valuables were stored. Perhaps other caves would be visited on the way back? As this was Kokopelli's last trip—or so he claimed—all of Kokopelli's turquoise might be retrieved on the return trip to carry back to his homeland.

Thorvald wondered if Kokopelli would be missed if it happened that he mysteriously disappeared. For a moment, his hand rested on the golden hilt of his sword.

But he must reach camp before the boat was finished. The men were eager to return home. They would not hesitate to leave without him if they had been doing enough trading of their own to accumulate the wealth they desired.

He quickened his pace.

Kwani sat to remove a pebble from her worn sandal. Thorvald and Kokopelli stopped a distance ahead and spoke quietly, scanning the landscape.

They watch for the tracker, Kwani thought. Her own eyes searched for a movement among the brush and the rocky upthrusts. How wide, how empty was this canyon. And how formidable with its tortured rock formations jutting high from the canyon floor. A tumbleweed rolled by, blown by a hot wind. Kwani listened for a sound of life in the canyon's silence. But she heard only the muted voices of her companions. The Toltec. The Northman.

Suddenly, she was overwhelmed with a longing for her own people. But Thorvald had said that the tracker was Anasazi. It was one of her own who wished them harm. It was her own people who drove her away. *I have no people, no clan,* she thought bitterly. I am like the tumbleweed, blown this way and that by the wind.

"What is wrong?"

Kokopelli bent over her. His eyes were warm with concern. He cared for her. She threw herself into his arms, clinging to him. She needed his caring, his love. She wanted no other people than his.

Thorvald stood waiting impatiently. "Look!" he pointed.

A group approached at a trotting gait, their drum beating a quick rhythm. "People from Puname, the next pueblo," Kokopelli said. He turned to Thorvald. "We must have a gift ready. Give me Kwani's pack." He rummaged in it, pulled out Kwani's feather blanket.

"But that is mine!" Kwani cried.

"Foolish one. All you make is mine, remember?"

Kwani bit her lips in sudden anger, remembering the long hours and days of meticulous work making the yucca threads, selecting the perfect feathers, weaving it all together as she sat beside her mother who worked with her. Part of her mother's spirit was in that blanket.

"I made that in my first home. Before you found me."

Kokopelli ignored her and handed a corner of the blanket to Thorvald. "Here, help me hold it up for them to see as they approach."

The blanket billowed gracefully in the wind.

"From now on, it becomes important to approach a city with care, and always with suitable offerings."

"But it's mine! Kwani cried, close to tears.

"You are my mate. I am yours. What we own, we own together. Therefore, this is mine, also."

Kwani stared at him without reply. She forced herself to see him as he was, not as she wished for him to be. He loved her—but in his own way. His ways were not her ways, and never would be. He was Toltec.

But she loved him. He was her only hope for realization of her heart's desire: a home, family, people of her own, protection from want and danger. Nevertheless, it was unjust of him to take her blanket. Kwani watched it waving as if in farewell.

It was hers. She resolved to get it back.

Boom-boom. *Boom*-boom!

The group was closer now. Kwani could see the runners approaching. They were of average height and wore fringed breechcloths with patterns of bright colors. They carried bows and quivers of arrows; the faces of some were painted in strange designs. They stopped some distance away.

Kokopelli made the sign for "friend" and the leader stepped forward. As Kokopelli handed the blanket to the leader, there was rapid conversation which Kwani could not hear. The drumbeat began again, *boom*-boom. The leader turned and trotted back up the path, followed by his men.

Thorvald said, "What was the talk?"

"They want me to use my magic tonight. Also"—he turned to Kwani—"they want you to do a Calling."

"Masau'u? No, I cannot—"

"Deer. There has not been enough game and they want you to bring more. And you, Thorvald—they want to see you use your bow when the deer come."

"You mean we wait for deer to come?" He snorted. "How many days?"

Kokopelli shrugged. "Who knows?"

"I say we go when we want to, deer or no deer."

"You forget. They are many, we are three, and one is a woman."

"A woman who would like to rest for a few days," Kwani said.

She had never called a deer, though she had seen it done. These people did not seem friendly. She hoped her protecting spirits would be with her. Perhaps the spirits of the Old One or of her mother would be near.

Puname was a large pueblo built on a hill overlooking a green valley. Narrow paths wound up and down and around the dwellings clustered on the steep slopes. Kwani, Kokopelli, and Thorvald sat with the people of Puname facing a sandstone cliff at the base of the hill. Before them stood the Medicine Chief and the Hunting Chief, chanting and shaking their gourd and bone rattles. It was late afternoon; soon, at evening, animals would come to drink at the river nearby—if animals were near. Hunting had been meager for too many moons; food grew scarce. It was necessary to beseech the gods.

The face of the Medicine Chief was painted in mystical patterns of red, black, and yellow. He had seen perhaps thirty years, each drier than the last, and he felt his responsibility keenly. The Hunting Chief wore the mask of the Spirit Hunter to facilitate communication with the spirits of the deer. To feed a city the size of Puname, hunters had to kill four deer or one elk each day. If no game was available, only food from the planting, or seeds, and other edibles gathered by the women would prevent starvation. When drought, prolonged and severe, stole the crops and sent the game to richer areas, bartering with other tribes became a necessity. When little was left to barter, disaster stalked.

They had greeted Kwani with warm courtesy, and she felt more at ease than she had thought she would. Although they were Pueblo, they did not have the Anasazi custom of bestowing breath-of-life, nor did they make the back of the head becomingly flat. They spoke in a rapid, breathless fashion, and they used many gestures as if words alone could not convey full meaning.

Now they sat spellbound as the Medicine Chief flourished his gourd rattle ornamented with cloud feathers, and the Spirit Hunter shook his bone rattle so that it hissed like a serpent. A drum throbbed with it.

Boom, sssss. Boom, sssss.

The Spirit Hunter and the Medicine Chief swayed and stamped their feet as they chanted.

> *Ho, towaha, ho towaha!*
> *Boom, sssss. Boom, sssss.*
> Ho, ya! Ho, ya!
> *Boom, boom, sssss.*

Kwani's blood quickened with the rhythm. Chanting rose to a crescendo and the Deer Dancer appeared, a muscular youth with a deer mask and antlers. He mimicked the steps, the hesitation, the anxious movements of a deer desperately afraid.

Flutes shrilled as hunters entered, chasing the deer. Each hunter carried a bow and danced to the rhythm of the rattles and the chanting, chasing the deer around and around the area between the watching people and the place where the Medicine Chief and the Spirit Hunter stood.

Ho, ya! Ho, ya!
Boom, boom, sssss.

The deer became more frightened. He paused, turning frantically from side to side, seeking escape. The drum quickened, flutes and rattles screamed with the blood lust, and every hunter in Puname became a predator, eyes gleaming.

Ho, towaha, ho towaha!
Boom, sssss. *Boom,* sssss.

People joined in the chanting, swaying from side to side, stamping their feet, waving their arms. Kwani felt the blood of the ancients rising within her. She rose, swaying, crying out the words of the chant as the hunters closed in on the deer. They drew their bows, shooting imaginary arrows. The deer staggered and fell; one leg twitched in dying convulsions while chanting rose to triumphant crescendo.

The Medicine Chief and the Spirit Hunter beckoned; Kwani approached as if in a dream. She had never called a deer, but the ancients in her blood had done so for centuries beyond counting. She clasped the shell in both hands, seeking to recall what she had seen of previous Calling ceremonies. She would be allowed no mistakes. Failure could mean a new accusation of witchcraft; game would not obey when called by witches.

The Medicine Chief spoke with ceremonial solemnity. "It is time for the Calling."

"I am ready."

The Medicine Chief extended his arm in a regal gesture, and three men stepped forward, each holding a small bowl from which a slender brush of yucca fiber protruded.

"The sacred pigments are here," the Medicine Chief said.

Slowly, Kwani approached the cliff. She had changed to the new robe and it shone white against the ruddy colors of the stone. The robe was of finely woven cotton ornamented with shell beads, and was tied at one shoulder, leaving the other bare. Her hair, freshly washed in yucca suds for the ceremonial cleansing, hung loose. Her cheeks were flushed and her eyes had an eerie luminosity.

She placed both hands on the cliff, communing with its ageless spirit. Sliding her hands over the stone, she sought permission to intrude upon it. For a time, there was no response. Then a mystical communication flowed through her hands and into her. She bowed her head in respectful gratitude, and turned to the Medicine Chief.

"The stone welcomes the sacred pigment. Bring it."

The men stepped forward, placed the bowls at her feet, and backed away. Again the rattles hissed, and the drum throbbed softly as she lifted each bowl in turn and offered it to the Six Sacred Directions. Holding a bowl of black pigment, she faced the cliff, and began her chant, singing each word to the rhythm of the drum. With a sweep of the brush she drew a zigzag mark.

> *Come to the river!*
> *Boom, boom.*

She drew another.

> *Boom, boom.*

Carefully, she painted an outline of a deer.

> *Come to your spirit brother! Come!*

She placed the bowl of black pigment at her feet. Taking the red, she painted an arrow on the deer's flank.

> *Accept the arrow, oh spirit deer.*
> *Boom, boom, boom, sssss.*

The people chanted, "Come! Drink at the river! Accept the arrow, oh spirit deer!" and turned to gaze toward the river, waiting for the deer to obey. Quietly, they waited. Sunfather sank below the horizon and birds flew swiftly to their nests. The river flowed slowly, silently, but no deer came.

Taking the last bowl, the one with white pigment, Kwani held it toward the direction of the river.

> *Come! Drink at the river!*
> *Sssss. Ssssss.*

She handed the bowl to the Medicine Chief who gestured over it, chanting, and held it toward the river. Then he handed it to the Hunting Chief, who did the same, and returned the bowl to Kwani. They peered up and down the river, but only a bird swooped low over the water.

Holding the bowl in her hand, Kwani turned to face the painting. Drums throbbed like a heartbeat as she sang.

Spirit One,
I give you myself,
My powers,
My solemn promise.
Your spirit shall live, immortal,
As long as this painting
Endures.

She dipped her hand into the white pigment and pressed it against the stone, leaving her handprint for eternity.

People rose, staring toward the river, waiting tensely. For a long time they waited; but no deer came.

Then a small boy whispered, pointing, "Father, look!"

Directly above them, on the hill of the city, a stag stood in profile, lifting proud antlers as he gazed toward the river. Swiftly Thorvald fitted an arrow into his bow, knelt, aimed, and let the arrow fly. The deer stumbled, rolled down the bank to the high cliff's brim, and fell, landing at Kwani's feet below the painting, with the arrow bleeding red in its flank.

There was stunned silence, gasps. Then a triumphant cry as from a single throat.

Feasting was underway. Already, the deer's skin was stretched taut upon the ground, held by stakes, awaiting further scraping by flint and bone scrapers. Kwani had been carried aloft on the shoulders of the shouting hunters, back up the hill, among awed congratulations. She protested that she was only a part of the Calling Ceremony's success and the Medicine Chief and Hunting Chief and Deer Dancers were equally responsible, but no one paid attention. Never had anyone seen such a Calling. The painting on the stone cliff would become a shrine.

Thorvald, too, was praised for his skill and the powers of his bow. He took it as his due, smiling at the women who edged closer.

Now they ate with gusto, discussing the Calling, talking and laughing, planning the evening's activities. Would Kwani tell a story?

She shook her head, pleading weariness.

Would Thorvald demonstrate his aim with the ax?

"Ja."

It was a new experience for Kokopelli to be practically ignored. No one had asked about his choosing, for example. He told himself this was his last trip; it was of no concern to him. But it was. Thorvald's youth and his vitality, and his massive beauty made Kokopelli feel even older than he was. And Kwani's Calling demonstrated powers his could not equal. Resentment was a lump in his stomach.

Moon Woman rose in splendor, illuminating the hilltop where they feasted, and the great spread of valley reaching into moonlit distance below. Kwani sighed. It was good to be here, feasting in the moonlight, surrounded by smiling faces; praised, appreciated. She wished this were her clan.

I have no clan, no people.

The baby moved inside her. Yes, Kwani thought. I have you. I will protect you, little one. I will give you a home, a family, all that I myself long for. When the feasting was over, and more wood added to the central fire, it was time for entertainment.

The Clan Chief, a pudgy man with a face as round as Moon Woman's, raised his hand in gesture-before-speaking.

"We are honored to have with us Kokopelli and his mate, she who calls the deer, and Thorvald, he of the ax and the Sunrise Sea." He turned to Thorvald who sat beaming with women close on either side. "We wish to see a demonstration of your skill with the ax."

Thorvald rose with a rippling of muscles. "Bring to me a squash. Large." Both hands showed how big.

There was hurried consultation and a woman scurried away. Soon she returned with a squash even larger than the size requested.

Thorvald gestured to a wall some distance away, and the squash was balanced there. People backed away, clearing an ax path. With one swift, powerful motion he threw the ax; it hissed through the air, splitting the squash precisely in the center, embedding the blade in the wall. The handle protruded like an arm with a severed hand.

"Aye-e-e-e!" What a fearsome weapon!

"Bring another squash, a little one."

The squash was brought and put upon the wall. Thorvald took his bow, inserted the arrow, knelt, aimed, and the squash spattered into fragments while the arrow sped beyond it into the darkness. Small boys ran eagerly to retrieve it.

People exclaimed in admiration and Thorvald smiled, glancing briefly at Kokopelli who sat silently.

"Now I shall tell a riddle," Thorvald said, glancing again at Kokopelli who ignored him.

> *"Who lives without breath?*
> *Who is never silent?"*

There was a pause, and a girl said, "Trees live without breath."
"That may be, but it is not the answer."

"Then tell the answer."

"Fish live without breath in water. Now, tell me who is never silent."

"My mate," a man said to uproarious laughter.

"The wind," said another.

"That is not the answer. It is the waterfall who is never silent."

They nodded. This one from the Sunrise Sea was better with weapons than with riddles. They turned to Kokopelli.

"Tell us your riddles."

"I shall confer with my flute."

He held the flute in both outstretched hands and gazed at it silently for a time. Then he said in a respectful tone, "Those who are gathered here wish for me to tell riddles."

People leaned closer, waiting for the flute to reply. They were eager to witness Kokopelli's fabled magic. But the flute remained silent.

He raised the flute overhead and turned from side to side. "See? The people await. Look at them."

They giggled self-consciously, enjoying the suspense.

He lowered the flute and brought it closer, as though to converse. "Shall I tell riddles tonight?"

"No. Who wants riddles on such a night? Moon Woman wishes to be wooed."

"Aye-e-e-e," they sighed, entranced.

"Very well." He held the flute up to the moon, and sang in his rich, deep voice.

> *"Does one live forever on earth?*
> *Not forever on earth, only a short while here.*
> *But thou, fairest one, shall live forever."*

He touched the flute to his lips and his fingers caressed it. Gently the flute sang to the moon, sweetly and with rising passion until the stars pulsated and the air quivered. Then, swaying, he began to dance, as birds dance for the mating, as flowers sway in offering pollen; bending, rising, forward and back, around and around, faster and faster, until at last the music reached a soaring crescendo, and ceased.

"Ah!" they sighed, and couples slipped away into the darkness. Kwani sat with lips parted, spellbound. Kokopelli, only Kokopelli could plunge his music into secret places of the heart.

She turned to see Thorvald's reaction. But he was not there. He had disappeared.

·42·

The man crouched on a high point above Puname, looking down at Thorvald who circled the mountain. If he could dispose of the big one with the ax that flew, he could then ambush Kokopelli along the trail. Kwani would be unprotected.

Thorvald paused to peer into the distance; in the moonlight he was plainly visible. The man fitted an arrow into his bow, but before he could release it, his quarry disappeared into shadow.

No matter. He would wait. He had patience, skill, and blessings of the gods to whom he had made generous sacrifices. Too much depended on the success of his plan for the gods to forget him.

He glanced into the distance, and froze. Warriors approached! Hurriedly, he made his way down the mountain and to the trail beyond the city. When Kwani and her protectors resumed their journey, he would be waiting.

Thorvald moved quietly, keeping close to the shadowed side of the hill. He paused now and then to listen and to scan the moonlit trail from where they had come. Whoever was tracking would soon learn that no Northman could be ambushed by a Skraeling.

Talk, laughter, and singing floated down from the hilltop. The people were relaxed and enjoying themselves—easy targets, totally vulnerable. Now, tonight, was an ideal time for an enemy to attack.

A light flickered on the trail in the far distance. Then another, and another. A group approached with torches! Even Skraelings would not be so stupid as to announce an attack with torches. But there was no drum, no chanting, or other sound. A silent approach.

He watched a moment longer, then returned to the top of the hill, to Kokopelli. "We must speak."

Kokopelli rose and followed him.

290

"We must leave at once," Thorvald said softly.

"Why?"

"Look." Thorvald pointed as they rounded the hill.

Kokopelli stood watching as torches grew closer. "There is something ominous about this. We must inform the people."

"They will find out soon enough. We leave now. Take our packs and go in the darkness before they get here." He seethed with impatience. This Toltec peddler knew nothing of battle. He, himself, was eager for it; he had been deprived too long. But Kokopelli would be useless in a fight. And Kwani . . . "We go *now.*"

"They have torches, we do not. They are many. We are not. We must use strategy."

They returned to where the Chiefs sat with the others. Something in Kokopelli's manner caused immediate silence.

"People approach on the trail. They carry torches and make no sound."

There were startled exclamations. Men hurried for bows and arrows. Women snatched children and scurried into their dwellings.

Kwani and Kokopelli were left alone as the men returned with their weapons and followed Thorvald, his ax in one hand, his sword in the other, and his bow slung over his back. His eyes gleamed with joy of battle. Action at last!

As they disappeared into the darkness, Kokopelli said, "Stay close to me. Here." Kwani stood with him by the fire. She was surprised to find she was not afraid.

"Who is coming?" she asked.

"I'm not certain, but it may be the people of the Raven Clan where we were last night."

"But why?"

"We shall soon learn."

Kwani strained to hear. At first there was only silence, then loud voices. Unmistakably, there was a woman's voice loud with anger, and men arguing. Thorvald and the men who had followed him appeared with a group of men from the Raven Clan bearing torches. A woman was with them.

Kwani had never seen such a woman. She was tall, nearly as tall as Thorvald. A raven's mask covered her head with the huge beak wide open through which her face appeared, black eyes ablaze. A long buckskin robe, fringed and painted with mystical designs, covered her from throat to foot. She carried a staff adorned with raven feathers, deerhorn rattles, and copper bells, which she brandished furiously as she saw Kwani.

"There she is!" she shouted.

Thorvald unsheathed his sword before Kwani to block passage. "Keep away," he said with cold command.

The Warrior Chief and his men pushed forward. In the torchlight, their painted faces were evil spirits.

Kokopelli said "What is happening here?"

The Warrior Chief threw Kokopelli a slashing glance. "This is Medicine Woman of the Raven Clan. She will speak."

"She has Sho-Kotl's robe. Give it back!"

The Clan Chief stepped forward and raised his hand. "We are friends. Let us discuss this like friends. Come to my kiva for a smoke." He bowed respectfully to Medicine Woman. "You will be welcome if you wish to come also."

"I want my daughter's robe! This one"—she jerked her staff at Thorvald—"stole it in the night. Give it back!"

"Your mate has that which is not hers," the Warrior Chief said to Kokopelli. "You told him to trade for it. Is this how you trade, stealing from women? In the night?" His voice dripped contempt.

Thorvald said, "I paid for it. I gave salt."

The woman spat in his face. "Salt was your meager gift for sharing Sho-Kotl's sleeping mat. You stole the robe. Give it back!"

"No."

Kwani stared at Thorvald. To steal a woman's robe was demeaning; it caused her and Kokopelli to lose face. How could she have assumed this thief, this ill-mannered barbarian, might be her kin? She pushed his sword aside, and stepped to the woman. The Raven warriors gathered closer, but Kwani ignored them. She looked into the woman's face hidden within the open beak. Black eyes returned her gaze, and Kwani sensed the maternal outrage in that fierce glance. She felt a pang of sympathy. But she must save face.

"Thorvald is a stranger here, as I am. We thought he had paid for the robe. If he did not, we apologize. He shall pay you now." She turned to Thorvald. "Pay."

"It is Kokopelli who pays, not I."

"You paid with *my* salt for the privilege of the sleeping mat. Now you pay for the robe."

Thorvald leaped to a nearby wall and stood with legs apart, ax in one hand, sword in the other. "And if I refuse?" He looked from one to the other, smiling grimly. Perhaps he would not be cheated of battle after all!

The Clan Chief raised his hand. "We shall discuss this in the kiva." He turned away, followed by others.

"It is not necessary." Kwani loved the fine weave and the shell ornamentation of the robe. But it was beneath her dignity and the dignity of her people to keep it now. "I shall return it." She began to untie the knot at her shoulder.

Kokopelli stopped her. "No. The robe is yours. In this robe you called the deer. It is the wish of the gods that the robe remain with the Caller." To Medicine Woman he said, gallantly, "Perhaps it was your daughter's spirit that helped to make the Calling successful."

The Warrior Chief stepped forward, scowling. But Medicine Woman raised her hand in an imperious gesture. He stopped and glared at Kokopelli and Thorvald who glared back. The men of Puname gathered closer, muttering threats.

Medicine Woman turned to Kwani. Her black eyes probed Kwani's, and Kwani felt her innermost being exposed. She returned Medicine Woman's gaze. A quick current of woman-to-woman understanding flashed between them; their spirits touched.

Medicine Woman said, "You are a Caller?"

"Yes."

"The deer came?"

"Yes."

The woman stood in silence. From within the open beak, eyes pierced Kwani's own. "You are also She Who Remembers?"

"I am."

"And she who tells of Eagle Boy?"

Kwani smiled. "Yes."

Medicine Woman turned away and stood silently for a time, fingering the fringe on her garment. Then she said, "I cannot accept the robe. I must be paid instead. Tell him"—she pointed her staff at Thorvald who still stood on the wall—"tell that one who hops about to come here." She jerked her staff and the copper bells jangled authoritatively. "I want turquoise."

Thorvald jumped down from the wall and met her eye to eye. "No."

There was sullen silence as the Raven people pushed forward. Behind Thorvald the villagers stood ready, bows in hand. Women and children crowded windows, watching fearfully.

"The kiva—"the Clan Chief said again.

"I am Northman. I do not squat in kivas." The ax swung slowly, back and forth.

Kwani was alarmed. She whispered to Kokopelli. "Do something!" A fight must be avoided at all cost.

He opened his pack and rummaged inside. Kwani gasped as he pulled out a necklace of turquoise, great shining stones alternating with glistening shells from the Sunset Sea. He held it up for all to see.

There were excited exclamations of admiration. The necklace was worth many robes. He thrust the necklace at Thorvald. "Here is a necklace of beauty to pay for a robe of beauty. Pay it."

Thorvald lifted his sword and Kokopelli looped the necklace over the tip. Thorvald strode nonchalantly to Medicine Woman, and extended the sword as though offering an unclean thing.

She ignored it. "I accept nothing when offered thus."

"Permit me to give it," Kwani said. Looping it carefully over the mask, she placed it around the woman's neck. She smiled. "It becomes you."

The fierce eyes softened only a little. "I accept this as payment—token payment—for insult to Sho-Kotl, to me, and to my clan. Now pay for the robe!"

"Enough is enough," Kokopelli said.

There were outraged shouts and angry voices.

"The kiva, the kiva!" the Clan Chief shouted.

Kwani swallowed hard and raised her hand. "Allow me to speak. Go to the kiva. Talk. Smoke. Remain friends. Leave me here with this honored one so we may talk also." She turned to Thorvald. "You go to a place alone and listen to your spirit."

"Wise words, mate of Kokopelli," the Clan Chief said. "Come." He led the way to his kiva and the men followed sullenly, extinguishing their torches.

The Warrior Chief was the last to leave. "You shall pay!" he snarled at Thorvald.

"I have paid!" Thorvald snarled back, and strode away.

When they had gone, Kwani and Medicine Woman stood looking at one another in silence. Again a current flowed between them.

"How like small boys men remain," Kwani said.

Medicine Woman's eyes glinted.

Kwani walked to the fire and sat down. The woman followed and sat gracefully, arranging her lavish robe around her. Venison remained in a bowl, and Kwani offered it. The woman took a piece and tried to eat it through the open beak, but it was awkward. She removed the mask and set it beside her.

Kwani tried not to stare. Medicine Woman was beautiful, the most beautiful woman Kwani had ever seen. Her large black eyes were pools over which dark brows hovered. The fine line of her cheek and aquiline nose was noble and serene. Her hair was in two shining black braids, each covered and wrapped with fine buckskin dyed bright red.

She chewed in silence, gazing impassively into the fire. From time to time she fingered the necklace, sliding her fingers over the stones.

Kwani felt that they had things to say to one another, but she hardly knew how to begin. She poked the fire, and sparks drifted upward to burn and die in the darkness. At last, Kwani said, "I am sorry about the robe. I have no other and must travel far to Kokopelli's homeland. Have you heard why I left the Eagle Clan?"

The woman nodded, still chewing.

"It is my blue eyes. They say I am a witch. But I have a baby here." She patted her abdomen. "I Call Masau'u and Motsni, I call the deer."

"You are not a witch. You are stupid only." She helped herself to more venison.

Kwani swallowed shocked surprise. "Why?"

"You are Pueblo. You leave your people, you go with these barbarians. Who will teach your son Earthmother's secrets? Who will teach him the hunting, the sacred ceremonies, the chants and dances, all he must know?" She shook her head. "It shames the gods."

"My baby may be a girl. I will teach—"

"It is a boy." She poked a finger into Kwani's stomach. "See how he lies. It is a boy."

There was silence for a time. In spite of Medicine Woman's blunt speech, Kwani was drawn to her. Their spirits recognized one another.

"I did not want to leave my people. They drove me away."

"Wakoni says she told you to stay with us, but you refused."

"My mate—"

"Not Pueblo." She took another piece of venison, and another. "Is there piki bread?"

"No, but here is corn cake." Kwani offered another basket.

Medicine Woman reached in the folds of her robe, brought out a woven bag, and stuffed the corn cake and venison inside. Kwani was surprised but made no comment. The moon rose higher and coyotes sang in the valley. The night breeze came, blowing the embers to a brighter flame. The women sat in silence, gazing into the wavering glow.

"My mate gave them my blanket," Kwani said at last. "My feather blanket I made with my mother long ago. She is in Sipapu now."

For a time, Medicine Woman did not reply. Then she said, "You want your blanket as Sho-Kotl wants her robe."

"Yes."

They glanced at one another, and Medicine Woman said, "It is men who cause the trouble."

"That is true."

From the kiva came the unexpected sound of Kokopelli's flute. Medicine Woman nodded. "Kokopelli knows medicine for the spirit. It is too bad he is not Pueblo."

Kwani did not reply, for what could she say?

The flute played, the coyotes sang, and a night bird called.

"I wonder where Thorvald is," Kwani said.

"Tell me about him. Why is he here?"

"Because he has blue eyes. I thought he might be my kinsman, and asked Kokopelli to take me to him, but he brought Thorvald to me, instead."

"Do you believe he is your kinsman?"

Kwani shook her head. "For a long time I hoped . . . When my people drove me away, my mother told me to find the Blue-eyed One who would be my protector. But—"

Medicine Woman gave Kwani a wise glance. "But he wants to possess you before he will protect. Is that not so?"

Kwani looked away. "He is hairy like a dog. And I am mate of Koko-pelli."

Medicine Woman smiled. "He is not your kin. He could not call Masau'u or Motsni or the deer. Who taught you these things?"

"I do not know. Perhaps the spirit of the Old One, She Who Remembers before me . . ."

"Ah."

The sound of the flute ceased. "They come," Medicine Woman said, and replaced the mask.

Kwani tensed as the men climbed from the kiva and stood in a silent group, facing her. Kokopelli and the Clan Chief approached.

"Where is Thorvald?" Kokopelli asked.

"We do not know."

"It is decided that Thorvald must pay for the robe," Kokopelli said.

Medicine Woman rose in magnificent dignity, summoning the Warrior Chief to her side with a gesture. "Light the torches. We leave now."

"But—" he choked. His men muttered and shifted uneasily. "You must be paid."

"I am paid." She patted the bulging bag beneath her robe, and looked at Kwani. "I shall ask Masau'u to protect you on your journey."

Kwani raised two fingers of her right hand and brought them to her heart. Medicine Woman did the same. Then they were gone down the trail, torches lighting the way.

The women and children came running. "What did you do? What did you give her?"

Kwani smiled and did not reply. She whispered to Kokopelli, "Take me where we can talk alone." She suspected he would not like what she had to say, but say it she must.

He led her to distant shadows. "What is it?"

"That beautiful turquoise necklace. It was wise of you to give it to Medicine Woman." She wanted to say, why didn't you give it to me, but she did not.

"Of course."

"I am sure that the Clan Chief here would like to have such a necklace for his mate."

Kokopelli cocked his head. "What are you trying to tell me?"

"I want my blanket back. It means much to me. Please buy it."

"It would be improper to suggest it."

"Then I shall!"

"I forbid it," he said in exasperation. "Let the matter be."

Kwani flushed with resentment. She was his mate, his equal, not his inferior. His attitude belittled her status. She would not allow it!

"You gave them my feather blanket that I made before I met you. You could have given the necklace. That is unjust. I want my blanket back!"

"The necklace was worth much more than your blanket. I shall not discuss this further." He turned away.

Kwani managed to keep her voice under control. "Please, Kokopelli, be reasonable. You said that all you own is mine—"

"And all you own is mine."

"You helped yourself to my blanket. Therefore, is it not fair that I help myself to your turquoise so that I may buy my blanket back?"

"I forbid it!" He strode away.

Kwani stood looking after him, burning with resentment. Among the Anasazi, women were highly regarded; a man's mate was his equal, even his superior. Thoughts churned in her mind.

To him I am not She Who Remembers. I am not his equal. It could be that in his homeland I shall be nothing more than a possession to be used and displayed as he sees fit. Why do I make this difficult journey to his distant home?

She knew why. Because she loved him. Because she did not want to be a woman alone again, without a mate, without a protector, without a home.

The baby moved, and Kwani wrapped both arms over it. "Do not be afraid," she whispered. "All will be well."

But worry nagged at her. Would Kokopelli welcome the child as his own? In Thorvald's camp there were sure to be women of neighboring tribes to help with the birthing. But what if the baby was born before they reached camp?

She clasped the shell for comfort. "Help me!"

Memory of the dream drifted into her mind. The White Buffalo.

"I await you. Come to me."

She concentrated on the dream, seeking its meaning. Slowly, knowledge and assurance welled up within her. The White Buffalo wished to tell her a wonderous truth. Somewhere she would meet the sacred one face to face and learn the truth, the magical secret, the Spirit Being waited to reveal.

It was her destiny.

* * *

Hidden in deep shadow, Thorvald congratulated himself on his restraint. He had been nearby the whole time, watching and listening to the threats of the Raven warriors while he burned with frustration at being deprived of battle. He understood why Berserks left their ships to avoid harming their shipmates when the battle rage was upon them, and wrestled with forest trees until the rage subsided. He could have thrown his ax or shot his arrow countless times. But he waited. Now he would be rewarded.

He had seen and heard the confrontation between Kokopelli and the Skraeling. He could help himself to Kokopelli's turquoise whenever he pleased, and the Skraeling who refused a Northman, and who presumed to order him about, would be blamed.

·43·

Kwani looked at the children clustered around her, eager faces turned up like open bowls waiting to be filled. Some sat crosslegged, some lay on fat little stomachs, some sat on their haunches, and two small ones were on her lap.

"Tell us about Eagle Boy!"

They loved that story, but she could not tell it again. She and Kokopelli and Thorvald had lingered in Puname for six days, and each day the children wanted stories. Always, someone wanted to hear about Eagle Boy again. Each telling became more painful as Kwani thought of how she, too, was leaving her people.

"That is all for today. I must talk with Makeeah."

She climbed the steep path to Makeeah's dwelling, wondering how she could bring up the matter of her feather blanket. She could not go away and leave it behind; it was part of her. Already, she had been forced to forsake many of her treasured things; she could not lose this. Makeeah, mate of Puname's Clan Chief, was the clan matriarch. Perhaps she could help.

The home of the Clan Chief was the highest on the hill. Makeeah, his mate, was sitting outside, sewing a little fur garment. "I greet you, Makeeah."

"I welcome you." Makeeah smiled, revealing wide gaps in her front teeth like open windows. "Come and sit beside me." Her bone needle moved in and out with the ease of long experience.

"I cannot stay. Kokopelli wants to leave in the morning and I must rearrange my pack."

Makeeah gave Kwani a shrewd and kindly glance. "Do you wish to leave?"

"No. I—"

"Stay with us. Allow your baby to be born here. We will give it many names, many presents."

"Thank you, Makeeah. I have been happy here. But—"

Makeeah nodded. "I understand. That is always the way, is it not?" She sighed in resignation. "If Kokopelli wishes to go, you must go. His people will be your people, your clan." She patted Kwani's shoulder. "They will be fortunate to have you." She bent again over her sewing. "We shall miss you."

"I shall always remember you and Puname, Makeeah."

They sat in silence for a time, while Makeeah's needle appeared and disappeared in the fur. Kwani said tentatively, "I have been wanting to ask your advice—"

The needle stopped.

"It's about my blanket. It has the spirit of my mother. Kokopelli did not know that when he gave it." She swallowed. "Would it be possible for me to buy it back?" She hurried on. "Kokopelli does not want to suggest it because it would not be proper. He does not want to offend. Nor do I."

"Allow me time to consider the matter." Makeeah sat back, looking thoughtful. "Come to my dwelling before you leave. I shall have an answer."

They were packed and ready to go. The people of Puname pushed packages of food and bags of water into their hands, saying goodbye, while girls clung to Thorvald, begging him to stay.

Kwani climbed to Makeeah's home, and entered. Makeeah sat, hands folded, smiling her gap-toothed grin. "I thought you had forgotten."

"Of course not. I come to say goodbye."

Makeeah removed a bundle on which she had been sitting. It was wrapped in a small robe of squirrel skins and fastened tightly with buckskin thongs.

"Here is my answer. The robe is for your baby; what is inside is for you. It is not permissible to buy back your blanket."

Kwani tried not to show her disappointment about the blanket. "Thank you for the gift, Makeeah." She leaned down and hugged the woman. "I shall remember you always."

Makeeah pointed her two forefingers at Kwani in the sign of "Until we meet again."

"I shall wait for your return."

Kwani made her way back down the hill. Tears welled up; to leave her feather blanket behind was like telling her mother's spirit goodbye.

Kokopelli and Thorvald waited impatiently; soon they were on the trail.

Beyond the hill, the valley unfolded with distant blue mountains on either side. White clouds soared against an awakening sky, and the breeze of early morning carried the fragrance of Earthmother's grasses. Thorvald wore his helmet and his tunic of iron links. He seemed in fine spirits as he strode ahead of them.

Kwani felt rested and refreshed. As they followed the trail she felt a new stirring of adventure in spite of the burden within her which grew heavier each day.

Subtly the landscape changed. Grasses grew taller, pinyon and juniper trees grew more thickly with other trees Kwani did not recognize. A running bird with a long tail dashed by, chased by mockingbirds diving at it with long swoops. Clouds billowed majestically, changing shape.

Kokopelli had removed his headdress of tall green feathers and wore, instead, the feathered cap with the fringe of turquoise beads. His bare, brown torso displayed his strong back and his legs were lean and muscular. He had magic for her—his voice, his music, his caress. If only—

If only what?

She wasn't sure. But she knew all would be well when they were in his homeland among his people. She wondered about them, often. Would they welcome her as the people of Puname had done?

Thinking of Makeeah made her remember the gift. She wanted to stop and unwrap the little robe and see what was inside the bundle, but Kokopelli and Thorvald were walking too fast; she was barely able to keep up. Sunfather was directly overhead when Kokopelli stopped. It must be time to eat, Kwani thought. But Thorvald and Kokopelli bent to look at the ground. Kwani came closer to see. It was a paw print.

"A bear!" she said.

Kokopelli nodded. "Grizzly. Two, maybe three days ago."

"How big?" Thorvald asked.

Kokopelli raised his arm waist high. "But when he stands on his hind legs, he is tall as you."

Thorvald hefted his ax. "I take his head."

"Not if he takes yours first," Kokopelli said drily.

They sat beneath a pinyon tree and took out the packs of food and the water bags given to them at Puname. Kwani drank thirstily, but she could not eat until she discovered what was in the bundle.

"See what Makeeah gave me." She untied the thongs and lifted the little robe. Beneath was her feather blanket, tightly rolled.

"My blanket! Look! She gave it back!" Kwani's voice trembled. "She gave it back!"

Kokopelli sat in stony silence, gazing at her with an unwavering stare. "What did you buy it with?"

"I did not buy it, Kokopelli. It was a gift."

"They would not give back a gift I gave them unless you asked for it."

Kwani felt herself flushing. She had asked, in a way. What could she say? "I . . . I did not ask for a gift."

They ate in frigid silence.

Thorvald said, "The bear will stay far away if he wants to keep his head. Ha!"

Kokopelli did not reply. His face was frozen in a grim line.

All day they followed a faint trail, and saw no one. It grew cooler as they climbed higher to foothills of the mountains. When they stopped to make camp and to eat, Thorvald sat with his back to the fire, watching. It would be easy for a tracker to hide among the trees.

At nightfall, while Thorvald's back was turned, Kokopelli reached into his pack for his bag of turquoise. Still leaving it concealed within the pack, he opened it and counted the necklaces and, one by one, the chunks of turquoise. A chunk as big as his palm was missing. Slowly, he returned the turquoise to the bag, fastened it, and shoved it deeper into his pack. He turned to confront Kwani but she was rolled in her feather blanket, already asleep.

Throughout the night, Thorvald and Kokopelli took turns watching. When it was Kokopelli's turn to sleep, he used his pack as a pillow. But sleep eluded him; Kwani's arrogant disobedience in stealing the turquoise to buy her blanket was an affront to his manhood.

And yet, of all the women with whom he had mated, some of whom he had loved—or thought he had—Kwani was the only one he wanted as mate. Her beauty, her spirit, her vulnerability . . . but there was more. She satisfied the mystical in him, the Toltec reverence for the unknown. How could she have betrayed him?

With dawn came distant thunder and dark clouds scudding low. Kwani sat up, fearing another flash flood. Thorvald was gnawing a piece of venison while he studied the sky. Kokopelli sat at a distance, rummaging in his pack. She rose and went to sit beside him.

"A storm comes."

He did not reply.

"How far is it to the next pueblo?"

He looked at her with hooded eyes. Finally he said in a controlled voice, "It is a dangerous pueblo. We shall avoid it and go directly to Cicuye."

"What people are there? In Cicuye?"

"Towa. It is the last Pueblo city before we get to the Plains where other tribes are." He stood and shouldered his pack as Thorvald approached. "Tiwa are south of here, and Tewa are in the canyon where we go."

Thorvald snorted. "Towa, Tiwa, Tewa. Only Skraelings would have names like that. It makes no sense."

"They are all Pueblo." Kokopelli's voice had a sarcastic edge.

Thorvald scanned the sky. "Big wind coming."

Kokopelli said, "We might reach the pass, where caves are. We will make a shortcut through the mountains to the pass which leads to Cicuye."

There was a boom of thunder, and Kwani cringed. "But the pueblo is closer. How dangerous is it?"

"Dangerous enough to avoid, obviously, or I would not avoid it."

"But you . . . your flute . . ."

"Times are changing. Last time I was there they allowed me to enter but they did not make me welcome. Trading was poor. We go to the pass."

Thorvald shifted from one foot to the other. "We waste time!"

A crash of thunder was followed by lightning. A gray curtain of rain descended over distant mountains. Wind rose; lightning flashed closer. With a groaning crack and loud rustle a tree fell nearby.

"Please!" Kwani cried. "The pueblo!"

The sky drew darker; clouds galloped wildly with the wind. Kwani clasped her necklace. It is the gods, she thought. They will punish me and the baby for leaving our people.

"Please!" she cried again. "The storm may be more dangerous than the pueblo."

"Very well," Kokopelli said. "We shall go to the pueblo, but we must be cautious. Stay close to me." He looked at Thorvald. "It would be wise to follow my instructions."

Thorvald looked scornful, but he did not reply.

The trail led up and down around hills and stony upthrusts, while the wind pushed and growled in their ears. Kwani followed as fast as she was able, and the baby squirmed as if in protest.

"Wait, little one," she whispered. "We shall be safe soon." Safety for the baby was what mattered now. Kwani bent to the wind and struggled on.

The man followed furtively. They would be forced to find shelter before they reached the pueblo. He searched uneasily for a rocky upthrust that might have a small cave. He was a stranger to this land. The farther he got from home, the more forbidding the land and its gods became. He wanted to turn back. But the thought of the riches and glory which would be his with the successful completion of his plan gave him courage.

* * *

Raindrops fell, big ones.

"Over there." Kokopelli pointed to a small, towerlike pile of rock jutting from the earth beyond the hill. "There may be a cave."

"I will see." Thorvald headed for it in a loping run.

Suddenly the rain became hail, huge chunks of ice big as bowls, growling, thudding, pounding down with stunning force, shattering into smaller chunks as they hit the earth. Trees shuddered and groaned as limbs were torn away.

Kwani bent forward in terror, wrapping her arms around herself, trying to protect the baby from the savage rage of the gods.

Thorvald came running, with hail bouncing off his helmet.

"A cave!"

He swept Kwani from her feet and ran with her to the cave. Kokopelli ran after them, trying to protect his head and face with both arms. In all his travels Kokopelli had never experienced hail like this.

"Tlaloc!" he beseeched the Rain God. "Be merciful!"

A chunk of ice hit the side of his head. He staggered and fell, lying unconscious as hail pummeled his body.

Kwani and Thorvald cowered in the cave, waiting for Kokopelli. The cave at the foot of the hill was low and shallow; they had to huddle on their haunches, but it offered some protection from the wind and the hail—except for occasional chunks of ice that rolled down from the hill and into the cave. Thorvald shoved the hail out with his foot, bumped his head with a clang, and cursed passionately in his own language.

Kwani shivered wretchedly. When Kokopelli did not appear, she said anxiously, "Where is he? Something must have happened."

Thorvald had already reached that conclusion. Perhaps the gods were assisting him, after all. But no, he needed Kokopelli a while longer.

"I find him."

Kwani huddled against the damp wall, fearful of what other punishments the gods would devise. She wished for her mother, for her childhood home, even for the peaceful times long ago when Wopio. . .

"Thorvald! Kokopelli!" she called.

There was no response. Huge chunks of hail rolled into the cave. She pushed them out to make room for Kokopelli and Thorvald when they returned.

If they returned.

"I will not be afraid," she said aloud. But she could not control her trembling.

She pressed the necklace to her, willing courage and serenity into her spirit, but she trembled still. She closed her eyes and called in silent desperation to the ancient ones.

Centuries flowed by, like rivers to the sea. Voices of all who had been She Who Remembers blended with the river sound. A murmuring, soft, insistent, became a single voice, that of the Old One.

"You are one of us, my daughter. Acquire wisdom. Learn the true purpose of your journey."

The voice dissolved into the river sound, and faded away.

Kwani opened her eyes, and realized she was no longer afraid. But she puzzled over the words of the Old One. Was not the purpose of her journey to find the White Buffalo, and to travel with Kokopelli to his homeland and become one of his people?

Thorvald appeared from around the hill, carrying Kokopelli who hung limp. Thorvald shoved the unconscious body into a seated position against the wall.

"He is wounded!" Kwani cried. A great, bloody bruise was swelling on one side of Kokopelli's forehead.

"Hail."

Thorvald pulled open Kokopelli's eyelids and inspected the eyes with the knowledge of one experienced with the blows of battle. He felt the pulse, and nodded.

"He is unconscious, but he will wake. We must stay here until he can walk again. Sometimes they walk crazy for a while."

Kwani pulled Kokopelli to her, and cradled his head on her shoulder. She loved this man, she needed him, and would go anywhere with him gladly! Her fear of deserting her Pueblo homeland and taking her child to a strange, far distant place, was forgotten. Surely the gods would understand that his people would be her people!

The storm abated, the clouds raced away, and Sunfather looked down on destruction. Thorvald stepped outside to see hail in piles and huge drifts with brush and grasses crushed underneath. A bird's nest lay on the ground with what was left of three little birds still in it. Tree limbs lay where they had been torn away, and other branches dangled helplessly.

Thorvald shook his head. He had seen many storms at home and at sea, but never hail like this. It was unnatural—an act of foreign gods. Never would he recommend colonization here. No crops could survive such battering. Unprotected animals would be hurt or killed.

He glanced at the sun; it was late afternoon. Another day wasted! He wondered if the storm had reached his camp, and if the boat were finished. Surely, his men would wait for his arrival before leaving; they would want to be paid.

He strode about in the icy hail, welcoming the chill of it after the heat of this cursed land. He thought of Kokopelli and Kwani in the cave, and was tempted to leave them and hurry on to his camp. But Kokopelli's riches—riches which could be his—made it necessary to keep the Toltec alive. And Kwani . . . he grinned, visualizing the envious astonishment of people at home when he displayed his exotic trophy. A newborn baby would be a nuisance but that would be no problem. Northmen knew how to dispose of an unwanted child.

Kwani sat close to Kokopelli, watching him with concern. He was awake but his eyes were glazed with pain. His pack was beside him and he opened it, feeling inside for his medicine bundle.

"Let me help you," Kwani said.

"No."

He found the bundle, pulled it out, and opened it. Kwani gazed in awe at its contents: strange surgical implements, rolled strips of soft buckskin, mysterious objects, and little bags and bundles of different sizes. He opened one, removed three dried leaves and a bit of root. They should be boiled to make a brew, but he could not wait. He put them into his mouth and chewed. This, and peyote, the "sun plant," would give relief from the pain in his head and the bruises on his body. He wondered if his skull was fractured, but his fingers found no suspicious ridges. Relief, and rest, would enable him to continue the journey. If only he were not so weary.

Kwani was outside, bent over a small fire where broth cooked in a small clay pot from her pack. Dried meat and beans and water melted from hail would be a meal to feed her and the baby, and give Kokopelli strength. She didn't worry about Thorvald; he could fend for himself.

They were eating when Thorvald returned. He sniffed eagerly and snatched the pot. It was nearly empty. He scowled.

"You do not have some for me?"

"You have food in your pack."

He tipped the bowl and drank the rest of the contents, scooping the remaining meat and beans into his mouth with his forefinger.

Kwani stared at him with contempt. "Strong men do not feel the need to take food from women and from men who are wounded."

"This strong man carried you here, carried him here in the storm." He swiveled his head at Kokopelli. "But for me, you both be dead. You begrudge me this trickle of slop? Ha!"

He threw the bowl to the ground where it broke in two. Each piece wobbled drunkenly in a different direction.

"My pot!" Kwani screamed in rage. She threw herself at Thorvald, clawing at him with both hands. "You killed my pot!"

He laughed, eyes glinting. He grabbed both her hands and pulled her to his lap. She wept in fury, and struggled to be free.

"Let me go!"

He held her arms behind her, and bent to nuzzle her breast.

"Stop!" Kokopelli was on his knees, holding Thorvald's ax overhead with both hands. "Let her go." His hands shook but his voice was steady and his eyes deadly.

Thorvald reached for the ax. Kwani jerked free, snatched the ax, and ran outside. Thorvald ran after her. Kwani heaved the ax to her shoulder. In her fury, the ax had no weight at all. "You killed my beautiful pot!" Her voice squeaked with rage. She swung the ax at him and he grabbed it easily.

"Ha!" he laughed. "You think to kill me, eh?"

He swung the ax overhead until it whistled. "It is Northman who kills, Skraeling."

Kwani stared at him with a surge of fear. She backed away, but he followed, still swinging the ax. His eyes glinted with mockery, and something more. The ax swung closer.

"Stop!" Kokopelli yelled.

Kwani whirled to see him staggering toward them. He faltered, tried to call again, and fell.

"Kokopelli!" Kwani ran and knelt beside him. He was unconscious again. Thorvald stood watching. After a moment he shoved his big foot into Kokopelli's side and rolled him to his back. The ax dangled above Kokopelli's stomach.

Kwani blazed up at him with fury that overcame fear. She pushed the ax aside with a gesture of contempt.

"Carry him back to the cave."

"Why?" he grinned.

"To show how strong and brave you are, you and your ax."

"Carry him yourself." Abruptly, he turned and strode to the cave.

She ran after him and grabbed his arm. "Don't leave him out there! Bring him back!"

"No."

He squatted and leaned against the wall, with the ax beside him. He rested his arms on his knees, and his big hands hung free. He gazed ahead, ignoring her.

Kwani stared at those hands. Brutal. And hairy, like the rest of him. She turned away, overcome with a feeling of helplessness. Her mate lay wounded and unconscious. What if he died? She would be stranded here with this Northman who would abandon her or kill her as his whim dictated. The baby kicked as if sensing her fear, and she wrapped both arms over it, forcing herself to be more calm for the baby's sake.

Thorvald glanced up at her with amused calculation. Deliberately, he reached for Kokopelli's pack and heaved it between his knees, preparing to open it.

"So the brave and strong Northman must steal, also?"

Kwani stared down at him as though he were something that even vultures would not consume. "How wise to wait until the owner is unconscious."

"He owes me his life. Not once, but twice. I take pay."

"What Kokopelli owes, Kokopelli pays. Bring him back."

Thorvald ignored her and rummaged in the pack, gloating. With a yelp of outrage, Kwani grabbed the pack and tried to pull it away. He held it easily with one hand and laughed, relishing her helpless fury. Her long hair fell free where the wind had whipped it, and her eyes blazed with blue fire.

Suddenly he tossed the pack aside and pulled Kwani down to him. She fought, enraged and frightened, while he kissed her savagely, fumbling at her breast. He pinned her down with one hand while he pulled off his undergarment with the other. The more she fought, the more he growled with pleasure.

"Kokopelli!" Kwani screamed.

"You have Northman now." He yanked her robe aside and forced himself into her with a brutal thrust.

Kwani lay rigid, biting her lips to keep from screaming again. She would not permit him to relish evidence of her fear and pain. She struggled to breathe against the hairy chest mashed to her face; the hair was in her mouth and nose, and she wanted to vomit.

Again and again he thrust. She forced herself to lie still, to tolerate, to endure, endure, until at last it was over.

He laughed in sated satisfaction.

"My woman now."

Outside the cave entrance Kokopelli lay where he had crawled. He had seen the open bag, he had seen the final act of mating when Kwani lay quietly—willingly!—beneath the man, the young man with body like a buffalo's. He had heard Thorvald's words and waited for Kwani's denial. Incredibly, none came.

His heart felt a blow more deadly than any the gods could bestow. He crawled back to where he had been, and closed his eyes. He did not want them to know what he had seen and heard.

How often had they mated before? How could he have been so naive, so blind? Why had he not realized that Kwani's rages at Thorvald and their loud confrontations were meaningless? Sex play!

They would pay for their betrayal! Within his innermost being he resolved that they would pay. When they reached Cicuye, the last Pueblo city before entering the Plains, another burden-bearer could be found. The Northman would suddenly disappear. Oh, yes.

As for Kwani . . . again his heart felt a blow . . . surely she could not believe that he, Kokopelli, would release his mate to anyone, let alone the Northman. If she did, she would learn differently when the body for which she lusted was abandoned to wolves and vultures.

He would take his revenge! Indeed! The birthing would be at Thorvald's camp as planned; that he would allow. But Okalake's child would not live to go with them to Tula. Kwani would learn what it meant to be mate of Kokopelli.

He smiled bitterly. Tears choked his throat; he ignored them. He had not wept since childhood.

·44·

T*he man watched as they approached the distant pueblo. For three days he had hidden upon a hill, waiting. Now that they had appeared, he saw they walked in single file instead of side by side as before. Kokopelli was in front, then Kwani, and the big stranger lagged behind. Kokopelli walked more slowly than usual. He did not talk to the others, nor did they talk to one another. Odd.*

Something had happened during those three days. Was one of them injured? He was not close enough to see. He, himself, had avoided injury by huddling against a large boulder. But his clothes and pack were soaked. Never had he experienced such fury of the gods!

He watched intently as they stopped and Kokopelli turned to face the big stranger. Hostility was in his stance; had there been a falling out between them? He hoped so. It would make his task easy.

As Kokopelli and Thorvald spoke in Thorvald's guttural language, Kwani gazed at the distant pueblo where smoke drifted against the horizon. It seemed peaceful and homelike, not dangerous at all. That is where I shall stay, she decided. I shall have my baby there. Kokopelli has turned against me. He may go or stay as he chooses; I don't care any more.

Her heart denied this. But she was weary, too weary to fight longer. It had been three days since Thorvald raped her, and although the baby moved and seemed unharmed, her own spirit hurt. Kokopelli had turned away when she confided what Thorvald had done. He pretended to believe, but his eyes were cold and he avoided her touch.

She had tried to help Kokopelli with his bruise, but he refused. She cooked for him, tried to embrace him, but he remained aloof. He seemed older, more foreign, and subtly dangerous. She avoided Thorvald, refusing to look at him or speak to him. He reacted with bored indifference.

Kokopelli and Thorvald were arguing. "My bow does not shoot arrows with feathers," Thorvald snorted.

"It will this time." Kokopelli smiled grimly. "Unless, of course, you prefer to approach the pueblo as an enemy and be attacked by the entire population." He removed a red feather from his pack. "This will say we come as friends. Send it."

"Skraelings!" Grumbling, Thorvald tied the feather to the iron tip of his arrow, and walked beside Kokopelli who began to play his flute. As they approached the pueblo, there were smoke signals and drum calls, but no one came to meet them.

"Can your arrow reach the pueblo from here?" Kokopelli asked.

Thorvald nodded, and shot the arrow high. It flew in a long arc, landing near the city. A figure ran to pick it up, and disappeared. Kokopelli continued to play, but they did not approach closer. No people came. Finally, another arrow was returned, a shorter one. It had no feather, only sharp flint on the point.

"We are not welcome here," Kokopelli said.

"What about my arrow? I want it back."

"Your bow is the only one that can send your arrow, as you know well. They do not want us here. If we go closer, more arrows will meet us." He turned north. "We go to Cicuye, through the pass."

"You go. I get my arrow and follow."

"You will get many arrows. They are good marksmen."

Kwani sat down. "I can go no farther."

"I carry you," Thorvald said.

"No!" She stood up, facing him. "No!"

He shrugged. Reluctantly, he followed Kokopelli who was already heading north, walking slowly but steadily.

Kwani forced herself to plod after them. She prayed she would encounter the White Buffalo soon. She knew it would reveal a truth to ease her troubled heart. As yet, the Spirit Being had come to her only in a dream, but it waited for her. Somewhere, some time, they would meet.

The pass was an ancient one, used for thousands of years by travelers to and from the land of the buffalo. Cicuye, at the north end of the pass, was the last Pueblo city, and the final outpost before the Southern Great Plains swallowed intruders in its vastness.

Kokopelli had been pushing them hard for two days, leading them up and down and around as the pass wound through the mountains. It was green and wildly beautiful, and Kwani would have enjoyed it had she not been so weary in body and spirit. *Cicuye. I shall go no farther. Cicuye.*

They stopped to eat what was left of food in their packs. Each sat apart from the others and ate in silence.

Kokopelli suddenly said sharply, "Do not move." He stared up the bank. Above them, a grizzly foraged in the bushes, its massive bulk nearly hidden. It rose on its hind legs, sniffing.

"He smells our food," Kokopelli said. "I shall talk with him. Do not move."

He stood up, gazing steadily at the bear. The animal started down the mountain at a loping gait.

"He wants to see us better," Kokopelli said. "Sit quietly." He continued to stare at the bear with a calm and steady gaze, communicating. The bear slowed to a walk, and lifted its nose, inhaling their scent. It was huge and shaggy, a creature of raw power. Kwani froze with fear.

Thorvald lifted his ax.

"No!" Kokopelli cried.

The ax hissed through the air and lodged in the bear's shoulder. He staggered with the impact and rose on his hind legs with a growl, trying to loosen the ax. It held. The bear dropped to all fours, laid back his ears, and lunged forward with a coughing sound, running so swiftly that Thorvald did not have time to use his bow.

He drew his sword as the grizzly came at him, head raised, jaws open, huge teeth gleaming. Thorvald jabbed the sword into the bear's chest. One swipe of a giant paw knocked Thorvald to the ground and the bear fell forward upon him, his weight thrusting the hilt of the sword into Thorvald's ribs. Kokopelli grabbed the ax, jerked it loose, and swung it at the animal's neck.

The grizzly shuddered and rolled to his side, blood gushing. The dying face turned to Kokopelli and stared into his eyes.

"Forgive me!" Kokopelli said huskily.

The bear's eyes did not close, but life ebbed from them.

Thorvald rose unsteadily. Deep gashes bled across his chest, and another gash was on his left cheek under the eye. Blood from his face and body mingling on the ground with that of the bear.

Kwani's legs shook. She looked at the shaggy beast sprawled upon the ground. Great jaws gapped open. Part of Thorvald's iron tunic clung to the curved claws, and the sword hilt jutted up from the shaggy chest. Already, flies converged on clotting blood, and vultures hovered. Thorvald pulled his sword out of the bear's great chest, and replaced it in its scabbard. He pressed both hands against his ribs. "Broken."

"Sit down," Kokopelli ordered. From his medicine bundle, he took out leaves and bark from a small packet.

"Make a brew." He handed them to Kwani.

"I have no pot."

"Take mine," Thorvald said.

Kokopelli inspected Thorvald's wounds. Kwani pulled open Thorvald's pack and saw the pot beneath a deerskin. A large chunk of turquoise lay underneath. How successful he must have been in his trading, she thought. He is wealthy.

Water from their water bags provided enough for the brew, and soon there was a pungent odor. Thorvald sat motionless and grim as Kokopelli cleansed his wounds and applied a healing poultice.

Kwani watched her mate working on Thorvald with experienced skill. A mottled bruise darkened one side of Kokopelli's face; the swelling had gone down somewhat, but Kwani knew it must be painful still. Yet, he seemed to have forgotten it in his effort to help Thorvald. She thought, this attack has shown how much we need one another, how much our spirits need . . .

The bear lay ignored. Kwani wondered how much of it they could salvage. The skin was valuable; even the claws would bring good trading, and the rich meat and fat would provide feasting for an entire clan. But it was too heavy for them to carry.

The brew was ready. Kokopelli poured some into a gourd cup. He tasted it, and nodded. "Drink." He handed it to Thorvald.

Thorvald tasted it, and spat.

"Drink, fool. It eases pain."

For a long moment, they gazed at one another in silence. Thorvald tilted the cup and drank it all. "Keep the pot," he told Kwani. "It is yours for the one I broke."

The brew began to take effect; Thorvald lay down and closed his eyes. "You saved my life," he said to Kokopelli.

"Yes. We are even now."

Thorvald's eyes opened.

"I saved you twice."

"Of course. My life is worth two of yours."

They grinned, and Kwani sighed with relief; the journey was too long and dangerous for them to be enemies.

Thorvald closed his eyes again. Kwani turned away. She did not see the grin dissolve to hatred on Kokopelli's face as he stared down at the Northman.

The man inched closer and fitted an arrow into his bow. He had seen the bear attack and was astonished that the big stranger was not dead. Now Kokopelli and Kwani were skinning the bear, absorbed in their work. They would not see him or his arrow until it was too late.

He stepped clear of the tree where he had been hiding, knelt, aimed, and watched his arrow fall short, landing beside the bear. Instantly, he darted again into hiding, but not before Kokopelli saw him.

"We are attacked!" Kokopelli pointed to where the man darted from bush to bush to tree, escaping.

"Who is it?" Kwani cried.

"I have not seen him before."

"Was there a wound, a deep wound on his cheek?"

Thorvald said, "I saw his face. He had no wound."

Who was it? Who moved that way, held his head at such an angle? Kwani asked herself. In a fathomless pool of memory, knowledge stirred. Almost, she grasped it. Then, like a fish darting into hiding, knowledge eluded her.

Kokopelli said, "We must find shelter. There is a safe place ahead. But . . ." He looked at Thorvald's pack on the ground. It would be dangerous for Thorvald to carry a heavy load, even though his massive strength might be equal to it, even now. The tunic of iron links had protected him from more severe injury, even death. But bleeding had to be controlled, and healing allowed to take place. He needed Thorvald—but only until they reached Cicuye. Another would take his place. Oh, yes.

The bear. Its skin and carcass were too valuable to leave. "We must prepare a travois."

"You make. I keep watch." Thorvald sat on a small boulder nearby, steadying himself with the bow held in readiness.

Kwani found her finest flint knife. "I will finish the skinning, and cut some meat for us to take. I shall choose the best parts. And the claws."

Kokopelli did not comment, but in his heart he could not restrain admiration. How valiant was her spirit! If only . . . He turned away, wishing he did not know what he knew about her and Thorvald . . . wishing he did not know she had stolen his turquoise to buy her blanket back.

With Thorvald's heavy ax, Kokopelli cut two trees tall enough to provide strong poles one and a half times his own height. He trimmed off the branches. Now he needed something to stretch between the two poles to carry a load. Thorvald's woolen blanket would be ideal. He strode to Thorvald's pack.

"No!" Thorvald shouted. "Do not touch my pack!"

But already Kokopelli had seen the great blue stone inside. He took it in his hand. He turned toward Thorvald with an icy stare. Thorvald stared back with a gaze equally cold, and pointed the bow in Kokopelli's direction.

Deliberately, Kokopelli dropped the stone into his own pack, while anger seethed in him. With hands that shook he bound an edge of Thorvald's blanket to each of the poles.

His mind raced. Kwani had not stolen the stone. Perhaps she also told the truth when she said Thorvald forced her. Thorvald. He turned to gaze at him again, and again Thorvald stared back. Kokopelli knew that only their need of one another kept the arrow in the bow.

He looked at Kwani, intent on her work. She paused to push the hair away from her face with both bloody hands. She felt his gaze and turned to smile. His heart skipped a beat. Never had he loved her more.

At the travois' burden end, the poles were closer together than at the other end, where they would be pulled and dragged along the ground. Meat was piled on Thorvald's fine blanket, four huge paws with claws were added, and all was covered with the bear's skin. Kokopelli laid the ax upon the load, adding Thorvald's pack, and Kwani's. He nodded at Thorvald. "I will help you pull."

"I need no help from a Toltec," Thorvald snorted. He slung the bow over his shoulder. As he bent to lift the poles, blood trickled from beneath the bandages across his chest. "We waste time!"

"You waste blood, fool." Kokopelli grasped one of the poles. The weight was enormous. "Wait." He rummaged in his pack and took out a length of yucca twine rope, and fastened it across the poles. He and Thorvald would stand side by side between the poles, with the rope at stomach level. "This will ease pressure on the chest muscles," he said to Thorvald. "Pull."

Together, they strained up the trail. Kwani followed, turning again and again to glance behind. Someone hid just out of sight.

Who was it?

·45·

Two Elk, Clan Chief of Cicuye, sat naked and crosslegged on the floor of his sweat lodge. He was no longer young, but his body was strong and well formed. His man part was one of the largest in Cicuye and renowed for its vigor—to which Two Elk credited the rejuvenating power of his sweat bath.

A fire burned in a small firepit at the back of the room, heating stones over which water would be poured to make steam. The room was small with a low roof, and smoke filled it before escaping through a little hole in the ceiling. He reached for a loosely woven bag of yucca fiber containing fresh grass, placed the bag in his mouth, bit down, and breathed through the grass until the smoke dissipated; grass filtered the smoke.

The heating stones were encircled by a mound of others. Waiting for the stones to heat, Two Elk pondered what to do about Tolonqua, his Hunting Chief. The young chief excelled as a hunter and as a leader of men—and therein lay the problem. He was pursuading the young men of the pueblo to build a new city across the stream on the flat-topped ridge soaring above them. A foolish idea, for had not the present pueblo served the people well for more moons than any young man could remember? The Hunting Chief was a trouble maker, no doubt about it.

The stones grew hot and Two Elk flicked a drop of water on them; the drop sizzled, danced, and vanished. It was time. He poured a ladle of water over the heated stones; immediately there was a crackling sound and a loud hissing as steam billowed.

He hunched forward, gasping, as the heat descended on his head, then his shoulders, down to his feet, enveloping him. The purification was beginning. A Clan Chief must make important decisions; a sweat bath cleansed the mind as well as the body. He closed his eyes and concentrated on making his mind responsive to messages from the gods.

He added more water, and more. Sweat poured from him. He reached for the stalk of an aromatic plant and flicked the leaves on his body, lingering in places where the medicinal quality in the leaves relieved pain in his joints.

Enervated, he stepped outside to sit and to rest, and to contemplate spiritual matters. But the problem of Tolonqua nagged at him. It was true enough that the ridge offered better fortification. But when rarely they were attacked by wandering hunters from the plains or by others from beyond the pass, Cicuye's own brave warriors drove them away. Besides, building a new pueblo would take farmers and hunters from their work, and they could not be spared.

He looked with pride over his pueblo on a bank sloping to a fine stream, and the fields of corn and squash and beans, and beyond to blue mountains for eyes to rest upon and calm the spirit. A party of Quere-chos had come for trading and had set up tipis near the pueblo at the base of the ridge. Two Elk observed them with a trace of unease. These were not the esteemed Querechos of the Plains, but a band from the south, given to thievery and ill temper. However, they were good trad-ers, and trading was trading. Tolonqua, however, said these southern Querechos were untrustworthy and should not be welcomed. Some of the young braves agreed with him. They agreed with everything he said since they learned of his vision of the White Buffalo.

Two Elk shifted uneasily. The White Buffalo was a powerful spirit. Perhaps he should seek a vision of his own. Preparations for the Snake Dance would begin soon. Maybe the Plumed Serpent god, Quetzalcoatl, would bestow wisdom as well as rain upon his people and show Tolon-qua the error of his ways. Yes, he, Two Elk, would seek a vision at the time of the Snake Dance.

He reentered the lodge and added water several times until the heat decreased to a damp, comforting warmth. Sighing in satisfaction, he left and strode to the stream. It was sacred, used only for drinking and cooking and for ceremonial purposes. So he sat on the bank and splashed water on himself. Naked children came running and helped with the splashing, while splashing one another and shouting and gig-gling, until Two Elk waved them away. He walked with great dignity back up the bank and to the ladder leading to his dwelling. His mate would rub him dry with a cotton cloth while enjoying the sight of his man part rising in appreciation.

He was half way up the ladder when two runners appeared.

"Two Elk! We bring news!"

"News will wait until I am ready. Go to the kiva."

The runners had come far since they left Kokopelli and his companions, and they were hot and thirsty in the midsummer heat. They yearned to bathe in the stream, but since it was forbidden, they splashed water on themselves. People stood by, agog for news, but they knew they would have to wait until the Clan Chief was informed.

A young girl with a water jug balanced on her head offered the jug, and they drank deeply and thanked her lavishly for she was pretty, with large, dark eyes that sparkled invitingly.

The runners went to the kiva and were about to climb down when they heard the voice of Tolonqua, the Hunting Chief, chanting the Prayer Stick song. They hesitated, reluctant to intrude upon a sacred occupation. Secretly they were in awe of the tall young Chief whose reputation as a hunter and a leader of men was formidable. And he was personable, so much so that it made them feel less attractive than they knew they were, for did not women look upon them with favor?

They peered down and saw that the prayer stick Tolonqua was making was circular—Sunfather's, Moonwoman's, the most powerful! They whispered in awed tones, and squatted by the ladder; they would wait until the chant was finished before descending.

Inside the kiva, Tolonqua bent reverently over his work. He had formed a slender willow twig into a circle, and fastened it to the center of a straight, slim rod as long as from hand to elbow. Now he took a short piece of hollow reed and stuffed it with sacred corn pollen and tobacco, and tied the reed at its center to the bottom of the willow circle.

He held the circular prayer stick before him, chanting. One more thing must be done, the most important of all. To the reed he added a cloud symbol, a fluffy white feather of eagle down that fluttered with the slightest movement. The feather would invoke the spirit of the Cloud People; they would cause the White Buffalo to appear before him. To possess the robe of the White Buffalo would assure him and his future sons, and their sons, wisdom, good fortune, and the protection of the White Buffalo, Chief of all buffalo, a Spirit Being. Ever since Tolonqua's manhood rites, when the White Buffalo appeared to him in a vision, Tolonqua had known that one day the White Buffalo would come to him. Twenty-two times he had seen Sunfather returned to his northern home, but the White Buffalo had not appeared.

Tolonqua placed the finished prayer stick upon the altar in front of the fire pit. The runners saw Two Elk approaching, and they waited respectfully for him to climb down the ladder before they followed. Tolonqua greeted them courteously and the runners sat at a polite distance.

Two Elk raised his hand in greeting. He wore a fine breechcloth of fringed buckskin painted in mystic designs. Feather ornaments hung from each ear. Several splendid necklaces and bracelets of carved bone and polished stone rattled impressively.

He sat down in his usual place of honor before the altar, and glanced at the runners. "I am ready."

The older of the two runners spoke. "Kokopelli, and he of the Sunrise Sea, and Kokopelli's mate—"

"He has a mate?" That was news, indeed.

"Yes. Her eyes are blue."

"Ah. She who is known as She Who Remembers of the Eagle Clan?"

"Yes. She is a Storyteller also—"

"Who calls Masau'u and Motsni and the deer," the other runner added.

Two Elk asked, "What do they want of us?" Important personages always had demands.

"They were attacked by a bear. A grizzly."

"Impossible! Kokopelli—"

"The hairy one threw his ax, and the bear attacked him. The hairy one is wounded, yet he pulls a travois—he and Kokopelli—with meat of the bear—"

"And he grows weary," the younger runner added. "They ask for help because Kokopelli's mate is with child." He showed with both hands how big her stomach was. "She also grows weary—"

"Kokopelli received a blow from ice-from-the-sky. The gods are angry."

"—And they were attacked by one who tracks them ever since they left the place of those who dwell among the cliffs," the younger runner added breathlessly, not to be outdone in the telling. "He sent an arrow, but it missed, and he ran away. They say the tracker still follows, but they do not know who it is."

"Where are they now?"

"At the Place of the Tall Stones. Kokopelli asks for men to carry the meat of the bear and for one to pull the travois with Kokopelli's mate on it."

"Are you certain she is his mate? It is hard to believe."

"We are. Beautiful, she is."

Two Elk pondered, rubbing his chin. This was important news. "We shall send bearers to carry the meat and to pull the travois."

He turned to Tolonqua who had been sitting in silence. "Assemble some of your hunters since they do not hunt today." His voice hinted at criticism. "It is proper for hunters to carry meat home."

Tolonqua's face remained impassive. "My hunters bring buffalo. However, inferior meat may be welcomed by our visitors." He rose, stretching his long legs, and looked down at the Clan Chief who returned his gaze with barely concealed hostility. The young Hunting Chief was not only disrupting harmony in the pueblo by his unwise insistence upon building another city, he was becoming too popular. There were whisperings of him becoming Clan Chief one day.

Tolonqua said, "I shall go with my hunters." He climbed from the kiva and disappeared.

Massive boulders formed an irregular V-shaped room; trees surrounded them, providing shade and a measure of shelter. Ashes of campfires from countless previous travelers and bits of bone and flint were strewn about.

Thorvald sat against a boulder, brushing away flies that sought his wounds. He gazed into the high blue sky where clouds sailed, wishing he were at sea, sailing home with wealth enough and exploration enough to restore his prestige and leadership. Memory of his humiliation and ostracism were more painful than his wounds. Surely, when he returned in triumph with Kwani as an exotic trophy, and with Kokopelli's riches, word of his discoveries and achievements would sweep the kingdom. He would be a hero, celebrated in the sagas, and honored with the High Seat in the dining hall of the king.

Kokopelli's riches . . . Even if there were no more trading, no secret storage places, what Kokopelli carried in his pack would be enough to dazzle people at home. He would dispose of the Toltec after they left Cicuye and entered the vast plains. Even a Northman could not stand alone against hordes. In that great, empty wilderness there were no pueblos, no people who regarded Kokopelli as a demigod and who would be quick to avenge his death.

As for Kwani . . . He smiled in his beard, remembering how she fought him when he possessed her. She would be eager for him after the baby was born and she could respond to him as all women did. The baby would be no problem; it would be disposed of according to the sensible custom of his people.

He glanced at the sun. When would help arrive? He was hot and sweaty, and his wounds hurt. He watched three vultures perch on top of the tall stones. Could they smell the blood of his wounds? He shouted at them in his native tongue but they did not fly away. Repulsive creatures!

He cursed. He hated this land. And he hated the arrogant Toltec who stood on the trail, waiting for help that did not come—and probably would not come.

He cursed again, and brushed away the flies.

* * *

Kokopelli watched the vultures finishing the last discarded parts of the bear. They flapped about, hovering, settling, stretching long necks to shred the carcass with hooked beaks. Some vultures lingered near the travois which was covered with the bear's hide. Occasionally, they perched on the travois to peck at the hide; Kokopelli shouted and they flew a short distance and squatted, waiting.

Kokopelli looked down the trail, wondering when help would come. Wondering if it would come. He did not want to spend the night with the bear's carcass; wolves would seek it. He could communicate with one or two or maybe even three, but he could not control a pack.

He wiped perspiration from his face with the back of his hand. Heat bothered him more than it used to, and he was weary, more weary than he should be. He must face it. Age was upon him. It was time, past time, for him to settle down in Tula. Some day there would be sons to whom he could reveal his secrets. But no longer could he travel the vast and lonely distances. His sons would conquer the horizons—his sons, and Kwani's.

Kwani, his mate. Raped by the Northman. Shame burned in him as he remembered how he had doubted Kwani when she said Thorvald had forced her. He would make it up to her when they reached Tula. There would be a great feast, a celebration, and a ceremony to establish her as his mate under Toltec law.

He heard Thorvald shouting at three vultures perched on top of the tall stones. The vultures shifted and stretched their ugly necks, but they did not leave. Some day they could have the Northman. Never again would Thorvald rape or steal or strut about, or brandish his weapons. When they left Cicuye for the plains, the Northman would simply disappear. How this would be arranged had not been decided, but Kokopelli knew a suitable method would be revealed to him. The gods did not look kindly upon evil men, especially foreigners. He, Kokopelli, would relish his revenge.

It was late afternoon. Why had help not come? Again, he thought uneasily of Thorvald's boat. If the men sailed before he and Kwani reached camp, a very great distance would have to be traveled on foot. More than could be done before winter came. Already, he was weary, and so was Kwani.

The baby. Okalake's child would not be worthy of a Toltec nobleman. It could not be permitted to live. Kwani would have to understand that.

He looked at her curled up against a boulder. How valiant she was! She would be a good mate to him in the years ahead, once she learned that the status of a Toltec woman was not the same as that of a Pueblo. She would forget about having been She Who Remembers once she had sons to keep her busy.

Again, vultures landed on the bear's hide. Kokopelli shouted them away, and sat where he could see down the trail and into the distance. Whoever sent the arrow might send it again.

Thorvald sauntered over, and circled the travois. He gave it a hard kick, scowling at Kokopelli. "Why did you tell the runners you give them meat? It is for trading."

"Yes. We trade meat for help. Unless you prefer to pull the load the rest of the way. It is uphill."

Kwani heard their sharp voices and came to stand nearby.

Thorvald said, "The meat will bring turquoise."

"You have need to steal more?"

"I am Northman. What I want, I take."

"I am Toltec. I allow theft from no one."

Amber eyes stared into blue ones. Their gaze locked. Hostility flared between them, a murderous presence.

Thorvald yanked out his sword, still stained with the bear's blood, and braced his legs. His blue eyes darkened with cold intensity. Kokopelli seized the ax from where it lay by the travois, holding it with both hands. "You raped my mate. You stole my turquoise. Now you presume to threaten me. Me, Kokopelli!" He raised the ax.

Kwani's heart lurched. These men would kill each other. She would be left defenseless against the one who lurked behind. The baby kicked, as if it were as frightened as she, as if it pleaded for protection and an opportunity to be born. She clutched the scallop shell to her, beseeching, demanding, to *remember*.

Of its own accord, her mouth opened and the singing cry emerged, fierce, wild, compelling. She stepped between the men and pushed them apart, while the terrible cry soared from her throat.

The men stared in awed astonishment. She was transfigured, an apparition with outstretched arms, head thrown back, mouth open in a primal cry—a priestess from a past ancient beyond remembering. They stood watching, listening. Ancestral memory stirred and spoke; ancestral blood responded. Their weapons dropped to the ground.

The cry faded, and was stilled. Kwani stood a moment as if awakened. Slowly, she faced them.

"You each saved the life of the other. You are brothers."

The men glanced at each other, and looked away. They watched in silence as Kwani returned to where she had been sitting against the stone. She slumped against it as if she were exhausted, and sat with her head on her arms.

A bird called sweetly on three descending notes.

* * *

Hours passed, and help did not come. Kwani drifted into sleep, and dreamed.

Her spirit left her body and traveled to an unknown place with cliffs of mysterious shapes and colors. There was water sound, and a cool mist carried fragrances she had not known before. It was early morning, or was it evening? She wasn't sure. Premonition and a feeling of awe made her turn. Enshrouded in misty haze was the White Buffalo. It came closer, and looked into her eyes, and spoke.

"I await you. Remember that when you are afraid."

"I am afraid now."

"I await you," it said again.

Slowly the mist rose and swirled; the head of the White Buffalo seemed to dissolve into that of a man. "Ah!" Kwani gasped, and she tried to see the face, but before it was revealed, the Spirit Being faded into the mist and was gone.

"Come back!" Kwani cried. "Tell me the secret!" But there were only the cliffs enfolding her, only the sense of a presence unseen.

Voices woke her. She sat up, enveloped by the spell of the dream. Thorvald and Kokopelli were outside on the trail, talking with someone. The dream was still with her as a Towa appeared from the trail. Kwani looked at him and could not look away. She had never seen him before, yet she felt that she knew him.

When he saw her, he stopped. He was tall, taller than Kokopelli. His strong body was bare but for a small fringed buckskin garment tied to his waist that covered him briefly before and behind, leaving his sides exposed. He was young, but his face had strong lines, and an expression of accustomed authority . . . handsome. With a proud hawk nose, high cheekbones, and a strong mouth set in a firm line. His expressive eyes, black as obsidian, burned as he looked at her.

She could no longer meet his gaze, but she could not look away. Her eyes lingered on the turquoise and shell necklaces gleaming against his bronze chest, and at the ear ornaments and the ornate band he wore across his forehead and fastened in the back. Eagle feathers were thrust into the band and stood upright. Tattooed on his shoulder was a strange design. His presence was overpowering.

Kokopelli and Thorvald returned, followed by a group of young hunters.

Kokopelli said, "Tolonqua is Hunting Chief of Cicuye. He and his hunters will take us to the city. Is your pack ready?"

Kwani nodded, speechless.

With a swift, fluid motion, Tolonqua picked up her pack and placed it in his own. The meat was loaded into burden-baskets carried by the hunters, and the packs of Thorvald and Kokopelli were transferred to the backs of others.

Only the bearskin and Thorvald's ax remained on the travois. Thorvald retrieved his ax, and swung it at his side.

Kokopelli said, "Leave the bearskin for my mate to sit upon."

It was smelly but soft, and Kwani sat awkwardly as Kokopelli held the poles. Tolonqua stepped forward.

"I will take her."

She felt his gaze like a lance as he took the poles and turned his back, preparing to pull. She stared at the line of wide shoulders sloping to a narrow waist; she wanted to reach out and touch the bronze skin.

Kokopelli was not unaware. He came to stand beside her, assuming a possessive stance. Up the trail Tolonqua and Kwani went first, followed by Kokopelli and Thorvald. The hunters strode behind, conversing softly among themselves. Kwani wished she could hear what they were saying. They had seemed startled by her blue eyes. Were they frightened? Now and then their Hunting Chief glanced back at her, and his glance was anything but afraid. It made her self-conscious.

It grew cooler as the trail rose gradually to higher altitude. One of the hunters carried a small cottonwood drum, and began to beat a steady rhythm to which they all kept step. Kokopelli picked up the rhythm with his flute.

Tolonqua began to sing, his voice, rich and strong, carried emotional overtones that echoed in Kwani's consciousness, compelling response. She began to sing too, a wordless accompaniment, and their voices blended like lovers in mating. He turned to smile at her, and she smiled back, still singing.

Kokopelli stopped playing. He felt suddenly helpless. A force confronted him over which he had no control—the power of youth to youth, Pueblo to Pueblo.

·46·

"That is Cicuye?"

"Of course."

Kwani stared, disappointed. She had looked forward to this city as a haven, a place to rest in comfort and security. She had hoped, even expected, a fine stone city of several stories and many kivas, like the Place of the Eagle Clan. What she saw was a modest pueblo of one-story adobe buildings with the usual ladders to rooftop entrances, and a small plaza with ladder poles protruding from a single kiva in the center.

Across a stream, at the base of a flat-topped ridge, were three tipis, triangular dwellings of buffalo hide wrapped around tall poles, the tops of which thrust through an opening at the top like pointed fingers. Naked children ran and played, and women bent over buffalo hides staked to the ground; they leaned forward and back, scraping, while their long, black braids swung to and fro.

As the procession approached, the women sat staring with opaque black eyes in dark, expressionless faces. Several men gathered, watching sullenly. They were squat and dirty, and their eyes fastened on Kwani like stinging insects. She felt a twinge of alarm, and turned to Kokopelli.

"Who are they?"

"Querechos. Related to Apaches."

"Are they . . . friendly?"

He looked down his nose. "With me, all tribes are friendly."

Tolonqua gave him an oblique glance. "Skraelings," Thorvald muttered, and took a tighter grip on his ax.

Kokopelli's flute played its usual announcement. As they passed the tipis, he ceased playing for a moment to raise a hand in greeting. One man responded; but his sullen expression did not change.

People had gathered in the plaza of the pueblo, and stood on the roofs

325

of their dwellings. Some shouted and waved their arms in greeting. Kwani felt battered and dirty from the ride, but at least she could arrive with dignity.

"I shall walk now."

The procession paused as she rose from the travois, and the loads of all the hunters were piled on it. There was goodnatured bantering about who would pull the load while Tolonqua stepped back to walk beside Kwani. Instantly, Kokopelli moved forward to walk on her other side.

As they approached the plaza, the Clan Chief met them. Beside him, a wizened figure sat in a litter carried by two young men who stood at respectful attention. The figure was bent, and only when they were closer could Kwani see that it was a very old woman. From beneath ragged white brows, dark eyes peered at her with sharp intelligence.

Tolonqua said, "I bring you Kokopelli from beyond the Great River of the South, Thorvald from beyond the Sunrise Sea, and Kwani, mate of Kokopelli, known also as She Who Remembers, who comes from those who dwell among the cliffs to the west. They bring meat of the bear." He turned to Kokopelli. "I am honored to bring you to Chief Two Elk of the Towa."

While greetings were exchanged, Thorvald looked beyond to the women and girls, who watched and giggled and whispered among themselves.

Kwani felt the gaze of the tiny, shriveled woman on the litter. She was old, so old that her face was furrowed with deep crevices, like land parched and cracked after long drought. Her hair was still black but for a few gray wisps over the ears. She beckoned, and Kwani stepped closer.

"I am Yellow Bird."

"My honored grandmother," Two Elk said.

Impulsively, Kwani took the clawlike hand and breathed on it. "I greet you, honored one."

The old woman nodded, pleased at the foreign gesture. This one had manners. She said, "A room is prepared for you. When you have rested you may come to me." It was a gracious invitation; but Kwani knew it was an order. Two Elk led them across the plaza where naked girls as well as children stood watching. Kwani knew of the custom. In warm weather, girls went unclothed until they married; an indiscretion such as her own could not be concealed.

Two Elk paused at the kiva, and motioned to a woman standing on a rooftop. "My mate will take you to your dwelling," he said to Kwani. He turned to Thorvald. "She and others will tend your wounds and provide a sleeping place. Kokopelli and I shall be in the kiva." He descended the ladder, followed by Kokopelli.

The mate of Two Elk approached shyly, beckoning other women who motioned for Thorvald to follow. He did so, grinning in pleased anticipation.

Kwani was led up a ladder, across the rooftops of several dwellings, and down into another. It was dim and cool, with a window.

"This is for you as long as you wish to stay."

"I thank you."

"My name is Aka-ti. Tell me if you need anything." She smiled and left.

Alone, Kwani sat on the smooth clay floor and looked around her. The room was divided into two parts; the smaller was a storage area with corn stacked like firewood to the ceiling. Storage bowls of beans and other edibles stood about. The other half of the room was a work area, with metate and mano and flint knives, round pots, and woven trays and baskets. A tall water jar stood filled, and bunches of dried herbs hung on the wall. All was in immaculate order. She wondered whose home it was.

She closed her eyes, willing herself to relax. How many days and weeks had it been since she left the Place of the Eagle Clan? She had lost track of time, walking endlessly into distant horizons. She felt that her spirit lagged behind somewhere, and needed time to catch up. She stared up at the heavy beams crossing the ceiling, and at the smooth, whitewashed clay walls . . . the orderly, comfortable, Pueblo room. What kind of a home would she have among Kokopelli's people? Would she and her child be happy there? Was she doing the right thing? What if the words of Medicine Woman of the Raven Clan were true? If the baby was a boy, who would teach him the sacred, secret, important things a man child must know? *Pueblo* things?

She fingered her necklace, remembering the words of the Old One. Could it be that the real purpose of this journey was to assure her child a Pueblo clan and people? How?

She closed her eyes and thought of the Place of Remembering in the House of the Sun. Again, she laid her arms upon it and pressed her cheek against the surface warmed by Sunfather's holy rays. She prayed.

"Give me wisdom. Show me the right path."

"The right path will be revealed." It was her mother's voice, but she was not there.

"Mother!" Kwani cried, and emotion welled up as from a bottomless pool.

"The White Buffalo . . ." The voice faded away.

"Mother! Wait!"

There was no answer.

Kwani opened her eyes. Had she slept and dreamed?

She looked about her with new awareness. For the first time, she realized her journey might also be a journey within, a search for wisdom and for understanding mysteries which would be revealed only to one who was She Who Remembers. She felt she was on the verge of discovering truths she had not known before.

A feeling of assurance and peace seeped into her. She drifted into deep, dreamless sleep.

Thorvald leaned against the wall of a small room and allowed a naked girl to smooth a healing unguent on his wounds. Supervising were two young matrons instructing the girl in correct procedure. The women wore only finely woven short skirts fastened with a belt at the waist. Necklaces dangled enticingly between ripe breasts. The girl was a beauty with curving thighs and luxurious long hair flowing over pretty shoulders. Thorvald wondered why she had no mate and was considering ways to volunteer. On a temporary basis, of course.

"Apply a little more under the eye," one woman said.

The girl nodded and touched the wound delicately with slender fingers. She leaned closer and he smelled the odor of her young body. Red-brown nipples of round little breasts pointed at him, and a bit of silky down barely concealed the cleft of her woman part. He yearned to taste it, to hold her blossoming body close, to teach her what a Northman knew.

He sighed, almost a groan, and the girl drew back quickly, thinking she had hurt him. He took her hand and pressed it again to his wound, wishing he could press it elsewhere.

She smiled and resumed her work. The women glanced at each other, and one said to the girl, "You have done well. You may go now."

Thorvald watched as the girl reluctantly climbed the ladder above him. Again, the women glanced at each other, and one of them took his hand.

"Come and rest."

She led him to a sleeping mat. He lay down, as slowly, languorously, both women untied their belts and let their garments fall to the floor.

Kokopelli and Two Elk were alone in the kiva. The chiefs and elders who joined them had departed, and Kokopelli and Two Elk were renewing old acquaintance, talking of preparations for the Snake Dance, the rain-bringing ceremony which would also honor Quetzalcoatl, the Plumed Serpent god introduced long ago by the pochtecas. Quetzalcoatl was not the rain god of the Toltecs; but he was a serpent, and as all Pueblos knew, serpents could intercede with the deities to bring rain.

Two Elk said, "The preparation will take eight days. I invite you to remain at Cicuye as long as you wish and to participate in the ceremony if you desire to do so. Afterward, the Querechos wish to trade. Perhaps you may care to trade also." He smiled at his joke; Kokopelli's trading expertise was legendary.

Kokopelli returned the smile, but he was thinking how meager was Two Elk's imagination and visualization of the future, and how different from Tolonqua's. During a previous visit the young Hunting Chief had agreed at once when Kokopelli pointed out the possibilities of expanding the trade and growth of Cicuye. The pueblo's location at the head of the pass between the plains and the many pueblos west of the pass assured vast trading potential—and inevitable attack by marauding tribes. A city on top of the ridge, surrounded by a wall, would become rich and secure. But Two Elk saw only into the past; he understood only the threat to his authority. His own future was doomed.

Kokopelli said, "I thank you for the invitation to remain here, old friend. But we must leave as soon as my mate has recovered sufficiently. Great distances face us. Meanwhile . . ." He paused, knowing that now was the time to bring up a delicate matter. "As you know, strange tribes from the north wander on the plains. I do not speak their tongues, nor am I fluent in sign language." It was a lie about the sign language, but the lie was necessary. "I would be grateful if one of your people could accompany us as interpreter, and help with our burdens until Thorvald's ribs mend." There was no point in mentioning the probability of Thorvald's future disappearance.

Two Elk nodded, his eyes glinting. "It shall be done." He smiled and reached for the tobacco; they would have another smoke before Kokopelli returned to his mate.

When Kokopelli found his way to Kwani's room, she lay on her back, one arm overhead. Her face, turned to the side, was partially hidden by hair that stirred a little over her mouth as she breathed. How vulnerable she seemed! Yet that lovely exterior harbored a spirit as strong as his own—a good thing, considering the distance still to travel that awaited them.

He thought of the vast plains, and beyond them to the green mountains and rivers that gushed wildly after rains, rivers that would not be easy to cross. There would be more mountains, more rivers, before they reached Thorvald's camp. From there, they would sail down to the gulf, and thence to the shores of his homeland. Burden-bearers would be easy to acquire for the journey inland to Tula. But Kwani . . .

She shifted to her side, easing the weight of her belly. It was obvious by now that the baby would be born before they reached camp. The problem of the pregnancy nagged at him. True, the baby would have to be disposed of, but how could he bring himself to let Kwani know he was responsible? She would never forgive him. Never.

Perhaps the infant could be found dead one morning; it would be assumed the child had died in its sleep. Yes, that would be the thing to do. The idea did not appeal to him for he was a healer. But it would have to be done—for the sake of them both.

He thought of his family at home, of his sisters and brothers and cousins and aunts and uncles, of their elegant attire and customs of nobility. He visualized their astonishment when they met his blue-eyed Anasazi bride. Would they allow Kwani to become one of them? For the first time, he wondered about this. Before, he had assumed that what he desired they would accept. But he had been gone a long time and had become accustomed to these people and their ways. Was it possible he had forgotten what the attitude might be of Toltec nobility?

He looked at Kwani as she slept. One foot twitched, one dirty small foot. He wanted to take her to the river and bathe her as he did when he found her. He wanted to hold her and make love and have her with him always. He loved her—her beauty, her spirit, everything about her—and have her he would. Always. Problems, if any, at home would be solved when the time came.

Sighing, he unrolled another mat and lay down beside her. He was more tired than he thought.

The man approached the tipis cautiously, giving the sign of friendship. He gestured that he wanted to see the Chief, and was taken to the painted tipi of a lean Querecho with a cruel mouth and eyes that glinted greedily as the man displayed turquoise and peyote. There was long bargaining in sign language. Turquoise and peyote, plus salt and obsidian, changed hands.

·47·

It was nearly dusk when Kwani woke. She saw that Kokopelli had slept beside her, but he was gone. She still felt tired deep in her bones. She splashed water on herself from the water jar, and smoothed her robe. Someone had brought her pack while she slept, and she found her brush and brushed her hair, arranging it in squash blossom coils over each ear. She must look presentable to visit Yellow Bird.

The aged woman was waiting upon the roof of her dwelling. She sat upon a mat, arms folded, face expressionless, as Kwani approached.

"I greet you, honored one," Kwani said.

Yellow Bird nodded acknowledgment. "Sit."

Kwani sat beside her in silence. From the kivas came chanting and sound of drums and flutes in preparation for the Snake Dance ceremonial. Children and dogs played in the small plaza, and voices singing the Corn Grinding Song rose above the commotion as women ground corn for the evening meal.

Finally, Yellow Bird said, "It is well that you are here. We have need of one who remembers. The young ignore the past."

"I am grateful for your hospitality."

"It is the past that must be remembered." She gazed over the plaza and to the fields beyond. "My grandson remembers, but there are those who will not listen," she added bitterly.

Kwani did not know what to say.

"Up there!" Yellow Bird pointed a shaking, bony finger at the ridge. "They want to build another pueblo up there." Her voice quavered in outrage. "Two Elk was born here, I was born here, my mother and my grandmother were born here. The past dwells in this place, by the stream, where ancestors come to us in dreams. This is where we shall enter Sipapu." She turned her ragged, fierce old face to Kwani. "You must tell them that."

Kwani thought the ridge was an excellent site for a pueblo, but she sympathized with the old woman and did not want to offend her. "I am an outsider," she said gently. "I am honored that you ask me to do this, but I cannot presume to tell your people what to do." She thought of one who had been on her mind since she first saw him. "Perhaps Tolonqua—"

"It is he! It is Tolonqua who abandons the home of our ancestors. Who seeks to divide us . . ." Her voice cracked.

"Perhaps this pueblo would not be abandoned and the new one would be merely an addition to this. As the population grows—"

"No, no! They will remove the strong beams from each dwelling to build the new . . . they will destroy . . ." She turned to Kwani with a pleading gesture. "You are She Who Remembers, mate of Kokopelli, a Caller, a respected person. Help us. Pursuade Tolonqua to forget a new pueblo." Sharp eyes peered at Kwani knowingly. "You are beautiful. He will listen to you."

Kwani looked away. What could she say? "Permit me to think about it, honored one."

"Of course. Then you will come to tell me you agree." She motioned a dismissal; and crossed her arms as though withdrawing into herself. Her eyes disappeared into the folds under her brows, and her face became expressionless. Yellow Bird had removed Kwani from her presence; it was as if she were no longer there.

At her own dwelling, Kwani lay on the sleeping mat and gazed up at the heavy beams across the ceiling, smoothed and fashioned with flint and stone tools. The whitewashed walls and clay floor were clean and beautiful; if this were her home she would not want it destroyed and abandoned. Was it really necessary to use the old beams? There were many fine trees in nearby forests. Of course, cutting timber with stone axes, carrying the heavy logs to the site, shaping and smoothing them involved much hard labor. But Pueblos never resisted labor. Maybe something more was involved. As for Tolonqua . . . She experienced a strange sensation, thinking of him. Captivated, that was it. As though he had made her captive. She did not want to confront him, to argue with him. Surely, he had good reasons for what he was doing.

How handsome he was!

She dismissed the thought. But she would discuss the matter with Kokopelli. Also—she braced herself—she had to tell him she was staying in Cicuye until the baby was born. He would not like it.

She reached for the medicine arrow in her pack. She held it in both hands, comforted by the knowledge of its protective powers. She wanted to carry it with her at all times. She would make a special little pack for it!

Her arrow, her necklace, and her protecting spirits would keep her and the baby from harm.

Cooking fires burned in the plaza and people gathered around to cut chunks of meat from bear roasts suspended over the coals. Fat dripped and spattered, and fragrant smoke rose to tantalize the appetite. Kwani realized how hungry she was. Corn and beans cooked together, squash dried in strips and cooked with herbs, and generous piles of corn cakes were being devoured.

Thorvald's laugh boomed out from the other side of the plaza, where he sat by a fire surrounded by women urging food upon him. Tolonqua sat at another fire; he too, had women with him, beautiful women and naked girls. Kwani felt a stab of strange emotion and looked quickly away. She watched as babies were nursed and changed and tucked back into cradle boards. Soon a baby would be at her breast. She looked about her at small children curled up like contented puppies while their older brothers and sisters played noisily in the firelight. Would it be like this in Tula? There she could not give her child the opportunity to be blessed by the sacred Sunfather Birthing Ceremony given to all who were born Pueblo.

Two Elk gave the usual introductions of guests, and announcements of evening festivities, but Kwani was not listening. She looked at the people gathered around the fire, faces lit by the glow of the flames and the pleasure of comradship, and her heart ached for her little one who would have no people, no clan, such as this.

She glanced at Kokopelli, splendid as always, in the firelight. He was impatient to reach the boat. What if he refused to linger here until the baby was born? Would he go on without her? She would be a woman alone, again, with no mate . . .

Tolonqua.

He came unbidden to her mind. She turned to gaze in his direction, and he met her gaze as though he had commanded it. Across the distance, his eyes burned into hers, an intimate embrace. She turned abruptly away—to see that Aka-ti, mate of Two Elk, had observed. Aka-ti smiled, a woman-to-woman communication and Kwani smiled back. Aka-ti moved closer and Kwani leaned to whisper, "Those women with the Hunting Chief . . . which of them is his mate?"

"No one. His mate died in childbirth. He grieves and will not take another."

Kwani was surprised. He did not seem to be grieving. Aka-ti must have read her mind, for she said, "He hides his sorrow where none can see."

Kokopelli told his news and his riddles, and the people listened raptly—all but Kwani. There was a clamoring in her consciousness and she was acutely aware of Tolonqua's gaze behind her.

Now Kokopelli was singing. She forced herself to attention.

> *My melodies shall not die, nor my songs perish.*
> *They spread. They scatter.*

A few people began to hum the melody. More joined, and more, until all were singing. Tolonqua's voice soared. Kwani sang with him; soon people quieted to hear the two of them in harmony.

Abruptly, Kokopelli stopped playing. Singing faded to awkward silence.

Thorvald rose. "I will sing Northman's song."

He stood with legs braced apart, great arms akimbo, bright hair and beard aflame in the light. Women had taken his tunic to mend, and he wore only a linen undergarment from waist to mid-thigh. The marks of the bear's claws were plain to see—marks of valor and triumph—but it was the magnificence of his body that commanded attention—envy from men, and admiring awe from women.

He was totally aware of the attention. He began to sing in his native tongue, in a deep voice resonant with emotion.

> *Let us head back*
> *To our countrymen at home.*
> *Let our ocean striding ship*
> *Explore the broad tracks of the sea.*
> *Tell women who wait on the watching towers*
> *The ship of the Northmen comes home.*

He sat down to warm comments of approval. They did not understand the words but they sensed his longing.

Coals had burned low; people drifted away. Stars hung bright and low. It was time for sleep, for lovemaking, for consummation.

Kokopelli took Kwani's hand, and she sensed his urgency. She followed him to their dwelling and stood silent as he undressed her bit by bit.

"There is something I must tell you," she began.

"Not now."

He laid her down. Hands and lips and murmured words caressed her, igniting inner fires. When at last he thrust deeply, deeply, the explosion within her was such that she feared the baby would be born then and there.

She held him close. "Kokopelli . . . Kokopelli . . ."

It was not yet daybreak. Kokopelli's breathing was peaceful and slow. Kwani had to relieve herself, and she made her way down from the rooftop and across the little plaza to a grassy field. She squatted awkwardly and was about to rise when she heard soft footsteps. She crouched low in the tall grass. A figure came closer, and passed. It was a Querecho, silent as a shadow. She watched until he disappeared beyond the ridge, then swiftly and quietly she hurried back to the roof of her dwelling. Only then did she feel safe. She sat huddled against a wall and waited for the dawn.

The sky paled and changed color. Gradually, a golden glow suffused the horizon, and Sunfather rose in grandeur. Simultaneously, she heard a man's voice singing.

Tolonqua stood on a roof across the plaza. He did not see her as he faced the sun, holding a bowl in outstretched hands. His song was a chant.

> Now this day,
> My sun father,
> Now that you have come out standing in your sacred place
> From where comes the water of life,
> Prayer meal,
> Here, I give you.

He tossed a handful of corn meal toward the sun.

> Your long life,
> Your old age,
> Your waters,
> Your seeds,
> Your riches,
> Your power,
> Your strong spirit,
> All these to me may you grant.

As he finished, there were echoing prayers from others who had heard his chant and emerged to greet Sunfather. Kwani was moved and impressed. How right it seemed!

Kokopelli came to sit beside her. For a time they watched the activities of the waking pueblo.

Kwani said, "It seems strange not to hear turkeys."

"You miss the Eagle Clan?"

"No." She watched the women preparing cooking fires and emptying the night pots. "I wonder what is happening there . . ."

"They say in the kivas that there has been quarreling among the clans. People are leaving."

"Where do they go?"

"Usually southeast to the rivers where other pueblos are."

"What are the quarrels about?"

"Crops, planting, food stores. The usual. Not enough water for crops. Hungry people reason with their bellies."

Again they sat in silence for a while.

Kwani said, "Zashue is Medicine Chief now."

"It is said he seeks revenge for his wounds."

She remembered the torn, bleeding face. "Is he . . . ugly?"

Kokopelli nodded. "Perhaps it is he who tracks us."

"It is not he."

"Then who?"

"Another who seeks revenge." She turned to him abruptly. "I must speak of something else. The baby." She placed both arms over her belly in an unconscious gesture of protection. "I cannot travel more until the baby is born. Can we not stay here for another moon?"

He shook his head. "You do not realize how far . . . The boat may be finished and the men waiting for Thorvald. If they tire of waiting, they may sail without him, without us. We would be stranded here with moons, many moons of walking to reach my home. We cannot linger here."

"What does it matter if we are stranded in Thorvald's camp? I have walked far with a baby inside me. After the baby is born, I can walk more. I want to stay here until the baby is born."

"No. We leave after the trading."

She turned away. *No matter what he said or what he did, she would not go.* She would change the subject, put his mind to other things.

"I must make new sandals. See?" She held out both feet, showing how worn and ragged her sandals were. "And I'm making a little carrying bag for my medicine arrow."

"Why?"

"I don't want to leave it in the pack that Thorvald carries—when I can carry a burden again." Actually, her pack would remain with her in Cicuye, but she wanted to have the arrow with her at all times. Why, she did not know exactly; some inner voice insisted.

"I will carry your pack."

"We shall have another burden-bearer. Two Elk has agreed to give us one."

He glanced at her sharply. "You do not trust me with your pack?"

"I do not trust Thorvald."

He nodded. "Nor do I."

There was another whom he did not trust. One whose eyes burned when he looked at Kwani.

·48·

The Querecho sat on top of the ridge, picking his teeth with a small twig. He was lean and scarred from battle; a finger was missing from his left hand. His hair was cut short on one side, but had been allowed to grow long on the other. The long hair was folded into a bundle, and tied with a leather thong dyed red. His ears were pierced in several places, and ornaments of shell, bone, and turquoise hung from each.

As he removed the remnants of his last meal from his teeth, he watched the activities of Cicuye below. It was the first of what would be four days of the snake hunt, four being the sacred Pueblo number. Today, men of the Snake Society hunted to the north. Next would be the east, then the south, and finally to the west. Searching every rock crevice, every hole, every chink in a cliff, and every refuge in a clump of brush, they pulled out rattlesnakes with their bare hands, and thrust them into a pouch they carried.

The Querecho had seen it all before. But he had never seen a man bitten. He was sure it would happen sooner or later, and he waited for that.

Meanwhile, he had to plan strategy. He fingered the handsome necklace of turquoise recently acquired, and wondered how he could fit his plans into the ceremonial activities. His eyes sought the pregnant, blue-eyed woman who sat on a roof with mate of Two Elk.

Kwani sensed someone's stare. She glanced up to see the figure on top of the ridge.

"Who is that up there?"

Aka-ti paused in her work; she was helping Kwani make new sandals. "That's one of the Querechos of the south who have come for trading." She squinted. "I think it's Running Wolf, the Chief." She shook her

338

head. "I don't like him, nor any of the southern Querechos. Tolonqua says they will attack one day, and I agree, but Two Elk thinks they want only to trade."

"Yellow Bird asked me to speak to Tolonqua. She wants him to forget about another pueblo on the ridge."

"Have you talked to him yet?"

"No . . ."

"I will arrange it. He is out with the hunters now. But I doubt if he will change his mind."

Kwani smiled at her. "That will be kind of you." She was growing fond of the small woman whose face was round as Moon Woman's and whose smile was so endearing. Aka-ti was a person one could confide in. "I have a secret . . ."

"Tell me!"

"I wish to stay here until the baby is born. I am tired. And I have nothing for the baby but one little squirrel skin robe. No cradle board—"

"Good! You are welcome here. I will help you prepare for the baby. But I am surprised that Kokopelli agrees—"

"I have not yet told him."

"Ah."

It was late afternoon when the hunters returned with game—a deer, two rabbits, and a squirrel. Shouting small boys ran to meet them, clustering around Tolonqua.

"Let me carry!" a boy pleaded.

Tolonqua handed him a rabbit. The boy strode proudly into the plaza, holding up the rabbit for all to see, as though he were the hunter.

Tolonqua said, "I will teach you to be a hunter," and the boy beamed. Those taught by the Hunting Chief would be master hunters themselves one day.

Aka-ti heard the hunters returning and summoned one of her sons, a boy not yet a man but both yearning and fearing to become one. "Tell Tolonqua I wish to speak with him."

"About what?" He tried to sound imperious as became a man, but his voice cracked.

"About a matter which does not concern you. Go."

Soon the Hunting Chief strode across the plaza and climbed to Aka-ti's roof. He had changed his garment and he wore his prized ear ornaments of red and blue feathers. Kwani was acutely aware of how handsome he was. She had to brace herself for his gaze. A fire lurked in his eyes, one he could ignite at will. Never had she seen eyes that burned like his. It made her feel selfconscious . . . and something more.

"I am here," he said.

"Come." Aka-ti led them down the ladder to the room below. When they had settled themselves comfortably, she said, "Yellow Bird requests that the mate of Kokopelli speak with you about a matter of importance. She is here to honor that request."

Tolonqua turned to Kwani with a cool gaze.

Kwani tried to hide her embarrassment, but that cool, penetrating gaze made it worse. She blurted, "I did not want to do this, but I must."

"Why?" His voice was expressionless.

"Because Yellow Bird asked me to, that's why. I am a guest here." Her blue eyes sparked.

His gaze warmed. "So. The aged and honorable one assumes that because you are beautiful you can make me change my mind about the new pueblo. Is that not so?"

Kwani was taken aback, and had to smile. "Yes. That is what she assumes. But—"

"Come." He held out his hand to pull her to her feet. "I will show you."

She followed Tolonqua around the end of the ridge and up a steep slope. Once or twice he took her hand in a strong grip, pulling her up after him to the top. Kwani stopped and gazed.

A narrow valley lay on either side, with blue-green mountains beyond. Below, Cicuye's adobe buildings surrounded the small rectangular plaza. Fields of beans and squash were being harvested, and although the altitude made it a gamble to grow corn, corn stood tall. A narrow stream glistened in the sun.

The ridge was flat on top, with steep sides, some too steep to climb. Kwani stood gazing into distance. Mountains shouldered turquoise sky and white clouds ran with the wind.

"See?" Tolonqua said. "What better place? Springs are down there at the base of the ridge, and also on the other side. A stream is nearby, as you can see, and the river is only a short distance away." He pointed eastward.

He stood looking toward Sunfather's rising place, and Kwani stood looking at him. He gestured with a sweep of his arm. "Beyond are the buffalo, and tribes that come from distant places to hunt. These people want to trade buffalo robes and hides and meat for salt and corn and turquoise and flint and fine bows and arrows and other things. Many other things. Where can they do so? And back the other way"—he faced westward—"where can hunters come for buffalo, or to trade with people of the plains?"

Again he turned to her, his face glowing. "You see? This is the place. Cicuye will become rich, the richest of all pueblos. Those tribes out there on the plains will want more than they can trade for. They will try to steal, to kill. So"—he strode to the edge of the ridge where it sloped steeply down,—"we shall build a wall, all around the new Cicuye, with only one place to enter. At the end of the ridge where we came up there will be a door in the wall, and warriors standing guard. And down there"—he pointed to where three tipis stood—"will be many tipis. Many. All coming to trade." He flung both arms wide. "You see?"

"Yes! Yes, I see. It will be beautiful!" She thought, I want to see it, to live in it.

They stood smiling at one another, glowing with shared enthusiasm. He stepped close and looked down into her eyes. Fires lit behind his own, and he spoke softly, almost singing. "The aged one is right. You are beautiful. Will you try to change my mind?"

She looked up into the proud young face with the band across the forehead. Eagle feathers thrust upward behind his head, and bright feathers were alive at his ears. She could not reply, nor could she stop gazing at him. She thought, he is a wild bird, soaring.

He slid a hand over her swollen belly. "I wish the baby were mine."

She pulled away, afraid her knees might buckle, she trembled so. She tried to say, "I am mate of Kokopelli," but she could only think, I am Anasazi. *Pueblo.* She looked for a place to sit and saw some large rocks nestled between junipers as though tossed there by a playful god. She sat down on one, and he came to sit beside her.

To change the subject and calm the irrational thudding of her heart, Kwani said, "What shall I tell Yellow Bird? She fears that her pueblo will be destroyed for use of the beams."

"Ah. She never mentioned that to me. I think it is an excuse. Her spirit dwells in the past, and she wants to be where her spirit is." He gestured toward the mountains. "There are more trees there than pebbles in the river. Why should we destroy the old pueblo for beams?"

"I don't know. The labor . . ."

"We have many men for labor. It will not be difficult."

They sat together in silence. A hawk swooped down and up, clutching a field mouse. Kwani thought, I am like that mouse, captured, carried away . . . by a wild bird.

"Shall I tell Yellow Bird the old pueblo will not be abandoned?" Kwani asked.

"Yes. Nor will it be destroyed. The pueblo is growing, and will grow more. The old one will not be large enough to provide homes for everyone. We will have warriors there, also, to protect. Tell her that."

"I shall."

The breeze of late afternoon rippled grasses soft and fine as baby hair. Tolonqua moved closer and she felt the warmth of him.

He said, "Must you go away?"

"Yellow Bird invites me to stay until the baby is born."

He seemed surprised. "Kokopelli agrees?"

"He does not know. I have not told him yet."

"What if he does not agree?"

She looked away. "I want to stay . . . until the baby is born." She wanted to stay always, near this wild bird.

"He will insist that you go, I think."

She nodded, and bit her lips.

"So," he smiled. "What will you do?"

She turned away to hide her face. "What can I do? He is my mate, my protector . . ." She swallowed. "I shall have a home . . ." She could not continue.

He leaned closer and she could smell the scent of him, a man scent she could not identify but could only respond to.

He said, "Kokopelli asked Two Elk for a burden-bearer and a guide. Two Elk chose me. So I will be with you when you go with Kokopelli and the hairy one. I will guide you across the Great Plains and to the green mountains and rivers beyond." His voice deepened. "I will protect you . . ."

"But the baby—"

"When will it come?"

"Sooner than another moon."

"There is a canyon where we go, a fine canyon with a stream and trees and many caves. It is a beautiful place for a baby to be born. Good spirits are there. And buffalo, sometimes. Maybe the White Buffalo . . ."

Her dream . . . the head of the White Buffalo dissolving to that of a man . . . She gazed into the face so near her own. Something in the eyes, the voice . . . She swallowed again. "The White Buffalo spoke to me in a dream. It waits for me."

His eyes shone. "The White Buffalo appeared to me. Many rains ago when I sought my manhood vision. It awaits me, also."

They stared at one another, marveling. How mysterious and wonderful were the ways of the gods! Obviously, the gods wanted them to find one another and seek the Spirit Being together.

Kwani said, "Take me with you."

With a crooning sound, he folded her in his arms. He did not kiss her, but held her close. He said, "I shall give your baby the Sunfather Birthing Ceremony. Your child will be born Pueblo."

He knew what was in her deepest heart! But to give the Sunfather ceremony would be to establish himself as the baby's father and, therefore, her mate. She was mate of Kokopelli. But she would not think of that now. She clung to him for a long time, feeling that something in her was healing at last, at last.

* * *

It was the fourth day of the snake hunt. Rattlesnakes had been captured, sprinkled with sacred meal so they might understand what was expected of them, and placed in storage jars in the kiva of the Snake Society. A sacred sand painting decorated the kiva floor; it was time for the Snake Washing ceremony.

Kokopelli was present as honored guest with members of the Snake Society. They sat on stone benches lining the kiva wall. Each member held a snake wand—two eagle feathers tied to a short stick. The snakes had been transferred to large woven bags, the altar was decorated, and the washing bowl of consecrated water stood beside it. All was ready.

Kokopelli looked about him and wondered where Thorvald was, and whom he might be raping now. Or perhaps the women and girls were willing, even eager. Not like Kwani who had to endure . . . Hatred welled in him, festering. He would relish his revenge on the Northman.

The Snake Washer entered. He was a proud, erect old man wearing a warrior's short garment and face and body paint. A ceremonial chant began as he stood beside the altar and was joined by two assistants, each holding a snake wand. Because snakes were terrified of eagles, the feathers on the wands controlled them.

The old Snake Washer thrust his hand into the basket, drew out a handful of squirming snakes, and dunked them in the sacred water, then, chanting, he threw them on the sand painting on the floor to absorb the painting's holy properties. Some coiled to strike, but a touch of the eagle feathers made them uncoil and move away.

As one old rattlesnake glided by Kokopelli, he spoke to it mentally. "Why do you allow this?" The snake cast him a dazed glance and did not respond.

When all the snakes were washed they were left upon the floor to dry, attended by boys who amused themselves by handling the snakes, tossing them about, and allowing them to crawl over their bare feet. None were bitten. When the snakes were dry, they were taken from the kiva and placed in the kisi, a cage of slender cottonwood boughs bound and fastened with yucca twine.

Meanwhile, the plaza was crowded. Everyone in the pueblo was there. People sat on roofs and against the walls; even the Querechos sat apart in a silent, expressionless group, waiting for the trading which would take place afterward. Thorvald was conspicuous, striding about, swinging his ax, laughing his booming laugh with the children, and smiling at the prettiest women and girls. Kwani sat with Aka-ti on a rooftop, and Kokopelli mingled with the Chiefs in the plaza.

A small hole was dug into the plaza floor and covered with a board. "What is that?" asked a small boy.

"The sipapu, of course."

"Why is it covered?"

"Learn to observe before asking questions. You will see."

"Look! The Antelope Society!"

To the beat of a drum and chanting, the Society members circled the plaza four times. As each passed the sipapu, he stomped on it.

Da-boom! Thump. *Da-boom!* Thump.

"Why do they do that?"

"So those of the Underworld will know the Snake Dance is about to begin."

"Why—"

"No more questions. Observe!"

Snake Dancers emerged from the kiva, one by one, in awesome array.

"Ah-h-h-h!" the people sighed.

Each dancer wore a cluster of bright feathers on the head, and a kilt from waist to knee, painted with a waving line indicating both snake and rain. A tortoise shell rattle fastened to the right leg below the knee rasped and clattered with each step. Eagle claws encircled both ankles, and a fox skin attached to the waist at the back dangled and swayed impressively. Gray and white painted lines zigzagged on chest, arms, and legs—homage to serpent deities.

People watched and listened, enraptured, as the Antelope Society began a new chant, commencing in low tones and increasing in volume. At a certain place in the chant, three Snake Dancers burst into a dance, followed by another three, and so on, each at a different place in the song.

Tension increased as the chant blended weirdly with the crisp, raspy chugging of tortoise shell rattles and the stamping of dancing feet.

Kwani saw that one of the dancers was Tolonqua. She felt a small pang of fear. "Do the snakes ever bite the dancers?"

"Very seldom, but it has happened."

"Does the dancer die?"

"Usually. But do not be concerned. All will go well."

In groups of three, dancing in a jerking half-step, the Snake Dancers lined up at the kisi. People gasped in awe as each dancer knelt, reached in, pulled out a snake, placed the center of the snake's body in his mouth, and held the dangling body with both hands. In a moment he was on his feet again, dancing four times around the plaza in time to the chant.

Kwani felt a tightening in her throat as Tolonqua knelt, drew out a snake, put it in his mouth with the head at the left, and grasped it behind the head with one hand, and the tail with the other. Her eyes never left him as he joined the others in the dance.

When a dancer completed the four circuits, he dropped the snake to the ground where it was picked up at once by a member of the Society and returned to the kisi. Women brought woven trays with corn meal to sprinkle on the dancers as they passed. Kwani noticed that not a single woman missed sprinkling Tolonqua.

Kwani shifted uncomfortably. The baby kicked repeatedly, and she felt nauseous. With a sense of foreboding, she remembered the snakes hacked to pieces in their sacred place. Had the deities accepted her plea for forgiveness? When she told Kokopelli what had happened, he had shrugged. "He is a fool." Now Thorvald ignored the snakes and ogled the girls.

It was time for the next ceremony. The head priest of the Snake Society accepted a bowl of corn meal from an attendant. Using a trickle of meal, he drew a picture on the ground.

"What is that, father?"

"Don't you see? It is a rain cloud and the Six Sacred Directions."

"Why are they bringing the kisi there? Why—"

"Must I be your eyes? Observe!"

With a final trickle of meal, the picture was completed. The priest raised his hand in a signal, and the snakes were dropped from the kisi onto the picture. There was a mad scramble as the snakes sought escape, and the handlers seized them to be returned to the four directions from which they had come. There was a babble of talk and laughter as people watched handlers chasing the snakes.

Kokopelli saw with interest that one snake escaped. While the handlers were occupied with the others, this one glided swiftly into the tall grasses. Thorvald lunged after it, floundering around in the grass. With a whoop of triumph, he held the snake high, grasped firmly behind the head as he had seen the handlers do. He threw the snake down on the corn meal picture. He would show these Skraelings how to handle snakes!

A handler stooped to grab the snake. But Kokopelli said, "Wait!" The snake coiled to strike, rattling a warning, and the handler stood back.

Kokopelli spoke to the snake mentally. "Come to me. I will protect you."

Slowly, the snake unwound and came to Kokopelli. He held out his hand. The snake climbed up on the hand and settled itself in a coil in the crook of Kokopelli's arm.

People gasped. They had seen Kokopelli's magic, but nothing like this! How wonderful was Kokopelli!

Thorvald was not pleased. He had gone bravely into the grasses, he had captured the rattlesnake and brought it back. But it was Kokopelli who received the awed and admiring glances, the congratulations. He strode away in a huff, following the path to the ridge.

Again, Kokopelli spoke mentally to the snake snuggled in his arm.

"He killed your brothers and sisters in their sacred place. Follow him."

He placed the snake on the ground. "He is an old friend. Let him go." The snake disappeared along the path Thorvald had taken. Kokopelli smiled. The gods would be gratified.

Thorvald reached the top of the ridge and gazed beyond, toward the plains, where he would go on his way to his camp, his boat, and home. Home.

He found a grassy spot and lay down, inspecting the sky with his mariner's eye. Good weather. Good traveling. If Kokopelli had valuables hidden in unknown caves he would get them now, on this final trip. Then one swing of the ax . . . Kwani would be his also. The baby would be no problem. He would do as they did at home and abandon the unwanted child before the third day, while it was not yet a person. He would leave it beside a stone with a piece of meat in its mouth. The gods would decide its fate.

White clouds floated in a dazzling sky. He watched them. Ships sailing . . . sailing home. Soon he would be striding the wide tracks of the sea. His secret was safe. These Skraelings would never know that he shamed himself and his men, and was taunted and ostracized because, during plunder and siege, he refused to impale children upon his sword.

Behind him, grasses hardly moved as the snake approached. Swiftly, silently, it coiled, darted forward, and plunged its fangs into Thorvald's throat.

The Snake Dance was over, rain was assured, and trading could begin. Querechos and Pueblos mingled in the plaza while members of the Snake and Antelope Societies retired to purify themselves with an emetic. There was much haggling in sign language as bargaining proceeded. Small boys played Snake Dance, using pieces of yucca rope for snakes, and little girls brought miniature trays made by their mothers, and tossed bits of grass for meal.

Kwani lay resting in her dwelling, exhausted from heat and emotional strain. Tolonqua with the snake in his mouth . . .

"Come! Come quickly!"

She sat up. "What is it?" But the one who called had disappeared. Slowly, she rose and climbed the ladder.

People stood staring as Thorvald staggered into the plaza. His face and neck were swollen, and turning black. His eyes bulged as though to escape the horror, and his swollen lips flapped in an effort to speak. With a guttural cry, he fell.

The Medicine Chief came running. His bundle contained the mountain plant that was the snakebite remedy, but he saw that it was too late. Nevertheless, he squeezed the fleshy stalk of the plant, allowing the sticky juice to flow into the punctured wound while he chanted healing incantations.

Thorvald's great body writhed in a convulsion and blood stained his lips. With a final hoarse cry, he lost consciousness.

·49·

Thorvald was buried immediately. It was not known what procedures were required for a Northman, so he was simply laid in the ground facing east toward the Sunrise Sea.

His death and burial dampened the festivities, but not the trading. Kokopelli assumed possession of Thorvald's belongings. The sword with its golden hilt and ornate scabbard he said he would keep in remembrance. Bargaining was brisk for the ax and the bow and arrows, and for the contents of Thorvald's pack although these had been reduced somewhat during his visits with feminine acquaintances. It was whispered that Cicuye would have several blue-eyed babies, come Spring.

Kwani spent much time in her dwelling. Thorvald's death brought memories of the death of Okalake, and her heart was heavy. How vengeful were the gods! Surely they would punish her if she left her own people, robbing her child of its Pueblo birthright. But what could she do?

She sought comfort from the ancient ones, but her spirit could not reach them. They eluded her as if in retribution.

Kokopelli sensed her depression and tried to console her. He took her in his arms. "Are you grieving?"

"Yes. In a way."

"For *Thorvald?*"

"For what has happened in my past. And for what I am denying my baby."

"Past is past, foolish one. And all will be well with the baby." He kissed her tenderly. "We leave day after tomorrow."

"What about the boat? Thorvald—"

"I will pay his men what is owed them, and more. They will take us where we want to go."

"But Thorvald was the navigator."

"Anyone can follow the shore. They will take us south in the gulf, and then head back north along the coast." He nodded at her pack. "Prepare to leave. We shall have a guide and burden-bearer to accompany us."

"I know. Tolonqua told me he would be with us."

He released her abruptly. "Tolonqua will be the guide?"

"Yes. He said—"

"I shall not permit it."

He climbed the ladder, muttering, and Kwani sighed. She suspected there would be trouble between her mate and Tolonqua. She needed to think, to get away from people for a while and commune with Earthmother and with her own spirit. She tucked her medicine arrow into the little bag she had made for it, and tied it to her waist.

The plaza was thronged with traders mingling with Querechos. Kwani headed for the ridge, to sit on the stone where Tolonqua had sat with her. The possibility of conflict between him and Kokopelli weighed on her spirit. She remembered the tense encounters between Thorvald and her mate. Would similar confrontations happen again? The thought filled her with foreboding, and she gazed over the valley to the blue mountains beyond, seeking reassurance in the peace and beauty.

Below, beyond the ridge, a red-brown, shaggy coat caught the sun. Brother Coyote! He stopped, and glanced up at her.

"I greet you, Brother Coyote."

He stared at Kwani a moment, then trotted away; she raised a hand in farewell. *He senses I am troubled. He was telling me something.* She tried to understand what it was, and concentrated, listening to an inner voice.

Realization welled up. Almost, she knew . . .

A vicious jerk from behind yanked her backward. With a cry of fright, she twisted to face a Querecho whose grim leer, revealing rotted teeth, made her cry out again. He shoved his hand over her mouth, pulled her to the edge of the steep bank, and dragged her down. Kwani fought to be free, kicking, clawing at the hand over her mouth. She bit down hard on his hand, and tasted blood.

A push sent her rolling down the bank. Sharp stones and thorny brush tore at her. He scrambled after her. She tried to rise; he kicked her down. He brandished a knife in her face, hissing warnings. Kwani could not understand the words but the meaning was unmistakable. Shouts for help would be silenced. Instantly and forever.

She bit her lips to keep from screaming, and lay on her side with legs curled up, trying to protect the baby. He shoved his foot down on her head, pressing her face into the dirt, while he bound his bleeding hand with a dirty rag.

Yanking her up, he poked the sharp point of the knife against her throat while he removed a leather thong from a pouch at his side. A warning thrust of the knife punctured her skin; he gripped the knife in his teeth and bound Kwani's hands behind her. She felt blood trickling down her neck. She bit her lips again.

With half the bloody rag from his hand, the Querecho forced open Kwani's mouth and gagged her. He pushed her ahead of him.

She stumbled ahead, disoriented, terrified, scratched and bruised, with the foul rag stretching her mouth wide. She feared she would vomit, and choke. The Querecho followed so quietly she had to turn to see if he were still there. When she faltered, she was pushed. Her heart pounded in her throat. She had visions of being stabbed and mutilated, the baby ripped from her womb; such things had happened.

She stopped. An involuntary cry became a muffled gurgle. Snarling dogs rushed at her. Each had a travois fastened by a collar to the dog's neck and shoulders; the travois held a round mesh bag between the poles, and the bags were piled high with the Querechos' belongings. The dogs jumped at Kwani but the man behind her ordered them back. They did not retreat, but they did not attack. They crouched, growling.

A Querecho woman followed the dogs. She was short, squat, and dirty, but she wore beautiful necklaces, bracelets, and ear ornaments of turquoise, shell, and polished claws and bone. The man was taller, equally dirty, and equally adorned. His hair was cut short on one side and left long on the other; it hung limply like the tail of an animal, fastened by a band around the forehead. Even at a distance, Kwani could see his rotted teeth as he spoke.

The woman saw Kwani's necklace, and came closer to see it better. She had a rank smell; Kwani turned her face away. The woman lifted the necklace from around Kwani's neck and put it over her own. Her eyes glittered in amusement as Kwani struggled in outrage, trying to free herself.

A man approached, walking swiftly. As he drew near, striding with obvious arrogance, Kwani knew it must be Running Wolf, the Querecho Chief whom she had seen as she sat on the roof with Aka-ti. Many ornaments hung from both ears which had been pierced in several places; much jewelery adorned his neck and both arms. His long hair on one side, folded into a neat bundle, was tied with a red thong. His breechcloth of fringed buckskin was handsomely painted and embroidered, and his sandals of buffalo hide were equally ornate.

The man and woman greeted him respectfully. He returned the greeting and came to stand before Kwani, inspecting her with an inpenetrable gaze. His face was flint-cold and hard, his mouth cruel. Instinctively, Kwani drew back.

Running Wolf turned to the woman and spoke sharply. He held out a hand with a finger missing; she shook her head. Again he spoke. Reluctantly she removed Kwani's necklace and handed it to him. He looked at it closely, turning the scallop shell with its turquoise inlay over and over. He lifted it to sniff at it like a dog. Satisfied, he slid his fingers over the smooth stone beads of many colors, grunted, put the necklace on, and admired the splendor of it upon his chest.

Kwani shook with fury. He gave her a contemptuous shove and spoke to the dogs who followed, pulling their burdens. The men and the woman headed east, prodding Kwani before them.

Gradually the ridge disappeared behind them. It grew hot; Kwani thought, surely this bloody rag binding my mouth is no longer necessary. She stopped and turned to face Running Wolf. With what dignity she could muster she turned around and lifted her bound hands. For a moment, he did nothing, then he sliced the thong with his flint knife, and her hands were free. She tore the gag from her mouth.

"Thank you," she said with cool courtesy.

If he understood, he gave no sign. His eyes slid over her and rested on the little pack at her side. He thrust out his hand for it.

No, she thought. He must not have it. But she had no choice. She reached into the pack. As though compelled by the painted arrow, her mouth opened with the singing, eerie cry she had used on the Medicine Chief who willed her to die. She held the arrow high in both hands as she sang, offering it. He saw the design on the arrow and recognized it as supernatural, a weapon to kill witches. He knocked it to the ground.

Still singing, she picked up the arrow and returned it to its pack. Only then did she stop singing. She stood immobile, gazing beyond them at something they could not see, surrounded with an aura of mystical power.

The Querechos shifted uneasily. Running Wolf barked a command, and again they headed east.

They walked all day. The dogs snarled at one another or sat and whined to have their loads adjusted. One dog darted after a rabbit; the man chased him, then punished him with a savage kick.

Kwani was so tired she could do no more than drag one foot after the other. Again and again she wondered where they were going, and why. Each time she looked at her necklace on the chest of Running Wolf, she burned with fierce resentment. Her feet hurt, her head ached, her back ached, she ached all over. Surely, the Querechos would stop to rest soon. But they did not. They strode along, talking rapidly to one another and to the dogs. If Kwani faltered, they prodded her; otherwise, she was ignored.

The gods are punishing me.

Or were they? Could it be that the trials of this journey, and the journey itself, had an ultimate goal worthy of all that was endured? Was she being challenged?

The landscape was changing, flattening out. There were fewer trees and shrubs, and different grasses. Earthmother's fragrance here was different than from where they had come. A flight of ducks swooped low; water must be near.

It was a marshy lake, a bit of turquoise sky fallen to earth. Ducks paddled upon it, iridescent feathers shimmering. Running Wolf drew an arrow from his quiver, raised his bow, and shot the arrow. The ducks flew away, all but one which dropped to the water with the arrow in its side. Running Wolf spoke to the man who removed his breechcloth and sandals reluctantly, and retrieved the duck; Running Wolf tucked it into one of the packs.

It was nearly dark when they stopped. Kwani sank to the ground and closed her eyes. The Querechos were setting up camp, and the woman was preparing a meal, but Kwani was too tired to care. She was asleep almost immediately.

It was dawn when she woke. She sat up, startled, and looked around. The Querechos were gone. She was alone but for a figure seated at a small fire with his back to her. *She knew that back, that figure.* It was he who had tracked them from the beginning. Wopio.

Wopio, her first mate. Who smiled and hid his face with a blanket when the Medicine Chief shot the arrow to kill witches, the arrow that was at her side. Wopio, who came to the Place of the Eagle Clan and tried to make her return to him. Did he think she would return to him now? She laughed in scorn.

Wopio swung around, startled. Kwani saw that he wore her necklace. For a moment, they stared at one another without speaking.

Kwani stood. "Give me my necklace."

"It is no longer yours." He grasped the shell and waved it tauntingly. "It is Tiopi's now."

Kwani had forgotten that mean look, that hangdog slouch. His small eyes were too close together, his mouth was flabby, and his body soft. How could she have loved him, cried for him?

She held out her hand. "Give it back."

"No. I told you. It is Tiopi's."

"So Yatosha sent you to do his stealing for him?" Her voice was scathing.

He flushed. "Zashue and Yatosha will leave the city and take the people south when I return with this necklace." He waved the shell again. "Then the city will have a new clan, and I will be Chief. I will bring my people there." He smiled smugly, not mentioning the various rich treasures Zashue and Yatosha promised in return for Kwani and the necklace. "Tiopi is She Who Remembers. The necklace belongs to her now."

Kwani turned away, pretending indifference. The situation demanded strategy. She said, "As you see, I am going to have a baby. Do you still accuse me of witchcraft?"

"Not I. The Eagle Clan. I shall return you to them for trial."

So that was it! Strategy was forgotten in rage. "You tracked us all this way, you tried to kill Thorvald and my mate with your arrows, you bribed—oh yes—you bribed the Querechos to kidnap me because you were afraid to do it yourself. Now you think you are going to take me back to those who want to kill me? As you wanted your Medicine Chief to kill me? You are more stupid than I thought." She stepped close to him and spat.

He wiped his face. "Zashue gives you this in exchange for what you gave him!" He drew a flint knife from its sheath and struck savagely at her face, but she ducked, and gave her singing-cry, eyes blazing.

He paused, surprised, and glanced at her belly.

"I give it to the child as well."

He slashed at her again, aiming for her belly. She twisted aside; the knife gashed her arm from elbow to wrist. Desperately, she kicked, and her sandaled foot hit him in the groin. He doubled over. She snatched the arrow from its pouch and gripped it with both hands. With all her strength, she plunged it into the artery below the side of his jaw, beneath his ear.

He wrenched the arrow out, and threw it down. Blood spurted and he tried to staunch it with his hands. Kwani picked up the arrow, and ran. She fell, rose, fell, and ran again, searching wildly for a hiding place where none existed.

Wopio did not follow. He sat, pressing both hands to his throat. Blood gushed through his fingers and ran down his arms. He rocked back and forth, chanting the death song he had planned and rehearsed all his life.

Kwani huddled under a bush, trying to make herself invisible. Her arm throbbed, and she wrapped it with a corner of her robe to make the bleeding stop. The blood still flowed, so she tore off a piece of her robe and bound her arm tightly, watching fearfully to see if Wopio followed. The breeze came, carrying the sound of his death song, a guttural wailing to freeze the blood. She felt sick, and vomited. She lay down, drained of strength. Wopio's song grew weaker, faded, and was gone.

For a long time she lay there, willing Earthmother's serenity to quiet her screaming brain and the pounding of her heart. The bandage on her arm was soaked red, but bleeding seemed to have stopped.

At last her mind cleared and she was able to think. Surely Tolonqua, Kokopelli, and the others had missed her and were searching by now. She reached for her necklace, then remembered where it was. Vultures circled, swooping low; she knew she could not go back for it.

She looked about her. Mountain ranges had spread apart like opening arms to the vast plains where buffalo ranged beyond. Here there were scattered trees, a few bushy shrubs, and grass, but that was all. What she feared the most had happened. She was alone again in the wilderness. But wounded this time, and over eight moons pregnant. With no pack, no food, no water, nothing but the medicine arrow which had saved her life once more.

Fear clutched at her. The baby moved as though changing position to be born.

"Not yet!" she cried aloud.

She pressed her hands to the place where the scallop shell had rested, and pretended the necklace was still there. She forced herself to concentrate, to seek the power, the wisdom the necklace gave her. Her spirit quieted, and she seemed to hear again the voice of the White Buffalo.

"I await you. Remember that when you are afraid."

The answer came. It was so simple, so obvious, she did not know why the thought had not occurred at once. She would send smoke signals to those who searched for her. On a day such as this, the smoke would rise high, it would be seen for miles. A fire must be built. But she had no fire stick—a wooden rod fitted into a base with a small cavity, and twirled by hand to create friction. She would make one. But she had no knife. At last she faced up to what she must do—return to Wopio and get his fire stick, his knife, and his pack with food and water.

Slowly, she headed back. Hovering vultures told her where he lay. As she approached, she saw movement which was not that of birds. She stopped, watching. No vultures descended. Cautiously, quietly, she drew closer.

Wolves!

She backed away in horror and sat waiting, trying not to be sick. One wolf trotted away, holding the lower part of an arm in his mouth. The hand flapped feebly as if waving goodbye. Other wolves lingered, growling as they fed; then they left one by one. When she was certain the wolves were gone, she went to look.

Only mangled remains were left, crawling with flies. Bones lay gnawed and scattered. The necklace was barely discernible in a bloody heap. The flint knife lay nearby, partially concealed.

Trying not to vomit again, Kwani extracted the knife and lifted out the necklace dripping with gore. Laying them aside, she looked for his pack. She had hardly turned her back when vultures descended, wings flapping.

His pack was by the remnants of the campfire. Perhaps a coal smouldered in the ashes; she looked for something to poke the ashes with. There was only Wopio's slimy knife. She forced herself to take it again, and leaned forward, blowing on the coals, turning them over, searching for a hint of glow.

There it was! The tiniest spark, but it was there! She fed it dried grasses, more and more, until the flame rose. She went to look for fallen branches—anything that would burn—but found a mere handful of twigs. Her arm throbbed with pain but she carried her find to the fire.

Something more was needed to make a fire big enough for smoke signals. Wopio's pack. What was in it? A blanket. Good, she would need that to make signals. A water bag. Corn cakes and dried venison. A fire stick and base. Yucca fiber sandals; she added them to the flames. A bag containing turquoise and obsidian. A small pouch of salt. A cotton robe.

Exultant, she pulled off her ragged, bloody robe and put on the other—too big and rather ugly, but it was clean. She fed her own robe to the fire bit by bit.

When the flames were high enough, she poured some water from the water bag on an armful of grass, and laid the damp grass on the flames. Immediately, smoke billowed.

Taking the blanket with both hands, Kwani flung it over the smoking fire, lifted it to allow a puff of smoke to rise, then covered it again. She did this over and over until she could bear the pain in her arm no longer. She replaced the contents of Wopio's pack and dragged it away as far as she could until exhaustion and pain forced her to stop.

She sat, waiting. It grew dark and the wolves returned. She saw their glowing eyes as they trotted by, but they did not stop. They had fed well.

·50·

In the pale light of dawn, Kokopelli, Tolonqua, and his hunters stood staring down at what was left of a body. Kokopelli's face was lined and circles smudged his eyes.

"Was it Kwani?"

Tolonqua pointed to a skull some distance away. It was nearly empty, but hair remained, three braids from a flattened head. "It was a man. Anasazi."

A hunter said, "He may have been returning from the plains, and was ambushed."

"Wolves," another hunter added.

"The wolves came later." Tolonqua pointed to the remains of a fire. "Something happened first to make him send smoke signals."

The oldest hunter nodded. His grizzled face bore the marks of many years. "He was followed from Cicuye."

"Yes." Tolonqua picked up a duck's webbed foot. "He came the way we did. See? The lake. He was killed for his pack."

"Querechos, tracking him."

The hunters agreed. One said, "They wanted his pack. We have been misled. We should return and start over; we have missed Kwani somewhere."

"Wait." By the remains of the fire Kokopelli stooped and picked up a bit of charred robe. A piece of shell clung to it. "Look!"

They examined it and a hunter said, "It is from a ceremonial robe. Why did he burn it?"

"It is Kwani's." Kokopelli's voice rasped with strain. Tolonqua nodded agreement. Again they turned to the mangled bones. Were there two bodies? If so, where was the other skull, and the bones? Did the wolves carry them away?

"If it was Kwani, where is the necklace?" Kokopelli asked.

"The Querechos took it."

Beyond the fire Tolonqua crouched, examining the ground. "The Querechos and dogs went that way." He pointed. "But something was dragged over there, and whoever, whatever, dragged it erased tracks with the dragging."

They looked at one another. Was it an animal?

Tolonqua bent low, inspecting every blade of grass, every hidden crevice of soil, and the hunters fanned out, searching.

Tolonqua grunted, and stood staring. Kokopelli strode to stand beside him, and the other hunters rushed to see. Kwani lay nestled under a bush like a young rabbit. One arm was swathed in a bloody bandage. She was asleep, in a man's white robe, with a bit of corn cake in her hand and the water bag beside her. The necklace and a flint knife lay in a bloody mess to one side. A rolled blanket was at her head, and a man's pack at her feet. Her mouth was slightly open, and she burbled a little in her sleep, like a baby.

They stared in stunned astonishment.

"Kwani!" Kokopelli knelt beside her.

She jolted awake, and Kokopelli folded her in his arms.

She clung to him. "You found me!"

"What happened?"

"Querechos. Kidnapped me and left me with Wopio."

"Who?"

"My first mate. Wopio—"

"What happened to him?"

"He did this—" She thrust out her wounded arm. "He tried to kill me. And the baby. With his knife. So the medicine arrow killed him—"

"You mean *you* killed *him* with an arrow?"

The hunters glanced at one another. What she was saying was impossible. She had no bow. She was a woman, and near her time . . .

Tolonqua knelt beside her. "How did you do it?"

"I kicked him here"—she pointed to herself—"and he bent over and I thrust the arrow here." Again, she pointed. "The wolves came . . ."

The hunters gawked. This would go down as legend.

Kokopelli said, "You burned your robe. Why?"

"To make fire for signals. Did you see?"

Tolonqua said, "Yes. Clearly." His eyes were warm with more than praise.

She held out her bandaged arm to Kokopelli. "It hurts."

"I know." He reached for his medicine bag.

"My necklace . . . the knife . . ."

"We will clean them," Tolonqua said. He turned to his men. "You will return by way of the lake so you can refill your water bags there." He handed a hunter the necklace and the knife. "Use water to get these clean."

Kokopelli frowned. "I need water here."

"There will be enough." He handed Kokopelli a water bag. Kwani lay back as Kokopelli unwrapped the bloody bandage. His touch was expert and gentle, but it was painful. During her ordeal, she had shed no tears; now they trickled down as Kokopelli cleaned the wound. To take her mind off the pain, she said, "I am sorry I had to burn the robe you gave me. But it was ragged and torn and I needed it for the fire . . ."

"It does not matter. I have brought you another." He glanced up, smiling.

Tolonqua said, "I have brought you something also. But I cannot give it to you now."

"Why not?"

"It is for when the baby comes."

Kwani smiled. Kokopelli did not.

The necklace and the knife were brought back clean, and Tolonqua drew the necklace over Kwani's head. "What shall I do with the knife?"

"You may keep it."

Kokopelli glanced up sharply. Tolonqua said, "Thank you, but I have no need of another knife. Perhaps Kokopelli can use it in trade."

"No," Kokopelli said coldly. "It would be more suitable if it were yours."

The two men stared at one another with expressionless faces. "Since neither of you wants it, I shall give it to the hunter who cleaned it for me," Kwani decided.

The boy ducked his head in shy pleasure. Tolonqua handed him the knife and he tucked it in the quiver with his arrows.

Kokopelli finished cleaning Kwani's wound, and applied a healing poultice. He bound her arm with a soft strip of buckskin—the same strip he had used when her leg was broken—and sat back and looked at her. The robe she wore was a square of woven cotton sewn at each side, with a hole in the center to slip over the head. Although the robe was clean, the rest of her was dirty. Her body was distorted in a late stage of pregnancy, yet she was beautiful. Amazing!

He said, "Tonight I will bathe you. Tomorrow, we continue on our journey to Thorvald's camp. They wait for him with the boat. We must tell them . . ." He paused, feeling an unaccustomed pang of regret. There had been times when Thorvald was a good companion. "Soon we shall be on the river, and then to the gulf, and home."

Kwani looked into the amber eyes and was torn with indecision. He was her mate and she loved him. But more and more she wondered about his distant homeland, and traveling far after the baby was born. His eyes searched her face, and she gazed at him silently. The sloping forehead, the eagle beak of a nose, the sensual, downturned mouth surrounded by ornamentation of black dots . . .

Compelling. *Foreign.* And older than she had ever realized.

She and Tolonqua glanced at one another, an exchange not missed by Kokopelli. He had disposed of one who desired his mate. Must he dispose of another?

It was three more days before they saw the buffalo, a long line of black specks against the far horizon. In every direction was distance—vast space filled only with golden grass waving in the hot wind, and enormous expanse of sky bending to meet it. Kwani had lived always among mountains and in canyons cradled by sheltering cliffs. Here she felt totally exposed. Vulnerable. There was nothing to lean the eyes against, no place to hide.

Behind them, dark clouds swelled. There was an ominous sound, like distant thunder. But the sound did not come from behind.

Tolonqua said, "Buffalo."

"The rutting season," Kokopelli added. "They bellow."

"And paw the ground and wallow and fight."

Kwani gazed at the wavering line of black specks. "Isn't it dangerous? To be near them, I mean."

"Yes," Tolonqua said. "But tomorrow they may not be there. They go and come."

"There is no danger." Kokopelli looked down his nose. "I am here."

Tolonqua turned away and did not comment. Kwani sensed tension between them and it increased her unease. She had made it a point to stay close to Kokopelli and avoid Tolonqua's glance. But she could feel it burning into her sometimes. She relished his presence. She enjoyed looking at him, listening to him, especially when he sang his morning chant to the sun. She liked the way he walked with long, easy strides as though he carried no burden. His pack contained hers as well as his own, and much of Kokopelli's. Kokopelli carried a heavy pack, also, with the golden hilt of Thorvald's sword protruding from the top.

Wolves! They slunk through the grass like shadows, avoiding them. A pack ran by, and another.

Tolonqua said, "They go for the buffalo."

Kwani shuddered. She wished she were back in Cicuye. "Do we have far to go?"

"To the canyon?"

"Yes."

"Which canyon?" Kokopelli asked sharply.

"The one with many colors, and caves. And buffalo."

"We do not have time for that. We shall bypass it."

Kwani said, "I want my baby to be born there."

"Why?" Kokopelli had seen women squat to have their babies anywhere, and continue traveling soon afterward with the baby in a cradle board. "We must reach the boat—"

Kwani flushed with anger. All he cared about was reaching the boat! She said hotly, "Look at me, Kokopelli. I have come all this way with you because that is what *you* wanted. I am tired, tired, tired. I need rest. I need a sheltered place. This baby is going to be born where there is water and shelter, and where I can rest comfortably afterward. In the canyon." She brushed the hair from her sweaty face, and glared at him.

He stared down at her in frozen silence. At last he said, "And what happens when we arrive at camp to discover the boat has gone without us? Do you have any idea at all of how far we would be forced to walk to reach Tula? No. You do not. I have brought you this way to make it easier for you. I could have taken you south through the deserts, over high mountains, among hostile tribes. But you insist on delay. You think only of yourself—"

"The baby—"

"Okalake's child, I remind you. This baby is not my doing, and I cannot accept responsibility for it."

Kwani gazed up at him, probing the secret place behind his eyes. With a flash of insight, she saw Kokopelli as he was—a powerful, magnetic, arrogant foreigner with magical skills and charms, but a Toltec whose ways would never be her ways. Why did she love him?

She lifted her chin. "I am your mate, am I not?"

His mouth set in a grim line.

"You must accept responsibility for me. And the baby is part of me whether you choose to admit it or not."

He thrust his face down to hers so that she could see the pores in the black dots ornamenting his cheeks and chin.

"I am Toltec. A nobleman. The mate of a Toltec does not presume to speak so. Never. You—"

"I am Anasazi. I am She Who Remembers, an Honored One. Not a dog to humbly follow a master."

"And I am not a dog to be ordered about!" he shouted. "Yes, you are my mate. Mate of a Toltec. It is your place to be humble. Whether *you* choose to admit it or not."

He whirled to confront Tolonqua, for it was he who had told Kwani about the canyon; otherwise, how would she know of it? But Tolonqua had tactfully walked some distance away, and peered at the sky where dark clouds hung low.

Abruptly, Kwani sat down. Her heart pounded, and her legs were shaky. Tears stung her eyes. He had shouted at her! What she wanted was for him to take her in his arms, comfort her, tell her he loved her and the baby would be born wherever she wished. Instead, he stood glaring down at her. She would not look at him, but gazed into distance—endless, empty, overwhelming distance shimmering in heat—heat that clouds pressed down as if to suffocate every living thing below.

Kokopelli saw that Kwani still wore the man's robe because the one he had given her would not fit over her swollen belly. Frustration and a strange feeling of helplessness fanned his anger. "Get up!"

Thunder rumbled. A deer ran by, and another. A hot wind seared the grass already parched from summer's heat.

Tolonqua hurried to them. He pointed behind.

Look!"

Again, lightning flashed. A line of smoke rose in the distance, and a bright band of fire approached on the ground.

"Hurry!"

Seizing Kwani's hand, the two men ran, lifting her off her feet when she could not keep up. She could smell the smoke as the golden grass, parched dry, was devoured by speeding flames.

"The river!" Tolonqua cried.

The land that seemed flat had small hills and gullies that made running difficult. They reached a wide path trampled smooth by herds of buffalo. Wolves sped by, and a herd of pronghorn antelope. Snakes and prairie dogs darted into their holes. A bobcat ran past, giving them hardly a glance.

Kwani looked back to see fire roaring upon them. Her heart leaped in terror, and she stumbled and fell. Tolonqua scooped her up in his arms.

"The river is down there!" he shouted as thunder boomed and crackled.

Countless buffalo had chosen the easiest place to cross the river, and had worn the bank to a gentle slope. Kwani choked with smoke as Tolonqua, half running, half sliding, plunged into the water. Kokopelli followed, panting, and sank to his knees at the river's edge.

Raindrops fell. Kwani huddled against Tolonqua's chest. Rain became a torrent, pounding down. Slowly, fire hissed and died, leaving the smell of its death on blackened earth.

Tolonqua sloshed up the bank. Kwani thought he would set her down, but he did not. He held her tightly; his breathing and the beat of his heart blended with her own. Her arms were around his neck, and her cheek was pressed against him while sheets of rain enfolded them. She knew he gazed at her, but she could not look up. She clung to him.

Here I am protected. Here I belong.

Kokopelli was downstream wading in the river, using rain and river water to wash away the detested accumulation of sweat and grime. He struggled up the bank as Tolonqua set Kwani on her feet.

"We must find shelter," Kokopelli said.

"Hunters should be around somewhere. They follow the buffalo. We can find shelter with them."

"But the buffalo are gone," Kwani said.

"No. They are everywhere. Huge herds. This is big country."

They plodded on, following the river and paths worn deep by buffalo. Gradually the rain ceased and a great rainbow arched across the sky. They stood gazing at it in wonder. Kokopelli took his flute from his soaked pack. He began to play, and it was as though he beckoned the sun to shine again and the birds to return singing. Clouds drifted away, Sunfather appeared, and but for the drenched ground and wet grasses, it was as if the storm had never been.

Behind them, a great stretch of blackened earth showed where the fire had raced. But small green sprouts would poke through, nourished by deep, dense roots reaching far below, and grass would grow again. It was Earthmother's way.

A puff of smoke appeared on the horizon, and another.

"Signals," Tolonqua said. "It is the Querechos of the plains. Friends. They know we come and they wait for us. They welcome you, Kokopelli."

"Of course."

He continued playing, and the hot wind came to carry the music away.

·51·

Early morning. Already the ground was dry from hot wind and sun, and dust hung low where vast herds of buffalo milled in the frenzy of the rutting season. Usually cows and bulls remained in separate groups, but not now. There was thunderous bellowing, loud clanking of horns in battle, and the thud of bodies hitting the ground in furious wallowing as bulls challenged one another.

A grizzled old bull, the leader of his herd, searched among the cows for one whose secretions invited mating. He was a magnificent beast, over six feet high at the shoulder and eleven feet long from nose to tail. Two thousand pounds of brute power lay beneath his shaggy brown coat, a power asserting itself with roaring bellows and threatening swings of his horns when other bulls presumed to approach a cow in which he was interested.

He found a cow in delectable heat. His neck stretched out, his upper lip curled back to expose the gums, and his nostrils distended. He was ready. He stood parallel to her, warning off rivals with bellows and brief charges, and placed his chin on her rump preparing to mount. She gave him a hard kick and galloped away to join another herd nearby.

He galloped after her, his short tail erect, followed by other bulls as eager as he. He turned to confront them in furious rage. He threw himself to the ground, wallowing, feet thrashing, clods flying, dust billowing.

With a mighty roar he faced a rival, pawed the earth, lowered his horns, and charged.

The infuriated young rival met the charge at top speed, and their skulls connected with an impact that made dirt fly from the pelts of both. They locked horns in a primordial battle grip. With humps arched in mighty curves of power and tails twitching rapidly, they shoved one another back and forth. Dust rose from their grinding hooves, horns clanked, and heads bent low until their beards touched the ground.

To and fro they surged while other buffalo paid no attention. Calves gamboled nearby; a wolf passed and was ignored.

The old bull's experience in countless battles and the power of his massive weight were too much for the young challenger. He backed off, swinging his horns, bellowing reprisals, and trotted away. With a roar of triumph, the old bull searched for another female in heat. He selected a fine one, drove away opponents, placed his chin on her rump and mounted her. He leaned his head against her side, wrapped his forelegs around her, and thrust steadily. A few seconds was all it took. He dismounted just as a commotion occurred at the edge of the herd.

A wolf was attacking a calf, and the calf bleated piteously. The cow which the old bull had mounted ran to the rescue, followed by the bull. As they drew near, the wolf and the calf suddenly became two-legged creatures—camouflaged hunters with bows and arrows.

The old bull faltered as arrows hit him. The cow fell kicking, and hunters came running from hiding places in the shallow gullies. The bull turned to run with other buffalo stampeding away, but more arrows found him and he fell to his knees. He tried to stand, but could not. Soon he lay dying.

Tolonqua rose with a shout, waving his wolf's pelt after the buffalo. The Querecho with the calf's skin shouted too, and they laughed together. They were friends of long standing; they had hunted this way before.

The butchering began. Tolonqua stood by, watching. Although his arrow caused the first mortal wound of this bull and he was, therefore, entitled to the pelt and his choice of meat parts, he had joined in the hunt as a gift to the tribe for their hospitality to him and to Kokopelli and Kwani. The pelt would go to the Clan Chief, and the meat would be divided among the tipis.

As they cut and slashed, the hunters snacked on raw morsels taken still warm from the buffalo—livers, kidneys, tongues, eyes, testicles, belly fat, parts of the stomach, gristle from snouts, and marrow from leg bones. A sprinkling of bile from the gall bladder added piquancy to liver portions. Some hunters bashed holes in the tops of skulls and scooped out the fresh brains. The belly was slit and entrails removed; men scooped up and drank handfuls of warm blood.

Then meat was piled on hides spread on the ground. Women and dogs with travois would come to haul the loads home.

Tolonqua said, "I will tell the women to bring the dogs now." He headed for camp.

*　*　*

Kwani sat with Kokopelli in the tipi of the Clan Chief. The Querechos here seemed different from those of the south who had kidnapped her. They were tall, well built, handsomely adorned, and clean. Still, she was uneasy and sat in silence as Kokopelli and the Chief conversed in eloquent sign language.

The tipi was surprisingly roomy. A circular fire pit sat beneath the smoke hole. Behind it was the family altar containing sacred objects; behind that, against the tipi wall, was an impressive collection of pipes and rattles, the Chief's feathered war bonnet, his painted rawhide shield, and his weapons. Three beds stood against the wall, and bundles of belongings were tucked neatly against the slanted base of the wall. This was a tipi owned by a family of wealth and importance, a dwelling that could be quickly dismantled, the buffalo hide covering rolled up, and the poles and all hauled away by dogs and travois.

A woman sat on one of the beds, mending a garment. She noticed Kwani's inspection, gave her a quick glance, and looked politely away. She wore a buffalo hide tunic, fringed and embroidered, and her hair was parted in the center and hung in two braids, the part was painted a bright red. It was becoming, Kwani thought.

The sign language talk continued. The baby moved within Kwani and she shifted uneasily. For several days it had seemed that the child moved differently than before. Did it want to be born ahead of time? She felt pressure on her bladder but was not sure of protocol here. She nudged Kokopelli who turned to her impatiently.

"I must relieve myself and I don't know where to go."

Kokopelli gestured a sign, and the woman rose, beckoning Kwani to follow. Outside, another woman who was about Kwani's age and who was six months pregnant smiled and beckoned for Kwani to follow her to a secluded spot by the river. It was a bowl-shaped indentation where buffalo had wallowed; it offered a measure of privacy.

As they returned to the camp, Kwani saw that some of the contents of their packs were spread on the grass to dry. Among Tolonqua's belongings was an altogether wonderful cradle board; Kwani knelt and took it in her arms. She had never seen one like it. Two slender boards formed a modified V upon which the enclosure for the baby was fastened. The top portions of the boards extended above, so that the mother could easily reach behind her to grasp the boards and lift the cradle board from her back. The baby's enclosure was of softest deerskin, laced all the way down the front so it could be easily opened, and diapering changed. It had a little bonnet with tassels and beads, and the skin was intricately embroidered all over with tiny shell beads, and painted in happy colors. A strip, fastened in the back of the V structure, slipped over the mother's shoulders for easy carrying. It was the most beautiful and the most practical cradle board Kwani had ever seen. She held it close, rocking back and forth, while the woman smiled in total understanding.

The dogs set up a loud commotion as Tolonqua returned. Women gathered to hear how many dogs and travois were needed to bring the meat home. He saw Kwani and went to her.

"You found it!" He smiled.

She was overcome. How perceptive of him to choose this as a gift! Her heart filled. It was almost the only thing she had for the baby, but it was enough. Kokopelli had given her nothing for the child; he seemed uninterested in what was the most important thing in her life. She could not speak but held the cradle board to her as if it were a baby.

Tolonqua's eyes glowed with a feeling that made her heart skip. He leaned close and whispered, "I will give the birthing ceremony."

She did not reply, and he tilted her chin, forcing her to look up at him. "The baby will be mine."

Kwani raised the cradle board to her cheek. She could not speak but her blue eyes spoke for her.

He said, "We will talk later. Tonight, by the river."

He turned away before she could say no.

It took ten dogs and their travois to haul the meat home. Usually four dogs sufficed for one buffalo. But the old bull was much larger than the cow, and bigger than many other bulls. Bringing home such a prize was a triumph. How fortunate that Kokopelli was there to lure the buffalo! And that Tolonqua was also there to hunt with Standing Eagle, their Hunting Chief! Tolonqua had devised the wolf-and-calf routine and pursuaded his long-time friend to be the calf because his bleating was so realistic. Word of their extraordinary technique had spread to far distant campfires, and was admired, laughed over, and copied—unsuccessfully.

Tolonqua and his hunters often encountered other tribes on the Plains as they followed the buffalo. Although Pueblos and Querechos were not friendly, Tolonqua's efforts to learn their language, his fair dealings, and his fine singing earned him welcome, especially when accompanied by generous gifts.

As the travois were unloaded, some of the less desirable portions of meat were tossed to the dogs as reward. The rest was exclaimed over, examined, tasted, and divided. There was talk and laughter and excited chatter of children as they begged for this or that tidbit.

Tolonqua looked for Kokopelli, but he was not there.

"Where is Kokopelli?"

There was no answer. Smiles and meaningful glances made Tolonqua look more closely at the women. A girl was missing, a pretty one who had once indicated to Tolonqua she would not be unwilling to share her bed. He had planned to do so until Kwani entered his life. Now it was Kwani, only Kwani, who consumed his thoughts, his being.

Mate of Kokopelli . . .

But the White Buffalo had appeared to her also, in a dream. Surely, this was an omen. And Kokopelli was with another.

He slipped away to the river to wait for darkness. And Kwani. There would be feasting and celebrating, but first he must hold Kwani in his arms . . .

Hours passed; Sunfather sank to the underworld, and Kwani did not come. A badger waddled to drink at the river; birds swooped low. Rich smells of roasting meat and shouts and laughter and the shrill notes of a bone flute were tantalizing, but he wanted only Kwani.

At last she came, hurrying, holding her belly with both hands. Her eyes were large and afraid. "I cannot find Kokopelli and I fear the baby is coming. Too soon!"

His heart contracted. When his mate died in childbirth, she had screamed and screamed in writhing agony.

"What do you feel?"

"Pains here." She indicated her lower back. "And here."

He picked her up and felt her trembling. "I will take you to the Medicine Chief."

"Hurry!"

The Medicine Chief was a tall man of stern and regal dignity. He sat with his mate and children at a community fire built for feasting. As Tolonqua came hurrying with Kwani, he realized something was amiss, and rose. Tolonqua set Kwani down, speaking in the halting Querecho he had learned over the years. The Chief led them into his Medicine Lodge, a large tipi with special painting and ornamentation indicating his powers.

Tolonqua pointed Kwani to a bed on the right. "He says to lie there."

It was a thick pad of blankets covered with a buffalo robe and a pillow stuffed with buffalo hair. Kwani stretched out; it was too soon for the baby, too soon! She closed her eyes and clasped the scallop shell for serenity, remembering her first pregnancy . . . the fall . . . Brother Coyote.

And Kokopelli. Where was he?

Tolonqua's face was taut with concern. "Do not be afraid. The Medicine Chief knows what to do."

"Please find Kokopelli and tell him—"

"Yes." His mouth set in a grim line as he left.

The Medicine Chief concocted a potion which he brought in a small bowl, motioning for her to drink. She drank some and gagged. He pushed it to her lips to drink again. She tried, but could not.

His mate entered with a small blanket that had been folded and soaked in hot water. She put the bowl aside, crooned comforting sounds, pulled Kwani's robe up to her neck, and placed the warm, wet blanket on Kwani's swollen abdomen, patting it as she did so, as though to comfort the baby as well.

She was a plump little woman, as genial as the Chief was taciturn. She smiled at Kwani who tried to smile back, but her lips trembled. She trembled all over, but made an effort to control it. She must not make a spectacle of herself here.

Tolonqua and Kokopelli arrived, and the Chief met them at the door. Kwani pulled her robe back down, but the wet blanket remained in place and made her look enormous.

Kokopelli knelt beside Kwani. "What is happening?" His voice was tense with concern.

"The baby . . . I think it wants to come too soon." She tried to hold back the tears, but her eyes filled. "I am afraid."

"Ah." He turned to wave Tolonqua away, but he did not go. He came to stand by Kwani.

"The Medicine Chief will conduct a Tipi Shaking Ceremony to call protecting spirits and soothe the child. I will be here then." He gave Kokopelli a glance, and left.

Kokopelli ignored him. He reached for the bowl, smelled the contents, and nodded. It was a potion to delay labor. He felt Kwani's pulse, examined her fingernails, pulled down her lower eyelids, and peered into her eyes.

"Are you hurting now?"

"No. Not now . . . except some in the back. Not much." her heart ached; she could not bear it if she lost this child.

He pulled up the robe—Wopio's hated robe. Putting the wet blanket aside, he examined her abdomen, pressing here, pressing there. He put his ear to her stomach.

"What do you hear?" Was the baby hurting?

He did not answer, but continued to listen. He spread her legs apart and examined her carefully for secretions, while the Medicine Chief tactfully turned aside. Satisfied, Kokopelli sat back on his heels and motioned for the woman to leave, and pulled down the robe.

"You are not in labor; the baby will not be born now."

She relaxed with a grateful sigh. Her protecting spirits were with her.

"You must rest." He frowned; there was no time to rest. They should depart in the morning.

Kwani saw the frown. "Where have you been? I searched for you—"

"I was busy," he said shortly.

"Busy with what?"

"You must rest," the Medicine Chief said quickly. Kokopelli was an important guest, and should not be embarrassed. "We will leave you so you can sleep. I will return to conduct the Tipi Shaking."

He ushered Kokopelli out, and Kwani lay looking up at the smoke hole of the tipi. Stars peeked through and light from the fire pit cast faint shadows. She trembled no longer. But a coal burned in her chest. Kokopelli. She knew very well what kept him busy all afternoon. She knew.

Was this what the ancient ones wanted her to learn—that she must share her mate with other women? Always? Was this the purpose of an unendurable, endless journey?

No. It could not be.

There was a rustle at the tipi door, and Tolonqua entered. He knelt beside her. Light from the fire pit shone faintly upon his face as he bent over her.

"Do you feel better?"

She looked up at the face so close to her own. Dark eyes burned into hers. She searched them deeply, and it was as though she listened to his secret heart.

He loved her. He was proud, honorable, strong. He was Pueblo. And he loved her, he loved her.

She reached up and pulled his face to her own. She kissed him as she had wanted to so many times before. He responded with passion that made her heart pound.

"Kwani," he whispered. "Let the child be mine. Kokopelli—"

"I know. For a long time, he chose no one else. But now—"

"Be my mate. Return with me to Cicuye."

"We must find the White Buffalo. And I am mate of Kokopelli." But she held him close. She longed for him. But she loved Kokopelli also, who had saved her life and who loved her—in his own way. She would have to choose. But she could not, not yet. "Take me to the canyon. The White Buffalo may be there."

"Yes," he said, kissing her throat. He slid his hands over her breasts, caressing. "Beautiful, beautiful." He pulled the neckline of the robe down to expose a breast and took the nipple in his mouth, groaning with desire.

They kissed again, and it was as if flames leaped in the fire pit, but only coals smouldered there.

* * *

The Tipi Shaking Ceremony was about to begin. It was early evening. Kwani had rested and was up and walking about. She had felt no more pain; it had been a false labor. Nevertheless, the Medicine Chief had conferred with his sacred objects, and decided that the ceremony was necessary to calm the restless spirit of the unborn child, and to overcome threatening influences.

Kwani, Kokopelli, Tolonqua, and priests of the Medicine Society sat in the tipi. The Medicine Chief was bound hand and foot. Coals in the fire pit were covered, so that all was in darkness. For a while they sat in silence.

In dim starlight from the smoke hole, Kwani saw the Chief sitting in his bonds, his head bowed. His chest rose and fell in spasms, as if something inside of him fought to escape. She shivered. There was no sound. The tipi was a world within a world, a dark, secret place awaiting spirits.

The Medicine Chief's voice suddenly pierced the silence like a knife. He writhed in his bonds, chanting, moaning, babbling, calling the spirits to possess him.

Strange animal sounds came from various places. Were animal spirits inside the tipi? Kwani could not tell. There was a low growling, an eerie whine, a grunt. An owl called from the underworld. The tipi began to shake. Chanting grew more intense, the moaning louder. Sparks flew up through the smoke hole although there was no fire in the pit. The tipi shook as if buffeted by winds of terrifying power.

Kwani wrapped both arms around herself and huddled in awe. Gradually the babbling ceased, the sparks disappeared, the tipi stopped shaking, and there was silence.

At last, the Medicine Chief spoke. Tolonqua translated. "He wants me to tell you and Kokopelli what the spirits say."

The Chief spoke again, in an eerie, singsong voice.

"He speaks to the child's spirit, commanding it to be born at the proper time."

Again, the singsong voice.

"He says it will be a boy who will become a great Chief. Your son will have a powerful protecting spirit."

Kwani gasped in joy.

Once more, the singsong.

"He says I must stay near you to protect you from one who would harm your child. The spirits have spoken."

The priests rose. "The Ceremony is finished. Go."

They left and stood together outside the tipi, looking at one another. Kwani was radiant.

"A son! Who will become a great Chief!"

Kokopelli snorted. "It was a performance, nothing more. He was demonstrating his expertise for my benefit, seeking to belittle my magic. Ha! I can do better."

Tolonqua gave him a level look. "I have been present at his Tipi Shaking before. The spirits do come, and what they say is true. I have seen it." He turned to Kwani with a protecting gesture. "I shall stay near you to protect your child."

"It is not necessary." Kokopelli pulled Kwani to his side, and put his arm around her. "I am her mate; it is I who will protect her. And her child."

Red stained Tolonqua's face from brow to chin. For a long moment he stared at Kokopelli in silence. Finally, he said, "A Hunting Chief and a Towa learns quickly to detect an enemy. Once detected, he tracks him down. I shall obey the spirits."

Kwani stepped between them. "I am grateful to you both." She tucked a hand in the arm of each. "Come, they wait for us at the campfire!"

She tugged at their arms, and reluctantly they walked with her to where the fire glowed in the darkness.

Several days passed; they lingered with the Querechos while Kwani regained her strength. Because she was constantly in the protection of the camp, Tolonqua felt free to join the hunters. Kokopelli traded and stalked glumly about, muttering that the boat would leave without them. He spent little time with Kwani.

She mingled with the women, made a tiny buffalo robe for the baby, and observed how pemmican was made. Her own people usually obtained this valuable food by trade, and she wanted to learn how to make it. It was delicious, lightweight, very nourishing. One handful thrown into a pot would swell three or four times in size.

She wished she knew the Querecho language, for the women chatted, told jokes, and laughed uproariously as they pounded dried strips of buffalo meat into a powder with a stonehead maul. The powder was packed in a large bag sewn from buffalo rawhide. Hot liquid marrow fat was poured in and seeped through the contents to form a film around each morsel. The bags were stitched up at the mouth and sealed with tallow along the seams.

The pemmican was being prepared in amazing quantities; bags were stacked like firewood.

One day Kwani asked Tolonqua how long the pemmican would keep.

He shrugged. "Fifteen, twenty years or more. If they add berries or other flavorings, not quite as long."

She was astonished. "Do they make pemmican in Cicuye?"

"Yes." He smiled. "Are you learning how?"

She nodded.

"Good. You can make it for us." A flame lit in his eyes and he leaned close. "You are Pueblo, as I am. How can you become Toltec when your spirit remains here? It is a good life in Cicuye. You will be my mate, She Who Remembers, a Caller, and a Storyteller. And I will teach your son—*our* son, our sons—all they should know." He leaned closer. "I will teach you, also. How a Towa loves."

She forced herself to turn away. How could she be mate of such a man as Kokopelli and have this overwhelming feeling for Tolonqua? She felt she had known him always. She wanted to be in Cicuye when he built the new pueblo. She wanted him to be father of her children, and yes, she wanted him beside her in the night. She did not know how to handle the situation. She loved Kokopelli and the thought of forsaking him was unbearable, yet she could not have both men. She would have to make a decision, a difficult decision, but she would postpone it as long as she could; perhaps the gods would intervene.

Kokopelli became more restless, and departure could be delayed no longer. He said to Kwani, "We leave tomorrow. At daybreak."

She was willing to go. She had been feeling twinges again. "Very well. I shall prepare my pack."

"Good. I go to finish trading." He strode out the door of the tipi which had been their temporary home.

She sighed. She was bone-weary of traveling. How many more moons would it be before they reached Tula? Again, she hoped the boat would be gone when they arrived at camp; maybe, then, Kokopelli would be willing to return to Cicuye.

Cicuye. Tolonqua.

Kokopelli did not belong in Cicuye. Their ways were not his ways. She knew this now.

You have much to learn, much to endure.

Yes, Kwani thought. But I am learning, and I endure.

The baby kicked and she wrapped both arms over it. She closed her eyes, straining to communicate with her unborn child.

"Wait, little one. It is not yet time. Soon we shall be in a beautiful canyon; that is where your birthing will be. Soon."

Softly, like sunlight through mist, the memory of a dream floated into her mind. The White Buffalo.

I await you. Come to me.

·52·

It was late morning of the second day since they had left the Querecho camp. Kwani plodded after Tolonqua and Kokopelli through the parched grass. The heat was ferocious and the searing wind never stopped blowing. Tumbleweeds rolled by. Prairie dogs barked alarms and disappeared into tunnels far below. Herds of buffalo without number galloped away at their approach, leaving clouds of dust.

The days spent lingering in the Querecho camp had rested her, and long days of walking had strengthened her study body, but the burden she carried within her grew heavier each hour. Time and distance were taking their toll.

Kwani stopped to wipe away sweat which searing wind had already dried. She gazed into the empty horizon which encircled them. The land was so flat that sky could be glimpsed beneath the bellies of the buffalo.

Kokopelli had discarded his finery and wore only his sandals (which needed repair) and a short cotton garment from waist to mid-thigh. He wore no cap and his hair was pinned in a knot on top of his head. Even necklaces and ear ornaments were in his pack. His face was streaked with sweat and dust; weariness creased his face and lined his eyes.

Tolonqua, also, wore only rawhide sandals and a breechcloth. The sweaty band across his forehead was dark with dust. But his step was still strong and his carriage erect. He came to stand beside Kwani.

"Is anything wrong?"

"I'm thirsty." She was exhausted, too. But so were they.

Tolonqua reached for a water bag. "It is still a long way to the spring, so drink only what you must have."

They had left the river when it turned northeast and now they headed southeast where there were only hidden springs. She handed him the water bag and wiped her mouth.

373

"How long to the canyon?"

"One day only. It will be cooler tonight; we will camp early. When it is this hot I think of the canyon and the stream and the trees. Tomorrow we shall be there."

Kwani remembered that through the endless day. When it grew too dark to travel more, they stopped at last. Tolonqua made a small fire, not for heat but for light and the feeling of comfort it gave. They ate pemmican washed down with fresh water from a small spring Tolonqua had led them to, and listened to sounds of the night.

The distant bellowing of the buffalo increased as it grew cooler; it would continue all night. The wind sighed in the grasses and wolves howled across the plain. Stars burned in a black sky so vast that the three people by a tiny fire drew closer together, silent with secret thoughts.

Kokopelli took his flute and played a lonesome melody. It spoke of time past, of childhood gone, and dreams not quite forgotten. Tolonqua and Kwani listened, remembering. The music ceased with a lingering, sweet note.

Tolonqua said, "I think of a song we sang when I was a boy. It is about a squirrel; there are many at Cicuye. Shall I sing it?" They nodded, and his rich voice floated into the night.

> *Slender and striped,*
> *Slender and striped,*
> *Look at him standing up there!*
> *He stands up there so slender in his stripes,*
> *The squirrel in his little, white shirt!*

They sat in silence again. The night was a blanket enfolding them, bringing them close together.

Kwani said, "Kokopelli, tell about when you were a boy."

Kokopelli gazed into the fire as though the past were revealed there.

"It was before the Chichimecas came. We lived in a city with a great stone temple, a pyramid." He demonstrated the shape with his hands. "It had many steps to the altar at the top. My father was a nobleman, permitted to bring his son to the altar. I climbed those steps, all of them, clear to the top. The altar was enclosed by a smaller temple, very beautiful. And outside stood three giant stone warriors gazing over the valley to the distant mountains, and beyond. Those stone figures were huge, especially to a small boy. I stood looking up at them, so beautiful were they, and I turned to look where they looked—into distance—and I told myself that one day I would go there." He paused. "Now I wish to be where I was then."

They watched the flames, thinking how mysterious life was. Tolonqua said, "Tell about when you were a child, Kwani."

"My mother said there was a storm when I was born and gods threw fire spears to earth as I left her womb. She said that is why my eyes are blue. My blue eyes . . ."

She stopped, then hurried on. "One day before I became a woman I found a shell, a wonderful little shell. I knew it waited there for me, and its spirit spoke to me. It said it was all right for my eyes to be blue, that I need not be ashamed nor afraid. I have it still. I shall give it to my son when he goes to seek his manhood vision."

Tolonqua said, "My vision was of the White Buffalo, the Spirit Being. Whenever I come to where buffalo are, I look for it. One day it will come to me and ask to be taken. Then I shall have the robe of the White Buffalo for my clan, my son . . ." His voice revealed his emotion.

Again they sat in silence, three people alone in a black sea. The wind fanned the flames and whispered in the grasses.

Tolonqua said, "The wind has changed direction. Tomorrow, clouds will come and it will be cooler."

As if by unspoken agreement, they lay down to sleep.

"Good night, Kokopelli," Kwani said.

"Good night, my love." He put an arm around her and drew her close.

Tolonqua lay with his arms under his head, gazing into the sky where clouds already blotted the stars. He faced the truth: the woman he wanted, the only one he longed for, was mate of Kokopelli. How foolish to assume he could lure her from such a man.

But he must.

The hidden stars walked their celestial paths, but he did not sleep for a long time.

They woke to a gray day. A heavy, yellowish-gray cloud bank hung low. The air was oppressive, hot, and strangely still. Tolonqua and Kokopelli studied the sky.

Tolonqua frowned. "I don't like the looks of that, do you?"

"No. Does the earth ever groan and shake here?"

"Not that I have heard of."

"In Tula, we would expect the earth to shake with this weather and such a sky."

Kwani made an attempt to brush her hair and tidy herself, but it was an effort. She did not feel as she usually did in the morning, refreshed and eager to meet the day. She had a sense of unease, an intuitive compulsion to hide.

"I hope it isn't another storm," she said. "There is no shelter."

Tolonqua agreed. "We must get to the canyon. Caves are there."

Kokopelli nodded. These empty plains begrudged shelter. The canyon offered the only possibility, but they could not linger there. Time grew short, they must reach camp.

They left without eating; they would nibble on the way. Shared experiences of the night before made them feel closer to one another. They were trespassers here, swallowed in the enormity of the plains, vulnerable specks at the mercy of unknown gods.

They plodded on for what seemed to be hours; Kwani lost track of time. The sound of buffalo came again, and a dark line surged against the horizon. The wind rose, stronger than before.

Tolonqua walked ahead with his usual easy stride. Kwani noticed he carried a larger load; Kokopelli must have given him more from his own pack. His was smaller, with the hilt of Thorvald's sword protruding. Kwani guessed the sword would bring many valuables in trade in Tula, but what these might be she had no idea.

Clouds changed formation. They looked as if they were punched from above; pockets protruded downward, changed shape, drifted. Tolonqua watched the sky and quickened his step.

Kwani called, "Please don't go so fast. I can't keep up."

"We must reach the canyon."

The wind grew stronger, pushing hard. It had a strange sound, an ominous undertone. Stalks of dried grass and bits of clod flew through the air. Clouds dipped lower; rain fell, big drops blown sidewise by the wind.

Kokopelli turned and pointed, unbelieving. In the far distance, a black, wavering finger poked down from the clouds and jabbed the earth, tearing a long swath. Slowly it lifted and dissolved.

"It can come again!" Tolonqua shouted. "Hurry!"

There was a rumbling sound and the earth vibrated. Kwani could feel it in the soles of her feet.

"Buffalo stampede!" Tolonqua yelled.

A wide, dark line approached, an onrushing avalanche of terrifying proportions. Tolonqua threw his pack to the ground and tore out blankets. Fighting the wind, he thrust a blanket at Kwani and at Kokopelli.

"Here! When they get closer, wave them aside!"

There was no place to run, no place to hide. Thousands of pounding feet shook the earth. Calves bawled, running with the herd. The dark avalanche drew closer. Kwani stood frozen, clutching the blanket to her as if for protection. The rain fell in torrents now; the wind pushed harder, daring them to resist.

"Stand there!" Tolonqua shouted at Kokopelli. "You, Kwani, stand over here. Wave the blankets! Now!"

Tolonqua and Kwani shouted and waved the blankets; they flapped in the wind with such force that Kwani had to use all her strength to keep her grip. Only Kokopelli stood calm, staring at the oncoming animals, his face tense with concentration.

The herd was nearly on them, heads bent low, great humped bodies rising and falling with terrible power. Kwani thought surely they would be trampled. One buffalo, just one, could squash them like insects.

At the last moment the herd split, passing on either side. Shaggy, heaving bodies surrounded them so closely that mud from their pounding hooves pelted like hail. The sound, the vibration, the smell, were overpowering. They thundered by, glazed eyes bulging. One swing of their horns and the puny creatures trapped in their midst would be tossed and trampled to muddy pulp.

"Keep waving!" Tolonqua yelled.

Kwani waved the heavy, flapping blanket until her wounded arm felt it would tear from its socket. Kokopelli continued to face the herd, issuing silent commands.

On and on came the buffalo until Kwani could lift the blanket no longer. Now, it was only Tolonqua who waved the buffalo aside; Kokopelli continued to stand, staring.

At last only a few stragglers pounded by. Slowly Tolonqua backed away, still waving the blanket, and Kwani followed. Kokopelli turned to hold her.

"They will not harm us; they go away."

Kwani slumped against him, panting with exhaustion. Rain poured in rivulets down her neck. What gods were these to punish them repeatedly and without mercy? The flood, the hail, the fire, and now this. Such gods were unnatural. Evil spirits!

Above the sound of thudding hooves receding came a thunderous roar as, ahead, a boiling black cloud dipped low. Stones, bushes, chunks of earth exploded upward. The black finger reached down again, jabbed the earth, and struck into the herd.

With bellows of terror, the buffalo ran for the horizon. The black finger followed, tossed great beasts into the air like toys, and threw them down to be trampled by those behind.

Kwani, pushed beyond terror, went blank, emerging after a moment with absolute calm. She was pale and her blue eyes unusually bright as she turned to Tolonqua. He stood gaping at buffalo being tossed high and mangled until the finger lifted, dissolved, and was gone.

"We must offer thanks," Kwani said matter-of-factly.

Tolonqua turned in surprise at her casual tone, and she handed him the dripping blanket. He and Kokopelli were shaking with strain. The wind had eased, but rain poured from them; it was as if they stood under a waterfall.

Kokopelli said hoarsely, "Let's get out of here. Take us to the canyon."

Kwani pointed to dead buffalo strewn about. "Look at them! Look at us; we are alive! We must offer thanks to the guardian spirits who saved us."

Kokopelli grabbed her arm. "We can give thanks in shelter. Come!"

She broke away. Head back, eyes closed, both arms outstretched, she began to sing, improvising.

> We give our thanks, sacred ones,
> Our thanks for turning the buffalo aside,
> Our thanks for turning the whirling cloud aside,
> For taking the whirling cloud away.
> We give our thanks, sacred beings,
> For protecting us on our journey.

Kokopelli and Tolonqua gazed at Kwani as though they had not seen her before. It seemed that one from an ancient past had assumed her form, commanding her spirit.

The rain was easing up as the song ended, and stopped almost as suddenly as it began. The wind cooled, blew more gently, and clouds raced into distance.

Tolonqua rolled the wet blankets and stuffed them into his pack. Sunfather appeared, and the soaked earth glowed. Tolonqua began to sing Kwani's song, keeping step with the melody as they continued their journey.

> We give our thanks, sacred ones,
> Our thanks for turning the buffalo aside.

Kwani's voice joined his, their voices blending as they walked together.

> We give our thanks, holy beings,
> For protecting us on our journey.

Kokopelli walked with them, but it was as if he were not there. Kwani and Tolonqua were absorbed in one another and in their song. Kwani strode with confidence in spite of her distorted body, in spite of the harrowing experience they had just endured. Her voice was clear and strong as she sang to the gods.

He shook his head. This woman was not the cowering, broken creature he had found and healed.

Who was she?

❖ 53 ❖

K wani, stared, unbelieving. "Ah!" she sighed. "Beautiful!"

Below was a narrow canyon, a great crack in the earth worn deep by erosion and millennia. They had been almost upon it before it was revealed. Sunlight on rain-washed walls revealed layers of brilliant color—red, gray, green, brown—undulating along the flanks. The canyon floor twisted and turned, divided by a glittering stream, with trees and shrubs and grasses growing profusely on either side.

Tolonqua smiled, seeing her pleasure. "Come this way."

He led them along a game trail down a steep slope. The air was fragrant with the smell of earth after rain. A golden eagle swooped and soared high above them. An omen, surely.

As they descended deeper into the canyon, Kwani saw that the floor was uneven, a jumbled mass. It would be slow and difficult to cross, but what did it matter? They were there, where Tolonqua had promised to take them. Where her child would be born, and where the White Buffalo might be.

The canyon turned in sharp angles; small buttes and mesas, capped by sandstone, humped from the canyon floor. One could not guess what was behind the next hill, or slope, or in a small ravine. It would be easy, very easy, to hide here.

They reached the floor at last, and drank at the stream. A deer bounded away; jays scolded.

Tolonqua said, "I know a fine cave. We will go there."

"Do you want to rest a while first?" Kokopelli asked. He looked as if he needed rest himself.

Kwani was anxious to find shelter. Instinct urged her to hide. "No. I want to go to the cave."

It was arduous walking on the uneven floor thick with brush, but the difficulty was forgotten when Kwani saw the cave—not large, but large enough, about the size of a room in a pueblo. It faced the stream and stood high on a bank, with trees arching over the entrance, and was protected on either side by jutting arms of the canyon wall. There were signs of old campfires; but nothing, no one, was there when she entered. It was cool and dim and smelled clean. The rocky walls had niches to hold things. It was ideal.

She sank to the floor. Tolonqua and Kokopelli stood looking down at her and she said, "This is the place. Thank you!"

Packs were removed and things spread in the sun to dry. Tolonqua propped the cradle board against the cave wall. He had wrapped it in buffalo hide to protect it from dampness.

"How are you feeling?" Kokopelli asked.

She could not reply. Now that she was where she had forced herself to go, now that she was safe, she suddenly felt drained. She shook, her teeth chattered.

"I feel . . . cold."

Kokopelli spoke quickly to Tolonqua. "Find kindling. We need fire."

Tolonqua hurried away, and Kokopelli searched for something dry to wrap her in. All he could find was his prized multicolored mantle; it had been in the center of his pack and was dry. He removed the robe from her trembling body and experienced a stab of concern at the grotesque bulge of her belly. Surely, this would be too large a child for her to deliver safely. *Okalake's child.* Never would he permit it to take Kwani from him.

He wrapped his mantle around her, swathing her like a papoose, and held her close until her trembling ceased. He laid her down, enfolded in his mantle.

"Rest now."

Tolonqua returned with twigs and dried buffalo chips which made a hot fire; soon a pot of water heated. He added a handful of pemmican and a few juniper berries he had picked on the way.

A rich aroma made Kwani realize how hungry she was. She sat up and leaned against the cave wall, watching Tolonqua preparing the meal, and Kokopelli reviewing the contents of his pack, studying his quipu, rearranging knots. She pulled his mantle closely about her, enjoying the odor of it, Kokopelli's unique scent.

These two men. She loved them both. Both wanted her; she would have to choose.

Tolonqua. Pueblo. Respected Hunting Chief of Cicuye, where she would be honored as She Who Remembers. A bold leader, builder of a new city. Young, with a bright future she could share. One who communed with her gods and who also sought the White Buffalo. A strong protector who took charge in emergencies; it was he who saved them from thousands of fear-crazed buffalo. Tender, generous, passionate. *Pueblo.*

Kokopelli. Who found her, who healed and cared for her. Magnetic, wise, wealthy, a masterful lover. One with mysterious powers . . .

How could she choose?

Tolonqua offered her a bowl of juniper-flavored pemmican and she ate it with relish, ignoring twinges and a heavy feeling in her back.

"That was good."

"Want more?"

"Not now. I'm sleepy."

Kokopelli said, "Sleep, then. But first I will inspect your wound." He unwrapped the bandage. "It is healing. Leave it exposed to the air."

She lay in her multicolored cocoon, and slept.

Her spirit left her body and wandered on the mesa. The Old One appeared, and spoke from within the folds of her feather blanket.

"Why do you come to me?"

"I did not leave my people willingly; they drove me away. But the gods have punished me. Why?"

"Do you not understand? We who are She Who Remembers, spiritually blessed by the gods and protected by the ancient ones, are not of one clan, one people. We are of all womenkind, and must endure much. It is struggle that strengthens and makes us aware, that tempers the spirit and opens the mind's eye."

"Is this the purpose of my journey?"

The Old One turned, and Kwani saw she was no longer blind. Her eyes, dark and luminous, glowed with inner light.

"Knowledge is within you, my daughter. Discover it." She wrapped her blanket about her, and was gone. Kwani was alone once more.

But not alone.

She woke at daybreak, filled with wonder, and looked about her with eyes that seemed new. She wanted to tell Kokopelli and Tolonqua of her dream, but they had left the cave. Their packs were there, and her cradle board and Thorvald's sword were propped against the wall.

Her dry robe lay beside her. She removed Kokopelli's mantle and slipped the robe over her head. As big as it was, it was snug across her stomach. She wondered where the men had gone; perhaps they had stepped outside or gone hunting. She still felt a need to remain hidden, but she wanted to see the canyon again. Cautiously she left the cave and stood looking at the stream, at the bank beyond, and on either side as far as the twisting canyon walls permitted. The men were not in sight.

It was cool and fresh, and smelled wonderful; Kwani went to the stream, knelt, and cupped the cool water in her hands, drinking deeply. As she rose, she saw it on the opposite bank.

The White Buffalo!

She stared in awe. The animal was shining white as it stood drinking at the stream in the light of daybreak. It raised its head, and slowly waded toward her, commanding her with its mystical pink eyes.

Kwani's heart beat hard; she did not dare to believe the Spirit Being was communicating with her. For a long moment, they faced one another.

"I knew you would come," she whispered.

The White Buffalo came closer. She stood spellbound, gazing into the pink eyes as though they were windows into another world, another reality.

Kwani felt an awareness like a seed sprouting, reaching toward the sun. Wisdom unfurled like a green leaf in her spirit.

"Open your mind's eye," the White Buffalo said.

She felt suffused in a pink glow as a secret, a wonderful secret, was revealed.

The Spirit Being bowed its head in farewell, and waded to the opposite bank. Slowly, regally, it disappeared around a bend in the stream.

Kwani stood transfixed, marveling at what the White Buffalo had disclosed. Now her child would be born. It would be a boy, and the White Buffalo would be his guardian spirit.

·54·

The Querecho sat on a hilly slope of the canyon, concealed by branches of a tree growing below. He watched the activity outside a cave on the opposite bank of the stream, and spat with contempt.

His tribe were canyon Querechos, related to those of the south. He wore his hair in their fashion, short on one side and long on the other. He was not tall, but he was muscular. His face was that of one who relished killing and had killed much.

His vulture's eye inspected the cave. He had seen the Towa and the pregnant woman and the foreigner when they entered the canyon. The woman was giving birth, and the men attended her like midwives. He spat again. Now, while the men were defiling themselves, was the time to achieve his objective—the sword. He had glimpsed its shining hilt in the pack of the foreigner. Soon, the sword would hang in splendor at his side.

Cautiously, he eased down the slope.

Soon after the encounter with the White Buffalo, Kwani's labor had begun. Instinct had told her to find a hiding place for the birthing, and she was grateful for the seclusion and security of the cave.

Kokopelli and Tolonqua, returned from briefly exploring the canyon, had brought a plant known to Kokopelli from which a tea could be brewed to ease labor. Tolonqua carried shredded cedar bark and fluffy shreds of long-dried buffalo chips for diapering.

"Are the pains closer together now?" Kokopelli asked.

"Yes. I'll need something to hang on to from above when the pains get worse. My people use a pole braced at either end." She turned to Tolonqua. "Could you find something?"

He looked at niches in the cave wall. "I'll cut a branch to reach from one side of the cave to the other, and fit each end into a niche. Will that do?"

"Yes."

He started to leave, and she said, "I saw it!"

"What?"

"The White Buffalo." Her voice was hushed with wonder.

"Ah!" He came close to stand looking down at her. "It is an omen."

"The Medicine Chief spoke truly. My child will be a boy. The White Buffalo told me."

"The baby isn't born yet," Kokopelli said drily. "Perhaps we had better postpone judgment."

"Perhaps." Tolonqua gave him a tart glance. "But you will see."

Kwani felt another pain, sharper. "I'll need the pole!"

Tolonqua took his stonehead ax and hurried outside.

"Have you eaten?" Kokopelli asked, preparing to make the tea.

"Pemmican." She sat down to relax between pains.

"Good. That will give you strength. Has the water broken?"

"No."

She unlaced the cradle board to fill the bottom with diapering. Kokopelli noticed how lovingly she handled it. Tolonqua's gift. From his pack he took the robe he had given her and held it up for her to admire again.

"I wrapped it so it didn't get wet. Soon you will be able to wear this and you won't have to wear that one any longer."

She smiled. "That will give me more strength than the pemmican."

The water boiled, and he cut the plant in bits and added them. He had learned of this plant from a Medicine Man on his travels; he hoped it would work. Kwani was ruggedly healthy, but her belly was huge. Could it be twins?

"Remove the robe. It is in the way. And lie down so I can listen."

She removed the robe and lay upon it. He put his ear to her stomach and pressed his hands over the swollen surface, but heard and felt nothing unusual.

"I want to stand. The pains are closer."

He pulled her to her feet and laid the robe aside. It would be useful for cleansing and for wrapping the baby's body for burial. He bent both his arms, elbows outstretched, and held them over her head.

"Hang on to me until Tolonqua brings the pole."

Tolonqua stood beside one of the outthrusts that protruded from either side of the cave. A young cottonwood tree grew there with a low branch of the right size. He hacked at it with his ax until it was nearly separated, then wrested it loose. Chopping off the leafy branches, he smoothed a place in the center for her hands to grasp. The ax fell to the ground. As he picked it up, an arrow whizzed by his head and embedded itself in the tree trunk.

He jerked upright. "An attack!" he yelled.

He dodged behind the outthrust. A steep bank led to an overhang high above the cave's opening. Brush grew there; it was a good place to hide while scanning the area below. He clawed his way up, concealed by the cottonwood and by brush. The soil was loose, with many small pebbles, and it took all his strength to reach the overhang.

He peered through the bushes. At first he saw no one. Then there was a movement upstream on the opposite bank. From where he lay, Tolonqua could see over a boulder behind which a man moved stealthily, bow in hand. A Querecho! Was he alone? Any number of warriors could hide in the canyon's twists and turns. Tolonqua looked back the other way and saw another movement, a quick glimpse of white. His heart leaped. Could it have been the White Buffalo? He fingered the talisman in a small pouch at his waist.

The Querecho eased around the boulder and slid like a shadow toward the cave.

Kokopelli struggled to brace Kwani with his upraised arms as she bore down, panting, moaning in agony. When they heard Tolonqua's yell Kwani threw herself against Kokopelli.

"Save me!" she screamed. Her eyes were wild with pain and fear. She was helpless to run, to do anything but push this child from her body— the baby that would not come.

Again pain knifed her; again she screamed. The water broke and ran down her legs in a warm flood.

Kokopelli said, "The baby will come more easily now."

In the back of the cave he stood her against the wall where niches would give her a hand-hold of sorts. "Stay here and do not be afraid. No one will enter. I promise you."

"Don't leave me!"

He pulled the sword from its sheath and stepped outside the cave.

Tolonqua looked down to see Kokopelli standing outside the cave beside the outthrust. From where Kokopelli stood, the Querecho could not see him, nor could Kokopelli see the Querecho wading the stream. There was no way of warning him without alerting the Querecho. Careful not to disturb a twig or a leaf, Tolonqua raised the ax.

Kwani clutched at the niches as grinding pain bore down again and again, more and more severe. She clawed at the niches, but they could not brace her now. She doubled over, unable to stand. She did not hear herself screaming.

Tolonqua cringed. Kwani's cries were like those of his mate who had died in anguish. Surely Kokopelli should be doing something to help her. But he stood there with the sword, waiting, straining to hear the enemy's silent approach.

Tolonqua held the ax in readiness. Sweat poured from him.

As Kwani's cries grew more agonized, the Querecho grew bolder. He ran along the bank until he reached the other side of the outthrust behind which Kokopelli stood. Drawn bow in hand, he inched around the outthrust to peer into the cave and confronted Kokopelli face to face.

At that moment Tolonqua threw the ax. It hit the Querecho a glancing blow on the shoulder, and he dropped his bow. Kokopelli lifted the sword to strike, but the Querecho grappled with him and pinned him to the wall, trying to wrest the sword from his grasp. They struggled in terrible silence, the young Querecho with the killer's face grinning with effort, and the older Toltec, hardened with years of walking, whose amber eyes glittered as he refused to relinquish his grasp on the sword.

Tolonqua climbed down, half sliding, to the ground as the Querecho, in a surge of strength, yanked the sword from Kokopelli. He stood back to lunge, aiming at Kokopelli's stomach.

With a yell, Tolonqua grabbed the severed branch, ran at the Querecho, and threw the branch like a spear. It hit him squarely on the side and knocked him down. Tolonqua snatched the sword. A mighty swing—a whacking sound, a great gush of blood, and the Querecho's head wobbled crazily down the bank, hair flapping, mouth open in a grotesque grimace. The head rolled to the stream and floated away, leaving a pink wake.

They stood shaken. The headless body lay on the sloping bank, blood trickling toward the stream. Tolonqua raised the sword and stared at it, not quite believing what it had done. He washed the blade in the stream, climbed back up the bank, and handed the sword to Kokopelli who stood staring at the headless body.

"Remove it. Take it somewhere for burial. We don't want wolves here," Kokopelli said hoarsely.

Only then did they realize there were no sounds from the cave.

When Kwani heard the fighting outside and Tolonqua's murderous yell, nightmare terror gripped her. She bore down harder. A head began to appear. Feeling she was being ripped in two, she squatted, and tried even harder. At last, the small body began to emerge. She reached down and tugged for it; but the slippery little form slid from her hands to the floor. She bent low to gaze at it. It was a boy, a large baby, a pink, wet, wonderful man child! She poked a gentle finger in his mouth to clear it of mucus, and he gave a lusty yell.

Her contractions continued so that the afterbirth might be expelled; but pain seemed bearable now. She picked up the child and held him close, comforting him and herself, and wrapped her arms around him to keep him warm.

The afterbirth emerged. It would be given to Earthmother, an offering of thanks for fertility—a gift from mother to mother, assuring continued fertility in the endless cycle of birth.

Unsteadily Kwani carried her son to the discarded robe spread on the floor. She lay down on it, cradling him close to her, pulling up a corner of the robe around him. Frightening sounds from outside were forgotten as she gazed and gazed at the wonder of him. His head had a downy fluff of black hair. He had stopped crying and his round little face was perfect in repose. How tiny his hands and feet were! She lifted one foot to admire it, and gasped. A mark was on the sole, the tiny figure of a buffalo's head!

The White Buffalo had marked him as his own! He would guide his steps for a lifetime! A miracle—too wonderful to believe!

She lay back, spent and radiant. Kokopelli and Tolonqua rushed in and stopped, gazing.

She looked up. "My son. Marked by the White Buffalo. Look!"

"Ah!" Tolonqua breathed. "He is a Chosen One!"

Kokopelli touched the baby gingerly. Kwani thought he did not seem pleased and it dampened her joy.

Tolonqua knelt beside her. She lay in naked, unadorned beauty. It was the first time he had seen her without pregnancy and his eyes lingered on the rich swell of her breasts and the sloping curves of the rest of her, and yearning burned in him. He wanted to touch her, but he touched the baby, instead.

"He will be a great Chief." His eyes caressed her. "You are all right?"

She nodded. She saw the longing in him. She looked into the lean face with dark brows arching over eyes that burned for her, in her weakness and exultation she could no longer deny the truth of her desire. This strong leader, this builder of a new city, saw into the future. He would teach her son the man things, the Pueblo things a boy must learn—this child he wanted as his own. The White Buffalo had come to him in a vision, and would come again. Surely this was a man chosen by the gods for a special destiny, as her son was chosen. She looked at the line of his jaw and his ardent mouth, and his wide shoulders and arms that had held her, protected her, and she wanted him to hold her for the rest of her life. This Pueblo Chief would be her mate and the father of her son and the children to come. Cicuye, the new Cicuye, would be their home. There she would be She Who Remembers.

She had made the difficult choice. But it would be more difficult to tell Kokopelli. She closed her eyes at the thought.

He nudged Tolonqua. "Take care of what must be done outside."

Tolonqua ignored him and gazed at Kwani as though he could not stop gazing.

Kokopelli pushed him aside. "I must care for her and the baby. You are in the way. Go outside."

Tolonqua rose. He smiled down at the baby. "A fine man cub."

"Go!" Kokopelli almost shouted.

Tolonqua took his bow and arrows before he left; he would not be caught weaponless again.

Kwani lay exhausted as Kokopelli cut and tied the umbilical cord and set the afterbirth aside, to be buried in the spot where the baby was born. Pieces torn from Wopio's robe were dipped in a bowl of water still warm from the morning's coals. Working quickly and gently, he washed the baby and Kwani and laid the baby in the crook of his mother's arm.

She was overcome with gratitude. How kind he was! How much he had done for her! How could she bring herself to tell him what she must?

A lump was in her throat as she looked up at him. "I am grateful to you, Kokopelli."

A look sparked in his amber eyes. Suddenly he leaned close, cupped her breasts with both hands, and kissed her with a desperate passion.

"I wait for you," he said huskily.

He took the new robe and laid it beside her. "It waits for you, also."

She brought the baby to her breast and smiled in contentment as he sucked, and she reveled in the beauty of him—and in the glory of her flat stomach. She touched the downy head and a tiny pink ear.

"He will be Sun Chief like his father. I shall name him . . ." She shook her head. "I cannot decide. What do you think Okalake would have liked it to be?"

Kokopelli turned away abruptly, and went outside. The Querecho's body was nowhere to be seen, nor was Tolonqua. He stood pondering how he might dispose of Okalake's child so it would seem to be a natural occurrence.

I'll wait until she sleeps.

Tolonqua stared at the headless body with distaste. The fine necklaces the Querecho had worn lay in a bloody heap by the stub of the neck. Tolonqua left them there, and dragged the body away. The rocky ground was uneven and covered with brush; it made the going difficult, but he had to find a burial place far from the cave. The best would be a shallow indentation in the cliff, one he could easily seal with rocks and brush. He left the body by a cliff wall while he searched. At last he found what he wanted, a small cave. He dragged the body to it, rolled it in, and sealed the opening with large rocks covered with brush. The burial was secure from wolves and vultures. That much, at least, he owed the man whose head he had taken.

He wondered uneasily about that head floating on the stream. Querechos and Tewas lived in the canyon's vast reaches. If a Querecho found it, there would be trouble. But it was likely the head would float downstream to where the stream joined the mother river. Or be lodged and buried in a sand bank or destroyed by predators. He and Kwani would be gone from the canyon by then, and on the way back to Cicuye.

But what if she decided to stay with Kokopelli? He groaned at the thought. He loved her, longed for her, so much that he refused to admit to himself that Kwani had every reason to stay with the man she had chosen.

Unless . . . unless Kokopelli did not want the child. But that could not be possible. Or could it?

With a stab of alarm he remembered the warning of the spirits during the Tipi Shaking Ceremony. *He must protect Kwani from one who would harm her child.*

He began to run.

Kwani slept with the baby beside her. Kokopelli went outside to be certain Tolonqua was not returning. It would not be easy to find a burial place; it would take a while.

Now was the time.

Okalake's child slept nuzzled to his mother's breast. Kokopelli resented that proximity; those lovely breasts were his. He knelt beside Kwani to judge the soundness of her sleep. Her dark lashes lay on her cheeks and her breathing was deep and slow. She would sleep soundly for a long time.

The baby twitched a tiny foot as if dreaming. Slowly, Kokopelli reached out his thumb. A firm pressure on the windpipe and the baby would not wake.

As if sensing his intention, the baby's eyes opened. The blue-gray eyes of a newborn seemed to focus and look into his own, and a fragile little hand waved up and down, hitting his thumb as if to push it away.

Just a quick pressure on the throat . . .

He stared at the child. For the first time, he saw that the brow, the placement of the eyes, the features of the face were a miniature of Kwani's.

This was *Kwani's* child.

He could not harm it.

He sat back on his heels, looking at the woman he loved. the only one he wanted as mate, the woman he knew, he knew, he had lost. Never would she take her son to his distant homeland, away from his people, away from all she wanted for him. He faced the bitter truth: Kwani was not of his world, nor was he of hers. She would not be welcome nor happy in Tula. And with her as his mate, his importance and prestige would be destroyed.

He could not bear to leave her, but he must.

He sorted through his belongings to select only what he could carry on the long journey ahead. Much would have to be left—his parting gift.

There should be a special gift for Kwani's son. He reached in his pack for the heavy gold necklace he usually wore and placed it upon the baby's body. It nearly covered him. He would wear it when he was a man.

Kwani still slept. Never had she seemed so heartbreakingly beautiful.

"Goodbye, my love," he whispered.

He walked quickly away. He would not allow himself to look back or to linger, nor would he acknowledge the poignant anguish of loss. He was, after all, Kokopelli.

He lifted the flute to his lips.

My melodies shall not die, nor my songs perish.
They spread, they scatter.

The White Buffalo saw him go, and stood waiting. For Tolonqua.

Time is a great circle,
there is no beginning, no end.
All returns again and again
forever.

Afterword

The Place of the Eagle Clan (Cliff Palace) and the Place of the
Wolf Clan (Spruce Tree House) and other cave cities among the cliffs
of Mesa Verde National Park in southwest Colorado still stand in crumbled glory. Ruins of the Great City (Pueblo Bonito) and Cicuye (Pecos)
in New Mexico speak mysteriously to those who listen. Traces of ancient
campfires endure in Palo Duro Canyon where the twisting stream still
flows. All the places of this story are real.

Kokopelli's enigmatic figure adorns enumerable rock art sites of the
Southwest, but who he really was is known only to you who encounter
him in the imagination. Perhaps you will hear his flute along the trail,
or Tolonqua's song at Cicuye high on the ridge.

Ancient handprints are everywhere—within dwellings, on the high
domed ceilings of caves, woven in textiles, and painted on cliff walls.
Which of these are the handprints of She Who Remembers? What is
their secret power?

Only you will know.

Bibliography

Ambler, Richard. *The Anasazi*. Flagstaff, AZ: Museum of Northern Arizona, 1977.

Ascher, Marcia and Robert. *Code of the Quipu*. Ann Arbor: University of Michigan Press, 1981.

Associated Press. *Arizona Archeological Finds Ring Bells With Researchers*. November 26, 1981.

Babcock, Barbara A. *Clay Changes: Helen Cordero and the Pueblo Storyteller*. American Indian Art Magazine.

Bahti, Tom. *Southwest Indian Tribes*. Las Vegas: KC Publications, 1968.

Bandelier, Adolf F. *Papers of the Archaeological Institute of America*, American Series III. Cambridge University Press, 1890.

Bandelier, Adolf F. *The Delight Makers*. New York and London: Harvest/HBJ, 1971.

Benedict, Ruth. *Patterns of Culture*. Boston: Houghton-Mifflin Co., 1961.

Benitez, Fernando. *In the Magic Land of Peyote*. Austin and London: University of Texas Press, 1975.

Boorstin, Daniel J. *The Discoverers*. New York: Random House, 1983.

Bunker, Robert. *Other Men's Skies*. Bloomington: Indiana University Press, 1956.

Campbell, Dennis. *Talking Wild Turkey*. Dallas Morning News, November 29, 1981.

Chapman, Paul H. *The Norse Discovery of America*. Atlanta: One Candle Press, 1981.

Cole, Robert. *Eskimos, Chicanos, Indians*. Boston: Little Brown, 1978.

Collier, John. *American Indian Ceremonial Dances*. NY: Bounty Books, 1972.

Curtin, L. S. M. "Healing Herbs of the Upper Rio Grande." Santa Fe, NM: Laboratory of Anthropology, 1947.

Dallas Morning News. "Vikings in Oklahoma?" July 26, 1981.

Davies, Nigel. *The Toltec Heritage*. Norman, OK: University of Oklahoma Press, 1980.

Davidson, Howard M. "The Occurrence of the Hand Motif in North American Indian Rock Art." In "American Indian Rock Art" (papers presented at the 1974 Rock Art Symposium), Farmington, NM, San Juan County Museum Assn., 1975.

Densmore, Francis. *How Indians Use Wild Plants for Food, Medicine and Crafts.* New York: Dover Publications, 1974.

Dickson, Bruce. *Prehistoric Settlement Patterns: The Arroyo Hondo.* New Mexico Site Survey: Santa Fe School of American Research Press, 1979.

Eddy, Frank W. *Metates and Manos.* Santa Fe: Museum of New Mexico Press, 1964.

Elmore, Francis H. *Shrubs and Trees of the Southwest Uplands.* Tucson, Arizona: Southwest Parks and Monuments Association, 1976.

Farley, Gloria Stewart. *The Heavener Runestone.* Oklahoma City: Oklahoma Tourism and Recreation Department.

Fehrenbach, T. R. *Comanches.* New York: Knopf, 1974.

Fell, Barry. "Columbus Was a Johnny-Come-Lately." *Saturday Review,* October 16, 1976.

Fell, Barry. *America B.C.* New York: Demeter Press Quadrangle/The New York Times Book Co., 1976.

Fisher, Helen E. *The Sex Contract.* New York: Morrow, 1982.

Foote, Peter. *The Viking Achievement.* London: Sidgwick & Jackson, 1970.

Fronval, George and Daniel Dubois. *Indian Signals and Sign Language.* New York: Bonanza Books, 1985.

Hayes, Alden C. *Archaeological Survey of Weatherhill Mesa.* Mesa Verde National Park, Colorado: National Park Service, U.S. Department of the Interior, 1964.

Hewett, Edgar L. and Bertha P. Dutton. "The Pueblo Indian World." Handbook of Archaeological History, University of New Mexico and the School of American Research, 1945.

Hultkrantz, Ake. *The Religion of the American Indians.* Trans. by Monica Setterwall. Berkeley, CA: University of California Press, 1967.

Hyde, George E. *Indians of the High Plains.* Norman, OK: University of Oklahoma Press, 1959.

Jennings, Jesse D. *Prehistory of Utah and the Eastern Great Basin.* Anthropological Papers, University of Utah, Salt Lake City, UT, 1973.

Kelly, George W. *Useful Native Plants of the 4-Corners States.* Cortez, Colorado: Rocky Mountain Horticulture Publishing Co., 1980.

Kessell, John. *Kiva, Cross and Crown.* Washington, D.C.: U.S. Dept. of the Interior, National Park Service, 1979.

Kidder, Alfred Vincent. *The Artifacts of Pecos.* New Haven: Yale University Press, 1932.

Lister, Robert H. and Florence C. Lister. *Those Who Came Before.* Tucson: University of Arizona Press, 1983.

Lowie, Robert C. *Indians of the Plains.* University of Nebraska Press, Lincoln NE, 1982.

Mackey, James and R. C. Green. "Largo-Gallina Towers." *American Antiquity:*

Journal of the Society for American Archaeology, Vol. 44, No. 1, Jan. 1979, pp. 144–53.

Marcus, Rebecca B. *First Book of the Cliff Dwellers.* New York: Franklin Watts, 1968.

Marriott, Alize and Carol K. Rachlin. *Plains Indian Mythology.* New York: New American Library, 1975.

Mays, Buddy. *Ancient Cities of the Southwest.* San Francisco: Chronicle Books, 1982.

McHugh, Tom. *The Time of the Buffalo.* Lincoln, Neb., and London: University of Nebraska Press, 1972.

Mead, Margaret and Ruth L. Bunzel, *The Golden Age of American Anthropology.* New York: George Braziller, 1960.

McLuhan, T.C. *Touch the Earth.* New York: Promontory Press, 1971.

Miller, Dorcas. *Track Finder.* Berkeley, California: Nature Study Guild, 1981.

Miller, Olive Beaupre. *A Picturesque Tale of Progress.* Chicago: The Book House for Children, 1953.

National Parkways. *Mesa Verde and Rocky Mountain National Parks.* Caspar, Wyoming: National Parks Division, World-Wide Research & Publishing Co., 1975.

Nelson, Dick and Sharon. *Easy Field Guide to Common Mammals of New Mexico.* Phoenix, Arizona: Primer Publishers, 1977.

Noble, David Grant. *Ancient Ruins of the Southwest.* Flagstaff, Arizona: Northland Press, 1981.

Nordenskiold, Gustaf. *The Cliff Dwellers of the Mesa Verde.* Glorieta, New Mexico: The Rio Grande Press, Inc., 1979.

Ortiz, Alfonso. *Handbook of the North American Indians* Washington, D.C.: Smithsonian Institution, 1979.

———. *Handbook of the North American Indians.* Vol. 9. Washington, D.C.: Smithsonian Institution, 1983.

———. *New Perspectives on the Pueblos.* Albuquerque: New Mexico University, 1972.

Parker, Arthur C. *The Indian How Book.* New York: Dover Publications, 1927, 1954.

Parsons, Elsie Clews. *Tewa Tales.* New York: American Folklore Society, G. E. Strechert & Co., 1926.

Patraw, Pauline M. "Flowers of the Southwest Mesas." Southwest Parks and Monuments Assn., 1970.

Peckham, Stewart. *Prehistoric Weapons in the Southwest.* Santa Fe, New Mexico: Museum of New Mexico Press, 1977.

Peterson, Frederick. *Ancient Mexico.* New York: Putnam's, 1959.

Ragghianti, Carlo Ludovico and Licia Ragghianti Collobi. *National Museum of Anthropology, Mexico City.* Newsweek, Inc. & Arnoldo Mondadori Editore, 1970.

Reed, Alma M. *The Ancient Past of Mexico.* New York: Crown, 1966.

Robbins, Don. "The Dragon Project and the Talking Stones." *New Scientist,* October 21, 1982.

Robbins, Wilfred William and John Peabody Harrington. *Ethnobotany of the Tewa Indians.* Washington, D.C.: U.S. Govt. Printing Office, Bureau of American Ethnology, 1916.

Rohn, Arthur H. *Cultural Change and Continuity on Chapin Mesa.* Lawrence, KS: The Regents Press of Kansas, 1977.

Schaafsma, Polly. *Indian Rock Art of the Southwest.* Albuquerque: University of New Mexico Press, 1980.

Schiller, Ronald. "When Did Civilization Begin?" *The Readers Digest,* May 1975.

School of American Research. *Pecos Ruins.* Santa Fe, New Mexico, 1981.

Stanislawki, Michael. "The American Southwest as Seen from Pecos." U.S. Dept. of the Interior, National Park Service, Southwest Regional Office, 1983.

Steward, Tyrone, Frederick Dockstader, and Barton Wright. *The Year of the Hopi.* Rizzoli, NYC: Smithsonian Institution Traveling Exhibition Service, 1979–81.

Stewart, George and Gene S. *Discovering Man's Past in the Americas.* Washington, D.C.: National Geographic Society, 1969.

Storm, Hyemeyohsts. *Seven Arrows.* New York: Ballantine Books, 1972.

Stuart, David E. and R. P. Gauthier. "Prehistoric New Mexico: Background for Survey." Santa Fe Historic Preservation Bureau, State of New Mexico, 1981.

Tanner, Clara Lee. *Prehistoric Southwestern Craft Arts.* Tucson: University of Arizona Press, 1976.

Terrell, John Upton. *American Indian Almanac.* New York and Cleveland: The World Publishing Company, 1961.

Tryckare, Tre. *The Viking.* Gothenburg, Sweden: Cagner & Co., 1966.

Tunis, Edwin. *Weapons.* Cleveland/New York, World Publishing Co., 1954.

Various Authors. *New Light on Chaco Canyon.* Several articles written by various authorities. Santa Fe, New Mexico: School of American Research Press, 1984.

Various Authors. *The World of the American Indian.* Chapters written by various authorities including Vine Deloria, Jr. and N. Scott Momaday. Washington, D.C.: The National Geographic Society, 1974.

Various Authors. *Vikings in the British Isles.* (Several articles by different authors.) A British Heritage Publication, 1983.

Watson, Don. *Indians of the Mesa Verde.* Mesa Verde National Park, Colorado, 1961.

Wellman, Klaus. *A Survey of North American Indian Rock Art.* Graz, Austria: Akademische Druck-u Verlagsanstalt, 1979.

Wenger, Gilbert R. *The Story of Mesa Verde.* Mesa Verde National Park, Colorado: Mesa Verde Museum Association, Inc., 1980.

Wenger, Stephen R. *Flowers of the Mesa Verde.* Mesa Verde National Park, Colorado: Mesa Verde Museum Association, Inc., 1976.

White, John Manchip. *Everyday Life of the North American Indian.* New York: Holmes & Meier Publishers, Inc., 1979.

Wormington, H.M. *Prehistoric Indians of the Southwest.* Denver Museum of Natural History, 1975.

Zeilik, Michael. *The Sunwatchers of Chaco Canyon.* Griffith Observer, Griffith Observatory, Los Angeles, California, June, 1983.